THE DADDY'S GIRL COLLECTION

THE DADDY'S GIRL SERIES, BOOKS 1-3

THREE NOVELS BY

NORMANDIE ALLEMAN

Copyright © 2015 by Normandie Alleman

All rights reserved. No part of this book may be reproduced or transmitted in any form or by any means, electronic or mechanical, including photocopying, recording, or by any information storage and retrieval system, without permission in writing from the publisher.

Published by Stormy Night Publications and Design, LLC.
www.StormyNightPublications.com

Alleman, Normandie

The Daddy's Girl Collection

Cover Design by Korey Mae Johnson

Images by Bigstock/Nataliia Natykach and RomanceNovelCovers.com/Jimmy Thomas

ISBN-13: 978-1515375623

ISBN-10: 1515375625

FOR AUDIENCES 18+ ONLY

This book is intended for adults only. Spanking and other sexual activities represented in this book are fantasies only, intended for adults.

Daddy Morebucks
The Daddy's Girl Series, Book One

Normandie Alleman

DEDICATION

To my darling husband, the most romantic man I've ever known. Without you, none of this would be possible.

CHAPTER ONE

Sitting on the barstool, Marley crossed her fingers and legs for luck. She tried, but couldn't quite get her toes to cross in high-heeled shoes. *Dear God, please let this be the right place for a score.*

In a flirtatious gesture, she tossed her jet-black hair over her shoulder and glanced around the swanky hotel bar for prospects. The sophisticated low lighting and the rich mahogany furnishings gave the place a cozy, yet elegant feel. Elaborate sconces dotted the walls. Exotic plants warmed the metallic, modern tables and the sleek bar at which she sat.

The other patrons were lost in conversation. No loners. No potential johns. Marley sighed deeply. With only enough money for one cocktail, she realized her time was limited. She couldn't nurse the same drink all night.

"What the hell," she thought and took a slug of her mojito.

She was about to ask the bartender if he knew where she could find some action when a nervous-looking gentleman carrying a briefcase walked into the lounge. He scanned the room like someone who had just realized he lost his wallet and was returning to the place where he hoped to God he'd find it.

Marley looked at him with interest. This guy had potential. The man glanced up, meeting her gaze. Relief washed over his face, and he stalked straight toward her.

"Um, may I help you?" Marley asked.

"Oh, I hope so. May I sit down?" He indicated the bar stool next to hers.

Upon further inspection he didn't look like her usual clients—businessmen far from home—but you never knew and she was desperate not to have to spend the night in the shelter again tonight. "Suit yourself." She shrugged.

He sat down heavily, mopping his brow with a napkin from a stack atop the bar. His head was shiny, bald as a cue ball, and he wore glasses with thick, black frames. Nerdy. Harmless.

Marley waited.

Finally, he stage-whispered, "Please don't throw a drink on me or anything, but you wouldn't happen to be a working girl, would you?"

The corners of her mouth turned up. She had the choice of being insulted or taking this question as a compliment. Marley chose to take it as a compliment. Nobody approached ugly, nasty girls in hotel bars and asked them such things. Did they?

She gave him her best come-hither look. "Who wants to know?" she asked in a sultry voice.

"I do. I mean, not for me. See, I was supposed to arrange a date for my boss, and she didn't show up. Oh my God, he's going to kill me." He jiggled his leg as he talked. The man was a bundle of nerves.

"Wait, what?" A boss. He had a boss. Now she was getting somewhere. Placing her hand on his shaking leg, she turned the charm up to max volume, purring, "Why don't you tell me all about it... and maybe you should have a drink."

He took a deep breath and ordered a scotch on the rocks.

"Okay, my employer." He cleared his throat and took a long draw on his drink before continuing. "He has certain tastes and my job, well, one of my jobs, is to occasionally procure a woman for him who can meet his needs."

"Interesting. And what needs might those be?" Marley had no doubt she could meet the man's needs, whatever they were. For a warm bed for the night and some cash, she would do just about anything. Had done just about anything.

When people get desperate enough, they'll surprise even themselves as to what they would do. She could attest to that.

"Do you know what a dom is?" he asked.

"Of course."

"Well, that's what he is. Doesn't usually like to play with the same girl twice. You'll have to sign a non-disclosure agreement, a contract, the works. But he pays well."

Never the same girl twice. That sucks. So much for finding Daddy Warbucks.

"What is *well*? And how rough does he get?" It was sad that she asked about the money before the safety issue, but there you were.

"I've never seen any of the girls hurt to look at 'em afterwards, and I always arrange for their transportation home. Depending on how pleased he is with you... most nights he pays five grand."

Marley's eyes widened in spite of herself. "Did you say five grand?"

"Yeah. You interested?" The glow of hope radiated from him, and he grabbed her delicate hands in his clammy paws.

Marley had to remind herself to blink. With five grand she could buy herself a place to stay for months. She could get back on her feet. Maybe even get a regular job. No more men with stinky breath laboring over her.

No more blowjobs in strangers' cars.

Wow, had she hit the jackpot or what? "I am."

"I usually hire from a service, but the one who was supposed to come tonight came down with food poisoning or something, and Miss Jay's has no staff available. All booked up for a senator's yacht party or something."

Marley made a mental note to self, Miss Jay's. If she did have to stay in this life, she'd rather do it on a yacht than in a dirty alley.

"So you're supposed to be vetted and all that. He can't know that I dropped the ball on this, so can you just play along like you're the girl from Miss Jay's?"

"Sure. How about you buy me a drink?"

"Oh, he won't want you to be drunk. How much have you had to drink, anyway?" he frowned.

She raised her eyebrows. "Really? I don't think you're in a position to be so demanding. I mean, I *am* doing you a favor," she said with a tilt of her shoulder. "What's your name, anyway?"

"Milton. Milton Barnes." He took a deep breath and asked the bartender to refill her glass.

"What about your boss? What's his name?"

He gulped down the last of his scotch. "That's not anything you need to know. Non-disclosure and all that." He opened the briefcase at his side and pulled out some papers. "Here, I need your John Hancock on these."

Boy, the rich really are different. A written contract for sex.

Marley perused the long paragraphs. All the words ran together, none of them making much sense to her. "What does it say?"

"Basically, that you aren't going to sue him or call the cops if he hits you, and that you will never tell anyone what transpires between you two."

"And what if I do?"

"He'll sue you."

Marley laughed so hard she almost fell off her barstool. "He will sue me? I haven't got anything."

Milton flashed a fake smile. "I don't care. Please, just sign it."

Shaking her head, she took the pen he offered her and signed her name at the bottom of the pages marked with an 'x.'

"Happy?" she asked.

"Deliriously." He quickly put the papers away and gave her a onceover.

"What? Don't I look okay?" Marley had spent her last twenty at the thrift shop on the heels and glittery emerald green cocktail shift she wore. She thought it was mighty classy for twenty dollars. She might have been broke, but she had style and she cleaned up nice. A chameleon, Marley prided herself on being able to fit in anywhere.

"It's not that. We need hair ties or something."

Marley found a few elastic bands in her purse. "Like these?"

"Yeah. Go in the bathroom and put your hair in pigtails and meet me outside. It's almost showtime," he said, looking at his watch.

"Pigtails? You're kidding me."

"No. He likes little girls. Just do it."

"Wait. He's a pedophile? You never said anything about that." Her voice wavered.

"No, no. He's *not* a pedophile. He's just that kind of dom. Likes to be a daddy to little girls. It's all fantasy. He's never been with a kid. He's not into that kind of thing. You know, he probably likes the Catholic schoolgirl thing. I don't *know*." Exasperated, he shooed her off her stool and toward the bathroom.

She marched ahead of him to the lobby, calling over her shoulder, "If you say so…"

"Don't worry. Just remember five grand."

"*Five grand. Five grand*," she repeated to herself. Milton was right. Heck, she could put her hair up in pigtails for that kind of coin.

"What about downstairs?" Milton pointed at her crotch, a spray of scarlet coloring his cheeks. "What kind of, um, haircut do you have?"

"Brazilian—with a landing strip," she said matter-of-factly.

"Let's get you a razor. It all needs to come off." He popped into the gift shop and purchased a package of disposable razors. "Think little girl," he whispered.

"Whatever you say." Marley rolled her eyes and ducked into the ladies' room to take care of her new client's special requests.

She returned moments later with twin ponytails, one on each side of her neck. The kind on the sides of her head looked ridiculous so she settled for these. She didn't want to draw any more attention to herself than was necessary in the lobby of the swanky hotel. Being asked to leave the premises was one of her fears.

"Where will I meet Daddy Morebucks?"

"In the penthouse suite. Come on, let's go." He took her by the elbow and guided her into the elevator. Once inside, he inserted his key before pressing the button for 'PH.'

Marley shifted her weight from one foot to the other. "When do I get paid?"

"I'll pay you after he calls me to arrange to have you transported home."

Home. She didn't have a home. Would she tell the driver to take her to the homeless shelter? No. She couldn't do that. Miss Jay's girls didn't live there, and neither would she once she had five G's in her hot little hand.

Her head began to pound. Forget it. She'd worry about where to go later.

Marley batted her eyelashes at Milton. "I usually get paid up front."

Milton snorted. "You *have* to be one of Miss Jay's girls. Or I'm done for. You too. And they get paid afterwards. That's how it's done."

"Okay, okay." She knew when not to push, but she felt uneasy not having the cash in hand.

The elevator car stopped and they stepped out into a small hallway.

Milton visibly gathered himself and checked his watch for the umpteenth time. "You ready?"

"Ready as I'll ever be."

He nodded at her and tapped on the door.

CHAPTER TWO

The door swung open. Behind it stood one of the most attractive men Marley had ever seen. His hair was black as midnight, like hers, but his eyes were the color of a deep, rich cup of dark roast coffee. Fancy coffee to be sure, for the man dripped wealth and privilege from every pore.

"Hello. Won't you please come inside?" he said with a tight smile. He wore a well-cut navy blue suit with a crisp white shirt and purple tie. Sharp.

"Thank you," Marley said and gave him one of her sweetest looks. His voice cemented her impression when he spoke with a cultured tone. He'd been born with money. She could tell.

"Milton, I will text you when she needs a ride. Keep your phone on you."

"Yes, Sir." Milton nodded and stared at Marley, beseeching her to remember everything they discussed.

"Bye." Marley dismissed Milton with a wave of her hand and wandered into the penthouse. It was nicer than most penthouses she had been in, not that there had been that many. The furniture was sleek and modern, yet warm and comfortable at the same time.

When volunteering in a hospital during high school, she spent her breaks poring over old *Architectural Digests* left in the waiting rooms. Interior design fascinated her. She noted how the green and cream color palette of the suite added to its calm luxuriousness. The artwork hanging on the walls appeared to be originals rather than the mass-produced pictures that passed for art in the hotels to which she was accustomed.

Decorative vases filled with delphiniums and roses left a heady floral scent in the air. The room smelled of spring, though it was the beginning of winter outdoors.

She heard him clear his throat. "Do you have a coat?"

"No."

"Okay." He looked puzzled, but shook it off. "You may call me Sir. What shall I call you?"

"Marley. That's my name." His eyes slid over her body, inspecting the merchandise. She was used to this part of the transaction. It didn't bother her anymore.

"Have you been informed of my particular requirements?"

"Yes, Sir," she lied. She wasn't sure exactly what he meant, but she was going to fake it. She'd make him think she was one of Miss Jay's call girls, or die trying.

He seemed satisfied. "Good. Let's have some dinner, shall we?"

Jackpot again! A meal. Thank you Lord! Marley hadn't eaten anything since the bowl of grits she ate early that morning at the shelter. No wonder those mojitos had gone to her head. Her belly rumbled. Tonight was turning out to be a good night.

"Yes, that sounds lovely, Sir." She knew dominant men loved it when you called them by whatever names they asked you to call them. Sir, Master, whatever. She aimed to please this one with the big checkbook as best as she could.

He led her to the dining room, where sumptuous blue and green draperies framed the Dallas skyline, the lights making it look like a Texas fairyland. The aroma of the food was so strong, it relegated the smell of the flowers on the table to a simple undernote.

The table was set with fine china, elegant crystal, and golden flatware. Goblets of icy cold water and several crystal wine glasses anchored beautiful place settings. Their plates had warmers over the top of them. *Ah, he's let the help go. It's only the two of us.* Marley made it a habit to know how many people were around. From a safety perspective, knowledge was power. She didn't expect this guy to be more than she could handle, but it was preferable to know ahead of time if someone else was going to pop out of the woodwork. She didn't like surprises when she was on the job.

He held the chair out for her. She sat down, then he pushed her back under the linen tablecloth.

"Thank you, Sir," she said politely.

Taking his seat across from her, he said, "I hope you aren't a vegetarian."

"Oh, no. I love meat." She raised an eyebrow suggestively.

He ignored the double entendre.

She opened the covering atop the food to peek at what was underneath it. She was famished.

"Marley, did I say you could look at your food?"

Is he serious? Chastised, she answered, "No, Sir."

"You will wait until I tell you to remove the cover."

"Okay, sorry," she grumbled.

"For tonight, I am your benefactor and you will do as I say. Is that clear?" His dark eyes stared into hers.

"Yes, Sir."

"Good. I prefer to say grace before we eat if that doesn't offend you." He reached for her hand.

"No, that's fine, Sir." She liked the feel of his clean, warm hand. A whiff of cologne or aftershave drifted past her nose. For some reason it gave her comfort. Though he appeared to be around thirty years old, the man had a commanding presence and she liked the way he took charge. It made her feel as though she could relax, a rarity for her.

Usually Marley had to be vigilant, not only when working, but in every aspect of her life. She was guarded with people. Friendly on the outside, but on the inside she was wary of everyone. Experience had taught her that. Count on no one but yourself. That was the only way to survive.

"Lord, bless this food and us to thine service. Please bless Marley in her endeavors and be with us this evening as we partake in your bounty. Amen."

Marley found it odd that a religious man would have a prostitute over and that he would pray over it. *It takes all kinds.* She found it kinda cute though. The fact that he did something so quirky made her warm to him. She didn't want to admit that it touched her that he said a prayer for her. No one had ever prayed for her before, that she knew of.

He leaned gracefully across the table and removed her plate cover to reveal a delicious-smelling entrée that consisted of some kind of beef tucked in a pastry shell, fluffy potatoes piped into a fancy swirled shape, and seasoned green beans.

"I'm glad you eat meat. I don't have much patience for salads myself, and you look like you could use a good meal." He chuckled.

He has no idea, she thought as she watched him cautiously, waiting until he picked up his fork first. She wasn't going to jump the gun again and risk looking like the starving indigent she was.

"You may go ahead." He motioned to her plate.

"Thank you, Sir." She dove in, starting with the meat, trying to remain ladylike while desperately wanting to eat like a famished farm hand after a long day's work.

They ate their meal in silence, the only noises being the clinks of silverware on plates and glasses tinkling as they drank and enjoyed the tasty meal.

"Do you care for any wine?" he asked.

Remembering what Milton had said about him not liking his girls to drink alcohol, she shook her head no.

"No, Sir," he corrected her.

She finished her bite and dutifully answered, "No, Sir. Thank you for offering, Sir." She could play that game with her eyes closed.

"Well, I'm going to have a glass of merlot, though I do like to keep my head about me during a scene. You should too."

"I'm fine, though I did have some drinks earlier."

"You did?"

"Yeah, but don't worry. Milton told me you don't like your girls drunk, and this food sopped up all the alcohol in my system, so no worries, Sir."

He sat quietly sipping his wine and considering her.

"Would you like dessert?"

"Sure! I mean, yes, Sir."

He looked surprised. "Oh, well, then I'll call down for something. Maybe we can have it later. What would you like? Cake? Crème brûlée? I could see what the specials are…"

"Crème brûlée. I've always wanted to try that."

He used a phone in the corner to order two crème brûlées before returning to his seat.

Marley finished her potatoes and leaned back in her chair, her tummy contented. "Thank you, Sir. That was delicious."

Unable to read him, Marley decided it was time to get this show on the road. The sooner he was finished with her, the sooner she could get some sleep. Lack of sleep was catching up with her. The different noises and random commotion that went on throughout the night at the shelter kept her awake. If she was lucky she could crash here and find a new place tomorrow.

Locking her eyes with his, she slipped out of her chair onto the floor and crawled on her hands and knees around to his side of the table. Setting her hands on his knee, she attempted to push back his chair. But it didn't go as smoothly as she had planned. The chair didn't budge.

"What are you doing?" He wore a bemused expression.

"I was going to ask you if I could please worship your cock, Daddy."

"Sir," he corrected. "And I will be the one to tell you what to do, young lady. You are out of line."

Marley sat back on her heels, deflated. "Oh. Sorry. Sir."

"My, my. You are a little slut. I think you've earned a spanking for that little stunt. Come up here and lie across my lap."

Obediently, Marley draped herself over his lap, her bottom over his knee.

Slowly, he pulled her dress up around her waist and yanked her panties down to just above her knees.

"Marley, do you know why I'm disciplining you?"

"Yes, Sir. Because I was naughty." Her voice sounded strange since she was upside down.

"It is because you are to do what I ask of you, not take the initiative."

"Yes, Sir. I'm sorry, Sir."

"The rules were explained to you before you got here?"

"Yes, Sir," she lied. She didn't have any idea she wasn't supposed to do that. Hell, she thought he would *like* what she did. But she'd lie there for a spanking for five G's.

"Then you have earned a punishment for your impudence. Do you understand?"

"Yes, Sir." She steeled herself for whatever was to come.

She flinched when his bare hand slammed down on her naked rear end. Another blow rained down, eliciting a cry from her lips. She clenched her muscles.

"Don't tense up. Relax. Ease into the pain. It will make it easier."

"Yes, Sir." Her voice a whimper, she took a deep breath and tried to do as he instructed.

More swats landed on her ass. She imagined it must be getting red by now.

He was right. Not resisting was helpful. Embracing the sting helped her ride the wave of pain as he smacked her posterior.

She moaned under his hand and was grateful when he ceased the spanking and began rubbing her aching cheeks. Gently, he slid his hands over her skin, massaging her hot globes, easing her distress.

"Mmm, thank you, Sir," she purred, disheveled and drunk with endorphins.

"You're welcome," he said quietly.

His fingers dipped down and brushed across her pussy lips. She strained, wanting him to touch her. This was strange. She didn't usually become aroused on her 'dates.' She carried lube for that reason.

When he inserted a finger into her opening, she was surprised that her cunt was so slick and welcoming.

"You must have liked your spanking, little girl. I can feel how wet you are."

Usually nothing a john said could get her motor running. She could fuck all day without becoming aroused. She could make up a grocery list in her head while pretending to have the time of her life. But there was something about this man's tone that awakened a place inside her. A place she wasn't familiar with.

She nodded, and this time he let that suffice as an answer.

Fucking her with one finger, then two, he pressed his thumb inside her asshole. Discomfort followed by unfiltered ecstasy overtook her, and Marley gave in to the experience. Why hold back? What was the point? She was here to get fucked; she might as well enjoy it.

Writhing on his lap, she could smell her own desire in the air. She wanted to burst, she was so filled with passion.

"Take the rest of your clothes off," he ordered her.

Dizzy, she took care not to fall over as she hurriedly pulled her dress over her head and removed her panties.

As she stood before him, undressed while he was completely clothed, the heat of the moment sunk in. She was vulnerable in a way that went beyond the fact that she was naked and he wasn't. He took control of her in a way no man ever had. She had interacted with doms before, but never like this. It had never affected her before. There was something about this man, the way he looked at her, the way he commanded her with merely his voice… it struck a chord with her and she wanted to play that chord at full volume.

She wanted him. She couldn't wait for him to have his way with her. Her cool persona melted away and left her a quaking puddle of unending need.

"Good girl. Now come over here and turn your back to me so I may bind your hands."

"Yes, Sir." She practically tripped over herself scurrying to comply. Putting her hands behind her, she eagerly awaited his tying her wrists.

Soft, silky rope passed over her wrists as he secured her hands at the base of her spine.

"Nicely done. Now bend forward at the waist so that I may inspect you."

As she leaned over, she realized she should have been humiliated by this request, but instead she felt her pussy lips and clit swell with her arousal. Her body felt as though it was on fire, and she thought she'd explode if he didn't touch her soon.

He must have meant a visual inspection because he didn't touch her. Not yet.

Circling around, he lifted her chin, raising her back to a standing position. A wicked gleam in his eye, he pulled out some frightening-looking nipple clamps. Without saying a word, he flicked her nipples, one at a time, with his index finger, transforming them into hard little nubs. He watched her face as he toyed with them.

She knew to keep eye contact with him, but what he was doing to her was so toe-curlingly delicious, she had to struggle not to close her eyes and get lost in the sensation.

"That's right. Keep your eyes up here. Now I'm going to clip these onto your nipples. They will hurt at first. Try not to scream." He stared at her as though she was catnip and he was a rollicking tomcat.

She nodded. "Yes, Sir."

One clip fastened around her left nipple. Sweet agony shot up into her chest. Gritting her teeth, she let out a yowl.

"Easy does it. One more," he said as he attached the other one to her right nipple.

"Oooh, hoo, hoo!" Marley cried out and tried to breathe deeply.

He lifted her chin and captured her lips with his. He held her face in his hands, burying his tongue in her mouth. With her hands bound, Marley was helpless to return his embrace, but she answered the call of his tongue, entering her own into the dance.

When he let her go, she tottered on her feet, woozy with lust. "Kneel," he told her.

In a chivalrous gesture, he held her arm so that she did not fall trying to get into a kneeling position with no hands to aid her. He laid a pillow on the floor in front of her.

Grabbing what looked like a riding crop off the mantel, he swatted her on the rear with it. "Head down, ass in the air."

Marley tipped herself forward, knees spread wide for balance. Her pulse erratic and her pussy throbbing, she laid her head on the cushy pillow, quivering in anticipation, praying that the rich playboy with the face of a movie star would give her the fucking she now craved so desperately.

• • • • • • • • • • • • • • •

James LeBlanc looked down at the heart-shaped behind of the adorable girl on the Aubusson rug before him. In his entire life, he had never seen such a delectable ass.

Where had this girl come from?

He knew she wasn't one of Miss Jay's girls. Did Milton think he was born yesterday? Or if she was, she was new to the game. This girl was real, not like the vacuous girls who worked for Miss Jay to supplement their allowances so they could buy the latest Birkin bag or yet another pair of Manolo Blahniks. He could tell by how hungry she was, how quickly she devoured her meal. Miss Jay's girls never ate more than three bites when they came to play with him. Marley's appetite impressed him in more ways than one.

At first he thought she was cute in her flashy dress with those big green eyes all rimmed with black kohl. But when she sank down onto her knees and asked if she could suck his cock, he lost his mind. Something clenched in his gut, and he panicked.

Afraid of losing control of the situation, he spanked her as though he could beat the seductiveness out of her… What was wrong with him?

James prided himself on his ability to control these interactions. He worked constantly, but knew that for the sake of his mental health he needed some down time to blow off steam. When he dealt with women who were 'professionals,' he got what he paid for, and he didn't have to deal with dating. Dating was a minefield, and he knew it was only a matter of time before the women he dated found out how much money he had. Things always got weird then, and not in a good way.

Although he didn't have time for a relationship, James did enjoy the company of women, and he liked to play kinky games with them. Several years back he discovered the ease of paid companionship. No hassles. Availability. And women who would go along with his kinks, no questions asked. The perfect way to play.

Then Milton brings this adorable little waif to my hotel room, and I get butterflies in my stomach like a teenager. James shook his head, disappointed with himself for experiencing human emotions. He prided himself in being able to distance himself from messy emotions.

"Mmm. Daddy, I mean, Sir. Aren't you going to fuck me?" She peered over her shoulder at him, beckoning him seductively. Was that a challenge?

Good God, why does she have to keep calling me Daddy? It made his cock throb, pressing hard against his pants.

He walked over and touched her porcelain cheek. "Is that what you want?"

She looked up at him through lust-filled eyes. "Yes, please, Sir."

He didn't always fuck the girls he played with. In fact, he usually didn't. Usually, he got his needs met without it. But he wanted to fuck this one. He wanted to fuck her hot little pussy for hours, until he made her raw and she begged him to stop.

In an instant he stripped down and donned a condom. Grabbing her by the hips, he burrowed inside her with a growl.

Her walls gripped him tightly, and he rocked her back onto his cock. Spurred on by the wet swirl of her cunt, he pounded into her. His bound captive offered herself to him, moans escaping her throat as she squirmed underneath him.

When he was balls deep inside her, he reached around and unclipped the clamps that confined her nipples. She shrieked as the blood rushed back into the sensitive tissues. He found her clit with his hand, rubbing tiny circles around her swollen womanhead.

She jerked with a body-rippling climax and came all over his rock-hard cock. He continued to impale her with long strokes until she stilled.

He was tempted to come, but he held back. First he needed to violate that pretty mouth of hers. Marley wore no lipstick, yet her lips were as red as the ripest apple. Probably just as juicy.

"Can you rise up to a kneeling position?" he asked.

The fucking had taken a lot out of her. With a dazed look, she nodded. "Can you help me up, please, Sir?" With her arms tied, she needed help getting into position. He gave her a hand and propped her up to kneel before him.

"Suck it." He tossed the condom aside and wagged his erect cock in front of her face. She bobbed her head down to capture the tip in her mouth. She licked the sides, gathered her lips around it, and enveloped it in her warm little mouth.

Placing a firm hand on the back of her head, he worked his way deeper into her throat. He was surprised that she was able to take him all the way in without gagging. Obviously this wasn't her first rodeo.

Tongue swirling, lips sucking, head bobbing—watching her work his cock made his heart sing. Grasping her ponytails in his fists, he took charge and fucked her throat to completion. He reared back and let out a harsh breath as he came.

She sank down, collapsing into a heap. With quick, deft motions, James untied her ropes and wrapped her up in his arms. Those amazing green eyes stared up into his, and he nibbled her bottom lip.

Marley responded with a passion of her own, her arms circled around his neck, and she held him close. Their lips met again, his tongue ran over hers. As he reveled in her kisses, James realized he had never made out with a prostitute before. Many of them didn't like to kiss. That never bothered him. Was he breaking one of his rules? Hell, he didn't know or care.

His mind was completely on Marley, appreciating the moment. He couldn't remember a time he had felt so happy.

CHAPTER THREE

Marley gazed up at her client. His eyes were closed, which afforded her the opportunity to study him.

That strong jawline could have been carved by a sculptor. Same with his abs. Cut with precision, as if chiseled by a professional. Worry lines creased his brow. Whatever he did for a living must cause him a lot of stress. Was this how he managed his stress? By playing with prostitutes? Judging by his physique, he worked out too.

Opening his eyes, he asked, "Marley, where did you come from?"

"Abilene."

He laughed.

"What? Somebody has to come from Abilene. Why not me?"

He chuckled, stroking her hair. He held her in his arms, and she had to admit she liked it. She felt safe there, though she had no idea why. She knew better than to get too comfortable with her clients. But this one was irresistible, even to her.

"Would you like to spend the night?" he asked.

She hesitated. Usually she tried to end her 'dates' as rapidly as possible. But in this case, she'd been hoping he'd ask. She wanted to spend the night between luxurious sheets and wake up to the possibility of breakfast. Plus, she wouldn't mind spending some more time with this enticing man, whatever his name was.

"We don't have to do anything else if you don't want. I just thought you might want to stay here instead of going home tonight. It *is* rather late."

How could she refuse? "Sure, I'd like that."

"Good, I'll let Milton know he can arrange to have you taken home in the morning."

She nodded and watched him put his pants on before going in the other room to call his assistant. She fumbled with her dress, pulling it over her head before retrieving her panties from across the room.

Walking back into the room, he frowned. "You got dressed."

"Was I not supposed to, Sir?"

"No, that's okay. We almost forgot our crème brûlée. Would you like some milk with that before bed?"

"Milk?"

"Yes, milk. It's good for a growing girl's bones."

"Okay then."

He smiled. "I'll be right back."

A few moments later he returned with their desserts, a glass of milk for her, and a glass of water for himself.

"What about *your* bones?" she teased.

"I drank mine this morning," he said, touching his glass to hers before lifting it to his full lips.

Dessert was divine. Marley had never had anything so yummy. She loved how the crystallized shell cracked when she pressed her spoon into the golden custard. "Mmm!"

He grinned at her. "Pretty good, huh?"

Marley nodded and gulped down her milk. He grazed her upper lip with his finger, wiping away her milk mustache.

She giggled. "Thank you, Sir."

He led her by the hand into the dark bedroom. They stripped down to their underwear and he lay down beside her.

In the stillness, she timidly asked, "Sir, what is your real name?"

"James." He put his arm around her and kissed her on the top of the head. "Now go to sleep, Marley."

"Yes, Sir." She curled up next to him like a drowsy kitten and drifted off to sleep.

• • • • • • • • • • • • • • •

The next morning Marley glanced over and saw the rumpled covers of an empty bed in the spot where James had slept the night before. Sleepily, she sat up, stretched her arms and saw a note on the bedside table closest to her.

Order anything you want for breakfast from room service. Enjoyed last night.
—James

Hooray! Room service. Marley couldn't remember the last time she had such a treat. Gleefully, she hopped out of bed, searching for the menu.

She found the remote control and turned on the television. It had been months since she had watched TV, at least being able to control what show was on. At the shelter she had to watch whatever the others chose. Before that, she and her roommate couldn't afford to have cable or satellite TV so they went without.

Snuggling back down under the fluffy, white cloud of a comforter, Marley flipped through the channels. Finally settling on *Live with Kelly and Michael*, she opened the menu and called room service. As she nestled under the covers, she got a whiff of his scent, pine and balsa wood with a hint of musk. Without thinking, she sniffed his pillow and hugged it to her. Damn, he did smell good, her sexy, *temporary*, fairy godfather.

This is the life. I could get used to this.

Soon a waiter brought in a rolling table groaning with the weight of her massive breakfast. She had him wheel it all the way through the suite into the bedroom so she could have breakfast in bed. Hey, it wasn't every day she got to eat like a queen and control the remote all at the same time. She intended to milk it for everything it was worth. Before she knew it she'd have to go back to her old life, so she would enjoy the life of leisure while she could.

Pushing the buzz-killing thought of her old life to the back of her mind, she devoured her western omelet, country potatoes, French toast, and bacon. She'd also ordered a side of fruit, some biscuits, and a pot of coffee. While Kelly and Michael interviewed Tom Cruise about his latest movie, Marley shoveled food into her mouth and tried to figure out how to take the rest home with her once she got too full.

She tucked bacon, cantaloupe, and a biscuit into a white cloth napkin before stuffing the stash into her pocketbook for later. She called down for a toothbrush and toothpaste, then took a relaxing shower, taking advantage of the hotel's French-milled soap and shampoo. Soon she was dressed for the day. Unfortunately, she wore the cocktail dress from the night before, but it couldn't be helped.

Flopping down on the bed, she flipped the controls until she found a soap opera to watch. The door to her room opened with a click, causing Marley to bolt upright and peek into the living room.

"Hello?" Milton's tinny voice rang through the empty suite.

"In here," Marley called back.

Walking into the bedroom, Milton said, "You ready to go?"

"I guess so..." Marley surveyed her opulent surroundings and sighed. *All good things must come to an end.*

"Here's your money." He handed her a wad of one hundred dollar bills.

Snatching up the cash, she followed him out of the room without looking back.

Downstairs Milton hustled her into the backseat of a waiting town car. "Thanks for saving my ass, Marley."

"Don't mention it." She gave him a wry smile and the car spirited her away. Milton stood on the sidewalk, his hand touching his brow in a mini salute.

So that was it. Marley counted the greenbacks. Yep, they were all there. She gave the driver the name of the street she had lived on the last time she had an apartment. With her newfound cash she had enough for first and last month's rent. She'd have a bed of her own to sleep in by nightfall.

Breathing a sigh of relief, she felt a peace she hadn't experienced in weeks, maybe months. She could start looking for a job tomorrow. A real job, maybe even one with benefits.

Don't get ahead of yourself. One step at a time. Just be careful about each dollar and make it go as far as you can. She knew that paydays like this only came along once in a lifetime, and that was if you were lucky.

When the driver pulled onto Oleander Drive, Marley thanked him and stepped out of the car, ready for a fresh start.

CHAPTER FOUR

James LeBlanc couldn't get Marley out of his mind.
This never happened to him. In the past, once a girl was out of his sight, she was out of his head. He didn't think about the women in his life unless they were standing in front of him. Even as a teenager, girls hadn't been a priority. Sports, school, and friends always took precedence over the fairer sex.

These days he was too busy building his empire. There was no time to be distracted by women. He tried having a live-in girlfriend once. Karen was more of a hassle than she was worth. In the end she ran off with a much older, wealthier dom. In hindsight he and Karen didn't have much in common. Good riddance, he said and moved on with his life. A life centered around work.

Several years ago, he invented an app that took off and his life changed overnight. The phone app allowed users to check on their pets when they were away from home. Like a portable feed for a nanny cam, but for pets. With all the updates his company had done, users could install up to four tiny cams in different locations. The four feeds showed up on the user's phone as a screen split so they could watch several different locations, or multiple pets.

Thanks to Americans' adoration for their pets, the app took off, making James a millionaire in its wake. Now he ran a multi-million dollar company centered around the app, but with dozens of offshoots including pet products galore. His company sold everything from doggie water bowls to ready-made outdoor dog runs, and his tech guys were constantly working on new apps in the product development section.

The Dallas skyline shone in the midday sun. Metallic skyscrapers reached to the stratosphere. Pictures of Marley flashed through his mind. Those haunting emerald eyes filled with lust gazing up at him. That incredible body bending over at his request, showing off her assets to their best advantage.

His cock stiffened, strained against his pants. He loved how she gave herself to him, allowed him to have his way with her. And that adorable cream mustache she sported after drinking her milk. Such a good little girl.

Moving away from the window, he shook his shoulders and tried to focus his brain on something else. Picking up the latest sales numbers off his desk, he read them without comprehension. His thoughts drew him back to Marley.

It was unfortunate a girl like her had to do that for a living. It never bothered him before—the working girls. But there was something about her. She wasn't just a nameless, faceless bimbo to him. A pang of guilt hit him in the gut. Was he a jerk for being so callous to the long line of prostitutes that had darkened his door?

Damn that Marley for making them human! But *she* was human, too special to be used by an endless number of men. Men who wanted her for their own pleasure with no regard for hers. He knew men like this. Perhaps he'd been one of them.

He had a younger sister. He would kill any man who treated his sister, Anna, that way. Marley brought out his protective nature. He wanted to take her in his arms and shield her from all of life's evils.

But that was ridiculous. She was just another girl who had gotten to him with those big green eyes of hers. She was a prostitute, he reminded himself, schooled in the ways of manipulating men to get what she wanted. He wouldn't let himself be played again. Better not to see her again.

He sat down at his desk, rapping his fingers on its cool, polished surface.

Maybe if he saw her again, he would learn something about her he didn't like. Then he could forget about her and move on with his life.

He called Milton and asked him to track her down.

Good. He'd done something to move the situation forward. Abandoning work for the day, he headed for the indoor swimming pool in the basement of his building. Maybe exercise would clear his head.

• • • • • • • • • • • • • • •

A week later, Marley opened the door of her new apartment to find James standing on the other side of it.

"What are you doing here?" she asked. Her hair was tied back in a ponytail, and she wore an old t-shirt and short jeans shorts. Paint smudged her arms and face, and she held a wet roller in her hand. "Hang on. I don't want to drip this on the carpet." She set the implement in a tray filled with creamy bright yellow.

"Have to admit I was hoping for a friendlier greeting." It had been difficult enough to find her. When Milton had no success, James hired a private investigator. It had taken the P.I. several days to find her. Days where James stayed distracted at work, tapping his foot awaiting news.

"Sorry." She looked him up and down. "I wasn't expecting you. I don't like surprises." She frowned.

"Okay. I get that." Now he felt stupid. What was he doing here? How could he explain it to her without sounding like a lovesick puppy dog or a stalker? He hated feeling like a fool.

Confidence. He had to suck it up and be confident. "I wondered if you might have lunch with me."

"Lunch? I'm kinda in the middle of something." She gestured to the half-painted room.

"I see that. How 'bout I help you? And then we go?"

"Really? Dressed like that?" She lifted an eyebrow.

He was wearing dress slacks and one of his best shirts. He'd taken off his tie in the car. "I can change. I've got my gym bag in the car."

"I've only got one roller…"

"Why don't I go get another roller, change, and I'll be back in a few?" He sounded desperate, even to himself. This was not how he intended this to go. But he didn't want to come across as though he thought he was too good for painting. Plus he wanted to help her, to spend time with her.

"Suit yourself." Marley shrugged and went back to painting.

"Back in a flash." This girl was tough. *You'd think she'd at least be grateful for his assistance…*

James spirited his Porsche over to the nearest big box store, picked up a couple of rollers and some blue tape. He changed in the restroom then made his way back to Marley's apartment.

He knocked on her door again.

"It's open," she called.

Glancing around the one-room apartment, he noticed a tiny kitchenette to the right, and surmised that the only door in the place led to the bathroom. A ratty futon, a glass coffee table, and a TV tray serving as an end table were the only pieces of furniture. Clearly, she was on a shoestring budget.

Something gnawed at his gut when he compared his sublime apartment in Prescott Tower to her meager dwelling. Why did there have to be so much poverty in the world? Why couldn't good, decent people have more? He spent many an evening attending charity events to assuage his guilt for being blessed with more than his share.

Damn, I've been lucky. He knew it was more than luck. He was also smart and talented with a huge drive to succeed. But fate had smiled upon him, of that there was no doubt.

As he looked at Marley, with all her spunk, beauty, and personality, he wondered why the fates had been so unkind to her.

"What's that?" she asked, pointing at the blue tape in his hand.

"Tape to keep you from getting paint on the ceiling or the baseboards."

"Huh," Marley said, as if that hadn't been a concern of hers.

He climbed up the stepladder and proceeded to affix tape to the ceiling, protecting it from her golden, sunny hue. "Where'd you get this ladder?"

"The super. He's real sweet."

Marley pushed the raven hair out of her face and picked up her roller to start painting again. A natural glow radiated from inside her. She was beautiful.

"Thank you for helping me." She peered at him shyly through her bangs.

"You're welcome. It's been ages since I've painted anything. It's kinda fun." He smiled warmly at her.

"Me too. I thought it would cheer the place up."

He nodded at the yellow wall. "It certainly brightens up the room. Like you." He couldn't resist speaking his thoughts aloud. She softened at the compliment. "How about I do the top part and you do the bottom?" As the words trickled out his mouth, he realized the double entendre.

"Sure," she said, apparently oblivious to any salacious meaning he might have had. But his mind flashed with a mental picture of him topping her. Marley beneath him, submissive and quivering with a desire to please him as he held her tightly, crop in one hand, the other wound around the back of her neck. His cock twitched.

"Okay." He moved to another section of the room, hoping to conceal his arousal. *Damn, this girl has a powerful effect on me.*

They worked together in a comfortable silence. The room was approximately eighteen by twenty-two and after an hour or so, they were a little over halfway done. James' stomach growled.

"What do you say we take a break for lunch, doll, and then come back to finish, more fortified?"

"Good idea," she said, wiping her brow.

"Where would you like to go?"

"Mmm. Mexican?"

"That sounds great, I love Mexican food. On the Border?"

"Margaritas?"

He shook his head. "It's the middle of a work day."

She stared at the paint trays. "Really? I think you can do this kind of work under the influence of a few margaritas."

He sighed. "Is it a deal-breaker?"

Crossing her arms over her chest, she nodded.

"Fine. But just so you know, I won't usually be such a pushover." It wasn't like him to let a girl call the shots. He was dominant by nature. But everything about this girl was new to him.

She lifted a brow. "Thank you, Sir," she said, gratitude dripping lazily from her lips like the sweetest honey.

He ushered her out the door, and held the car door open for her. She thanked him. Walking around to his side of the car, James puzzled, *"What am I getting myself into?"*

Shaking his head, he drove them to the restaurant. Marley was quiet. Odd for someone with such a bubbly personality. It was in there, he'd seen glimpses of it the night they'd spent together.

Ah, perhaps she's being guarded. Understandable. How do I break through that careful façade she's wearing? Maybe those blasted margaritas will help.

His hunch proved correct. Margaritas turned out to be the key to loosening her up. Marley ordered a frozen margarita. It came in a huge bowl of a glass that was bigger than her head. The more she drank, the friendlier she got.

The waiter brought a plate of nachos to their table. Between the two of them, the chips loaded with cheese, sour cream, beans, beef, and guacamole disappeared rapidly.

"Why did you *really* come to see me? Milton said you don't see the same girl twice," she asked between bites.

Startled by Milton's lack of discretion, he scowled. "What else did Milton tell you?"

"That you liked the whole daddy and little girl thing, pigtails, stuff like that." She took a sip from the icy concoction in front of her.

He froze. Heat radiated from his face.

"That's okay. To each his own," she said, nonchalantly popping a tortilla chip in her mouth. She signaled the waiter. "Can we please have some queso for our chips?"

"No problem," the waiter said and hurried away.

"Milton needs to keep his mouth shut," he muttered. Though he thought his heart would come out of his chest when she talked about calling him Daddy.

Marley reached across the table and laid her hand on his arm. "Don't worry about it. Doesn't bother me." She bit into another chip.

She's so flippant. What all had she been exposed to in her line of work? He shuddered to think. He regarded his kinks as rather harmless, but he knew some doms really liked to beat women. His gut twisted. A lot of hardcore things that went on in the world, and he hated to imagine Marley being subjected to some of them.

"You know, you weren't easy to find. Especially since your real name is Harley, not Marley."

It was her turn to freeze. She choked on her chip and took a slug of her icy beverage to wash it down.

She stiffened. "How did you find that out?"

"Had to hire a P.I. No one could find a Marley living anywhere on the street where the driver took you, but we did find a Harley. Cool name by the way; why'd you change it?"

She laughed. "Wouldn't you?"

He grinned. "Possibly. What, was your mom a biker babe?" He could picture that.

"My dad. Only thing he ever gave me was that stupid name. Then he left us."

"I'm sorry."

"Yeah, don't be. It was probably the best thing he could have done for me. I mean leave, not give me that dumb name." She giggled.

"Why? What was wrong with him?"

"Oh, I don't know. Sounds like he was a real asshole. My mom doesn't have a lot of nice things to say about him. My brother remembered liking him, but he was little. All kids love their parents when they're young."

"So you have a brother?"

A cloud settled over her face. "Did. He got killed in Afghanistan last year. His name was Paul." She stared at the table, her fingers fiddling with a paper straw wrapper.

"Oh, Marley, I'm so sorry." He reached out and took her hands in his.

She smiled bravely. "Enough about me. Tell me about you. How did you get so rich? You were born to it, right?"

James almost spit out the water he was about to swallow. "Me? Born with money? No, no, no. I grew up middle class, public schools, regular neighborhood. What makes you say that?"

"I don't know. You just seem… cultured." She shrugged.

"Well, thanks, I guess. But no, I invented an app. Like for your phone."

She gave him a blank look.

"Where's your phone? I'll show you."

She blushed crimson. "Lost mine."

She doesn't have a phone. The reality sunk in like a stone attached to his foot, sinking him. "Doesn't matter."

He wanted to change the subject fast, to put her at ease. "So, what have you been up to since I saw you last?"

Her face brightened. "I got a job." Her chest puffed with pride.

"You did? Doing what?" *God, please don't let it be a one-on-one job hooking for another guy.*

"Waiting tables. At the pancake house. It's not glamorous, but it pays the bills." She crossed her fingers. "I hope."

"Good. Good for you. So you're not doing the other thing…?"

Marley made a face. "Nope. Moving onward and upward," she said, her voice determined. She slurped down the last of her drink.

A crackling sizzle interrupted their conversation, and the waitress set down a platter of beef fajitas with all the accoutrements.

Their server out of earshot, James whispered conspiratorially, "You never worked for Miss Jay, did you?"

Her eyes widened. "What? How did you know?"

"Doll, you're nothing like Miss Jay's girls," he chuckled.

She tossed her napkin on the table in a huff, lower lip protruding. "Why? What do you *mean*?"

He shrugged. In a low voice he said, "Just… you're not like them. Her girls were all very professional, mechanical almost. Snotty too. You… you were different."

He paused. "You seemed to actually *enjoy* what we were doing."

"Well, that's not how it usually was!" she snapped.

"Oh." He didn't know what to say to that, and he had obviously pissed her off. Squirming in his chair, he tried to focus on building his fajita in the tortilla. Out of the corner of his eye he could see that she was sitting, stock still, with her arms crossed and a snarl on her face. *Just eat.*

He ate three huge steak fajitas before assessing her mood again. Her face had softened some, but she still looked angry. "Marley, please eat your lunch. We have to get back to painting soon. Remember?"

With an exaggerated sigh, she started to build her own fajita.

That was more like it. He knew this girl could eat. He liked that about her. He had spent the past week fantasizing about her voracious appetite, in the bedroom as well as at the dinner table.

"Marley, I know I've made you mad, but that wasn't my intention. I like you, and there are some things that are awkward to discuss with someone when you first get to know them."

She bowed her head. "I'm sorry." Her face glowed with pure submission.

How did she do that? This firecracker of a girl went from feisty to demure in less than sixty seconds. He wanted to kiss her in the worst way.

He took her hand and squeezed. "It's okay. You know, you please me very much."

"I do?" She scrunched her eyebrows. "I thought I was just a pain in the ass."

"Oh, you probably are a pain in the ass, but I enjoy your company."

The smile on her face made his gut tighten. Marley aroused feelings in him that he couldn't name. He wanted to hold her in his arms and protect her. That beautiful, independent creature that life had dumped on. She acted as though she had life by the tail, but James knew better. He wanted to make things better for her, but as independent as she was, she was bound to resist.

He scratched his head. *How in the world am I going to persuade her?*

CHAPTER FIVE

What was Daddy Morebucks doing showing up on her doorstep? Did he want to hire her again or was he looking for a freebie? *That's so not happening.*

She was shocked when he offered to help her paint. What was up with that? *People don't do things for you without expecting something in return.* Then he bought her lunch on top of that.

The way he treated her at lunch was almost the way she'd expect him to treat a date. As the meal went on, she forgot to be so guarded and found herself having a decent time. *Damn those margaritas.*

On the ride back to her place, she cloaked her invisible armor back around her shoulders. "Thanks for lunch. You really don't have to help me finish painting."

James reached over and stroked her hair. "Try to stop me." His gaze was intense, focused. She felt like a wildebeest facing a hungry lion.

Something fluttered in her stomach. Involuntarily, she leaned into his hand that petted her head.

What is it about this guy? Earlier when he called her doll, her blood had warmed all the way down to her toes. Even though the idea of her being a doll was comical.

Over the next couple of hours, they finished painting. There wasn't much conversation, but the connection in the air between them was electric. Several times Marley looked over and saw him staring at her.

"Stop it," she finally said, laughing.

"Stop what?" He feigned innocence, but they both knew he wanted her. Hell, she wanted him too.

"Stop looking at me like that." She wielded her wet paintbrush in her hand, threatening to flick him with it.

"Like what?" He sidled up to her and took the brush out of her hand, setting it on a tray. When he moved, she caught a glimpse of the muscular physique that lurked beneath the thin fabric of his shirt. The scent of his deodorant mixed with sweat tickled her nose as he came closer.

"Like you're a tiger and I'm your dinner." Her voice faltered when he took her face in his hands and kissed her.

The velvety softness of his face and lips told her he must have shaved before coming to see her. That gave her a little thrill. He dipped his tongue between her lips. Surrendering to him, she kissed him back with a ferocity that surprised her.

As quickly as he advanced upon her, he let her go. Raising his eyebrows, he turned away and picked up his paint roller, returning to work.

It took a moment to catch her breath. Gathering herself, she returned to painting too. A bit dizzier, and a bit giddier.

Watching him roll the paint up and down the wall, she swallowed. The sensuous movement sent a shiver through her.

It had been so long since someone had helped her with anything. Not since Paul.

Her brother forced his way into her consciousness every day. She'd see something to remind her of him, or she'd think of a joke they'd shared. When you grew up like they did, you banded together. And they had. Even though she couldn't count on her mom, she'd always been able to count on her big brother. He sheltered her, made sure she was safe and cared for. As she grew older she had done the same for him. They had each other's backs.

When he died, he left a hole in her heart so big she wasn't sure it would ever close.

"Almost done," James said, jolting her back to the present.

"About time. This was a bigger job than I thought it would be. I'm glad you were here."

He put the finishing touch on his section, and she did the same on her wall. "Whew! Want a beer?" she asked.

"Sure." Stretching his arms, he walked over and sat on the edge of the futon.

She took two cold ones out of the fridge and sat down beside him. They each took a long sip. Her body relaxed and she linked her arm with his.

He didn't seem surprised. *We have already been naked together*, she reminded herself.

His eyes met hers. "Marley, I'd really like to play with you today." There was a raw honesty there she wasn't accustomed to.

"Okay," she said reflexively. The heat between them was palpable. *Why am I throwing caution to the wind?*

Because you need to experience life every once in a while instead of always holding back, a voice inside her answered.

He took her hand. "I need you to be submissive to me. Is that a problem?"

Butterflies took flight in her stomach. She shook her head no.

"Good." She could tell by his sly grin that he was practically licking his chops with anticipation.

Reclining on the futon, he ordered her in a firm, low voice, "Remove your clothes."

"Yes, Sir." His command stirred her sex. She could feel the moisture between her legs as she disrobed.

After months of hooking, Marley was comfortable in the nude. Her body was thin, with smallish breasts, slightly curved at the waist, with an ample behind. She wouldn't be starring on the cover of any men's magazines, but she'd never had any complaints.

James observed her, then flipped over onto his back and beckoned her toward him. "Stand here and lean over."

He lay with his face below her, and she stood at the head of the futon, bent so her tits dangled in his face.

"Good girl."

Reaching up with both hands, he fondled her breasts. Her nipples hardened at his first touch. He flicked and pinched them between his fingers. A groan escaped her lips.

He worked her little buds, pulling and twisting them. Her breathing grew heavier, the sensations so heavenly she thought she'd lose her mind.

Pulling her by the nipples, he brought her face down to his. Obeying his silent command, she leaned down and met his lips for an upside-down kiss.

She'd never kissed this way before. His tongue in her mouth was foreign, curving against hers instead of with it. It was softer and more insistent at the same time. He was delicious, tasting of barley and hops. Covering his mouth with hers, she couldn't get enough.

The more intently she kissed him back, the rougher he played with her. She moaned into his mouth over and over again.

Overcome with lust, she reached down and pressed her hand against the large bulge in his shorts. She squeezed the sides and rubbed the length of his erection over the fabric of his shorts.

He gripped her wrist with a growl and removed her hand. "My dear, you need permission to touch me."

What the fuck? Clearly he was enjoying it. Why did he have to do that?

He rose from the makeshift bed. "Change places with me. Lie down. Legs down here," he said, pointing at the edge of the bed.

She didn't like being reprimanded and it must have shown on her face because he said, "You will learn. I can be more lenient on you because you are new at this, but you must gain an understanding of my rules. Do not touch me sexually unless you have been given permission. Do you understand?"

She nodded.

"Please answer with 'Yes, Sir' or 'No, Sir.'"

Her face felt hot. "Yes, Sir."

"That's better. Lay back and spread your legs for me. Arms by your sides."

It felt so naughty to lie there and keep her legs apart. Extremely vulnerable. The sheer immodesty and boldness of opening her sex to him for whatever purpose he had in mind made her feel like the sexiest woman alive.

He crossed the room to the paint supplies and returned with one of the wooden paint stirrers that hadn't been used. Lightly, he tapped her breast with it.

Marley stretched like a cat, purring in sensual delight.

He rapped her on her bosom with the stick; staccato blows stung her skin, bringing it to life.

Try as she did to hold back, a whimper crept from her lips as her body absorbed the smacks.

He moved to her legs, swatting her inner thighs, his face intensely focused on the task.

It tingled. Smarted more than it actually hurt. The stick hit up the inside of one leg, conspicuously passing over her sex, before travelling down the other leg. Each time he missed her mound she arched her back, straining, beseeching him to hit her there.

Tapping her cunt, he asked, "Is this what you want?"

Biting her lip, she nodded.

He hit her pussy lips harder. "I'm sorry. I didn't hear that."

"Yes, Sir!" she screeched.

Her skin beaded with a light film of sweat. The combination of pleasure and pain he elicited in her was intoxicating.

He inserted one, then two fingers into her aching channel. He fucked her hard with merciless thrusts, while she writhed underneath him.

More swats up and down her inner thigh, teasing her hungry pussy. Finally he landed a blow to her sweet spot, making her jerk and wiggle like crazy.

"You will learn to be still and take this like a good sub," he said.

Marley couldn't imagine being still for this. Her body trembled with lust, needing him to fill her, to make her come.

"Yes, Sir. Sir, will you please fuck me now? Please!" Every nerve ending in her body pulsed. Adrenaline coursed through her. She was laid bare before him, quaking with desire, and she didn't care if she had to beg. She didn't care about anything except having him inside her.

"I think I will have you fuck me, my little doll." He set down the improvised toy, rolled a condom onto his erection, and lay down next to her. "Get on top of me."

Marley usually hated to be on top. When she was working, she'd always wanted the john to do all the work. It was bad enough she had to even be involved; the less energy she had to expend the better. But this was different. Her lust for James consumed her. She would gladly climb on top of this incredibly gorgeous man who had worked her into such a wanton state.

She straddled him, grinding her pubis against his hard cock. Rubbing his length against her clit made her want to come. She looked to him for direction.

"No, don't you dare come yet."

"Yes, Sir." She glided back and forth over the tip of his penis with her cunt.

"Take my cock inside you."

Greedily she swallowed him up inside her. Slippery as an eel, she raised and lowered herself onto him. She prepared to set the pace, her arms on either side of his head, bracing herself.

He caught her breasts in both hands, squeezed them together, and pulled them into his mouth. His tongue caressed her sensitive tips, sending a luscious wave of pleasure through her whole body.

The nip of his teeth jolted her. He bit down, gnawing at both nipples at the same time, one in each corner of his mouth. Pain mixed with ecstasy enveloped her. She was caught in that position, her breasts locked down, held captive by his strong jaw. All her senses intensified, and she fucked him harder.

A slap landed on her ass, making her cry out. He slapped her again and bit down harder. Her hips ground down against his, fucking him with a desperation intensified by her plight.

Repeated blows rained down on her ass. She was his prisoner, his fucktoy. He ran his tongue over her tight little nubs and then bit down gently, sending her over the edge.

As she climaxed she kept riding him, not daring to stop even when the reverberations had stopped.

He let her tits go, then took both her wrists in one hand, holding them tightly, pushing her to sit up straight atop him.

"Yeah, that's a good girl," he said, pumping his hips into her. His upward thrusts hit her g-spot time and time again. She was limp as a rag doll, her legs wobbly, unable to keep up with him.

"Be still, doll." She forced herself to hold still and he sent his hips driving into her at such a frantic pace she could only hold on so as not to fall off him.

He held her wrists clasped in front of her. Pushing down on her shoulder with his other hand, he fucked her like a stallion.

With a final burst, he jetted into her with long strokes.

When he let her go, Marley collapsed into his arms, stretching her legs out beside him.

"You were a very good girl." He played with her hair and held her close. "I like playing with you."

"Thank you, Sir." It felt so good to be snuggled up, safe in his arms. Lying there in contented bliss, Marley couldn't remember the last time she felt so peaceful.

"Marley, Marley, Marley, what am I going to do with you?" he asked, kissing her forehead.

Truthfully, she answered, "I have absolutely no idea."

CHAPTER SIX

Her feet were killing her. She'd bought some new, serviceable shoes for her waitressing job. Hopefully, they would help her breeze through eight-hour shifts, but so far they'd only given her blisters.

Marley stopped along the sidewalk and rubbed her sore heel. Broken pieces of cement and debris littered the grass along the path. Rundown buildings loitered on both sides of her. The seedy neighborhood was sparsely lit with streetlights.

Just a few more blocks. Then I can soak in a steaming tub.

Trudging along, her mind drifted to James. He was on her mind a lot these days. Why did he come over and help her paint that day? Was it for the sex? They did have good sex, but part of her dared to dream there was more to it.

Okay, damn it, she liked him. Shaking her head, she admitted it. She'd developed a crush on the handsome dom. Images of him flashed through her mind. His thick head of black hair. Those piercing dark eyes. Something fluttered in her gut.

He was a sexy man. He turned her on more than any man ever had. But it was more than his obvious physical attributes... It was like they had a connection.

How had that happened? She was so careful to keep a wall up between herself and other people; she needed to protect herself. *Life throws you enough pain as it is. Why go asking for more by investing yourself in others? You're bound to get hurt.*

Yet, she'd let down her defenses. Being honest with herself, she had feelings for Daddy Morebucks.

It's okay. I doubt I'll ever see him again. He hasn't called.

It occurred to her she didn't have a phone.

Probably should get one. She had to be one of the few people with a job who didn't even have a phone. But she could pay her electric bill for six months for what they wanted for the latest phone these days. She shrugged.

Anyway, who would I call?

She left Abilene with the intention of never coming back. When she first got to Dallas she had a roommate, but she and Sarah hadn't been fast friends. Once they got evicted, they parted ways. Sarah was living with a cousin in California last Marley had heard.

Sarah was a kind person, but they'd both been working double shifts to pay the bills, and there was never much time to develop a friendship. They were both either sleeping or working.

Besides, getting close to people was something Marley avoided. It annoyed her that she couldn't keep her mind off James.

She reached her apartment door, cursing under her breath while she fumbled for the key in her purse. *Why can't they have better lighting?*

"Hi," a low voice said from the darkness.

Marley whirled around, aiming her handbag toward the voice. "Stop right there. I have mace!"

"Whoa, whoa. No need for that." James stepped out of the shadows under the dim, flickering glow.

Her hand flew to her chest. "Oh my God! You scared the crap out of me!" She punched him in the arm.

"Ow, sorry." He rubbed his bicep where she'd struck him.

Marley scowled, still shaken. Grudgingly, she invited him inside.

They sat down in the living room, her only room. "What are you doing here?" she asked.

"You know, you could really use some work on your manners. How about 'Hi, Sir, it's nice to see you'?" he said, disapproval written all over his face.

Her shoulders rose and fell as she exhaled. "Okay. Hi, Sir, it's nice to see you. Now, why are you here?"

"You are suspicious, aren't you?"

"Yes, I *am*," she said, folding her arms smugly.

"Okay, I missed you, and since you don't have a phone I didn't have a choice but to drop by unannounced."

"Oh."

"And I've been thinking… I have a proposition for you."

"A proposition?" One eyebrow shot up quizzically.

"Yes." He reached across the space between them and picked up her hand. She didn't shy away.

"I'd like you to come live with me."

Her jaw fell open. "Live with you? What do you mean?"

"When you came to the hotel that night and we played—it was amazing. Since then I haven't wanted to play with anyone else."

A tingle spread through her down into her extremities, and she smiled in spite of herself.

"I know you've started a new job and you just got this apartment, but I can get you out of your lease and you won't have to work at the restaurant anymore."

Her forehead creased. "I won't? Why not?"

"Because I will pay for your expenses." He lifted his shoulder in a half shrug, tilting his head.

"You mean be a kept woman. And what would I *do* all day?" The idea was slightly offensive, but considering her previous career, righteous indignation didn't feel like the best response.

"I don't know. We'd think of something. How about go to school? How far did you get in high school?"

That he'd used the term 'we' was not lost on her.

"I have a high school diploma," she huffed.

"Good. Then you can attend college. What kind of grades did you have?"

"Mostly B's with a few A's and C's."

"Great."

"What if I don't want to go to college?" A thundercloud settled on her face, her lips jutted out.

"Then we'll figure out something else for you to do." He patted her on the knee. "I only want what's best for you, Marley."

For some reason, she believed him.

"Let me think about it." She bit down on her bottom lip.

He rose. "Of course. If you agree, you will be my sub. There will be rules. I'll expect you to follow them. If you do not, there will be consequences."

She stared at him. *Rules. Consequences.* She hated rules and consequences. But maybe not so much when *he* came up with them…

He pulled a phone out of his pants pocket and handed it to her. "Call me when you decide."

She stood up to take the phone. "For me?" Her voice squeaked.

His eyes rolled toward the ceiling. "Yeah, it's a real hassle not being able to get in touch with you. Feels like I need to hitch up my covered wagon to even speak with you. My phone number is in there. It has Internet as well. Knock yourself out."

"But…"

He touched his index finger to her lips. "Just think about it." He leaned in closer and whispered in her ear, "I think we could have lots of fun."

She became aware of the heat between her legs.

Not trusting herself to speak, she nodded.

He kissed her on the forehead, and left.

Marley plopped down on the futon, her mind racing. James wanted her to live with him. Numerous questions popped into her head. Would she have her own room or would they sleep in separate beds? Would she be 'on call' for his sexual whims like a live-in prostitute or would she have a say in when she was available?

Did any of that matter? From a practical perspective, this was like winning the lottery. He must have a cool pad. She'd have a nice place to live, her bills paid, time to do whatever she wanted. Live a life of leisure. Maybe go to school. Vast possibilities were in reach.

College had never been an option for her. She needed money too badly. Now it was something to explore. The world was opening up to her.

But there was something bothering her. A niggling doubt played in the back of her head.

He was doing this because he liked playing with her. Naked playing. This wasn't because he loved her, or really cared about her. This was about what she could do for him. An uncomfortable sinking began in her brain, inched lower and lower until it landed heavily in her stomach.

That's the way the world works. You don't get something for nothing.

A small, vulnerable part of her wished James wanted her for herself, not for her erotic skills or her willingness to spread her legs whenever he snapped his fingers.

No sense crying over unrequited feelings. Not when an opportunity this rare stood before her. James didn't know she had feelings for him. She'd do her best to treat this as a business transaction. Perhaps they could both get what they wanted.

He could use her, but she'd use him too. There were way worse things in life than spending time playing with a handsome millionaire who paid your bills.

Suddenly her feet didn't hurt so badly anymore. The bath could wait. She kicked off her shoes and started to pack.

· · · · · · · · · · · · · · · ·

A driver picked her up and whisked her to a massive tower that appeared to climb upwards for days. Shielding her eyes from the sun, Marley gazed up at the monstrous building, feeling like she was in a modern version of Jack and the Beanstalk.

Nerves jangled inside her. Would she be able to pull this off? Could she fit into this world of high rollers and high society? The self-confident air that was her constant companion fled the minute the driver opened her door. She was out of her element. It was one thing to pretend to fit in, another thing to actually have to do it.

The elevator ride to James' penthouse apartment was surprisingly short. She expected it to take five minutes or longer to reach the top, but it felt more like seconds. Did that thing run at warp speed?

On the top floor, the doorman ushered her into a large apartment with an open floor plan and an incredible view. One edge of the massive room consisted of a wall of windows overlooking downtown Dallas. It had to be stunning at night.

The furniture was oversized, cozy. She expected it to be more modern and sleek, austere. But the huge sectional sofas, and chairs in chocolate and cinnamon hues created a warm and welcoming atmosphere. A reflection of their owner. There were crimson accents around the room, and unique art on the walls. A few sculptures graced side tables. The biggest television Marley had ever seen hung over a fireplace on another wall. Above her, a vaulted glass ceiling offered a view of the clouds.

Books lined the bookshelves. Curious, she wandered over to peruse James' reading preferences. Footsteps sounded and she turned, her nerves on the outside of her skin.

"Hello, Marley, I'm glad you're here." James radiated warmth as he closed the distance between them. He held her at arms' length and inspected her from head to foot before bringing her into his arms for a bear hug. He kissed her on the lips.

"Welcome, little girl." For a split second he resembled a wolf salivating over his dinner.

"Thanks, happy to be here. I love your place."

"It's yours now as well. I want you to make yourself at home. Let me show you around."

He took her on a tour of the penthouse. The spaces were so large, each one beautifully decorated. The laundry room alone was almost as big as her apartment. There was a wine closet, a massive walk-in pantry, and two guest bedrooms. The bathrooms were huge. Everything was clean and new. At least it looked new.

The place wasn't exactly lived in, but it wasn't too sterile or pristine either.

The kitchen sported all the modern conveniences—two massive stainless steel built-in refrigerators, a high-end cooktop and range, multiple sinks. Warm, brown swirled granite counters sparkled atop cream-colored wood cabinets. An iron pot rack groaned overhead with copper cookware.

"Do you cook?" she asked.

"Occasionally. Sucks cooking for one." He scrunched up the corner of his luscious mouth. "Maybe I'll do it more now that you're here."

"Sounds nice." She smiled.

"Why don't we sit down and go over some of the rules?" He motioned for her to perch on one of the wrought-iron barstools tucked under the overhang of the island.

Sweat tingled in her armpits, and she climbed tentatively onto the seat. He joined her with all the confidence of a man who ruled his castle.

"I guess I should have discussed these rules with you earlier. I apologize for not doing so. If there is anything here that you feel that you truly cannot agree to, we can discuss it. However, these rules are important. For this to go smoothly I'd like you to do your best to follow them."

"Let's hear 'em." She smoothed her skirt with sweaty palms.

"Okay, first of all, I will be your daddy, and you will be my little girl. You will be mine and only mine. You will do what I say, without complaint. Do your best to be a good girl."

"Okay, Daddy," she said, flipping her hair. In part it felt like play acting, answering him this way. At the same time it was like falling into a pit of marshmallows, knowing there was a soft, sweet place to land.

"You'll need to keep me informed about your comings and goings, who you're with, what you are doing. You can text me. I also want you to eat a nutritious diet and get enough sleep at night. Take care of yourself."

She nodded. That didn't sound too bad. Controlling? Maybe, but not too big of a price to pay. It had been ages since anyone had cared about her enough to make sure she slept and ate properly. Was this what it felt like to have 'security'? It was easy to see why some women craved it.

"No drugs. When drinking, limit yourself to two alcoholic drinks."

She balled her fists. "Hey, that's not fair."

"Why? How many do you think you should be allowed?"

Sticking her lip out, she replied, "As many as I want!"

"I disagree. When you drink too much your judgment becomes impaired, and that's not good for you. You might make poor decisions."

"What do you think is going to happen, *Daddy*?" she hissed.

"You will speak to me with respect or you will get a spanking." The humor was gone from his face.

"Really?"

"Yes, really."

"Well, I still think it's stupid."

"Marley, you have every right to your opinion, but you are pushing your luck with me."

"Tough." Why was she continuing to push so hard? She was out of control.

"That's enough. Come here."

As if in a trance, Marley obeyed. He slid his stool back and laid her over his knee. The stool was so high that her feet dangled, unable to touch the floor.

He flipped up her skirt. She grabbed the spindly iron legs of the stool and held them. Gritting her teeth, she prepared herself for his onslaught.

He pulled down her panties slowly, inch by inch. The anticipation overtaking her, Marley stopped breathing for a minute. Seeing the kitchen from this upside-down angle disoriented her. The smell of his cologne mixed with a lemony aroma coming from the spotless kitchen floor. A ripple of desire skittered through her, and the whole situation took on a surreal quality.

"I hate to have to do this, Marley. But I hope you will learn a lesson about being respectful." He placed his hand gently on her bottom. She'd underestimated how much she liked feeling his skin on hers.

Then he struck her bottom with his open palm.

She flinched at the blow.

"I will start with twelve swats because I know this is new to you. In the future, bad behavior will earn you more."

Wincing, she bit her lower lip. He hit her harder than the last time, and she bit down harder, breaking the skin.

Tasting blood, she decided that hadn't been the smartest idea. She told herself no biting, but it was difficult not to clench her rear molars together.

He smacked her again.

She whimpered. He wasn't holding back. These blows stung. How was she supposed to just take this?

Remembering to breathe helped, but her ass was on fire. Hadn't he told her to ease into it? Easier said than done.

She must think of something else. Take her mind elsewhere. The pretty penthouse. The super-fast elevator. Anything else but the pain of her backside.

About the tenth slap, she'd given up. Her body was almost growing accustomed to the agony. She lay limp over his knee, not really caring how many more were left.

Then it was over as quickly as it had begun. He righted her, eyeing her sternly. "Do you think you can be more appropriate now?"

Cowed, she fixed her hair and stared at him through wide eyes. "Yes, Sir." She rubbed a hand across her bottom, wishing it was his hand. Wishing that he would comfort her after her ordeal. But there were no signs of that happening. Her spirits fell.

"Good. Then have a seat and we'll finish up."

Marley plopped into her chair, dejected. *Ah, at least the seat is cushy.* Her rear sang with the consequences of her actions. Ouch.

"Are you okay?" He touched her arm. Finally, some compassion.

She brightened. "Yes, Sir."

"All right, Marley. You must always be honest with me. I care about your feelings and your well-being. I want you to communicate with me and I will do the same with you."

Feelings? He wants to know about my feelings? What man does that? There's hope for him yet...

He continued, "We will discuss your interests and goals and make some plans to help you meet those goals."

"I don't think I have any goals, Sir." Life had always been about solving immediate problems. The future wasn't something she had the luxury to contemplate before now.

"Surely there must be something you'd like to do."

She shrugged. What kind of loser didn't have any goals? She wracked her brain, but came up with nothing.

"When you were a kid, what did you want to be when you grew up?"

"A ballerina?" As soon as the words left her mouth she regretted them. Her mother hadn't been able to afford dance lessons. And high school dances had always ended with her stepping on more toes than she cared to remember.

"Can you dance?"

She shook her head, fidgeting on her stool. "Can we move on?"

"Yes. We'll get back to that later. From now on, your body is mine sexually. No other men, or women for that matter."

She made a face.

"Your orgasms are mine as well. Little girls need their daddy's permission to touch themselves."

"Seriously?"

"Seriously. Do you have a problem with that?"

"Not really."

"Good. Now let's talk about punishments. If you break the rules, there will be a punishment." He reached over and stroked her hair. His voice softened. "I will never give you more than you can take. I will stretch your limits, and I will respect your hard limits. You will always be able to use your safeword. What is your safeword?"

"Bluebird."

"All right, Marley, bluebird it is." He cupped her chin. "Trust that I have your best interests at heart."

"So I'm to be available to you whenever you want?"

He nodded. "You are to comply with my requests. You will still be able to have your own life, but being my submissive, my little girl, will be your top priority. Do you have any more questions?"

Chewing on her bottom lip, she shook her head. It was kinda like being a slave. But not. A knot formed in her belly.

"How's your ass?"

A sigh escaped her lips. "It's okay."

"I'm glad. Now let me show you to your room."

CHAPTER SEVEN

James threw open the door to the most beautiful room Marley had ever seen. A huge mirrored wall framed the bed. Aged with a lacy gray finish, it gave the room an antique vibe. Floor-to-ceiling windows showcasing the view made up another wall. An expensive-looking taupe rug covered the cool, gray stone tile floor.

A deep plum upholstered headboard rested atop the king-sized bed, outfitted with platinum and pale lavender shantung linens as soft and shiny as cupid's wings. A lone, fuzzy aubergine pillow centered the bed. Gray damask draperies anchored the view. An upholstered bench butted up to the foot of the bed, and a lamp topped with a stylish white shade was conveniently positioned on a substantial oak chest. A crystal chandelier dripped glamour from the ceiling, and a velvet chaise lounge added voluptuous seating to the room.

A bedroom fit for a Hollywood starlet... and it was all for her. Wrapping her arms around herself, Marley did a small pirouette.

"I take it you like it?" James asked.

"Like it? I love it!" Throwing her arms around his neck, she kissed his cheek. "Thank you, Daddy." The words slid off her tongue like a Slinky rolling down an incline. He could be her 'daddy.' She could get used to that.

"Have you always had a bedroom like this?" She gazed into his eyes.

He laughed. "Of course not. It's a touch too feminine for me. I had it designed especially for you. The designer complained about the turnaround time, but I think she did a fine job on short notice, don't you?"

"Absolutely!"

"If there's anything you don't like, it can be changed. Or anything else you need..."

Surveying the room, she noted a television, a stereo, and a desk. Exquisite details were everywhere she looked.

A realization lit up her brain. She belonged here. "It's perfect."

She walked over to the windowed wall. So many buildings, so many people out there. Usually a view like this made her feel small. Not today. Today she didn't feel like a nobody. James made her feel important from the forehead he liked to kiss all the way down to her heels.

Goosebumps rose on her skin as she sensed him approaching her from behind. His arms encircled her waist, his lips nuzzled her neck. "Oh, Marley, I'm so glad you're here."

"Me too."

She shifted in his arms and pressed her lips to his. He answered hungrily, exploring her mouth with his tongue. Welcoming him, she sucked on his lip, dancing a slow, sensuous tango with nips and flicks of her own.

He released her and stepped back. "You're good to humor me and give this a try. I'm sure you have some reservations."

She pursed her lips. "I guess I just don't know what it's going to be like…"

"I understand that. I don't know either. Every daddy and his little girl must find their own way. But I want to pleasure you. Show you what it can be like to be my little girl."

He strode over to the closet and came back with a copious amount of rope. Hemp, perhaps? She wasn't sure.

"How familiar are you with rope?" His eyes gleamed.

"N-not very." She swallowed. Having her hands tied was one thing, but what did he plan to do with all that rope? Control was slipping away from her; she could feel it in her gut.

"That's okay. I will show you. Take off your clothes."

Every time he gave her that order, butterflies took flight in her stomach. She dropped her skirt and panties to the floor. Pulling her top over her head, she felt his warm hands on her back, unhooking her bra.

Cool air whooshed over her body. The hairs on her arms stood on end, and her nipples sprung to attention.

James ran his hands over her upper arms and shoulders, warming her. "Don't worry, your body heat will rise before long. Would you like me to close the drapes?"

She shrugged. "That's up to you, Daddy."

His erection pressed against the small of her back. A sigh crept from her lips. Damn, he felt good.

"All of Dallas could see you up here if they had a telescope and they wanted to. That doesn't bother you?"

"It doesn't matter to me. I just want to please my daddy." She hoped that was the right answer.

"Marley, it's not safe for you to be in your room naked for all to see. You must always close the draperies if you intend to be undressed. Do you understand me?" His voice was firm.

Another rule. Gosh, he was uptight. "Yes, Sir."

"Good girl." He crossed the room and pulled the cord to close out the rest of the world. Turning back to her, he asked, "Where were we?"

"I think you were about to tie me up."

"Oh, yes. I was." He grinned at her.

Taking a deep breath, she tried to relax. She trusted him. Why? She wasn't sure. But she did.

He stood in front of her. "Lift your arms to your sides."

She obeyed. The rope he draped over her shoulders was softer than it looked. It had a distinct smell. She wasn't sure what it was, but the raw freshness of it reminded her of the lumber section at the hardware store.

She stood there quietly watching him make a crisscross between her breasts. The air filled with electricity as he looped the rope around her body several times.

He wound it around her torso, bringing it behind her back, then to the front again, layering the ropes. The process continued, back to front, then back to front again.

A sense of calm enveloped the two of them. With every loop, every wrap, Marley relaxed. His movements were purposeful and repetitive—hypnotic. The ropes hugged her body like a cocoon. Swaddled in his creation of cords, she felt safe.

Looking down, her breasts were bound with ropes surrounding them, displaying them in a distorted, yet sexy fashion. The image was so bold, she felt almost obscene. To her surprise, she liked it.

"Would you like to be blindfolded?" James' voice broke the silent spell between them.

"Not this time, if that's okay, Sir." This was all so new. She wanted to understand what he was doing to her.

"That's fine. But I will probably blindfold you next time. It enhances the senses." He went back to work.

Starting above her knee, he wrapped a loop over her several times around her leg, catching it with the end of the rope and pulling it taut. Then he repeated the process with her other leg. He bound her wrists behind her back, attaching them to the bottom of the harness. He glanced at the ceiling, then disappeared into the closet again.

He came back with a stepladder. What?

Marley's eyes followed his to the rings coming out of the ceiling. Her heart raced. Her upper lip beaded with sweat. Oh my God! He was going to suspend her. She'd seen this before on the Internet, but never imagined anyone would do that to her.

She watched as he set up a fairly complex pulley system and had four groups of rope billowing down from the ceiling.

"You're going to lift me off the floor with those?"

He nodded and kept working.

"But I'm too heavy. I'll fall."

He touched her cheek gently. "Don't worry. It will hold. I know what I'm doing. You have to trust me, Marley."

Adrenaline pumped through her veins. Trust him? It was a matter of physics, wasn't it? She considered this. She didn't doubt he knew more about physics than she did. Plus it appeared he'd done this before. A twinge of jealousy irked her. She hated thinking of him doing this to another girl.

After asking her to kneel on the bench at the end of her bed, he bent down and wrapped rope around her calves, one at a time. Then he bent her leg back and bound an ankle to the ropes he had tied around her thigh. Two of the ceiling ropes connected to her harness and he attached another to her calves.

He secured her other leg the same way. "I'm going to lift you now. Do not be alarmed. Once you're off the floor, I don't want you to struggle. You are safe. I will not allow you to fall. Those hooks are secured in the roof of this building. They're rated for over six hundred pounds, so they can handle you."

She nodded. Sweat pricked her armpits, and she willed her nerves to chill out and trust him.

Slowly she left the floor. Her body jerked instinctively, aching for the safety of land.

"Uh-uh-uh," he chided. "You want to be a good girl for me, Marley. As you can see, you are clearly at my mercy now. I recommend you follow my directions."

"Yes, Sir. I'm sorry, Sir." Concern vibrated in her voice. He ignored it and made the finishing touches that put her in a semi-hogtied position. Her legs were spread, back arched, with her feet bound up behind her, same as her wrists that rested on the small of her back.

"What if I fall on my face?" she shrieked. In addition to the adrenaline coursing through her veins, she also had full-fledged panic to add to the list.

"Shhh!" He put a finger to her lips. "Take a deep breath. I'm not going to drop you." He lifted her torso to a more upright position. It reminded her of being at the head of a ship's bow. Suspended above everything, her tits jutting out proudly in front of her.

Taking a deep breath, she closed her eyes, and concentrated on her breathing. She opened her eyes to see him secure the rope tails to some pegs on the wall she hadn't noticed before, but then she promptly closed them again. She was starting to understand the value of a blindfold.

Supple lips pressed against hers. She relaxed a little. He dallied with her breasts for a moment, flicking her nipples, pinching them. She wiggled at the attention. Desire raged in her. She was so sensitive! Her bound breasts were like globes of fire, urging him on. He bent and took one, then the other in his mouth. Suckling, licking, then punctuating his attention with a sharp bite. Marley groaned, praying he would play with the rest of her.

Pulled up and positioned, her legs splayed, she was completely open to him and helpless to do anything about it. Her cunt ached for his touch.

"Please, Daddy," she heard herself saying.

"Please what?"

"Please touch me." She was in his hands, ready to surrender to him.

"Touch you where?" He prodded.

"My pussy. I want to feel your fingers inside me."

"What a little slut you are."

Color rose in her cheeks, but her cunt tingled at his words.

She nodded. "Yes, Sir. Your little slut."

He smacked her ass. "Good girl. You're starting to catch on. You're my prisoner. At my mercy, little one. You look incredible, all strung up for me. Delectable." A jolt of electricity ripped through her. She loved hearing that she pleased him.

Tugging on the ropes, he lifted her higher in the air. It was like flying. Being suspended in midair gave her a rush.

He slid underneath her and gave her pussy a lick. Her body jerked, pulled against the ropes, wanting more. Her breasts stuck out, eager and ripe. Her cunt pulsed with need. Another wet graze of the tongue and he stopped.

Damn him! She wanted him to keep going, but she dared not ask for it. Her role was that of a submissive, to take whatever he doled out. Not to make demands.

As nerve-wracking as it was to be out of control, she liked giving him total access to all parts of her body. It released her of any responsibility, any need to perform. For so long she had been the one to give the pleasure to men… this was a novel experience for her.

"Close your eyes."

She obeyed.

A moment later something pushed against her mouth. "Open."

Unsure, she parted her lips tentatively. A cool, hard object forced its way in. Covered in nubs, the phallic rod kept her curious tongue busy.

"Suck it. Make it really wet for Daddy."

She quivered, working hard for him.

He withdrew the object. Dying to see what it was, she peeked.

A beautiful blown-glass dildo. The rainbow-colored nubs covered the shaft, ending in a red glass heart handle.

"That's lovely," she said.

"Nothing but the best for my doll. Now close your eyes like I told you to unless you want a punishment."

She shut them tight.

The dildo stroked the outside of her pussy lips. Up and down. Her muscles clenched down on it as it entered her.

He fucked her with it. Slowly at first, then he picked up the pace.

He rolled his tongue lazily over her pussy folds, nipping her clit as he traveled over her most intimate terrain, using the dildo at the same time. Lapping at her sweet nectar, he pushed her to the edge, nudging his nose over her tender button.

"Oh, Daddy. I want to come, Daddy! Please, can I come?" she screeched.

"Yes, baby. Come all over me," he mumbled into her folds.

She let go with a low guttural cry. Pleasure overtook her and she trembled in her hemp hammock. Having an orgasm in midair intensified the experience. Tremors rocked her all the way to her toes. She experienced a freedom she'd never known.

She descended from the ceiling. He fondled her tits from behind, his hips pressed between her legs. His erection jammed into her butt cheeks.

"Oh, Daddy!"

"Yes, doll?"

"Are you gonna fuck me?"

He laughed. "What do you think?"

His rock-hard cock thrust into her soaking wet slit. He grabbed her torso and pulled her down onto him. Working her on and off his rod, he whispered, "You feel so good, doll. I need you so bad."

She moaned as her hips flew up and down on his cock, controlled completely by him. Another orgasmic wave hit her, her convulsions stirred James. He thrust once more, finding his release.

He hugged her, then lowered her gently to the carpet where he tenderly removed her bindings.

"Stretch," he told her.

Gingerly, she wiggled her arms and legs. Were they made of rubber?

James scooped her up into his arms and carried her to her luxurious bed. He tore back the covers and lay her down on top. Climbing in beside her, he held her close.

His arms snuggled her tight. Marley's body was worn out, but she felt more safe and secure in his arms than she had in her whole life.

"Marley?" Her skin tingled as his fingernails barely scratched her, stroking her forearm.

"Yes?" Her lids were heavy. She wanted to fall away into his dreamy embrace.

He repositioned himself, leaning over so that he could see her face. "If your real name is Harley, how did you come up with the name Marley? And why would you change your name?"

She chuckled. "You mean other than the obvious?"

He smiled. "Yeah."

"When I left home I wanted to forget. Both the good and the bad. My brother got killed over in Afghanistan, and I missed him terribly. I didn't want to remember him. It was too painful."

"I'm sorry, Marley." He smoothed her hair and kissed her temple.

"Yeah. And my mom. Well, my mom's a drunk. I wanted to forget her, and leave all of that behind me. So I decided a fresh start needed a new name."

"What about your driver's license? What does it say?"

"It says Harley. To change that I'd have to go to a judge. Too much of a hassle."

"So where did you get Marley?" She rolled onto her back, and he propped up on his elbow. His other arm slid down to hold her at the waist, their legs entwined.

"When I was in high school I used to volunteer at our local hospital. It got me out of the house, away from Mom and all her crap. I liked it, doing nice things for sick people."

"Like a candy striper or something?"

"Yeah, kinda like that. But no cute uniforms." She giggled.

"That's too bad. I can dream up some hot visuals of you in a candy striper uniform."

Giving him a playful shove on the arm, she continued. "Anyway, I worked with lots of people, but one patient was my favorite."

"Yeah? Which one?"

"Her name was Tricia. She was a three-year-old little girl with AIDS."

James' face grew serious.

"Tricia's mom was a drug addict, a prostitute too. She had AIDS and passed it on to Tricia. When she was pregnant, she was on the streets and didn't take any of the medications that could have prevented her from passing the HIV on to her child. They have those now, so no babies really have to be born with it, but her mom was out of that loop."

"Oh my God. How sad."

"Yeah. It was heartbreaking. She was the most adorable child. Even though she was three, she had the developmental skills of an eighteen-month-old. Apparently she had walked and talked in the past, but by the time I met her she had started going backwards in her development. She smiled all the time. Had the sweetest temperament." Her voice broke. Marley's eyes filled with tears. "I'm sorry," she croaked.

"No, don't apologize. Go on when you can."

She took a deep breath. "I used to pull Tricia around the children's ward in a wagon, and I'd hold her and read to her or we'd watch TV. She was always happy to see me, and I loved spending time with her. One day we were watching that sad movie about the dog named Marley and she pointed at me and started saying, 'Marley. Marley.' Those were the first words I'd ever heard her say." She swallowed. "It really touched my heart, her calling me

Marley. Just hearing her speak was incredible enough, but that she gave me a nickname... she was so smart. I loved that child."

"That's sweet. What happened to her?"

Marley sniffed. "She died."

His jaw fell. "She died? I thought you were going to say she got better and left the hospital."

She shook her head. "No, she died. Just before her fourth birthday. I went to her funeral. Thought I never would stop crying."

He hugged her close. "I'm sorry, Marley."

She squeezed him back. "Thanks. It's weird, but I relate to 'Marley' in a way I never did to being called 'Harley.' I believe when Tricia named me, she knew what she was doing. And it makes me feel connected to her. Like in some way a part of her lives on, in my name."

Kissing her head, he breathed, "My poor, poor girl. You've seen more than your share of sorrows, haven't you?"

Her eyes stung. "Yes." She smiled wryly.

"My dear Marley girl." He held her close until she fell asleep.

CHAPTER EIGHT

Marley woke up alone the next morning. A quick peek around the place told her she was the only one home. That gave her the opportunity to snoop in James' room. He hadn't taken her in there when he'd given her the tour yesterday, and she was curious.

His suite matched hers in luxury, but it was more masculine. A king-sized, dark mahogany sleigh bed anchored the room, outfitted with sumptuous blue and white patterned linens. The bedspread and wallpaper shared different, yet complementary shapes swirling across the surface. While the prints were a bit fussy, the lines of the furniture and the expanse of glass looking out onto the city added a sophisticated tone to the space. Silken rope ties held back golden draperies, and another exquisite chandelier added a bright spark to the dark room. Unlike her room, there was no mirror. For that she had to go into his bathroom.

Appointed with a massive whirlpool tub and huge walk-in shower, the bathroom housed a separate closet for the toilet. Brown and cream granite abounded, accented by navy towels. When she saw there were two sinks, Marley's spirits soared. *Stop that*, she cautioned herself. *He gave you your own room for a reason.* Though what that reason was, she wasn't sure.

His closet was unbelievable. One of those professional closet companies must have designed it. Row upon row of shirts and jackets hung from what seemed like an endless wall. At least thirty pairs of shoes rested on shelves lining another wall. The ends were capped with built-in drawers from floor to ceiling. Marley peeked in several of them, only finding socks, folded t-shirts, and underwear. The sexy boxer-brief kind she liked. How could he be so perfect?

She shouldn't be in here. A shadow of guilt passed over her as she made her way to the kitchen. He'd left her alone. Surely he knew she would look in his room…

It took effort to open the heavy door of the enormous refrigerator. She pulled out a carton of orange juice and poured herself a glass. Padding her way into the living room, she tucked her feet under her and switched on the television.

Nothing held her attention. She flipped through the channels several times, marveling at the sheer number of them. She'd only had basic cable before. Over eight hundred channels and she still couldn't find anything to watch. How could that be? Finally she settled on a Johnny Depp movie in which he was fighting the devil. At least that's what she gathered. She'd tuned in during the middle so she was slightly confused.

When the program ended, she went to her bathroom to shower. Hers was similar to James', but the counters and shower were made of a sparkly white stone. Marble? The fluffy periwinkle towels were soft as velvet against her skin. She considered an inviting soak in the tub, but decided against it. She was too amped up to take a relaxing bath.

Her shower was well equipped with shampoo, conditioner, and body wash, as well as bar soaps and a shower cap. He'd thought of everything. Or someone had.

Hundreds of tiny jets sent water beating down on her ever so gently. Like a rain shower. After drying off, she applied one of the lotions she found in one of the cabinets, immersing her skin in the sweet berry scent. She blow-dried her hair and applied mascara and lip gloss.

Marley remembered to take her birth control pill. James had seen to it they were both tested for STDs before she moved in. He'd found her a doctor who had put her on the pill so they could enjoy their intimacy uninterrupted by condoms.

The clock read 11:43. She considered calling James, but what would she say? She missed him, but he was at work. Better not to bother him.

After getting dressed, she went into the kitchen and made herself a turkey sandwich. Sitting at the island, eating, her mind drifted back to the night before. Those ropes. They felt amazing on her skin, and she loved letting go and giving herself to James. There was an allure to submitting. It took the pressure off her and allowed her to release her inhibitions.

What he'd done to her was mind-blowing. Who knew being tied up could be so exhilarating, so freeing? The men she knew were only interested in having a good time themselves. Until she met James, she hadn't known that there were men who found enjoyment in satisfying a woman. It turned him on to get her off.

Damn, that was so hot! Her panties moistened. *Maybe I'll go in my room and find that vibrator…* James' words echoed in her ear—"Little girls are not allowed to touch themselves without Daddy's permission." Double damn! That made her even hotter. She sucked an index finger into her mouth.

Taking a deep breath, she decided to obey his rules. For some strange reason she wanted to please him. But why? He would never know if she touched herself or not. She hadn't seen any hidden cameras. She could always play with herself and then lie if he asked her about it.

But she didn't want to. Being honest with him was important.

Shaking herself, she took the key James had given her and left the apartment. She needed a distraction, maybe some exploring. Anything to take her mind off James. Off sex.

Marley took the supersonic elevator to the ground floor. She exited into the beautiful lobby. The floor gleamed, the chandeliers sparkled. The place shone like a new car lot.

Hmm. No gift shop or bar. She approached a uniformed man sitting behind a desk near the front door.

"Excuse me, is there anything to do around here?" she asked, tilting her head.

The man glanced up from his newspaper. "Like what?" His nametag read 'Stan.'

"Oh, I dunno. Exercise. Shop. Eat. Anything, really. I'm new to the building." Marley twirled her hair and tossed him a sugary smile.

"Exercise. Yeah, there's a gym on the third floor and an indoor pool in the basement. What apartment are you in?"

Her sweat glands started working overtime. Crap. She didn't remember the number. Should have checked before she left the apartment!

Cupping her hand over her mouth, her eyes widened and she said, "Oh no, I completely forgot."

Stan laughed. "What's your name? I can look it up for you."

"Marley. It's on the top floor… the penthouse. Is there more than one?"

Stan brightened. "You're Mr. LeBlanc's girl. He told me to get you anything you needed. You need anything?"

She flipped her hair. "No, I'm fine. Just bored. Thought I'd get the lay of the land."

"Well, the mailboxes are back there around the corner." He pointed toward the back of the building. "And the exercise facilities are on three, the pool's in the basement. Here, let me get you a map." He grabbed one from behind his desk and handed it to her along with some other papers. "We don't do food service here, but here's a list of restaurants that either deliver or we can send someone to pick up take-out for you."

"No kidding?"

"No kidding. All you need to do is call me and let me know what you need. I'm here from four in the morning until Ken comes in at three. He's here 'til two. From two to four in the morning you're on your own." He winked.

She giggled. "Good to know." Tucking the papers under her arm, she turned to go. Over her shoulder she called, "Thanks, Stan."

"Anytime, Miss Marley. Happy to be of help any way I can."

Next, she visited the pool. It was dead. Everyone must be at work. The vast expanse of blue water looked to be an Olympic-sized pool for lap swimming. From a practical standpoint, it was nice that you could swim in the winter, or when it rained. But Marley preferred the sun and lounge chairs to come with her swimming, thank you very much, so the fact that the pool was underground removed any allure it would have otherwise held.

The gym was more her speed, but the personal trainers milling around made her uncomfortable so she gave the place a quick onceover. Row after row of elliptical machines, stationary bikes, and treadmills loomed in the front. At least seven large screen TVs were mounted to the wall in front of them. The sides and the back of the gym were reserved for weight machines and free weights.

She discovered a small spa with a limited menu of services that included massages, pedicures, manicures, waxing, and facials. They were open only three days a week, but that sounded fun. She'd never had a pedicure before. Maybe she'd ask Daddy if she could get one.

Daddy. In her head she was growing accustomed to referring to him that way. In some ways it was an endearment. Like honey or sweetheart. She relished being able to call him something so intimate.

It was good to get out of the apartment, but she was still restless. She went back upstairs to wait for James. He was planted at the forefront of her mind, and she couldn't think of much else.

Back in the penthouse, she parked herself on the couch in front of the television. She watched reruns of old shows until she got so hungry she called down for Ken to order her a pizza.

She ate half of the pepperoni pie herself, holding out hope that James would come home soon and join her.

With each passing hour her spirits sank lower. Where was he? Why didn't he call and tell her where he was?

Check yourself, Marley. You're not his wife. You have no claim on him or his time, she chided herself. *In fact, it's the other way around.* He was the one who had a claim on her. That was both exciting and frustrating at the same time.

She stayed at loose ends for the rest of the evening. Rattling around the apartment all day wasn't for her. She'd have to find something to do during the day or she was going to go bananas.

Around eleven o' clock she finally gave up waiting for James and went to bed.

She was sound asleep when something woke her. Something rubbed and caressed her legs and buttocks. Someone. Her eyes cracked open. Pitch black. What was *that*?

"Sorry to wake you, darlin'," a voice whispered in her ear. Hot, wet lips pressed against her neck. A familiar, masculine scent registered in her brain.

James. She had missed him. As mad as she had been earlier, when he touched her now, her irritation fell away.

He scooped her up from behind, contouring his body to fit hers. His hand glided over her, warm and enticing. She found herself anticipating what he would do next, leaving her slumber for later.

Kisses sprinkled her shoulders and neck. Soft, butterfly kisses mixed with more passionate suckling and nipping. She wriggled with pleasure.

"Hi, Daddy," she said shyly.

"Hi," he rasped into her ear, taking it between his lips.

"What are you doing?"

"Coming to see my little girl. I missed you today."

She smiled. *He had missed her.* "I missed you too. Where were you all day?"

"Work. I'm sorry. I realized on the way home I should have told you that you could use the car service if you wanted to go anywhere. You probably had some questions as to where some things were. I'm afraid I wasn't a very good daddy."

His apology alleviated many of her concerns and she gave him a squeeze. "That's okay, Daddy."

He caressed her buttocks. "No panties. That's a good girl." She had gone to sleep in a big old t-shirt and that was it. She never wore underwear to sleep.

"Mmm," she purred.

His fingers found her core. He insinuated one, then two inside of her, stroking her pebbled walls languorously.

She fidgeted, shifting her body to give him better access.

"Oh, so you like this?"

"Mm-hmm," she squeaked.

"Yes, Daddy," he corrected.

"Yes, Daddy."

"You're so wet, baby. You feel so good."

Coated with her juices, he rubbed back and forth over her clit as she writhed in front of him. "Daddy!"

"Yes, baby?"

"Daddy, you're going to make me come."

"Not yet, princess." He chuckled.

"Turn over on your back."

She rolled toward him. He captured her mouth with his, plundering it with his tongue. She responded with a fire of her own.

"Sit up."

He lifted the t-shirt over her head and tossed it on the floor. He laid her back on the bed, suckling her erect nipples, one at a time, pinching the other one as he went back and forth giving them equal attention.

Marley raised her hips, wanting him. Her brain, and all its calculations, had abandoned her. He had turned her into a voracious animal aching for him to take her.

"What a wanton little girl you are. Are you going to be Daddy's little whore?" he growled.

The word punched her in the gut. Yes, she had been a whore. She hadn't wanted to do those things before. She put up with it—for the money.

Now James was keeping her. She was a kept woman. Still a whore. But somehow this was different. This time she wasn't doing it for the money. She did it *for him*. She wanted *him*. More than anything she'd ever wanted in her life.

"Yes, Daddy. Only yours."

At that, he breached her defenses, forcing himself into her with a ferocity that took her breath away. She groaned as he rocked her body in his arms, filling her with every thrust.

He lifted her legs onto his shoulders. She wrapped them around his neck, urging him to plunge deeper and deeper into her.

His cock banged against her g-spot, then rammed into her cervix. Each time he hit that sensitive spot, she twitched with a combination of pain and elation. The exquisite combination led to a rush of fluid flooding from her cunt.

What the hell? Did she just pee herself? Heat rose in her face. She was glad it was dark.

He cupped the base of her head with his hand and kissed her. "You are such a good girl, Marley. I love when you squirt all over my dick."

Was that what it was? She'd heard about squirting, but she didn't think she'd ever done it before now.

His praise made her forget her embarrassment, and she surrendered to the sensation. He plowed into her at a rapid pace, and her orgasms took control. Wave after wave of bliss fluttered through her, encompassing her whole being.

With a gurgle in his throat, he pushed into her one last time, then stilled. His seed warmed her insides and seeped out onto her legs. Who knew it would be so satisfying to have a man come inside you?

Wrapping her arms around his neck, she nuzzled him. "Thank you, Daddy." And she meant it.

He withdrew and fell onto the bed next to her. "You're welcome, baby."

Her pussy clenched at his absence. She wished he could stay inside her. It felt so right. She wasn't able to get enough of him.

He held her for a few minutes, then gave her a peck on the forehead. "Goodnight, Marley." With that, he left her room, closing the door behind him.

Tears formed in her eyes. Why had he gone and left her all alone again? She craved his arms around her shoulders, his voice whispering huskily in her ear.

You are still just a whore to him. Salty tears leaked from her eyes onto the cushy down pillow.

Her practical side resurfaced. *Be grateful for what you have, Marley. You hit the jackpot with this arrangement. Be happy*, she chided herself.

The pep talk didn't help. She was falling in love with him.

CHAPTER NINE

The next morning James woke Marley when he entered her room carrying a tray. On it he'd piled a plate full of cinnamon rolls, accompanied by a glass of water and a glass of juice. The dishes were white and light blue with the faintest of white dots around the edges.

"I wish I had some pretty flowers to add to your tray, but I'm all out of rosebushes up here," he said, setting the tray down next to her on the bed.

She giggled. "That's okay, Daddy. Breakfast in bed… I wasn't expecting that."

The corners of his mouth turned up. "Well, it's not something I can do every day, but I want to pamper my little girl when I can."

She grinned back at him. "I like that!"

"I'll bet you do."

He sat down on the bed.

"Aren't you going to join me?"

"I've already eaten."

"Oh." She took a bite of the pastry. "You've got an awful lot of style for a bachelor." She indicated the china plates.

"Oh, that. Yeah. I used to have a sub who liked to spend my money. She bought those."

"You did? Tell me about her."

Alarm bells rang in his head. It's never a good idea to discuss one woman with another. He would tread lightly with this topic. "Not much to tell. I tried having a relationship like this before, and it didn't work out too well." He rubbed his chin.

"Why? What happened?"

He snickered. "First of all, she was a bitch. Submissive in the bedroom, like she was supposed to be, but hell on wheels out of it. I'm not sure how I got into that arrangement. It was a mess. In the end I think she was after my money. She moved in here, took over, then left me for an older, richer guy. Married him, actually."

"No way! I'm sorry." Her mouth hung open. "How could someone do that to you? You're wonderful."

He gave her a quick kiss. "Thanks. You're sweet. But she wasn't a true sub; she just played the part when she needed to. Helped her get what she wanted." He sighed. "She was a social climber too. Really not my thing."

"I see. What is your thing?" Her eyes widened.

He moved the tray out of the way and tickled around her waist, answering firmly, "You."

She squirmed underneath him and gurgled with laughter. "Stop!"

He kept tickling. "You're my thing."

Giggling, she fought to catch her breath. "Stop, Daddy!"

"Do you need to use your safeword?" He nuzzled her neck as he counted her ribs, sending her into tickling hell.

"No, Daddy. Please!"

He stopped and put on a stern face. "Marley, you can always use your safeword and I will stop."

"Okay, Daddy. I'm just afraid you'll think less of me if I do." She bit her lip.

"I won't. I need to know and understand your limits. I want to push them, but not take you over that edge. I never want to hurt you or make you too uncomfortable."

She took a deep breath. "Thank you, Daddy."

"Sure." He put her tray back in front of her. "Now eat your breakfast like a good girl. I'm going to take you out today."

"Really?" She shoved a bite into her mouth enthusiastically. Today was starting out well.

"Yep. So eat and get dressed. I'm going to send a few emails and then we'll go."

"Where are we going?" Her eyes shone with anticipation.

"Shopping," he said, closing the door behind him.

He checked his emails, threw on a polo shirt and some khakis, and went to wait for her in the living room. Not long after he sat down, she strolled out of her room. Popping up like a jack-in-the-box, he took her by the arms and inspected her.

"Lovely, Marley." He hugged her tight. This morning he'd been surprised when the first thing that popped into his head was her. He'd woken up longing to see her, smell her, touch her. "Do you know how glad I am that you are here?"

"No." She sounded puzzled.

He let her go. "I think you're the best thing that's happened to me in a long time."

"Ditto," she said.

They walked into the hallway and onto the elevator.

"But, if you tried this before, what makes you think it's going to work this time?" she asked. "Not to say it won't, but I'm just wondering why you're so optimistic?"

"You're different, Marley. Different from any woman I've ever met."

"How?"

He considered how to answer her. It was hard to put into words. They reached the ground floor. He led her through the lobby, where she spoke to Stan.

"Hi, Stan." She waved.

Stan gave her a big grin. "Good day, Miss Marley."

"See? Most women I know would not be friendly with the doorman," he whispered as he opened the door of his black Porsche 911 for her.

"Why not?" she asked before he closed her door.

He opened his door and slid into the driver's seat. "I don't know, they just wouldn't."

Once they buckled their seatbelts, James continued, "Marley, you are a breath of fresh air. Thanks to Milton you must know that I hired prostitutes on occasion after Karen left. And that was fine for a while. I don't do much socializing. I'm more of a workaholic." He glanced fondly at her. "Then I met you. You've awakened something in me, and it feels great."

"Really?" She appeared skeptical.

"Really," he smiled. "Face it; you are an amazing girl, my dear."

Marley lit up. His spirits soared that she cared what he thought about her.

He turned the radio on and flipped around until they agreed upon a channel. Marley sat back and took in the sights. Had she seen these parts of Dallas? So much of her experience was foreign to him.

He pulled the car into the huge parking lot at Northpark Center. Recently renovated, the mall had a fresh new vibe.

Inside, they were greeted by massive works of art that rose up in the center of each section. A red metal object as high as the second floor towered over them. Stores of all kinds lined each side of the main walkway. Marley stood with her mouth open.

James asked, "Are you all right?"

"Yeah. We don't have malls like this in Abilene." She grinned.

"Gotcha." He took her hand and led her into a store dedicated to sunglasses.

"Sunglasses?" she asked.

"Yes, I'm tired of watching you squint when we go outdoors. You have to take better care of your eyes. Let's find some you like."

Twenty minutes later, they exited the store with Marley wearing a pair of designer sunglasses. "What's next?" she asked.

He looked at his watch. "We actually have an appointment at Neiman Marcus in about thirty minutes."

"An appointment? Why would we need an appointment?"

"It's with a personal shopper. I contacted her in advance with your sizes. She's pre-selected things she thinks you might like."

She narrowed her eyes. "You're serious?"

"Yes. Why wouldn't I be? I don't know what to buy for you. I thought professional help might be in order."

She crossed her arms in front of her chest, tapping her toe on the floor. "What about me? Why can't I shop for myself? Are you afraid I won't pick out the right thing?"

Wow. Sometimes women could be so difficult. He'd tried to do something for her and now she was offended. Great. "No, Marley. It's nothing like that. You can pick out whatever you want. I just thought it would be helpful. If it's not, you don't have to buy anything. Please, let's have a nice time." He let go an exasperated sigh.

Marley stood on her tiptoes and kissed him on the cheek. "Sorry, Daddy. Thank you for the sunglasses. I'm just not used to anybody doing things for me. Please forgive me."

"Of course," he said, taking her hand.

They strolled along, window shopping, until she paused in front of a lingerie store. With a wicked grin she asked, "Can we stop in here? I do need some things, Daddy."

How could he say no? His dick stiffened at the picture in his head of Marley wearing the items on display in the window. "Sure."

He followed her inside like a puppy on a leash. There was nowhere to sit so he trailed along behind her, hoping to prevent himself from drooling.

Occasionally she'd ask his opinion as she sashayed by the tables of pretty panties and bras. He nodded and smiled, overwhelmed by the sheer number of choices. Bras in an endless array of colors lined the walls. Alluring teddies in various animal prints spilled out of an open armoire. Marabou slippers teetered atop a cascade of silky chemises, calling out for him to touch them. After making sure no one was looking, he reached out and stroked the turquoise feathers, vowing to get a pair of those for Marley. The things he could do with those feathers...

Hmm. Where was she? Marley had disappeared the moment he'd turned away. He searched each room for her and was about to give up when a perky salesgirl approached him. "Sir, are you looking for the girl with the black hair? She's in the dressing room. She asked me to come get you."

"Thanks." He followed her to a hallway, each side lined with pink and black doors. "Marley?" He called, clueless as to which door she was behind and terrified at the prospect of walking in on a stranger. Pulling at his collar, he began to perspire. Was it super hot in here or was it just him?

"Yes, Daddy?" Her voice lilted over a dressing room door near the end of the hallway. Part of him wished he could shut her little mouth for calling him that here. The other part was proud of her, wanting her to shout to everyone they saw that she was his little girl and he was her daddy.

"Marley! Where are you?" he hissed.

She opened the door and traipsed into the hallway wearing nothing but a bra and panties. The skimpy underwear was red plaid, trimmed with white eyelet. She twirled around, showing off for him. "Do you like it, Daddy?"

She was a vision. Her beauty squeezed him deep in his heart.

Jolted back to reality, he answered, "Yes. You look incredible." He shooed her back into the dressing room. "But you don't need to show the whole world."

"I don't?" she asked, playing with his collar.

"No, you don't. Now be a good girl and stay in here. This is only for me to see." He pointed two fingers at her.

"Yes, Daddy. I'll be good." She turned her back and removed her clothing. She wore a white thong underneath, but was naked other than that. He tried to look away, but glanced into the mirror instead where he got a view of her from the front. *Hmm. I could get used to this.*

She tried on a variety of things. Everything got a thumbs-up except a stretch lace bodysuit he thought made her look cheap.

It took monumental restraint not to slam her up against the wall and take her right there in the dressing room, but he summoned all his willpower and refrained. They were sure to have hidden cameras and the last thing he needed was a scandal. Instead he took mental pictures of her in the skimpy lingerie. Later he could call them up when he needed a Marley fix.

Checking his watch, he noticed they were about to be late for their appointment. He hurried her along, taking her finds to the cash register while she got dressed. He laid on the counter a pair of emerald green ruffled rhumba panties, a black bra, black panties with a heart cut out in the ass (his favorite), a frilly short black nightgown, a red ruffled bra and panty set dotted with black hearts, and the plaid bra and panties.

At the last minute, Marley rushed to the counter, out of breath, with more in her hand. "Can I get these too, Daddy? Pretty please?" She held up a see-through lavender babydoll nightie and a couple of beige bras.

"You most certainly can, but we need to hurry. I hate being late."

She hugged his arm tight. "Thank you," she whispered.

The salesgirl was nonplused by her referring to him as Daddy, but she did step up the pace folding their purchases and finished ringing them up in record time. He relaxed his shoulders.

"Anything else, Mr. LeBlanc?" she asked.

"No, thank you."

Marley had grabbed one of the shopping bags when they headed into the mall.

"Here, give me that," he commanded.

"Why? I can carry things."

"I know you *can*, but I want to do it for you. Now don't argue with me."

She reluctantly handed the bag back to him. "But now I have nothing to carry. And you have all those bags. It makes me feel useless." She frowned.

"Doll, you are anything but useless. Do you have any idea how hot you got me back there?"

She shook her head.

"I'll have wet dreams all week." He gave her ass a quick slap.

She giggled. "Daddy!"

He smiled at her. "Let me spoil you today. Okay?"

Beaming, she drawled, "Okaaaay."

Looking down at her tiny little handbag, he made a mental note to get her a new one at Neiman's.

His hands were full of bags, but she unwrapped his pinky finger and circled her dainty little hand around it.

She gazed into his eyes with an intimacy foreign to him. A warm breeze of happiness blew through him. He knew he was infatuated with her, but this was something more…

When they arrived at Neiman's, they took the elevator to the top floor where they met Beverly, their personal shopper for the day.

Beverly wore a smart navy blue suit with high heels that clicked when she walked. "Hi, Mr. LeBlanc. I'm glad you could come in today. I believe we may have met before. I'm a friend of Sloane's." She extended her hand.

"Nice to see you." He shook her hand. "This is Marley Middlebrooks."

Marley greeted Beverly with a smile. "Nice to meet you."

"Likewise. Mr. LeBlanc called in your sizes and I've set aside several things, but you tell me what you think. Let me know if we're on the right track."

Marley nodded. "Okay."

Beverly showed them to a massive private dressing room with a chaise lounge, a sofa, and table. There were several full-length mirrors placed specifically to show off a person from every angle.

"Make yourself comfortable, and I'll be right back," she said, disappearing behind a swath of curtains.

The moment she was out of site, Marley asked, "Who's Sloane?"

Was she jealous? He smiled at the possibility. "A friend of mine. We went to school together. She's a clothing designer, I guess she knows Beverly." He shrugged.

"Oh. Where did you go to school?" She laced her fingers with his, caressing his hand with hers.

"UT—Austin. How about you?" As soon as the words came out of his mouth, he wished he could take them back. He already knew the answer to that. But it was such a knee-jerk reaction in his world. Like when someone asks how you're doing and you automatically say, "Fine. How're you?"

She laughed, but there was no mirth in her eyes. "Abilene High School."

He clasped her hand. "That's something I want to talk with you about later. Maybe over dinner."

Her eyes lit up. "Dinner! You *are* spoiling me today. Where are we having dinner?"

"We'll see." He loved how excited she got about things he took for granted, like going out to dinner. Her childlike enthusiasm was enchanting.

A hefty rack of clothes pushed through the curtains. Beverly followed behind, steering the colorful vehicle.

"Oh my!" Marley exclaimed.

"You can start by looking through these. Tell me what you like and what you don't. Let me know if there are any special occasion items you need. Mr. LeBlanc said you mostly needed everyday wear so that's what I've brought out first. Now, what can I get you to drink? Bottled water, champagne, a Coke?" Beverly asked.

A devious grin spread across Marley's face. She turned to him, pursing her lips adorably. "Daddy, can I please have some champagne?"

"Yes, but no more than two glasses." He held a finger up, warning her. "You know the rules."

Enthusiasm bubbled from her lips. "Yes, Daddy, I know." Marley hopped up and began rifling through the clothes. "Wow! Look at this, Daddy; wouldn't it look cute on me?"

"Yeah, doll. That is cute. And Beverly, I'll have some water, please." The situation was getting too girly for him. That looked like a colossal amount of clothes for her to go through… Maybe he'd send her shopping alone next time, or with a girlfriend.

While Marley oohed and aahed and tried on countless dresses and sweaters, James checked his portfolio, his email, and finally the Dallas Vipers sports news on his phone.

James was a huge football fan, and his buddy, Natron Dakers, was the star wide receiver on the team. The Vipers needed to win only one more game to make it to the playoffs.

He lifted his gaze to see Marley dressed in a short gray sweater dress topped with a zebra print scarf, gray leg warmers, and sexy black knee-high boots. *She looks great, but I'd rather see her in only the boots.*

"What do you think?" she asked.

"Love it, especially the boots."

She scrunched her shoulders happily and turned back to Beverly. "I think I need more things like this. Things I'd wear every day. I don't really need anything fancy, do I, Daddy?"

"No," he replied absentmindedly, then changed his mind. "Now that I think of it, maybe a ball gown and a cocktail dress, Beverly." There would be occasions coming up where she would need to be dressed up.

"A ball gown?" Marley's eyes grew big as saucers.

"Yes. I go to charity events on occasion. I'd like you to come with me."

"I've got just the dress," Beverly told Marley.

The University of Texas fight song jangled in his hand. Saved by the phone. He excused himself. The girls didn't even notice his exit.

It was his friend Charles. "Hey, J, what's goin' on?"

Charles had recently returned from Iraq. He and his girlfriend Kimberly were engaged and they had asked James to be the best man in the wedding. Charles hadn't said much about the wedding yet, but James expected the planning would begin in full force after the holidays. "Not much. What's up?"

"Sloane texted Kimberly that you were at Neiman's shopping with a new girlfriend. She wants me to get the scoop."

"Already? I've only been here an hour." The gossip pipeline flowed remarkably fast. Guess there wasn't much you could keep private in this town. Not that he'd want to. Marley wasn't a dirty little secret, he was proud of her. He'd want to show her off to his friends. Just maybe not so soon…

Charles laughed. "I know, right? Kimberly wants to meet her. Do you think she would get along with the other girls?"

"I don't see why not."

"Okay, will you give her Kimberly's number? The girls are having lunch next week and she and Sloane are dying to meet her."

"Gotcha. I will pass that along." They spoke for a few more minutes about work and the Vipers before they hung up.

James poked his head back into the dressing room. Marley viewed herself from all angles in a khaki trench coat with ruffles at the bottom, her face plastered with pure delight. His chest tightened. He wanted to see her happy like this always.

He closed the curtain back and called Milton, who complained he wasn't at the office.

James considered cutting their day short and going in to work for a couple of hours, then brushed aside the idea. When was the last time he'd taken the day off? It had been ages. Maybe for some dental surgery last year. It felt strange not being at the office, but he was looking forward to spending the rest of the day with Marley.

The next time he checked on her, Marley stood in front of the mirror in a flowing floor-length gown with a portrait collar. Billows of red surrounded her, like flames licking the air. She was stunning.

"That one for sure," he said to Beverly. Marley beamed.

Next she slipped into a deep green beaded cocktail dress with three-quarter sleeves. It reminded him of the panties they'd purchased earlier.

"It matches your eyes. It was made for you," Beverly enthused.

"We're almost through, Daddy," Marley said.

"Oh, Beverly, she needs a new bag, too. Can you show us some choices?"

"Sure. Be right back." Beverly scurried to the back.

"Come sit in Daddy's lap." James sat down and patted his legs.

"Yes, Sir." She sidled over and settled herself onto his waiting lap. Wrapping her arms around his neck, she kissed him on the mouth, then let her lips travel to his neck. Nibbling on his ear, she whispered, "Thank you, Daddy. You're so good to me, so generous."

"Marley, this is the least I can do for you. You give yourself to me so completely. It makes me want to always be this good to you. Makes me want to spoil you rotten." He spanked her bottom playfully.

She giggled. "Can't argue with that."

Holding her in his arms, he felt centered, content. His mind filled with peace. Taking care of her made him feel whole. He nipped at her lips, found her tongue with his.

Beverly cleared her throat, and Marley stood up. "Oh, those are fabulous. Daddy, are you sure we can get all this?"

He nodded. "Whatever you want, doll."

She chose a black Gucci shoulder bag. Elegant and casual, it complemented the rest of her selections perfectly. The three of them decided that Marley should wear the last outfit home.

A black leather jacket with a hint of a peplum and white and black plaid wool skirt. The transformation was significant. Marley looked more sophisticated than he'd ever seen her. With her hair pulled back into a long ponytail and her new sunglasses on, he hardly recognized her.

He noticed she wore the boots he favored. It sent a shiver down his spine. His pulse raced. *I need to get her alone.*

Aloud he said, "Here, Beverly. This ought to take care of everything." He handed Beverly a credit card, and she hustled away with the heaping armload of garments Marley had amassed.

Standing up, he pulled Marley into his arms, asking, "Is my baby hungry yet?"

She nodded.

Since they were alone again, he let his hands drift down to her ample ass. He leaned in for a kiss; her lips parted, ready for him. God, he could kiss her all day long.

Beverly interrupted their embrace when she discreetly placed a padded folio and pen upon the table. With a flourish of a pen, James took care of the five-figure bill he and Marley had rung up. What good was money if you had no one to spend it on?

He arranged with Beverly to have someone deliver their purchases to his address. There wasn't room in his car for all of their boxes and bags. Marley and James thanked her for her time, and they set off for an early dinner.

CHAPTER TEN

After discovering they both loved Italian food, James decided to take Marley to Maggiano's Little Italy. Even though the restaurant was in a mall, white linens covered the tables and the service was impeccable. Marley raised an eyebrow when he ordered a bottle of wine. She'd already had champagne that afternoon.

"I'll watch you. I won't let you get too drunk," he told her, flaring his nostrils.

"Okay, Daddy."

She balked when he ordered calamari as an appetizer. "Isn't that squid?" she asked.

"Yes. Sometimes I may ask you to try new things…" He placed his hand over hers, giving her a knowing glance.

"Yes, Sir."

Marley's behavior had been exemplary so far. *She's going to deserve a reward once we get home.* The wheels in his brain turned over one another as he conjured up new ways he could take advantage of her enticing charms.

He ordered the rustic chicken and shrimp for himself and the lobster carbonara for her.

"Thank you, Daddy. I don't get a chance to eat lobster very often." Her face glowed in anticipation of such a treat.

"You're welcome, doll. I hope you enjoy it. Now, there are a few things I'd like to talk with you about."

Her face grew serious. "Did I do something wrong? Did I pick out too much stuff? Because if I did, you can take it back." She chewed on her bottom lip.

"No, Marley. Nothing like that. All of the things you picked out today are yours. We're not going to take them back. I just wanted to talk to you about some of the rules and the way we do things at home."

"Oh." She breathed deeply. "Okay."

"I'm not sure how much you know about being a sub or how familiar you are with the lifestyle."

She shrugged and set the piece of bread she was eating down on her plate.

"Well, everyone does things differently. Some doms would have you greet them naked at the door every day on your hands and knees, wearing a collar."

She looked shocked, but she remained silent.

"But that's not how I am. I don't think either one of us wants you to open the door like that to Stan or Milton. It wouldn't do for us to become known as the kinkiest couple in the building. I like to operate with more discretion than that."

Her head bobbed in agreement. "What about a collar? You haven't put one of those on me yet."

"It's not a big thing for me to drag you around by a leash." The corner of his mouth curled. "However, I *would* like to see you crawl around on all fours for me."

Her cheeks turned crimson. "Daddy!" She looked around to see if anyone else could hear their conversation.

Chuckling, he continued, "I expect you to do certain chores around the house. I'll make you a list. I have a housekeeper who comes to clean weekly and a service to do my laundry. They can do yours as well. But I do ask that you pick up after yourself, keep things tidy, and wash your dishes."

"No problem. I'm used to doing a lot more than that!"

"Good. Some days I will give you other tasks to do, and I will expect you to do them or risk punishment."

"Yes, Sir."

"Also, while we were shopping, a friend of mine called. His fiancé wants to meet you. In fact, several of the girls I know want to meet you. Sloane, too. The designer who knows Beverly."

"Really? I don't know." She fidgeted in her chair.

"As much as I like having you all to myself, it would be great if you could make some friends. And these girls are subs, like you. They can help show you the ropes."

"Show me the ropes?" she repeated, skepticism storming her face.

"Okay, offering you support. They have a sort of club. They call it the Daddy's Little Girls club."

Marley stared, agape. "For real?"

He nodded. "Yeah. I guess they sit around and talk about their daddies and gossip, same as any other women."

"Only they all have daddies?"

"Well, maybe not all, but they're all subs who like being taken care of, who like daddy-type doms. I suppose some of them might be between daddies…"

The calamari arrived at the table. She waited for him to begin eating. He dipped a piece in the marinara sauce and popped it into his mouth. She followed suit.

"What do you think?" he asked.

"It's pretty good. Kinda chewy, but the flavor is good."

"See? Daddy can teach you new things." He smiled, dipped another, then inserted it into her waiting mouth. She closed her eyes as she chewed, savoring it. Damn, he loved her like that—eyes shut, overtaken by pleasure. He felt his cock harden.

"So what should I do about these girls again?"

"I'll give you Kimberly's number. Give her a call. I think they're having lunch next week. Just go and see what you think. If you don't like it, that's okay. I suspect it would be nice for you to have some friends that understand what you're into, what it's like to be in a relationship like ours."

"Okay, but what about what I used to do... Do they know about that?"

"No. Marley, the only people who know about that are me and Milton. And he's sworn to secrecy. Besides, things are different now. That's in the past. You're with me." He reached across the table and clasped her hand in his. "Those days are behind you."

Gratitude shone in her eyes. "Thanks, Daddy."

Her words only aroused him more. That adoring face calling him daddy made him want to take her right there.

"Something else I want you to consider. Have you thought about enrolling in school? Going to college?"

She convulsed with laughter. "Um, no. How would I pay for it? I've always had to work." She gazed up at the ceiling. "Always."

"Well, you don't have to work now. You need something to keep you busy, and I find that people with a purpose are much happier than those who have no direction. Wouldn't you agree?"

"I never thought of that... a purpose? What kind of purpose do you mean?"

"Well, what are you good at? What gets you excited?"

She giggled.

He smirked and forced himself to push aside a visual image of her consumed by passion. "You know what I mean, you little vixen."

More giggles. "Yes, I do. And I don't know. I've never really thought about it. I've had to get whatever job I could for as long as I remember."

"What about your mom?"

"What about her? She's always drunk on the couch. Couldn't hold down a job for more than a week. Paul and I always took care of things once we got old enough."

"Oh, Marley. I'm sorry. It doesn't sound like you had much of a childhood."

"Nope." She agreed.

How does she do that? Refuse to feel sorry for herself. So many people would be bitter and angry if they'd been given that lot in life. But not Marley. The girl forged ahead and triumphed over whatever obstacles got in her way. You had to admire that.

"Even if you don't know what you want to do, it would be good for you to start taking classes. Basic courses can count toward any degree. I'll have Milton bring over a laptop and you can start researching. Figure out what you want to do."

"Okay."

"Unless you have any other ideas…?"

"No, I'm good." She winked at him.

The server brought their entrees. The food smelled divine. He watched as Marley dove into her meal the way she dove into everything—with abandon.

• • • • • • • • • • • • • • •

They fell through the doorway, exploring, groping, kissing. Their bodies writhed with the need to become one. An urgency filled Marley as she staggered to untangle herself from James in order to remove her coat.

"Take off your clothes, all of them, right here," he ordered.

Never taking her eyes from his, she slowly and deliberately disrobed right there in the foyer.

"Kneel and unfasten my pants," he commanded.

Kicking the pile of clothes to the side, she knelt down in front on him. Breathing in his musky scent, she unbuckled his belt and unzipped his fly.

Clearing the opening of his boxers, his rock-hard cock sprung out of his pants. She bent to take it in her mouth, then paused.

"Daddy, may I please suck your cock?"

"Yes, you may. And what a good girl for asking." He patted her head, then curled his fingers into her hair, controlling her.

A warm tingle ran down her legs. His praise never failed to arouse her.

She licked up and down his shaft before swallowing him deep inside her mouth. He forced her head back and forth on his rod, hitting the back of her throat with each motion. She took a breath when he pulled back and focused on the wetness between her legs to keep herself from choking.

"Such a good little cocksucker for Daddy." He reached down and pinched her nipple, twisted it.

He muffled her squeal with the cock in her throat.

He pulled out, moved over to one of the couches in the living room, and removed his pants. "Come over here." He crooked his finger, coaxing her.

She began to stand up, but he stopped her. "No, no, no. Crawl. I want to see you crawl over here to me. I've been thinking about it all night."

Crawl? Oh Lord, this is awkward. Creeping across the floor on her hands and knees felt funny at first, vulnerable.

"Good girl," he said encouragingly.

Relaxing more with each move, she embraced the posture, her position. She trusted him. Wanted to please him, and in some ways it was freeing to follow his orders, to let him control the situation.

She crawled the last few inches slowly, watching him. His eyes were glued to hers. "You are so beautiful, Marley. Do you know that?"

She shook her head and knelt in front of him.

"Sit back," he told her.

His cock preceded him as he leaned forward over her. "Open your mouth."

Parting her lips, she waited for him to shove it inside her waiting hole.

Instead she felt the rap of his erection on her cheek.

Thud! Thud! Thud! It hit her face in rapid succession. She melted under the onslaught. Her cunt throbbed. Her nipples begged for attention. A whimper rose from within.

"Do you like that?" He grabbed her hair and tugged. "Does my little whore like to be dick slapped?"

"Yes, Daddy," she whined, her breath coming fast.

He assailed her once again, thumping across her face. Opening her mouth, she tried to catch it; she wanted him in her mouth. Wanted to suck him dry. Wanted him to come all over her.

"Please come on my face, Daddy," she rasped in a hushed whisper.

He planted his pole in her eager mouth.

She curled her lips around it, suckling him with great aplomb.

"You want me to come on your face?"

She nodded, water forming in her eyes as she worked his cock. Her mouth drooled their combined juices.

"Lie back." She unfolded her legs and lay on her back. He straddled her face, re-entered her throat, thrusting in and out until he withdrew and stroked himself, his seed spraying her lips and chin.

She opened her lips wide to taste his cum. The bitter saltiness on her tongue made her shiver as she swallowed it. She licked the sides of her mouth.

He presented her with his half-mast erection. "Clean Daddy's cock like a good little girl."

She obediently lapped up the remaining cum.

"Good girl." Sliding down beside her, he cupped her face and kissed her.

Quaking with need, she kissed him back feverishly.

He laughed. "Do I have a horny little girl on my hands?"

"Yes, Sir."

He sighed. "You have earned an orgasm, I believe. You've been a very good girl today." Kissing her again, he trailed his fingers down her stomach, toward the center of her aching need.

Then he popped up. "I'll be right back."

She groaned softly. Where was he going? She felt as if she might die of desire at this point, if that was even possible. Every nerve ending was alive. All the blood in her body had rushed between her legs.

He came back carrying a huge dildo.

"Daddy, that looks too big for me." She stiffened.

"Relax. Trust Daddy. It never hurts a girl to stretch a little."

She closed her eyes.

"Clasp your hands and hold them behind your head."

She obliged.

She heard the squish of a bottle of lube. Then cold assaulted her between her legs. Damn, that thing was cold! She squeaked as he inserted the massive dong inside her.

At first her vaginal muscles complained, fought the intrusion. *Relax. Be calm. Breathe deeply.*

He fucked her with it. Slowly at first, then picked up the pace.

It was hard to be still. She wanted to wiggle with pleasure, but she knew better. He wanted her still. She bit the inside of her lip instead.

While he was fucking her, he ran his fingers over her clit. The combined sensations took her to a new place. The pleasure was intense, almost too intense. Within a matter of minutes, she was begging him to let her come.

"Okay, doll, you can come now." He pinched her little nub, rolled his fingers over it. She moaned in ecstasy.

Arching her back, she let the orgasm flow through her, convulsing with his every touch.

He worked her until the climax ebbed. Then he pulled her onto the couch with him, encircling her in his arms.

"Thank you, Daddy." It was weird to be thanking him, but it seemed right. She was grateful. As demanding as he was for her to service him, he was just as focused on meeting *her* needs. This thing between them was so, so… caring. Thoughtful.

Did he really care about her and her needs? Or was he just a good man who believed in the golden rule?

She puzzled this as she snuggled in his arms and fell asleep.

CHAPTER ELEVEN

Bile threatened to rise up in her throat. Marley had been unable to eat this morning, she was so nervous about meeting this group of girls for lunch. She sat in the back seat. The smell of the car's leather seats soothed her. Definitely new. If not, how did they keep the car smelling this good?

She crossed and uncrossed her legs, picked at her fingernails. *Bet these girls have nice manicures, and here I am, turning mine into nubs.* Taking a deep breath, she sat on her hands and tried to regain control.

In high school, Marley had lots of friends. She got along with most people. But that was then. Before she balled guys for a living. Now, she felt... less than. And Lord help her—what if these girls *knew*? If there was one thing she was sure of, it was that women didn't like hookers. They were threatened by them. Everyone thought men cheat on their wives with hookers. It was like the kiss of death, even worse than being a stripper or a waitress at Hooter's. Women would find out you're a hooker and they'd write you off that instant. Hate you on sight.

Dear Lord, please don't let that happen today. She clutched the driver's phone number in her hand. At least she could call him if she needed a quick getaway.

Why had she let James talk her into this?

Because she was crazy about him. She'd do almost anything to please him, and he wanted her to go. He'd done so much for her, given her so much, and he asked for so little in return.

Well, just her body. But she'd give that to him anyway. She smiled to herself, her mind wandering to the things he had done to her last night. A squiggle of delight coursed through her. He was *so* damned good to her.

The car pulled up in front of Hillstone Restaurant, and the driver opened the door for her. Marley tentatively stepped out onto the pavement.

Time to cowgirl up and walk through those doors.

She had spoken to Kimberly on the phone a few days ago. Kimberly had said that she would meet her a few minutes early so Marley would at least 'know' someone when she arrived.

Marley had to admit that Kimberly was warm and welcoming. She wasn't scared of her. It was the rest of them that worried her.

As soon as Marley entered the restaurant she saw her. Sitting at a large table all by herself was an attractive brunette with big dark eyes. The girl rose and approached her.

"Marley?" she asked.

"Yes." Marley nodded. The girl took her by the arm, all smiles and enthusiasm. "Hi! I'm Kimberly. It's so nice to meet you, glad you could come. C'mon. We're over here."

She led Marley back to a large round table in the middle of the restaurant. So much for being inconspicuous.

They sat down. Kimberly was having iced tea. Marley ordered the same. *Daddy would be proud.* She had texted him to let him know where she was going and with whom. He'd replied, telling her to have a nice time and to text him when she got home. Originally she thought checking in would be irritating. Instead, it made her feel that someone cared. Most of her life, no one had been concerned with what she was doing. Except maybe her brother.

"So I hear you're getting married." Marley said, knowing that most women would talk a blue streak about their weddings. She'd rather put the spotlight on Kimberly and refrain from talking about herself.

"Yes, next fall. Plans are slow right now, but at least we have a date. I think." Kimberly's eyes danced with a warmth that put Marley at ease. She didn't have anything to fear from this girl.

"You *think*?" Marley asked.

"Yes," Kimberly sighed. "It's Charles' ex. We want his son to be in the wedding and she's not cooperating."

At that moment a striking young blonde breezed up to the table, setting down a huge black portfolio case with a thud. "Hi! You must be Marley."

The blonde looked like she was holding back a secret.

"Marley, this is Sloane. Sloane, Marley," Kimberly introduced them.

Sloane proffered her hand and Marley took it. "It's nice to meet you."

"Likewise." Sloane found a seat on the other side of Marley. Sitting down, she flipped the sleek mane behind her shoulder. "What are you girls drinking?"

"Iced tea," Kimberly answered.

"I'll have one too. Long Island." Sloane captured the waiter's attention and ordered her libation, her waist-length hair swinging like a curtain down her back.

"That sounds good. I think I'll have one, too." Marley happily ordered the adult version of the tea in front of her.

Sloane turned her attention back to Marley. "So you and James? Wow, that's cool. He hasn't had a sub since Karen ran off with that old guy. I thought he'd given up on women."

Marley smiled, shifting in her chair.

"Tell us about yourself, Marley. Are you from Dallas? How did you meet James?"

Maybe they didn't know. Good! "I'm from Abilene, and his assistant Milton introduced us. He thought we might hit it off."

"Obviously ole Milty was right. You moved in with him. Is that right?" Sloane leaned forward.

"Sloane! We don't need to give Marley the third degree," Kimberly said, smoothing a napkin in her lap.

Shaking her head, Marley replied, "No, Kimberly, it's okay. Yes, we're living together. I moved in a couple of weeks ago."

"Damn, he works fast. I've never heard of you, and James and I go back forever." Sloane furrowed her brow.

"It was rather sudden." She laughed nervously. "So how do you and James know each other?"

"College. We both went to the University of Texas in Austin. It just doesn't seem like him... such a workaholic. He never goes out with us anymore. I didn't think he had time for women." The waiter brought their drinks and Sloane took a big sip.

"Sloane, not everybody needs to work all the time like you," Kimberly pointed out.

"Well, I know that, Kimberly, I just thought... well, anyway, I'm happy for you two. If anyone deserves a good woman, it's James. He's a great guy."

Marley beamed. "He is."

Two more young women walked through the door. They waved when they saw the group and approached their table. Kimberly introduced them as Carmen and Nellie.

Carmen mouthed 'hi,' waving as she came toward the table. A halo of chocolate curls surrounded her cherubic face. Marley liked her right away.

"You wouldn't believe the traffic! Are we the last ones here?" Nellie's entrance was more dramatic. She spoke louder than was necessary with a thick Southern accent. She reminded Marley of a beauty queen, poised with 'fixed' blond hair.

Nellie flounced the latest Louis Vuitton bag onto the floor beside her seat and peered intently at Marley. "You must be Marley!" Her broad smile seemed rehearsed. Marley hoped it was genuine because this one intimidated her.

Marley nodded wordlessly.

Sloane addressed Nellie's question. "Charmaine's supposed to be coming. You don't really think you'd be later than her, do you?" She rolled her eyes.

Nellie twittered. "Oh no, I guess not." She fussed with the napkin she'd just pulled into her lap. "What are you girls having?"

"Tea and Long Island iced tea," Kimberly answered.

"Ooh! I'll have one of those," Nellie said.

"Sweet tea for me," Carmen said. "I have to work this afternoon."

"Oh? What do you do?" Marley asked, seizing the opportunity to take the attention off her.

"I'm an artist." Carmen said.

"Fascinating. What kind of art?" Marley asked, determined to steer the conversation.

"Painting. Portraits, among other things. I have a deadline so I'm working a lot lately. Can't believe I came out to lunch today." She fidgeted with her fingers.

"Carmen, you can't stay in that loft all day long every day with all those paint fumes and never leave your studio!" Nellie shook her head, beseeching the other girls, "Am I right?"

"It is important to take a break every once in a while," Kimberly agreed.

"I know. I know. That's why I'm here today. And to meet Marley." She smiled at Marley.

The attention was back on her. A droplet of sweat rolled down Marley's back. She smiled at the group.

"Lucinda's on tour, but you know she knows James," Nellie said to Marley.

"Oh, who's Lucinda?" Marley asked.

"She's a member of the club, too. She's a pianist, a former student of James' mom. She and James have known each other forever. I think she started lessons around age five. James is kind of like a big brother to her," Sloane said.

So James' mother was a piano teacher? And this Lucinda was like a sister to him? Why hadn't he mentioned that to her?

Thrown, Marley nodded. "Oh. So y'all have a club?"

They nodded. Nellie said, "Yes, it's loads of fun! We tell each other everything." Nellie had been a cheerleader and a sorority girl in school. Marley would lay money on it.

"Nellie! Marley does not have to tell us everything. You'll scare the poor girl off," Kimberly said.

Thank God for Kimberly. Marley exhaled.

"A few years ago, I met a few girls who were in relationships similar to mine. We talked about how our other girlfriends didn't really understand the daddy/little girl dynamics we had in our relationships," Kimberly explained. "So we made a point to get together. It evolved slowly, but eventually it became a kind of club. Nothing formal. Just a way for us to be around other girls who have similar interests."

"So how did you know that you wanted to be in a relationship like that?"

Marley asked.

Kimberly laughed. "I didn't. For me it just kind of evolved into that." She shrugged.

"I met my daddy, and he showed me the ropes," Nellie said.

Sloane snorted. "Ropes."

The other girls laughed. Marley did too. She'd been shown some ropes. Recently.

"I'm between daddies right now," Sloane said. "So is Charmaine. Where is that twerp? It would be nice if she could be on time just once." She glanced at the diamond watch that dangled from her thin wrist.

Kimberly explained to Marley, "Charmaine's a professional party girl. She usually sleeps all day."

"She doesn't have a job?" Marley asked.

"Oh, no. Charmaine has a trust fund. A big one. I can't picture her working. She'd be a disaster." Kimberly laughed.

"What about you, Carmen? What's your daddy like?" Marley asked.

Carmen gazed at Marley with eyes that were either green or blue. It was hard to tell.

"Carmen has the Mac Daddy!" Nellie giggled.

"What?" Marley knitted her brows.

Sloane looked around to be sure she wasn't overheard. "Carmen's daddy plays for the Dallas Vipers." She put a finger to her lips. "We keep quiet about everybody's business, because it's the right thing to do, but also because some people in the club date celebrities."

"Oh." Marley's ears perked up. "What position does he play?"

"Wide receiver," Carmen said.

"It's not Natron Dakers, is it?" Marley teased.

Carmen nodded reverently.

"You're kidding!" Marley squealed. Natron Dakers was one of the most famous football players in the country. Even though Marley wasn't a huge football fan, she knew about him. The man was featured in at least three commercials every time she turned on the television.

Carmen weighed a good thirty pounds more than the swimsuit models most celebrities seemed to prefer. Good for her. Hell, good for him! Carmen was darling, and she exuded a great energy that made Marley want to get to know her better.

Just then, one of the most gorgeous girls Marley had ever seen stepped inside the door and removed her sunglasses. Charmaine. Had to be.

The beauty stalked over to their table and tossed out an unenthusiastic, "Hello."

The girls greeted her and introduced Marley.

Charmaine smiled wanly at Marley, then slunk down into a chair and slipped back on the sunglasses.

"Really?" Sloane asked. "You're twenty minutes late."

"Sorry," Charmaine mumbled.

"Hungover?" Carmen asked sympathetically.

"God, yes. Who do you gotta screw around here to get a Bloody Mary?" Charmaine bellowed. A waiter scampered over and took her order.

"What's got you so grumpy?" Sloane asked.

"Nothing. I was just up all night. I could use some sleep, that's all."

"What did you do last night?" Kimberly asked cheerfully.

"Went to hear that new band, the Plaid Richies," Charmaine said with little enthusiasm.

"How was it? I heard they're amazeballs!" Nellie said.

"They are." Charmaine sipped her Bloody Mary, which arrived in record time. "Amazeballs. Don't let me interrupt. What were y'all talking about? Anything juicy?"

"We were just telling Marley about our club," Kimberly said.

Charmaine nodded. "These are some good girls, Marley. You'll like them." She offered Marley a crooked grin. "So where's Lucy?"

"On tour," Kimberly answered.

"Figures. I wanted to know what's up with that dom of hers." Charmaine slid a celery stalk between her full, red lips.

Marley thought Nellie had high maintenance hair. But she couldn't stop staring at Charmaine's. It was impossible to tell what the original color might be. Charmaine's hair was streaked with several shades of golden brown and honey blond. It was striped. Like a tiger.

Charmaine took her sunglasses off again, this time zipping them into her purse. Her blue eyes were bloodshot, but they were a striking blue so deep, Marley wondered if they were contact lenses.

"Lucy's dom?" Marley asked.

"Yeah. Her daddy." Charmaine placed her menu in the center of the table. "Have y'all ordered? I'm dying for a cheeseburger."

After they ordered lunch Marley asked, "So what's going on with Lucinda's daddy?" It might not be fair to talk about Lucinda when she wasn't there, but it was safer than asking the girls about their own situations.

Sloane cut her eyes at Charmaine. "We really shouldn't talk about Lucy when she's not here."

"Fine." Charmaine turned to Marley. "It's nothing. Last time she complained that her daddy was too controlling."

"I know I'm new at this, but isn't that how they are, these daddies?"

Charmaine choked on her drink. When she recovered, she said, "Good point, Marley." Looking at the other girls, she added, "I like her."

Kimberly said, "Yes, Marley. That is one of the points. But every relationship is different, and all of us have different levels of control we're comfortable with. For example, some of the things that define my relationship with Charles might not work for some of the other girls. Some of the things Mason does with Nellie might creep me out. There are degrees…"

Nellie pursed her lips. "What does Mason do to me that creeps you out?"

Kimberly sighed. "Nothing. It was just an example."

"If you say so," Nellie pouted.

"I see," Marley replied.

"Sorry I brought it up. What else is new?" Charmaine asked.

Sloane told them about her upcoming fashion show and asked them to mark the date in their calendars. Kimberly shared her problems getting her wedding plans started. Charles' ex-wife had stalled progress by not cooperating about committing to a date for Charles' son to be available to be in the wedding.

"I'm afraid we'll have to get the lawyers involved," Kimberly sighed.

"That's what my father does. With all his ex-wives. Easier that way, and less messy," Charmaine said.

"But that's so cold," Kimberly said.

Charmaine raised a shoulder as if to say, "So what?"

Carmen talked about her current project, a portrait of a country music star and the young soap opera star he was engaged to marry. "It's supposed to be a surprise for her birthday so I've got to make it happen." She sighed. "You can't exactly move someone's birthday. I'm having trouble with her nose. If I could just get that nose…"

"Nellie, what's new with you?" Sloane asked.

"Not much. I'm redecorating the downstairs, we're getting new hardwood floors next week, and Mason's taking me to Paris in the spring. I'm trying to learn French before we go." Nellie said.

"Must be nice," Kimberly said.

"Oh, it is. What about you, Marley? You don't work, do you? Maybe you and I can have some fun. Do you like to shop?" Nellie's face brightened.

"No. I'm not working right now. I'm going back to school in January," Marley said. Going shopping with James had been fun, but she wasn't sure about spending an entire day shopping with Nellie.

"What about shopping? Do you like to shop?" Nellie pressed.

"A little. James took me last week. I don't think there's much else that I need, thanks." Marley fumbled over the words. She didn't want to offend Nellie.

"Oh. Well, maybe we can do something else," Nellie said, undeterred by the attempted brushoff.

"Don't worry, Marley. No one likes to shop as much as Nellie. Not even me," Charmaine noted. Marley was grateful for Charmaine's intervention. Something drew her to the surly girl of the bad attitude.

"Okay, enough with the boring stuff—I want to know who's got something juicy to spill," Charmaine said.

The girls all looked at each other.

"Nothing? C'mon. I haven't had sex in weeks. Surely someone's got something fresh to tell me about," Charmaine prodded.

"Natron's either practicing or on the road this time of year. We barely see each other," Carmen said.

Nellie shrugged. Kimberly shook her head.

Marley spoke up. "What about punishments? Do you guys get lots of punishments? I'm kinda worried about that."

"Only when I'm naughty. Or bratty. Which happens about once a week. I usually get a spanking, but if I'm really bad, Daddy will withhold my orgasms. I hate that!" Nellie shook her head slowly. "That's the worst."

The other girls agreed.

"I had one daddy who wouldn't let me pee." Charmaine said.

"Oh my God!" Marley exclaimed.

"Eewww!" Nellie squealed.

"Yeah. That was the end of that." Charmaine laughed and slammed her empty glass on the table. She scanned the room and signaled to a waiter for a refill.

"That's horrible. You'd get a bladder infection," Kimberly said.

The other girls nodded.

"Charles mostly spanks me, but sometimes he tickles me. I hate tickling! It's so perverse that tickling makes you laugh. There is nothing funny about it." Kimberly shuddered.

"Oh my God, he tickles you?" Sloane asked.

"Yes, and it's the worst!" Kimberly exclaimed.

Charmaine turned to Marley. "Most daddy doms use spankings and orgasm denial as punishments. There are all sorts of other creative things, and some do whip their subs, but daddies are generally not sadistic doms. They love their little girls too much, and true pain sluts usually want doms who are more into pain."

"So it's a dominant/submissive relationship. Just a lighter version?" Marley quizzed.

"I'm not sure if it's lighter because some of them can be intense, but it usually has less pain involved for pain's sake," Kimberly said. "But I'm sure some girls who love pain might find having a daddy dom attractive too."

"There's still a power exchange, punishments when you get out of line, and some daddies are into bondage," Carmen added.

"The bottom line is that you surrender yourself to your daddy. Your main goal is to obey and please him. And a good daddy wants a happy girl, so he pleases her too." Nellie's eyes sparkled. "I don't know why more people don't do this. There would be fewer divorces if married people put their spouses' needs above their own." She frowned.

"Amen to that," Charmaine said in a bored tone.

"You mentioned bondage… have any of you ever been suspended?" The Long Island tea had given Marley liquid courage.

"You mean with rope bondage?" Charmaine leaned in. "No, but I've always wanted to."

Sloane lifted an eyebrow. "That's so hot!"

"Charles and I've done it. Did James do it to you?" Kimberly grinned.

Marley nodded shyly.

"Well, tell us about it, bitch! God, getting the good stuff out of you guys is like pulling teeth." Charmaine smacked her hand down on the table. "C'mon. Details."

Marley recounted the experience, the girls giving her their rapt attention. The more they listened without judging her, the better Marley felt. Maybe she could be friends with these girls. Her heart soared at the thought.

"It sounds like James is really good to you, Marley," Carmen fanned herself after Marley finished sharing her exploits.

Marley smiled. "He is. I think I'm incredibly lucky."

Sloane winked at her. "You are. James is a good man. I have something to tell y'all."

"Ugh. You've been holding out on us?" Charmaine scrunched up her face.

"Well, it's not that big of a deal. It's just that I saw Rocco the other day, and I think he may have split from his sub," Sloane said, a twinkle in her eye.

"No way. I thought they were hot and heavy," Carmen said.

"Sloane has a major crush on this dom Rocco. She's had it bad for him for years." Kimberly whispered to Marley.

Marley nodded.

"Where was he? What was he doing?" Nellie leaned forward to catch every detail.

"Pumping gas, of all places," Sloane said. "I flagged him down from a few pumps away like a giddy schoolgirl. It was embarrassing."

"Hey, lots of doms like schoolgirls," Charmaine noted.

"Okay. But I mean I probably made a fool of myself being too eager." Sloane winced.

"I doubt it," Carmen said.

"Anyway, I said hi, asked him what was new. He said not much, and when I asked about Angelique, he said they were taking a break." Sloane grinned. "I said I was sorry to hear that and said, 'Oh, we'll have to get together.' That was too forward, wasn't it?"

"Depends on if he calls you," Charmaine said.

"He hasn't yet. That was about a week ago." Sloane's shoulders slumped.

"Maybe he'll call you real soon, sugar," Nellie said reassuringly. The other girls made noises, encouraging and sympathetic.

For the rest of the meal, Marley felt wrapped in the arms of belonging.

She radiated in the warmth of the conversation. It was wonderful to feel like she was a part of a circle of 'normal' women, even if it was only for a couple of hours.

After lunch, Kimberly walked Marley to James' waiting car.

"So how many times has Charmaine's dad been married?" Marley asked.

"I think he's on his fifth wife. He goes through them." Kimberly sighed. "He makes a new family with each of them. Charmaine's his oldest child, but last I heard she had six half-brothers and sisters. I don't know how she deals with it. Maybe that's why she's so tough. Her dad's always trying to buy her love. I guess he doesn't know what else to do." She shrugged.

"That's sad," Marley said.

"Yeah, you know what they say: 'Money doesn't buy happiness.'"

Marley nodded.

She got into the car and waved goodbye to Kimberly.

Glad that James had urged her to come meet the girls, Marley hugged herself. How incredible not to feel so alone anymore. She had James, and now she had some new friends. Things were finally going her way.

CHAPTER TWELVE

The next day Marley pored over the University of Texas—Dallas catalog. In the Behavioral and Brain Sciences department, they had a Child Development program. The more she contemplated it, the more Marley wanted to work with young children. It seemed like a good fit for her, and the application was straightforward.

The doorbell interrupted her thoughts. Expecting it to be the doorman with a delivery, she was surprised to see Milton standing there.

"Hi, Milton. What can I do for you?"

"It's more like what I can do for you." The bald man edged by her into the living room.

The top of his head was shiny, like a cue ball. Marley held back a grin.

"Okay… what does that mean?"

"It means that I'm supposed to take you to the car dealership and pick you out a car." He sighed.

Marley's eyes rounded. "A car?"

"Yep. You can drive, can't you? You have a license and all that?"

"Yes."

"Great! Get your things and let's go."

"Shouldn't I talk to James about this? I mean, I have some questions…" A knot formed in her stomach.

"Talk to him later. He wanted to take you himself, but he got tied up in meetings all day so he asked me to take you."

"But I don't understand. Why am I picking out a car?"

"*To drive*," he said slowly, as though she were hard of hearing or incredibly stupid.

"I know that. But why do I need a car to drive? James' driver always takes me places."

"I don't know, Marley. I'm only doing my job. Can you please hurry?" He let go another exasperated sigh.

"Okay, okay. It will be just a minute." She disappeared into her bedroom to spruce up a bit.

Moments later she slipped on her shoes and they were out the door.

On the way, Marley asked, "So what dealership are we going to?"

"Audi. James thinks they're safe. Believes they make a quality product."

"I bet they do." She couldn't imagine herself driving an Audi. It seemed way too upscale. "Can't I choose what type of car?"

"Yes," he hissed, gripping the steering wheel tightly.

"Well, can I have a Volkswagen or something? I've always wanted to have a cute little bug."

"Dammit, Marley! Why can't you be happy with an Audi? Who wouldn't be happy with an Audi?" he snapped at her.

"What is wrong with you? Why do you care what kind of car I get? You get paid no matter what." She eyed him suspiciously.

Milton pulled the car off the road and glared at her. "I don't want you taking advantage of him!"

Marley was quiet for a moment and let his words sink in.

"Is that what you think?" she asked.

He ran a hand over his slick head. "I don't know what to think. But I'm concerned."

"Why are you concerned?"

"Hello! Rich daddy takes girl in off the streets. She's after him for his money... the last time this happened, it didn't end well."

Marley bit down on her lip. "He found Karen on the streets?"

"No, but you know what I mean. She took him for lots of money and then left!"

"Yeah. I heard about that."

"Well, I don't want it to happen again. Do you understand? If you break his heart, it will be my fault. I'm the one who introduced you to him."

Marley breathed deeply. "Listen, Milton. I have no intention of hurting James. In fact, I'm more worried that he's going to dump me at some point and find a girl more his class."

"He's nuts about you." Milton rolled his eyes. "I've never seen him like this before."

Her spirits lifted. "I feel that way about him, too. I'm just not sure about all this. I... it doesn't seem like I deserve all this."

"What are you talking about?"

"This lifestyle. It all seems so, I don't know—above me. I don't feel like I fit in."

"Who's to say anyone deserves it? Most rich people are born into it. The luck of the draw." He shook his head. "But not James, he earned it. Works like a slave, that guy." His face shone with admiration as he spoke of his boss.

"He is wonderful." Marley stared out her window. "I wish I could be the kind of woman he deserves."

"Are you serious?"

"Sure." She raised her shoulders slightly.

He studied her like a bird inspecting a worm. "You like him for real?"

"Yeah, what's not to like? Of course I do." She frowned. "I'm just scared it won't last."

Milton nodded. "I understand. Not many relationships do. But if you break his heart, I'll kill you."

His words didn't trouble her. She had no intention of leaving James, and she doubted Milton could kill a butterfly. However, it made James all the more attractive that he inspired such loyalty in the people around him.

"Got it." Marley touched her fingers to her brow in a mock salute.

He maneuvered the vehicle back onto the roadway. "Then accept the gift he gives you."

"You mean the Audi?"

He nodded. "Yep."

Marley heaved a sigh. "O-kay."

"Don't be so depressed. It's not every day you get a new Audi."

True. She smiled to herself.

• • • • • • • • • • • • • • •

For once *he* had to wait. James was accustomed to everyone waiting for him to arrive, but he got home to find an empty apartment this afternoon. It was too quiet. Every day he looked forward to coming home to Marley. It was the highlight of his day. He'd gotten used to Marley's hip-hop music playing in her room, the smell of nail polish lingering in the air. The energy she brought to everything she did.

Impatiently, he checked his phone for the time. Milton had texted him that they were on their way. At least he would see her soon.

He fixed himself a bourbon and coke. Surveying the Dallas skyline from the window, James considered his success. He'd always dreamed of rising to the top. He'd been driven ever since he was a child, excelling in sports, making straight A's.

They'd had a pleasant enough existence. His father was an insurance salesman and his mother taught piano lessons after school. Their home had been filled with love, but James always knew he was destined for a bigger life.

His success had knocked him upside the head. A beneficiary of technological advances, he'd stumbled into his career. The idea for his app had been a lark.

He was possibly at the height of his career. It was a great place to be. But something had been missing. The love that filled his boyhood home. Until

Marley came into his life, he was alone. His friendships and charities gave him an active social life and he'd been quite content. But once he met that raven-haired siren, he was smitten.

Now he had someone to share his wealth with, someone to help him enjoy life. That was why he'd bought her the car.

He wanted to give her everything. He wished he could bring her brother back, make her mother whole, take away everything from her past that haunted her. But that was impossible. All the money in the world couldn't change those things. So he did his best to make her happy in the present.

Yes, he could have spared his driver, or ordered her a car service. But he wanted her to have nice things. Things she'd never had before. Things she wouldn't have without him.

Was he trying to buy her love? *Maybe.* Was that arrogant? *Perhaps.* But what good was fighting the war if you couldn't enjoy the spoils?

Being with Marley was so different than it had been with other women. She didn't want to bleed him dry. If he gave her a gift she appreciated it, but she didn't ask to go on huge spending sprees. She was grateful for what he gave her, not looking for the next handout.

The fact that she was gorgeous with an enchanting personality to match didn't hurt. He wanted to take her places, show her off. Hell, he was proud of her. It delighted him that such a lovely, spirited creature wanted to spend time with him.

He gulped his drink. She made him happy. Not just sexually. She nurtured his soul as well. She seemed to care about *him*, or was he imagining that? Was that just something he wanted to see?

His ears pricked at the sound of a key rattling in the door. Marley breezed in, all smiles.

"Hi, Daddy," she called in a sing-songy voice.

"Hey, doll. Do you pick out something you liked?" He raised an eyebrow.

She sashayed over and gave him a peck on the cheek. "Yes."

Setting his drink down, he moved over to a sofa, dragging her into his lap. "Tell me all about it."

She giggled and wrapped her arm around his neck. He snuggled close and fondled her breast with one hand.

She laughed but didn't push him away. "Daddy, you're distracting me."

"I don't care. Tell me about it." He pinched the hardening bud through her shirt.

"Okay. Thank you for the car, by the way." She kissed him again.

"You're welcome. So which one did you choose?"

"The TT." She snorted. "That name cracks me up. Why would they name a car that?"

"No idea, but that's a hot car, baby. You'll look good driving it. What color?"

"Red. I've always wanted a red car."

"Did they already have one or do they have to order it?"

"They say there's one in Houston so it should be here in a couple of days." Wonder shone in her eyes. "This is the nicest thing anyone has ever done for me. But why did you do it, Daddy?"

His arms clamped down on her. "I've got to spoil my girl," he said, giving her a squeeze.

"That's sweet, but a car? I mean, couldn't you just send your driver for me like you have been?"

"Sure. But I wanted to do something special for you, and I thought a vehicle would be more practical than jewelry."

She chuckled. "Yeah, a car is definitely better than jewelry."

It felt so good to hold her in his arms, to be able to give her things. She gave so much to him. More than she knew.

Her fingers fiddled with his tie. "Is there anything I can do for you, Daddy?" she asked in a husky voice.

"Oh, I have some ideas. Would you like a drink first?"

She shook her head no and started to pull her shirt over her head.

He sat back to enjoy the show. "Good girl."

Once she had removed all her clothes, he asked her to get down on all fours. Marley dropped to her knees then planted her hands on the floor, her eyes never leaving his.

His temperature inched up, degree by degree as he surveyed her luscious body. Her posture so inviting, so tempting.

"Bring me your underwear."

She grabbed for it with her hands.

"Uh-uh-uh." He shook his finger at her. "No hands."

Her brows knit together. He watched her forehead crease as she processed his reprimand.

Dutifully she retrieved the panties in her mouth and brought them to him.

He patted her on the top of the head and crooned, "Good girl."

He took them from her, bunched them into a ball, dipped them into the rest of his bourbon to give his new toy weight, and he threw them across the room. He cupped her chin. "Fetch."

A glint of defiance reflected in her eyes before she dutifully crawled across the floor, giving him the view he'd been dying to see. Her cunt shone with her lust as she slunk toward her goal.

"Damn, you've got a gorgeous ass." He unzipped his fly and stroked himself.

She added a wiggle to her strides in response.

Bending to take the damp panties in her mouth, she chomped down on them and turned back toward him, eyes downcast.

"No. Look at me. Always keep your eyes on me."

Green orbs glanced up through a fringe of black lashes.

"Good girl," he encouraged. "Now bring them to me."

She slowly made her way to him, their connection burning brighter with each thud of her knee on the floor.

When she reached him, he removed the alcohol-stained rag from her mouth and instructed, "Now I want you to suck Daddy's cock."

Her tongue swirled around his cock, base to tip, moistening him before she took him deep into her mouth. She grasped him with one hand, jerking him with it as she shoved him to the back of her throat.

Gently, he peeled back her grip. "No hands."

Her head bobbed up and down on his cock. In a display of compliance, she clasped her hands behind her back.

He leaned back and closed his eyes. Her perfume wafted past his nose. She smelled of jasmine and honeysuckle. It was girly and youthful, not expensive or sophisticated like the women he was familiar with. It reminded him of playing outdoors on a spring day.

He loved her transparency. It ran across all aspects of her life. She kept nothing veiled. Nothing except her feelings for him.

As he watched her delicate lips work him into a frenzy, he wondered. *Is she doing this because she wants to or because this is part of the bargain that she made?*

Internally he shook his thoughts loose. *I want to enjoy this, not analyze it.*

"Come sit on Daddy's lap. Straddle me."

Saliva dripped from the sides of her mouth. She wiped it as she stood up, swallowing.

He smiled. The sight sent a jolt of electricity through him. Lifting himself off the couch, he shifted his pants down around his ankles and she climbed aboard.

He shifted to the edge of his seat in order to give her leverage with her legs. "Lower your cunt onto me."

Her warmth engulfed him and he had to hold himself back from shooting his load into her right away. He bit the inside of his lip. Damn, she felt like a dream. Only he'd never had a dream this incredible.

"Now fuck me, you little bitch," he growled.

Her hips rose then lowered, her tight little hole sucking hard on him with each motion. Her long black swath of hair begged to be pulled.

He snatched her mane all into one hand and held her by it. She dropped onto him, co-mingling their juices and grinding her clit against his pelvis.

The next time she came down, he gave her hair a firm yank, forcing an exclamation from her lips. "Daddy!"

"Yes, baby?"

"Nothing, Daddy. Thank you again for the car." The movement of her hips intensified. "You're so sweet to me."

"You really are a good little slut for Daddy, aren't you?" He slapped her ass hard.

She nodded. Her brow furrowed in concentration. She was close.

"Such a good little whore for Daddy." He grabbed her hips and helped raise and lower them. Their pace increased furiously until he felt her vaginal walls contract wildly around him. Her face tightened, then softened as she rode the afterwaves of her orgasm. She collapsed onto him, hugging him close, spent. He thrust into her several more times before emptying himself into her.

Pulling back, he studied her face. Flushed from their lovemaking, she was the most beautiful he'd ever seen her. "You know you are the best little girl I could wish for, don't you?" He kissed her on the tip of the nose.

"Yes, Daddy." She shifted, his cum seeping out of her onto his leg. She rooted up into the crook between his arm and his torso, tucking her legs up to her chest. Snuggling against him, she added, "And you're the best daddy."

Within minutes her breathing slowed to a rhythmic pace. She was asleep.

Just as he would a child, he picked her up and carried her to her bed. He tucked her in and told her goodnight. She didn't stir.

He stood over her, filled with a sense of contentment. This was where she belonged. Here with him. He bent and touched his lips to hers, then silently left the room.

CHAPTER THIRTEEN

Marley sipped a cup of coffee and tried to focus on her application for UT—Dallas. But this morning her mind kept drifting back to last night with James.

He sure knew how to make a girl feel good. A tiny shiver danced down her spine. As demanding as he was, he always made sure *she* had a good time. Her orgasm seemed important to him. That always blew her mind. She wasn't familiar with anybody putting her first.

She hugged herself. She was a lucky girl.

Lucky in so many ways.

But why did *she* get to benefit from all of this? Her eyes scanned the upscale kitchen with its fancy refrigerators and zillion-dollar copper cookware.

What had she ever done to live in a place like this?

She wasn't worthy.

How would she ever be able to repay him for all that he did for her? The man had given her a car, for heaven's sake!

Taking a deep breath, she tapped her fingernails on the counter. She'd never be able to pay him back for that. Never.

Blowing her bangs in the air with a heavy sigh, she lowered her shoulders in defeat. She was not in his league and that was all there was to it. *Hopefully, it will be a while before he realizes that.* Thinking about life without him was too painful.

Footsteps in the hall got her attention and she looked up to see James enter the kitchen.

He looked as handsome as ever, freshly shaven, smelling woodsy from his sexy aftershave.

"Good morning, Daddy," she chirped, hopping up to hug his neck. Every time she used the word, it passed her lips as an endearment. His asking her to call him that had been a step. A step in the right direction. It gave her a way to express her feelings for him.

His arm encircled her waist, his lips finding hers. "Good morning, doll. You taste delicious."

"Thanks."

"Working on your application?"

She bobbed her head to the side. "Trying. I'm a little distracted today. Would you like some breakfast? I could scramble you some eggs." Though she wasn't about to set the culinary world on fire, she'd been making her own breakfast since she was eight. Eggs were especially easy.

"Sure. Thanks."

"I made some coffee, too. Want some?"

"You are a dream, you know that? Sure. I'll take some."

"Black?" she asked, pouring him a cup.

He nodded. "I'd like to talk to you about Christmas."

"Christmas?" Her ears perked up.

"Yes. It's coming up in a couple of weeks and I wanted to know if you'd like to go over and meet my family? We have a big tree, a big ham, stockings, my mom plays the piano and we all sing Christmas carols. Embarrassing, I know, but it's a lot of fun. You can meet my sister Anna, and I know my parents are dying to meet you." He paused. "But if you've got plans to go home to Abilene, I understand."

A sarcastic laugh escaped her. "Abilene? Home? Not hardly." She tucked her hair behind her ear.

"Well, I thought… your mom. Maybe you'd want to see her." He shrugged.

She handed him his coffee and sat down next to him. "Let me tell you about the Christmases I had in Abilene. They usually involved Mom drunk on the couch and whatever food Paul and I could scrounge."

He grimaced.

"Yeah. One year she forgot to buy us presents so she went to the 7-Eleven at midnight and bought us some stuff. We were thrilled when Santa brought us beef jerky, gum, and a comic book. But when we got older we realized that she'd forgotten us that year. As the years went by, she stopped trying and Santa quit coming."

Concern flashed across his face. "Oh, Marley…"

She focused her attention toward a speck on the floor. "It's okay. I'm used to it."

He tilted her chin so she had no choice but to meet his gaze. "You're not used to being cared for, are you?"

She shook her head and willed the unshed tears to remain, stinging, in her eyes.

"All that's in the past. From now on, I'll take care of you." He pulled her head close to his, pressed his lips to her forehead.

A salty drop escaped onto her cheek. That was what she wanted more than anything.

She wanted to take care of him, too.

She wiped her face. "I'd like to meet your family and spend Christmas with you." She hesitated. "If that's what you meant."

"That's exactly what I meant."

"Sounds nice." This topic was uncomfortable. She needed to change the subject. Giving him a peck on the cheek, she bolted to the other side of the kitchen and reached for a pan. "Poached or scrambled?"

• • • • • • • • • • • • • • •

That afternoon Ken called up to tell her that Charmaine's driver was there to pick her up.

Kimberly had invited Marley to join her and Charmaine for a movie. Marley jumped at the chance to have something to do and to get to know these girls a bit better. She had lunched with them a couple of times since their first meeting and she liked them more all the time. It was nice to be able to talk with girls in relationships like hers. Heck, it was awesome to have some friends.

The elevator beamed her to the ground floor, and she waved goodbye to Ken as she left.

Charmaine's ride was a tricked-out stretch Lincoln Navigator. She'd heard Charmaine say countless times, "Limos are so passé, chère." The vehicle was the traditional black, equipped with fancy rims and a privacy window. The rich girl's palace on wheels was stocked. With a full bar, of course. Would Charmaine travel any other way?

Charmaine was pouring herself a glass of champagne when Marley embarked into her mobile lair.

"Want some bubbly, hon?" Charmaine glowed. Whether it was from the champagne or some tropical vacation, Marley wasn't certain. It was the middle of winter so knowing Charmaine, probably the former.

"Sure," Marley agreed, settling herself into her supple leather seat.

"Good. Kimberly won't have any. Sometimes she can be a bit of a doormat, ya know?" Charmaine filled up another flute and handed it to Marley. "Be careful. Sometimes George hits the brakes too hard." She rolled her eyes, swinging her head in the direction of the chauffeur. "But he's a good egg." Charmaine took a swig.

"Thanks." Marley took a sip, the fizzy bubbles tickling her nose.

"So how are things going with Mr. Wonderful?" Charmaine teased.

Heat rose in Marley's cheeks. "Fine, I guess."

"Fine? *Just* fine?" Charmaine's icy blue eyes pierced her.

The car pulled up to Kimberly's place and they stopped.

"Yikes! I've got to go to the bathroom. I'm going to run into Kimberly's. Here, would you hold this?" Charmaine shoved her champagne flute at Marley, who took it before Charmaine scurried out of the car.

Whew. Saved by the next stop. What was her problem? Nothing was wrong with her and James.

Or was there?

Nothing, other than the fact that she constantly felt like she was a good-for-nothing freeloader. She wished she had some way to pay him back for everything he did for her.

But what could *she* do?

The only thing she knew was sex. And she already gave him that. She would have given that to him anyway. *If only I could do more…*

Kimberly climbed into the car, greeting Marley warmly. Charmaine followed and invited Kimberly to join them in having some bubbly.

"No, thanks," Kimberly said.

Charmaine giggled. "See? What'd I tell you?" she asked Marley.

"It'll make me fall asleep during the movie!" Kimberly popped Charmaine on the bicep.

"Okay, okay. You don't have to go all *Million Dollar Baby* on me." Charmaine rubbed her arm.

"I'll have some after the movie, how 'bout that? Y'all want to go for dinner afterwards?" Kimberly asked.

"Sure. Where's Charles?"

"With his kiddo. How about you, Marley?"

"Yeah. Dinner sounds good."

The girls laughed and joked all the way to the movie theater. Once there they purchased tickets and drinks. Marley and Charmaine ordered sodas, while Kimberly got an inordinately expensive bottle of water. Charmaine excused herself to go to the bathroom.

"She just went to the bathroom at your house," Marley observed.

"She might be spiking her drink," Kimberly sighed.

"Really?"

"Yeah. That girl has a tolerance I can't even begin to wrap my head around."

"She doesn't seem drunk."

"That's what I mean. I'm not sure if she has a problem, but what can we do about it?" Kimberly whispered.

"Hmm. I'm not sure. Maybe ask her about it."

Charmaine came out of the restroom and strolled toward them.

"Hey, did you go in there to liven up your drink?" Marley asked, half-joking.

"No," Charmaine answered, looking nonplussed. "Tuna for lunch. Has my stomach all torn up if you must know, Miss Nosypants." She linked her arm with Marley's and marched them into the movie theater.

After a particularly long epic romance, the girls headed to a local burger joint for dinner. Charmaine had vetoed sushi, so they decided on hamburgers.

Once they were seated and had heaping plates of burgers and fries in front of them, Charmaine started in. "So, Marley, you were going to tell me what's going on with you and James."

"Now who's Miss Nosypants?" Marley teased.

"What do you mean? Is something wrong?" Kimberly asked, worry lines indenting her forehead.

Marley swallowed a bite of her cheeseburger. "No, there's nothing wrong exactly," she said, dabbing the corner of her mouth with her napkin.

"Then what?" Kimberly asked.

"It's just that he does so much for me... Hell, he gave me a car last week. And I'd like to give him something back. But I don't have anything," Marley explained.

"But he has *you*. Isn't that enough?" Kimberly asked. "I mean, Marley, I know you're good to him. Charles told me he's never seen James so happy."

"Yes, I am good to him, but I'd like to do more."

"Like what?" Charmaine asked, sipping on a beer.

"I don't know. Give him a three-way." Marley laughed.

"Seriously?" Kimberly's eyes grew wide.

"Why not?" Charmaine shrugged.

"I don't know. Sex is the only thing I can think of. And guys all want to be with two women. It's like the universal male fantasy, right?" Marley asked.

Kimberly shook her head. "I don't know, Marley. Who would you get to do it?"

Charmaine grinned. "I'm in."

"Really?" Marley's heart raced.

"Sure, why not?" Charmaine's nonchalance intrigued Marley.

Marley hesitated. Would it be weird with someone she knew? Or would that make it easier, better?

Kimberly said, "I could never do that. I don't know how you girls can deal with that. I'd be too jealous. It would be too weird."

"This wouldn't be my first time. I respect their relationship so I won't get in the way. No need to worry about me being a third wheel afterwards." Charmaine chuckled.

"Do you even know James?" Kimberly asked.

"No, it's hard to believe. You and Sloane talk about him so much, but I've never even met him," Charmaine said.

"You haven't?" Marley was surprised.

"No."

"Are you sure you didn't meet him at Sloane's Christmas party last year?"

Kimberly asked.

Charmaine inspected her zebra-stripe manicure. "I was in the Swiss Alps, remember?"

"Oh, yeah." Kimberly turned to Marley. "He doesn't know her. Seems like that would make it easier…"

"Yeeeesss." Marley stalled. "I guess I'm down with that." Charmaine was beautiful. A gorgeous, exotic woman who seemed to have everything. Surely Charmaine had men knocking down her door. She didn't need James. She didn't need his money either. Maybe she *would* be a good choice.

Scratching her chin, Marley considered. Charmaine batted her eyes at Marley.

Yes, she trusted her. Charmaine didn't have designs on James. She only wanted to have a good time.

Marley sighed. "We'll set up something next week?"

Charmaine winked in response.

It wasn't until they were on the way home that Marley realized she'd forgotten to check in with James.

CHAPTER FOURTEEN

James paced the floor. Back and forth. His shoes threatened to wear a path into the rug.

Where was she? She knew she was supposed to check in, but she hadn't.

She said she was going to a movie. Had texted him about that. But the showing should have been over hours ago. Where could she be?

And why didn't she answer her phone? Or respond to his texts? His stomach tightened.

Her car was in the garage. She must have ridden with someone else. Supposedly she was with Charmaine, but he didn't know that number…

His gut lurched. What if she wasn't with Charmaine? What if she were with another guy? Or worse, injured in an accident…

Grab a hold of yourself. People are late all the time for good reasons. Traffic. Things happen. It could be anything.

Forcing himself to sit down, he reached for the remote control. Maybe watching television would distract him. He took a deep breath and tried to concentrate on SportsCenter. How did he keep finding himself in this predicament? He frowned. Usually women waited for him. His time was valuable. Too valuable to be stuck waiting around for a girl too self-involved or headstrong to obey his rules. His anger swelled.

The jangle of the phone startled him. It was a text from Marley.

"Sorry, Daddy. Went to dinner with Charmaine and Kimberly and forgot to tell you. Please forgive me. On my way home now."

A wave of relief washed over him. Thank God. She was okay.

Now that he knew she was okay, his thoughts turned to consequences. He'd never really had to punish Marley. He'd spanked her a few times, but nothing significant. She was a well-behaved sub most of the time, but this kind of mistake could not be repeated. It was important that she understand the rules; that he was in charge. She must obey them. Or there would be repercussions.

Rules with no consequences were ineffective. He'd have to come up with something that would serve as a deterrent. He tapped a finger on the side table and considered the possibilities. When he heard her enter the apartment, he was prepared.

"Daddy, I'm so sorry." She tossed her purse to the side and rushed to him, showering him with kisses. "I totally forgot to call you. I'm so sorry," she repeated, her face forlorn.

He hugged her to him. "I'm glad you're okay. I was worried. Are you aware of that?" His voice was firm, almost harsh.

Fidgeting, she replied, "I guess, but I didn't mean to upset you."

"It doesn't matter if you didn't intend to do it; the point is you broke the rule. Rules are in place for a reason, Marley. This rule is for your safety and my peace of mind. I'm disappointed that you selfishly disregarded it. In this case you caused me unnecessary worry. And for that you shall be punished."

"But Daddy…" she protested.

"But Daddy what?"

She lowered her head. "It's just—I didn't mean to, and I'm sorry. Isn't that enough?"

"No. It is not enough. Now go into your bedroom and strip naked. When I come in there I want you naked and kneeling on the floor with your hands behind your back."

"But Daddy!" Her voice shook with fear.

"Just do it," he barked.

Keeping an eye on his watch, he let fifteen minutes pass before going to her room. He wanted her to wait, just as he had waited. He wanted her to wonder what he was going to do to her, what was going to happen next.

After giving her plenty of time to stew, he marched purposely toward her door.

Inside he found her kneeling on the floor, facing him, eyes lowered, hands clasped at the small of her back.

"Nice. You followed my instructions perfectly. Good girl." Marley's posture relaxed somewhat at his encouragement.

He strode to the closet and brought back several coils of rope. Moving the bench at the end of the bed, he asked her to kneel in front of the footboard facing him.

Slowly James draped rope around her chest, running it around her back, and pulling it through. He could tell by her countenance that Marley enjoyed the sensuality of the rope's caress. Good. Pleasure coupled with pain was always ideal. He created a bra-like harness with it, accentuating her breasts.

He bent to suckle a nipple before he progressed to her hands. His nostrils inhaled her scent. Damn, she smelled good—like fresh honeysuckle, and she was just as wild. Tasted sweet too.

Teasing her was part of the fun. He loved watching her become aroused, then leaving her wanting more. Tying each wrist to the top of the footboard, he secured her position so her arms dangled by her wrists, giving her plenty of room to adjust if they became sore.

Her legs were another issue. He wanted her on her knees, legs spread, so he lifted her ankles behind her and connected them to her thighs, hindering her ability to use her calves to scoot around.

Marley had been quiet while he secured her. She watched him work as if in a trance. He sensed she knew this was a good time to be silent. Her submission meant everything to him. The fact that she didn't complain, didn't question—it appeared she trusted him. It was never easy to hurt another person, particularly one he cared about, but her trust centered him and gave him the strength to do what he needed to do.

He pulled a dark scarf out of his pocket and her eyes widened. "A blindfold?" she asked.

He nodded. "Close your eyes, little girl." She shut them and he tied the scarf snugly around her head. "Too tight?" he asked.

"No, Sir. It's fine."

"Can you see?"

She shook her head, then realized her mistake. "No, Sir."

"Good."

He went back to the closet and retrieved the flogger with its black leather tails. This particular flogger packed a wallop, but it was nowhere near as intense as others in his collection. He wanted to punish her, not injure her. He knew Marley was in the process of adjusting to his rules. She was unaccustomed with having someone to answer to.

"Now I'm going to flog you for not telling me your whereabouts. Do you understand?"

"Yes, Sir." Her muscles tensed and her voice trembled as she spoke.

The leather fingers slapped her thigh, and her body jerked involuntarily at the insult.

"Relax into it. You'll find that helps, and the pain won't be so bad. Remember to breathe."

He struck her on the stomach. This time she controlled her instinct better and only flinched slightly.

"Good." He could tell she was trying to please him. To submit to her punishment, whether she agreed with it or not.

His heart went out to her and he began flogging her with a repetitive motion, knowing the pattern would make it easier for her to withstand.

Each time the flogger met her skin, it deepened his connection to her. Using it as an extension of himself, he reached out and claimed his sub, relishing every stroke she endured. Each one an acceptance of him, his lifestyle, his choices, and his feelings for her.

Thin, pink marks striped her breasts, stomach, and upper thighs. No raised welts. No need to blister her. Watching her dig deep into herself to withstand his reprimand was enough. It stirred something in him. Lust, yes, but more than that.

He desired to own this woman. He wanted her all for himself. Controlling her was heady. Irresistible. His breathing quickened. *I'm becoming addicted to her.*

Undressing from the waist down, James approached her, his cock leading the charge.

"Open your mouth, doll."

Those gorgeous wet lips parted. She opened wide, welcoming him.

He stroked himself, memorizing the picture before him—Marley tied up, blindfolded, spread wide, waiting to service him any way he saw fit. The image would stay with him; that he knew.

He ran his hand down her rope-decorated flesh to the triangle between her legs. Her slick, ready pussy drenched him as he entered her with his hand. Fingerbanging her hard and fast, he captured a nipple in his mouth and reacted to the noises she made. Oooh's and aaahhh's poured from her throat as he rubbed her clit with his thumb and fingerfucked her vigorously.

Sensing she was close to orgasm, he stopped. Pulling away, he observed her panting and sweating with lust. She wanted to come badly, but she wasn't begging for it. Not yet.

"Keep that mouth open. Did I say you could close it?"

She shook her head no rather than giving him a verbal response, but he let it slide since it would be unfair to ask her to talk and keep her mouth open at the same time.

He struck her on the side of the mouth with his cock. She turned her head to accept him.

"No. Be still," he said in a firm voice.

Slapping her cheek with his cock as he stroked it got her attention. She settled down. Her face wore an expression of pure bliss. Her gaping lips formed a half-smile as he pummeled her with his rock-hard shaft. He loved being so close to her mouth, taunting her and taking pleasure from her all the same. Hitting his cock on her face aroused him. He loved being able to use her entire body for his own enjoyment.

Finally he fed her eager mouth. Hungrily she took him in, licking, sucking, bobbing her head as best she could, considering her bondage.

Her velvety lips enveloped him. Little teeth grazed him ever so slightly, driving him wild. His hips bucked into her, shoving to the back of her throat. Occasionally she made a strangled sound. He'd pull back, appreciating the strings of saliva connecting his rod and her talented mouth.

"You're such a good little slut for Daddy," he said, breaching her again.

She nodded vigorously, mumbling something unintelligible around his dick. "Yes, Daddy" or something to that effect. Clutching her head, he controlled her and thrust himself inside her until he was on the verge of completion.

Taking his cock in his hand, he jerked himself until he was ready to spew.

"Open that mouth. Stick out your tongue," he ordered her.

Her tongue reached out and captured the salty white substance he gave her. Some dripped down her cheek. What a glorious sight—his baby girl covered in his cum.

"Lick it up, doll." He wiped the silky fluid from her face with his finger and offered it to her.

Lapping it up, she shivered in anticipation. She was expecting it to be her turn next.

"There's only one more part to your punishment, love. It's almost over."

"What is it?"

"Be patient. You'll see. I'll be right back."

He returned with a vibrator and some clothespins.

He fondled her breasts, flicking her nipples until they hardened into tight little nubs. Then he slowly placed a clothespin on each of them.

Marley whimpered, but kept her composure.

Until he started the vibrator. Inserting it was no problem. She was as wet as a Slip 'n Slide. But the finger that flicked her clit each time he sunk the vibe into her sent her into orbit.

She struggled against the ropes, pelvis gyrating, pleading for more.

"I can tell you like this," he taunted, working her aching cunt.

Each time the vibrator glided across her engorged clit, she whimpered helplessly.

He removed it and flipped the off switch. "You really like that, don't you, doll?" He grabbed a handful of her hair and tugged gently, his face almost touching hers. "You're such a dirty little slut, aren't you?"

She nodded wildly, her moans indicating she liked the dirty talk. "Yes, Daddy," she almost screamed. "Please, Daddy."

"Please what?"

"Please keep doing that!"

"Such a greedy little whore for Daddy. I love that." He kissed her deeply, her tongue eagerly joining his.

"You want to come, don't you?" he asked, removing her blindfold.

"Yes, Daddy, please, Daddy. Please make me come."

He began to untie her arms.

"No. You are not allowed to come tonight. That is the last part of your punishment. No orgasm for you."

Eyes bulging, she squeaked, "You're not serious."

Kissing her on the top of the head, he replied, "Oh, I'm very serious."

He released her from the bindings and went to the closet to put the toys away. He brought her a modest white cotton nightgown and handed it to her.

"Put this on and get into bed." He pointed to her bed.

"But Daddy, you got me all excited!" she whined.

"Yes, I did. Orgasm denial is a punishment that should work wonders with your thoughtless behavior." He pulled back the covers for her. "Now hop in. And don't even *think* of masturbating tonight. You are under strict orders *not* to do that."

Dazed, Marley put the nightgown over her head and trudged to bed. Once under the covers, she asked with a mischievous grin, "Not even a little bit?"

"You are not to even touch yourself. At all. Do you hear me?"

Crossing her arms over her chest, giving him an exaggerated pout, she agreed. "Fine. But that's an awfully mean punishment, Daddy."

He leaned down to kiss her and clutched her to him. Stroking her hair, he said, "It's not intended to be mean, but to get your attention. To teach you something. To stop you from making the same mistake again. Perhaps next time you will think about it and remember to check in with me."

Heaving a big sigh, she agreed. "You're right, Daddy. I was wrong. I'm sorry and I won't play with myself."

"There's a good girl. Sleep tight, my dear. I'll see you in the morning." He gave her a chaste kiss goodnight and left the room.

• • • • • • • • • • • • • • •

It was all Daddy's fault.

Marley changed positions, slinging the covers across the bed. Lying on her side, she couldn't get comfortable. First she was cold, then she was hot. Nothing seemed to help.

James had gotten her so aroused, she thought she would jump right out of her skin. For hours she'd tried to distract herself from the wicked thoughts that kept playing in her mind. James touching her in all the right places, fucking her brains out. To her dismay, her brain insisted on replaying scenes from their lovemaking over the past month, ramping up her level of excitement.

But she didn't dare touch herself. And she didn't go to the closet to find that marvelous vibrator he'd used on her. Why? She wasn't exactly sure. Ultimately, it was more important to obey Daddy than it was to satisfy herself.

What did that say about her feelings for him? She had it bad.

Frowning, she punched her pillow a few times. She'd fallen in love with him. Why else would she put his desires, his requests above her own needs?

Then there was the way her stomach fell to the floor anytime he walked into the room. And the way it made her ecstatic when he called her his little slut or kissed her on the forehead. Who knew things like *that* would make her heart sing?

The more she considered it, the more certain she was he would like the surprise ménage she had planned for his Christmas present. What else could she give him? She didn't have any money of her own. Yes, he'd given her a credit card, but it would feel silly buying a present for him with his own money.

No, it was best to give of yourself. And in this case, Charmaine.

Charmaine. Marley had to admit she was quite taken by Charmaine's considerable charms. The girl was larger than life. Wealthier than anyone Marley had ever met. She had more money than James, and while James was a self-made man, Charmaine grew up with all the spoils of the rich and privileged.

From what Marley had gathered, Charmaine's father used money to tie her to the family. The man used money as a symbol for his love, while he gallivanted all over, making more brothers and sisters for Charmaine, acquiring then disposing of wives left and right. According to Kimberly, Charmaine's father was currently working on marriage number six. Charmaine had joked there was actually a legal limit on how many times one could be married and her father was edging perilously close to that limit.

While Charmaine's wealth was impressive, her beauty was staggering. She reminded Marley of a lion, with her bright, sharp eyes and gorgeous mane, her lithe body all poised and curled up ready to strike. On the surface Charmaine was a wild tangle of fun, but Marley knew a dark sadness lurked behind her blasé exterior.

Marley saw in her a kindred spirit. Way down deep, Charmaine was wounded. Her troubled nature appealed to Marley. Even though Charmaine had many advantages in life, Marley was certain that, like herself, Charmaine had seen the uglier side of human nature. She wanted to believe that if Charmaine knew the truth about her past, her friend would be able to relate. Not as a whore, but as a fellow recipient of the garbage life can throw at you.

When it came to sex with women, Marley had been a party to a few threesomes. It had always been staged, and it usually paid well. In her personal life she'd never been interested in women, but when she was working, a body was a body. Man or woman. It didn't really matter. It was all for the money.

But if you were going to bump and grind with a woman, Charmaine was a gorgeous one to do it with. And her feline grace made it something Marley was almost looking forward to. It would be fun. And James would love it. Men always fantasized about being with two women adoring them, wanting them, begging for their cock. How awesome for her to give that to him.

A thorough understanding of sex and a lack of hang-ups were some of the benefits of her previous occupation. Marley congratulated herself on her mature, progressive approach to sex. This practicality set her apart from most women.

Her mind drifted back to James and how much she wanted him. The spell he'd cast over her was almost unbearable. By telling her she couldn't touch herself, he made her unquenched lust the sole focus of her attention, both mentally and physically.

Damn that Daddy! She snarled, and hurled herself out of bed. This had gone far enough.

Her bare feet padded through the dark, silent living room. Standing outside his closed bedroom door, she paused. Did she dare enter uninvited? Could she wake him up in the middle of the night?

Heart pounding, she screwed up all her courage and turned the door handle.

Inside she could hear his breathing. Steady, like the man himself.

When she tried to speak, only a strangled whisper came out. Her pulse throbbed just under the surface of her skin, which was beginning to perspire. What would he do once he realized she'd come into his room unannounced?

What if he yelled at her and sent her back to her room? That would be worse than the suffering she had endured for the last several hours. She wasn't sure she could take that kind of rejection.

Surely he would be kind to her, even if he sent her away. It was this hope that gave her the chutzpah to pull back the blankets and crawl into bed with him.

He lay facing away from her. Slowly, she inched toward him until they were touching.

Still he didn't stir.

She lay there for a while, relishing the quiet intimacy of being in bed with the man she loved, watching him sleep.

But his back was to her. Sigh. *Maybe I should just try to fall asleep.*

After a few minutes, she realized that wasn't going to happen. She had unfinished business with her daddy and there would be no sleeping on her part until it was settled.

Gently, she draped her arm across his chest and snuggled up like a spoon against his backside.

Finally, he moved. His hand reached up and pulled her arm to his chest, holding it close. He mumbled something unintelligible and let out a snore.

This would not do. Frustrated, she whisper-hissed into his ear, "Daddy!"

"Huh? What is it?" he asked, half-asleep.

"Nothing, Daddy. It's me, Marley."

He readjusted, rolling back over toward her. "Marley." He rubbed his eyes. "What are you doing here?"

How to answer that...?

"I couldn't sleep."

He reached over and ran a hand over her hip. "You couldn't, huh?" A lecherous tone snuck into his voice.

"No, Daddy. You told me I couldn't touch myself, so that's all I've been able to think about. Sex. And you," she said petulantly.

"So you understand the punishment now and you don't like it, do you?"

"Yes, I understand, and no, I don't like it, Daddy." She gently traced the chiseled planes of his face with one finger. "I get very lonely, all by myself in my room."

"You do?" he teased.

"I do, Daddy, and I miss you."

He pulled her to him, covering her mouth with his. Even though he'd been sleeping, he tasted delicious, clean and fresh as a spring breeze.

"My poor girl."

She nodded her assent and kissed him back, her tongue darting into his mouth, lolling in a dance with his.

"Let's get this thing off." He tugged her gown over her head then tossed it on the floor.

"So tell Daddy what it is you want."

"I just want you, Daddy. However you want to take me." She loved being submissive to him; that was what brought her the most pleasure of all, letting him do what he wished with her body.

"Uh-uh. This is your show, princess. You're the one who woke me up. Now tell me what you want, what you've been fantasizing about."

She furrowed her brow in the dark. Clearly she hadn't thought this all the way through. What *did* she want?

"I want you to lick my pussy." The words tumbled out before she could stop them. When he had done that before, it felt amazing.

"That's such a good girl, telling Daddy what she wants. I'm very proud of you, Marley. If you're not honest with Daddy, I can't please you."

Shifting himself atop her, he slid down her torso. "Spread your legs."

She pulled her knees up and opened her legs.

"Wider," he barked.

She stretched them as wide as they would go. "That's the best I can do, Daddy."

"That's fine. You should start stretching yourself when you're watching television. Daddy likes you to open wide for me, understand?"

"Yes, Daddy," she whimpered with anticipation, the adrenaline already pumping at the vulnerable position she was in. Being spread like this had her juices flowing.

He burrowed his head between her legs, and caressed the insides of her thighs with his hands.

Marley involuntarily tensed. She felt incredibly vulnerable, her naked pussy in his face, and after she'd asked him to do this, too. How embarrassing.

"Relax," he said, stroking her, tracing the outside folds of her southernmost lips.

Tilting her head back, Marley shut her eyes and took a deep breath. She was more comfortable giving. It was difficult for her to accept the gift he was about to give her, but she knew she must. She had asked for it, after all.

She forced herself to let go and enjoy the experience as he nipped at her lips with his. Boldly, Marley wound her fingers into his full head of hair. James took this as a green light, employing his tongue with a gusto that surprised her. He seemed to truly be enjoying himself.

His tongue was thick, wide, and meaty. He lapped up her whole sex, the way a Labrador would drink a bowl of water—thirsty, with passion abounding. Then he pointed his tongue and hit only certain spots of her labia. At first Marley was consciously aware of what he was doing, and with what part of his body.

But before long, the pleasure became so intense, spreading out over so many nerve endings, she couldn't keep it straight in her mind. She moaned, crying out constantly, her body overtaken by the most delicious sensations she'd ever felt in her life.

He licked her clit, swirled all around it. Was he using his fingers, maybe his nose? Hell, she didn't care! He was so passionate, like her body was an ice cream store filled with all of his favorite flavors. She spread her legs even wider, open for business.

His mouth made her buck hard underneath him, and she came, wave after wave of pleasure lasting for what seemed like an eternity while he licked, nipped, and stroked her pussy. Slowly she came back to earth.

Afterwards, he marveled at how much pleasure he'd brought her. "Wow! You really liked that. Why didn't you tell me how much you like that, naughty little girl?"

She giggled, threw her arms around his neck, and said, "I didn't know I did." Her lips found his and she tasted her own tart nectar. Holding him tightly to her, she hoped he wouldn't banish her from his bedroom. The endorphins pinging through her body gave her confidence. "Daddy, can I sleep here tonight? Please."

He kissed her neck and gave her a squeeze. "Yes, you may. Snuggle up to Daddy and go to sleep now." He tapped her on the nose. "We have a big day later today. I'm taking you out for brunch and then we're going to a football game."

"For real?"

"For real. Now let's get some sleep."

Dutifully, she rolled into the crook of his arm and slept better than she had in weeks.

CHAPTER FIFTEEN

James took Marley to brunch at Nick & Sam's. He wanted some time alone with her, so he planned to meet their friends later at the game.

They sipped mimosas and grazed at the various culinary stations. James ordered a slab of prime rib, while Marley enjoyed a custom-made omelet with ham, cheese, and two kinds of onion. The dessert table groaned with scrumptious selections, but they both settled on the chocolate mousse, which was heavenly and thankfully light.

After they were satiated, James had his driver take them to the Dallas Vipers' gigantic stadium. The facility boasted some of the world's most lavish accommodations, and last year he had treated himself to season tickets with his own skybox.

For the last few games he'd given his tickets to some of the higher-ups in his company as a perk and a gesture of good will. But today, he looked forward to showing off Marley and watching the game with her.

The box seating offered a bird's-eye view of the playing field and gave the event a party vibe. Luxurious midnight blue upholstered furniture, several high-definition monitors, and parquet flooring provided a comfortable atmosphere.

James had invited Charles and Kimberly. Carmen would be joining them as well. From what she had said, Carmen preferred to watch with them rather than the 'players' wives.' It didn't sound like that group was one in which she felt at ease. To hear her tell it, those ladies had nothing on any of the housewives from those reality shows in the drama department.

The home team played the Houston Honeybadgers that afternoon. The game opened with a kickoff return for a touchdown by the Vipers. They set the tempo from the beginning, held down the throttle and never looked back. Just before the half, Carmen's boyfriend, Natron Dakers, caught a pass at the twenty-five yard line and ran it in for a touchdown, making the score 21-0.

Mugging for the cameras, Natron unveiled a new touchdown dance that had him shimmying in the end zone. The crowd went wild.

"He's quite the showman," James said to Carmen.

She laughed. "Don't I know it!"

Mushroom snowcaps, breaded parmesan asparagus tips, stuffed shrimp, and other appetizers were served on the buffet. Ice-cold beer flowed, and a wine selection was available for some of the ladies who preferred vino.

James watched Marley mingle. Every move she made dripped style and grace. Truly, seeing her today, it blew his mind that she had ever been a prostitute, walking the streets. The woman could shine in any setting. From homeless shelter to the most high-end charity ball, she found her niche and made her delightful presence known. Seeing her today, a stranger might have thought she'd grown up in the toniest neighborhood in Dallas.

None of that mattered to him. He didn't care about her past. Hell, there were times when he forgot about it completely.

On the other side of the room, Marley sparkled in a green sweater that enhanced her emerald eyes. Engaged in conversation with Kimberly and Charles, she tucked a strand of raven hair behind her ear. James' chest tightened. He couldn't imagine life without her. She'd become as essential to him as breathing.

He must tell her.

Talking about his emotions wasn't his strong suit, but he'd find a way.

James crossed the room and slid his arm around Marley's waist.

"Hey." She turned to him and smiled. "What have you been up to?"

"Watching you." It was halftime and people were milling around, out of their seats.

Kimberly and Charles shared a knowing look, then rushed off, making some excuse about needing some more champagne.

"Ah, now I have you all to myself." He wrapped his arms around her.

"Daddy, *here*?" she protested feebly.

"Anywhere I want," he growled in her ear. "This is *my* box, anyway."

He tickled her ear, nibbling just behind it.

"You're right, Daddy."

He nuzzled her neck, leaving a trail of kisses behind. They huddled together on a sofa and watched the rest of the game. The Vipers destroyed the Honeybadgers with the final score reading 42-7. Natron had two hundred all-purpose yards. Viper fans were jubilant. Their team was going to the playoffs.

Amidst all the high-fiving and the congratulatory hugs, Marley whispered in James' ear, "Daddy, there's something I want to run by you."

Leaning back to look at her, he said, "I'm listening."

"I'd like to have a friend over to spend the night this week. Kind of a slumber party. If that's okay…"

Stroking his chin pensively, he answered, "I don't see why not."

She threw her arms round his neck and kissed him hard on the cheek.

"Oh, thank you, Daddy. You won't regret it."

"Okay."

"And I have a special early Christmas present for you, too." An impish grin lit up her face.

"Great." What was his little vixen up to now?

• • • • • • • • • • • • • • •

James couldn't decide if he should go for a swim or a run. Swimming was his workout of choice, but he liked to break up the monotony occasionally. While it was chilly outside now, it wasn't terribly cold, and it was only going to get colder out the further they got into winter.

A run, then. He walked into his closet and took out his running shoes.

Marley was having her friend over tonight, and he was planning to stay out of their way. Let them do their girly things. He'd brought some work home with him. Maybe he'd get a pizza and hole up in his room.

Dressed in a long-sleeved Under Armor shirt and jogging shorts, mp3 player in hand, he was almost at the door when the bell rang. He opened it to see an attractive girl with tiger-striped hair, dripping with designer labels and sex appeal.

"Hi, I'm Charmaine. You must be James." She extended a hand palm down as if she expected him to kiss her ring.

He gave her a firm businesslike handshake and invited her in. Offering to take her bag, he called for Marley. "Charmaine's here."

Marley's head popped out of her room. "Okay. Hey, Charmaine." She then turned to James. "Where are you going?"

"Running."

"Oh, okay." Was that a look of disappointment he saw on her face?

It was sweet she would miss him. "I'll be back soon. You girls have fun."

With that, he plugged in his earbuds and set off for his workout.

Six miles and one hour later, James came through the door, dropped his mp3 player on the hall table, and went to his bathroom to clean up.

His hair still dripping from his shower, he threw on a t-shirt and shorts. Parched, he padded barefoot to the kitchen to get some water.

A gale of giggles erupted from Marley's room. He smiled to himself, glad she was having fun.

Full glass of ice water in hand, he trudged into the living room, sat down, and turned on the sports channel.

Momentarily Marley and her friend came out of her bedroom. They were laughing and stealing glances at one another, as if they had a secret they weren't going to share with him. Both girls wore short tight t-shirts, panties, and long striped knee socks. Marley's hair was tied back in ponytails.

It unnerved him to see Marley's guest partially undressed. Not wanting to be accused of ogling her friend, he averted his eyes and focused on Marley. He wanted Marley and her friend to have a good time, to make themselves at home. This was *her* slumber party, after all.

Marley sat down next to him on the couch, her friend taking the adjoining sofa. He started to get up and give them the room, but Marley put a hand out to stop him.

"Don't go, Daddy. How was your run?" Marley purred, caressing his leg.

"Not bad," he said, offering her a peck on the cheek. "What are you girls up to?"

"Well, we're getting a little bored, Daddy, and wondered if you would play with us." she said, managing to look both innocent and seductive at the same time.

"I guess. What did you have in mind? Monopoly? Cards?"

Her laughter tinkled in the air. "Well... Charmaine is between daddies right now. I thought maybe you might like it if she played with *us*." She dipped her hand down to his crotch and squeezed. She whispered in his ear, "Think of it as an early Christmas present, Daddy."

He swallowed hard, his throat dry. Charmaine nodded, wearing an angelic expression.

"Uh," he stalled. Glaring at Marley, he asked in a stage whisper, "Are you sure you want to do this?"

Marley smiled sweetly. "Sure, Daddy. I just want to make you happy." She slithered down between his legs and tugged at his shorts. Intent on what she was doing, she peeked over at Charmaine. "I'll show you what Daddy likes."

"Okay." Charmaine responded, crossing and uncrossing her legs suggestively.

He closed his eyes, trying to wrap his head around the situation. Blood rushed to his brain rather than below the waist. Two girls. They wanted him to play with both of them.

His heart raced. Was Marley really okay with this? He didn't want to be unfaithful to her, but she was the one bringing another girl into their bed, so to speak. Was this something she *needed*? If so, he didn't want to disappoint her.

He'd been with two prostitutes once. The sex had been good enough, but it had been so impersonal that he'd never repeated the experience. He liked having some sort of connection with his partner, however fleeting, and the threesome had been more mechanical, just another way to get off.

But he and Marley had an amazing connection. If she wanted to play out this fantasy, he was willing to go along.

She was playing with his cock, which had yet to respond. Taking a deep breath, he realized he would have to channel his best inner dom to give these girls a good time.

"Take off your shirts, both of you," he ordered them firmly.

Charmaine's eyes stayed locked with his as she pulled the thin fabric over her head. She had small, firm breasts with tiny pink nipples that were already erect. Slowly, she sunk down on the floor next to Marley.

Marley removed her top quickly, intent on making him hard. She moved aside for him to stand and take down his shorts. He was damp and sweaty from the run, but the girls didn't look as if they minded. Bottomless, he turned off the television and walked away from the furniture.

Standing in the middle of the room, he said, "Both of you crawl over here to me."

On hands and knees, both girls slowly, sensuously inched toward him.

He held each girl's chin, and rubbed their cheeks as he would a kitten.

Marley nuzzled against his hand while Charmaine watched.

"Marley, show Charmaine how to worship Daddy's cock."

Her eyes lit up, and she took him into her mouth. He felt himself thicken in her wet, warm tunnel. He was tempted to close his eyes and enjoy it, but he was distracted by Charmaine nuzzling his hand as Marley had done.

Aha. Charmaine was a quick study.

Charmaine looked up at him and winked saucily.

Studying the new girl, he noted her bright blue eyes and wild, wavy hair and all its plethora of colors. She was sinfully beautiful and he could tell she knew it. This one was trouble.

He reminded himself this was Marley's idea, pulled himself out of her mouth, and shoved his rod in Charmaine's face. "Suck it, little girl."

Charmaine opened her mouth, which was much larger than Marley's, and took him to the back of her throat, holding his gaze the whole time.

Not a novice, this one. He clutched the back of her head, pulling her toward him, fucking her mouth deep.

"Charmaine, hands behind your back. Marley, go behind me and lick my balls." Adjusting his stance, he made room for her between his legs.

In no time he felt the lap-lapping of her warm, soft tongue.

He thrust in and out of Charmaine's mouth, causing drool to trickle out the side. Her dripping mouth spurred him on. Exquisite sensations engulfed him as one girl worked him from the front, the other from the back.

He wanted to come, but knew he needed to hold back. Wanting to put on a better show for these girls, he gathered himself and told them to stop. Charmaine kept sucking until he held her by the shoulders and slid out from between her lips.

"I said to stop. Do you need a spanking?"

A twinkle in her eye, she replied, "Yes, Marley's daddy. I think I do."

He glanced at Marley for her reaction. Gleefully she said, "Yes, Daddy. I do think she deserves a spanking!"

James nodded. "Charmaine, come over here and lean over the edge of this chair."

Charmaine cut her eyes at Marley, but draped herself over the side of the chair.

"Marley, go in your closet and bring me the paddle out of the second drawer."

Her eyes rounded but she scurried into her room, and came back with a wooden paddle. "Is this it?"

"Yes. Charmaine, stretch your hands out in front of you and Marley will hold them."

The girls followed his instructions, Marley clasping Charmaine's hands in hers.

"I will give you ten strokes. Charmaine, would you like to count or would you prefer Marley to do it?"

Charmaine looked to Marley. "Would you do it, please?"

Marley nodded. "Sure."

"Marley, come behind her and take down her panties."

Marley moved behind Charmaine. "How far down, Daddy?" she asked as she began sliding Charmaine's underwear down her hips.

"To her ankles."

Charmaine wiggled as her delectable ass was revealed. Marley came back around to hold her friend's hands.

"Be still, girl, or you will wish you had obeyed. If you want to play with me, you will have to accept my authority."

"Sorry, Sir," Charmaine squeaked.

He raised the paddle and brought it down on Charmaine's taut butt cheeks.

She flinched.

As he punished Charmaine, he observed her reactions, reading her signals. A good dom knew how to push his sub to the limits, but not cross them. He swatted her hard enough to get her attention, but not hard enough to break her.

Charmaine took her spanking like a good sub, but didn't appear to relish the pain of the beating. That was the case with most little girl subs. They generally weren't pain sluts. Those who loved pain usually gravitated to more sadistic doms. On a mission to be a good dom, he didn't want to leave her wanting more, in case she'd been angling for a severe punishment.

"Marley, come look at your slutty little friend's cherry red ass."

"Wow, it *is* red."

"Feels red." Charmaine rubbed her bottom.

"Marley, do that for her. Rub Charmaine's ass. Make her feel better."

"Yes, Daddy." Marley stroked the hot cheeks gently. Charmaine stretched underneath her in a uniquely feline motion.

"Now go into Marley's bedroom, both of you, and take off everything but your socks. You may leave them on. Then lie on the bed, face down, ass up in the air."

"Yes, Sir," they said in unison.

James drank the rest of his water. He needed to stay hydrated. He took off his shirt and threw it on the floor. Naked, he walked into Marley's room.

The girls had positioned themselves so when he walked through the doorway he was presented with their eager cunts, legs spread, bottoms ready for him. Their heads turned toward one another, they whispered and stifled giggles.

"Let's see what we've got here." With a hand on each girl, he caressed the outsides of their thighs, ran his hand over their backsides and down between their legs.

He stroked each girl's inner thighs, one leg at a time. Anticipation built as the room filled with the scent of desire. An electric current sparked in the air, connecting them all in a lusty conspiracy.

James started his pussy inspection with Marley. He traced the outline of her lips with his finger. Using two hands, he spread those lips apart, inserting a finger into her slick, wet cunny.

She gasped into a pillow and shook her ass at him. She wanted more.

"No, you little whore. I have to inspect your friend now." He spanked her flank before turning his attention to Charmaine.

It intrigued him that women's cunts could be so different. Marley had a longer slit, darker in color. Charmaine's was wider, more plump and pink.

They were both beautiful. Both completely shaved the way he liked. Both made him want to bury himself, nuts deep, in them. But there would be plenty of time for that.

He inserted one, then two fingers inside Charmaine. Since she was new to him, he needed to feel out her likes and tolerances. She barely responded until he inserted the second finger. Then she rocked back onto his hand, wanting it deeper.

Climbing on the bed, James planted his knees between the two girls' heads. This gave him the best angle to smack their pussies, which he did. The girls grunted and groaned as he smacked their exposed clits repeatedly. Then he fingerfucked them until he had them writhing on the bed, dripping with need.

"Please fuck us, Daddy. Please!" Marley begged.

"In a minute, doll. Don't be so greedy. Roll over onto your back and bring your legs down so they dangle off the side of the bed."

Her breath heavy with lust, Marley repositioned herself.

"Now Charmaine, straddle her face. Marley, I want to see you lick her pussy good."

A hint of defiance flashed across her face, but Marley lay back and accepted the other girl lowering herself over Marley's lips.

"Good girl, Charmaine." He swatted her still-pink ass.

"Now, Marley. Let me see you eat her pussy," he growled.

Marley stuck her tongue out, reaching toward Charmaine, who lowered herself further. Her red little tongue dipped into the other girl's folds. She pointed it, jabbing at Charmaine's clit, eliciting a moan. Then she offered a flatter, looser tool, lapping at the other girl's length. Charmaine ground her hips into Marley's face, saying, "Yes, yes," urging her on.

"Good girl, Marley. Eat that pussy." James grabbed Marley's legs and impaled her with his rod. Fucking her fast and hard, he felt her muscles clench around him almost instantly in a climax. God, she was so turned on, and she had him stiff as a board. He pounded into her with great force. She usually liked it rough and today that's what he gave her.

Marley's body grew rigid again, then limp. "Don't forget your job, little slut. Did you make her come?"

Charmaine piped up, "Nearly there." She ground against Marley, who seemed to have wilted.

"Stick your tongue out, you little bitch, and lick her," James barked menacingly. He slapped her thigh to get her attention.

Marley came to life under Charmaine, nipping and sucking her swollen button.

Charmaine screamed out and her hips bucked uncontrollably. James held her by the shoulders, crooning, "It's okay. It's okay," into her hair.

This was as close as he'd gotten to Charmaine. The exotic perfume of her flowing mane was intoxicating, like Asian blossoms and cinnamon. When her body stopped trembling, he let her go.

"I'm going to get water. When I get back, I'm going to fuck you," he said to Charmaine, who shifted her position and answered him with a passionate kiss.

CHAPTER SIXTEEN

Charmaine chewed on a perfectly manicured fingernail. "I'm sorry. I forgot to ask if you minded if I kissed him. I got carried away."

James had left to get some water.

"That's okay." Marley brushed a hand in front of her face.

"Okay, because I don't want to piss you off. By the way, you were awesome." Charmaine winked at Marley.

"Thanks." The whole situation was surreal. She heard James call to her from the other room.

"Be right back," she told Charmaine before bolting to the kitchen.

Marley took a deep breath. She needed a break from the threesome. She'd been surprised at how intense it had gotten.

James handed her two bottles of water. "Can you please take these back in there? For you and Charmaine. It's important to drink fluids."

She searched his face. He looked happy. Content. No signs of uncertainty, doubt.

Did she really expect to see any? He was a red-blooded American male whose girlfriend had gifted him another woman, a three-way. What guy wouldn't be happy in that situation? Thrilled, even.

And it had been her idea. So why did she feel so crappy all of a sudden?

At first it had been a silly game. She and Charmaine giggling, trying to seduce her daddy.

Then, somewhere along the way, it started to feel wrong.

Maybe when James said he was going to fuck Charmaine next. Marley was not looking forward to that. Could she even watch? She wasn't sure.

"C'mon, Marley." James' face brightened as he gestured to her, and her heart lurched. He looked so handsome—his coal-black hair wild, his piercing brown eyes focused on her.

She loved him so much. Why hadn't it occurred to her that she'd be miserable having to share him with another woman?

Slowly she skulked back to her room. Charmaine was perched on the edge of the bed, glamorous as a showgirl in her nudity. Marley's stomach dropped. She cursed herself for coming up with this idea.

Charmaine took the water bottle out of Marley's hand. She frowned. "You okay, Marley?"

"Sure. I'm fine." Marley plastered on a fake smile.

The three of them sipped their water silently.

Charmaine broke the silence. "That was fun, Marley. You have a pretty cool daddy." She traced the hair on James' chest with a blood-red fingernail.

Marley's blood pressure rose and she fought to keep her emotions under control. "I do." She didn't trust herself to say more. She thought if Charmaine didn't remove her hands from James' muscles, she might scream.

"Give Marley a kiss, Charmaine."

Charmaine took Marley's drink out of her hand and set it aside. Then taking Marley's face in both hands, she pressed her lips hard onto Marley's. Her friend slipped her tongue inside her mouth, gently, then more insistently.

Marley resisted at first. At that moment she had mixed feelings about Charmaine. She didn't want to be kissing her. But her body betrayed her, relaxing into the kiss, enjoying the girl's soft lips and warm, invading tongue.

None of this is Charmaine's fault. I asked her to do this. No reason to punish her or James for my own idiocy.

"That's it. Now play with each other's titties." James stood back and watched.

Charmaine's hands traveled over Marley's chest. Instinctively, her nipples pebbled under Charmaine's touch. Marley clumsily groped Charmaine's breasts in response.

Sighs of ecstasy erupted from Charmaine's throat. She was really getting into this.

"Good job, girls. Get on the bed and play with each other." By this time, James' cock had joined the party and he stroked his shaft while watching the girls obey his commands.

Marley tried to put aside her misgivings and get into the groove of things. She and Charmaine made out and continued to fondle each other.

"Marley, it doesn't look like you're having much fun. Lie back and spread your legs. Charmaine, I want you to show me what a good girl you can be. I want you to make Marley come with your mouth. I know how much my little girl likes that." He winked at Marley, who awarded him a weak smile in return.

He moved closer to the bed. "Marley, take care of this for Daddy." James placed her hand on his erection.

Grateful for something to do, Marley closed her hand around his shaft and jerked it the way he liked.

Charmaine licked her sex from top to bottom and back up again. She nipped and pulled at Marley's lips, eliciting praise from Marley's daddy.

"Nice, Charmaine. I believe your behavior has improved. I think you deserve a good fucking, what do you think, Marley?"

"Sure," Marley answered miserably.

James was too busy with Charmaine to notice Marley's lack of enthusiasm. "Give me your cunt, girl. Raise it up high so I can fuck it."

Like a horror movie in slow motion, Marley watched Charmaine toss him a flirtatious look over her shoulder as she offered herself up to him. She watched James grab Charmaine's hips and force himself into her. Watched him pump into her, grinding his hips against her ass.

The pleasure on his face was unbearable. Nausea churned in Marley's belly, and she struggled to get up.

But Charmaine pushed her back down. "Where are you going? You're gonna get me in trouble with Daddy." She giggled between groans.

"Yeah, you'd better make Marley come, you little slut, or it'll be another punishment for you. And I won't go as easy on you this time."

Marley froze. Charmaine dropped her head back down between Marley's legs.

Marley wasn't feeling it. Charmaine was a woman, so she knew all the right buttons to hit, but Marley's stomach hurt so much she wasn't getting aroused.

"Put your fingers inside her. Use them. Spread her." James ordered Charmaine.

Marley felt what must have been most of Charmaine's hand inside her. Her friend poked and prodded at her poor pussy until her juices began to flow. Once Charmaine had a rhythm going, Marley responded, her hips thrusting to meet Charmaine.

"That's it. Good girls. Both of you," James said. "Keep going. Keep fucking her. Now suck on her little clit."

His words alone knocked Marley's excitement up a notch. She loved when he talked dirty. It made her moist every time.

Charmaine's velvet lips clamped down on Marley's tender nub and sucked the skin around it into her mouth. The tip of her tongue dabbed that most tender spot, making the tiniest of circles, round and round until Marley climaxed with a scream.

"Keep licking," James ordered Charmaine.

Marley's entire body shuddered and shook as a gigantic orgasm took her on a ride that seemed endless. She jerked and cried out, "Daddy, thank you, Daddy."

"You're welcome, doll." He leaned down and stroked her arm, still fucking Charmaine.

Marley slammed her eyes shut. She didn't want to see anymore of her friend and the love of her life in this intimate embrace. Even if she was involved. Even if they did just make sure she had a brain-bending orgasm.

Weak from her climax, Marley struggled to free herself from Charmaine's attentions. "I have to go to the bathroom," she muttered.

With that, Charmaine lifted up, and Marley scrambled for the bathroom.

While sitting on the toilet, she made a quick decision. She threw on some dirty clothes from the hamper and snuck out the other door. Carnal sounds of grunting and panting drifted into the front hallway. Marley shoved her feet into her shoes and threw a bag over her shoulder. Tears streamed down her face as she closed the front door behind her.

• • • • • • • • • • • • • • •

Marley's knuckles whitened as she gripped the steering wheel, weaving in and out of Dallas holiday traffic. She'd forgotten it was the weekend before Christmas, and shoppers were out in droves. Her plan, short term though it was, had been to drive around to clear her head.

Snarling congestion encompassed her, intent on robbing her of what little peace she had left. She had to get out of it. But where could she go?

She knew it was immature to leave in the middle of the tryst, but she hadn't been able to help herself. Her armor had begun to crack and she couldn't bear for James to see her like that. Charmaine either, for that matter.

James had always been too good for her, she chided herself. Too wealthy, too upscale, too generous. And she'd been naïve enough to think things could work out between them. That it was possible for her to have a man like him. That she was worthy of being loved.

Marley snorted. Yeah, that was a joke. She and James were from different worlds and it had been foolish of her to believe it didn't matter.

She'd brought her past 'occupation' into their bedroom and cheapened what they had. Before, things with James had seemed special. Had she imagined that?

Now it felt like their whole relationship boiled down to sex. Maybe the threesome was what she needed to open her eyes to the reality of the situation. She had an agreement with him to sleep with him, in exchange for a place to live. That was it.

What was she supposed to do now?

As she contemplated being homeless again, a sense of dread permeated her consciousness. If she left James, she'd have nowhere to live. She'd have to give back the car, she realized with a grimace. And she'd have to forget going back to school.

At least she had some friends now. Who could she call? Sloane was too close with James. Carmen was busy with Natron. The two of them were going to visit his family for Christmas in Florida. Kimberly's plate was full with the wedding, but she had nowhere else to turn.

She pulled off the highway and coasted into a parking lot, then dialed Kimberly's number.

"Hello." It calmed her to hear Kimberly's friendly voice.

"Hi, Kimberly, it's Marley."

"Hey, girl. Oh my gosh, are you calling to tell me about your ménage with Charmaine? How was it?"

"Not so good," Marley said, deflated.

"Oh, crap. What happened?"

"It was going pretty well, and then I lost it and skipped out. I hate to impose, but do you think I could come over and talk about it?"

"Absolutely. Come on over."

"I'm on my way."

Thirty minutes later Marley found herself sitting on Kimberly's couch, sipping white wine and telling Kimberly all the gory details from her rendezvous with James and Charmaine.

Her face creased with worry, Kimberly made clucking noises at all the right places during Marley's story. At one point she reached over and laid a comforting hand on Marley's arm.

"So what has you the most upset about the whole thing?" Kimberly asked.

"James fucking Charmaine. It made me ill to see that. I wasn't able to 'just have fun' or separate myself from the situation. All of a sudden, I realized the man I loved was screwing another woman, right in front of me." Marley dropped her head in her hands.

"I hate to ask," Kimberly said, "but, um, didn't you consider that might be a problem *beforehand*? I know I couldn't handle Charles doing that."

"*Now* I get that, but when I planned it, I guess I didn't think it would affect me like that. I thought I could be professional about it." Marley shrugged.

Kimberly laughed. "Professional, what a funny way to look at it."

Heat rose in Marley's cheeks. She was swimming in dangerous waters. Time to backtrack before Kimberly grew suspicious. It was nice to have a friend she could talk to. Having a girlfriend she could confide in was a luxury she hadn't had in years. The idea of losing this new friendship made her stomach churn harder. And that's what would happen if Kimberly found out she used to be a hooker.

Marley's phone buzzed. Another text. James and Charmaine had both left dozens of texts and voice messages. Not that she listened to any of them. The incessant beeping and binging of the phone was driving her nuts. Finally, she turned the blasted thing off.

She didn't want to talk with them. Not now. Her nerves were so frazzled, her feelings so hurt—she couldn't.

"Marley?" Kimberly asked. "Are you okay?"

Marley realized that she'd just zoned out while talking to Kimberly. "I'm sorry. I'm just distracted…"

She finished giving Kimberly the blow by blow of what went down at James' apartment that afternoon. Just as she wound down, a knock sounded at Kimberly's front door.

CHAPTER SEVENTEEN

"Kimberly! It's me, James. Is Marley here?"

The room fell silent, with the exception of the fist banging against the other side of the door.

Marley scrambled off the couch and mouthed to Kimberly, "I don't want to see him." She rushed into the hallway, hoping she'd be able to eavesdrop.

Kimberly opened the door. "Hi, James. I'm sorry you came all the way out here. Marley's having a hard time. She doesn't want to see you right now."

James burst past her. "I don't care. I need to see her, Kimberly. Do you know why she left?" Marley heard the pain in his voice.

"I guess the thing with you and her and Charmaine didn't work out so well," Kimberly said.

"But I don't understand. She set it up. It was her idea!" he protested.

"I know. She's confused. She didn't know it would make her jealous, but it did. You know how sometimes things don't work out the way you plan them."

"Fine. It's over and it won't happen again. But I want her to come home. She and I need to work through this." Marley peeked around the corner.

"I know." Kimberly patted him on the back.

He ran his fingers through his hair. "Are you sure she won't see me?"

Kimberly shook her head. "She just needs time. Be patient with her."

James turned and Marley quickly slipped back into the hallway before he saw her. It made her heart lurch, seeing him in such a state. But she was so messed up. He'd be better off with someone else.

"Tell her to call me. Tell her I need to see her. Kimberly, please talk with her," James pleaded.

Kimberly agreed and told him goodbye. She closed the door and rounded the corner to find Marley in the hallway. Kimberly didn't have to say a word. The disapproving look on her face said it all.

"I'm sorry. Thanks for fending him off for me."

Kimberly exhaled loudly. "I just hope you know what you're doing. He really cares for you."

Later, in the privacy of Kimberly's guest room, Marley mustered the courage to return Charmaine's phone calls.

Charmaine apologized for not realizing that her presence in Marley and James' lovemaking was intrusive. "I'm sorry, babe. I got lost in the scene and wasn't paying enough attention. I should have realized that you weren't comfortable with it. My bad."

"No, mine." Marley shook her head. "I asked you to do it. You had no way of knowing. Heck, I didn't have a clue it would affect me that way."

"You have to know that I'm not interested in James. I mean, he's a hot dom and all, but he's not my type. Plus I know he's your daddy. And honey, he's crazy about you."

"Really? What makes you say that?"

"Well, for starters, he only had eyes for you. I might as well have been invisible."

"That's not how it seemed to me," Marley grumbled.

"Well, you must have been in a different room then. I usually get much more of a reaction from guys than I did from him," Charmaine snorted.

"I can see that," Marley admitted.

"Plus when he found out you had left the apartment, the man was beside himself. It was sad. He was like a lost puppy or a kid whose ice cream cone just fell on the sidewalk. I felt sorry for him. For you both. I know threesomes can be complicated, but this one ended worse than any I've ever experienced. No offense."

"None taken."

"So what are you going to do?"

"I don't know."

"Well, honey, if I were you, I'd run back over there to him. It's clear he adores you, and he treats you like a princess. There aren't a lot out there like him. Believe me, I know."

"He *is* wonderful, but sometimes it feels crappy, like I'm a 'kept woman.'"

"You know what, Marley? I'm always worried that guys are after me for my money. Money gives people so many hang-ups. Hell, I go to a psychologist for mine. But I can tell you care about James for who he is, not for his cash. Don't let money get in the way. Fuck convention. Embrace the relationship. Accept it for what it is. It's okay to like his money. As a rich bitch, I can tell you it's okay to like the money. It won't take the place of love, but it's a good thing to have."

"I heard that." Marley chuckled softly. Charmaine had no idea how well Marley knew the value of money.

"I'm leaving for Switzerland in a couple of days. If you don't go back to

James, you're welcome to come."

"Thanks, Charmaine. That's awfully sweet, but I don't think so."

"Well, it's the least I can do. Don't make me feel guilty for breaking y'all up," she whined. "If you don't go with me, you have to go back to him. So he fucked somebody else. You were *there*. You know it didn't mean anything. If it's not your thing, just don't do it again."

"I'll think about it, Charmaine. You're a good friend, you know that?"

"Sure am, hon. Let me know if you change your mind about coming with us. It will be a blast. Skiing, partying with hot European guys and some cute baseball players I met last week."

"Baseball players?"

"Yeah. It's the off season."

"Okay. Well, Merry Christmas if I don't talk with you before."

"You too, hon."

Marley said goodnight and hung up the phone. She was relieved the conversation had ended on a positive note. She didn't blame Charmaine. Or James. If she blamed anyone, it was herself.

The thought of meeting James' parents for the holidays made her blanch. She contemplated Kimberly and Charles' brightly decorated home, all ready for Christmas. Colorful stockings hung cheerily over their fireplace. The tree was decked with silvery icicles, glass balls, and handmade ornaments complete with handprints. There were even holiday towels in her guest bathroom.

The festive environment that should have brought her cheer instead depressed her. Christmas Eve was the next day. She would only dampen any celebration Kimberly and her little family would have. What in the world was she going to do?

• • • • • • • • • • • • • • •

James' voice rang hollow, even to his own ears. His family, caught up in the festivities of the evening, didn't seem to notice he was less than enthusiastic as they sang Christmas carols.

Of course, when he had shown up without Marley, they'd been disappointed. But he played it off as though even though he and his girlfriend were in a fight—he was fine. His parents didn't pry into his personal life. If he said he was okay, they took him at his word.

His younger sister, Anna, being a typical teenager, was too involved in her own life to be concerned with his. She'd spent the whole drive home from the Christmas Eve church service trying to convince her parents to let her pierce her nose. When she tried to get James on her side, he refused to get in the middle of the argument. He had enough drama in his life.

Now he and his father and Anna stood around the piano. His mother glided her fingers masterfully across the keyboard, making it look effortless.

Music had always been a part of life in this home. Usually it brightened his mood. As a child it had given him comfort. He and Anna had been musical children, always learning to play one instrument or another.

But tonight he feared nothing would be able to lift his spirits. Breathing deeply he plowed through the last round of 'O Come All Ye Faithful.' When the song ended, his dad clapped him on the shoulder. "Good to have you home, son. You staying the night? You know your mom has a delicious breakfast planned for tomorrow morning. Macadamia nut French toast. Your favorite."

"No. I think I'm going to head home soon. Got a lot of work to do," James replied with a lie.

He wouldn't be doing work. He'd probably go home and watch television by himself, maybe drink himself into Christmas Day. Ever since Marley left he'd been depressed. He'd missed work. Milton was driving him crazy pestering him to come in, but it didn't matter.

Nothing seemed to matter except Marley. He'd gone to Kimberly's hoping to find her, but she wouldn't see him. Why would she be so cruel? Not only did she leave without a word, but she refused to explain her behavior.

He tried to figure out what went wrong by talking with Charmaine and Kimberly. They both told him that the ménage was what had sent Marley over the edge. It had made her jealous. But if that was the case, why would she have arranged it? That baffled him. He'd never understand women.

If he'd known Marley would have a problem with including Charmaine, he never would have gone along with the scene in the first place. And for her to have just disappeared from his life so easily, with no explanation—it was clear she'd never cared for him at all. She had wanted the money, and now she'd moved on. Probably to bigger and better prospects. Had she been using him the whole time?

That made sense. It was the only thing that made sense. He'd been a fool to fall for her. He should have known better.

An elbow nudged him in the ribs. His mother was speaking to him. "Where are you tonight, James? Definitely not here with us." She brushed a lock of hair off his forehead, as she'd been doing since he was a boy. His father and sister had gone into the kitchen for some more pie.

"I'm sorry, Mom. You're right. It's this girl."

"The one you were going to bring tonight?"

"Yes. I can't get her off my mind." He made a wry face.

"She must be pretty special, then." She patted his arm. "James, all couples have fights. And if you care for her as much as I think you do, you should try to work things out."

"Yeah. It's just that I don't know where she is. She's not returning my calls."

"It is Christmas Eve. You don't think she'd be with her family?"

"No, I don't. She's had a rough life. She's not close with her mother and she lost her brother in the war."

"Oh, that's awful."

"Yeah. I might have one idea where she might be…" he said hesitantly.

"Well, go find her."

"Are you sure? What about opening presents? We haven't done that yet."

"Take yours with you. We'll open ours and call you tomorrow. Maybe come back by, and we'll have leftovers. I have to be sure you're eating well," she teased.

"Hey, I may take you up on that." He smiled.

"I hope you will. Heaven knows your father and I don't need all this food, and Anna eats like a bird these days."

James agreed to stop by the next day for some leftovers and more pie. His mom told him she'd save a piece of French toast for him.

He bent to pick up his presents from under the tree, inhaling the scent of the massive Douglas fir. The tree sat nestled in the corner of the living room, twinkling with hundreds of tiny lights in magical colors. He thought about the measly little desktop tree he'd set on the coffee table in his penthouse.

He hugged everyone and made his way to his car. As he drove, he began wishing he had gotten Marley a real tree.

She'd asked him to go with her to pick out a tree, but he'd been too busy working to find time. Now he wished he had *made* time. He imagined her face shining in the dim glow of a Christmas tree. She would have loved it. Marley found the greatest pleasures in the simplest of things. He could only imagine how happy a tree would have made her.

Why hadn't he dropped everything and gotten her one?

Would she be here with him tonight if he had? He doubted it.

The more he thought about Marley and how grateful she was for all the things he'd done for her, the more confused he became. In many ways, she was uncomplicated and easy to please. If all she needed were the simple things in life to make her happy, why had she left him?

As he drove, these questions pinged around in his head.

CHAPTER EIGHTEEN

Knowing James would be spending Christmas with his family, Marley decided to spend the evening at the only home she knew. The one she shared with James.

She called Ken and asked him to let her know when James left. "I have a surprise for him," she said. It wasn't a fib, exactly. *I did have a surprise for him. It just didn't turn out like I'd planned.*

Once she got word that James had left the building, Marley came over. She gave Ken a generous Christmas bonus, courtesy of a cash advance from the credit card James had given her, then made her way up to the apartment.

Crossing the threshold, she realized how much she'd missed the place. She loved living here with James. Yes, this was the perfect place for her to spend Christmas, even if she was alone and would probably be packing her things soon.

She'd figure out the rest later. Her brain was mush from rehashing the situation with James over and over in her mind until she was dizzy from it all. A soothing glass of wine and the crackle of a fire in the fireplace was what she needed. She needed to relax.

A bottle of red wine and a glass in hand, she made a nest for herself on the couch and clicked on the fireplace. Not quite as traditional as a wood-burning fire, but the gas flames were a lot less trouble than climbing to the penthouse with an armload of logs.

Staring into the flames, she thought of Paul. They had always spent Christmas together. A dull ache throbbed in her heart. She would never spend another holiday with her brother. Yesterday, feeling desperate, she'd called her mother. Apparently, Mom had taken up with some boozehound she'd met at the local bar and planned to spend Christmas with him. Marley was all alone.

She had just switched on some holiday music when James walked through the door.

"Marley!?" His voice was a mixture of surprise and elation. He scooped her into his arms, but her body remained stiff.

"Hi, James. I, uh, didn't think you'd be home." She shifted uncomfortably in his grasp.

"I was at my parents' house, but I wasn't good company so I left. All I could do was think about you. I'm so glad you're here. I hoped you would be, but I feared it was wishful thinking on my part."

"Yeah." She looked away.

He held her by the shoulders. "Marley, what's wrong? Why haven't you been returning my calls? Why wouldn't you see me when I went over to Kimberly's the other night?"

"I'm sorry, the other day, with Charmaine… it got me so confused. I got so jealous. It tore me up to see you with her." Tears welled in her eyes. She willed them away.

"But that whole thing was your idea. You instigated it." He threw his hands in the air. "Why in the world would you do something like that if it was going to upset you so much?"

"I know and I'm sorry. It sounds crazy. The idea came to me because I felt like I could never repay you for all the things you have done for me, all the things you've bought for me. I tried to come up with something I could do for you, something I could give you." She sniffed. "The man who has everything."

"But Marley, you don't have to repay me. Not for anything. I do things for you because I care about you, because I want to. Not so you will give me things in return. Your submission is more than enough." He reached out to stroke her cheek, but she stepped away.

"No, let me finish. I don't feel like I deserve you. I know the reason I'm here—to be the plaything on your payroll." He tried to protest, but she held up a hand. "The only thing I know is sex, James. That's all I have to give—so that's what I did. Tried to give you the sexual experience all men fantasize about."

"Thank you, Marley. And it was great. I'm not going to lie. But mostly because having sex with you is always outstanding."

"What about Charmaine?" she asked.

"What about her?"

"She's easily the most gorgeous girl I've ever seen. She has an insane body. And she's so charming." She found a tissue in her purse and blew into it.

"Doll, I hardly noticed Charmaine. I only want you. Surely you know that." He whisked her into his arms.

Marley gave in and pressed against him, her frame shaking with breath-altering sobs. "This, this relationship or whatever we have, feels so one-sided." She beat her tiny fists on his broad chest. The force of her blows wavered, the protests of a defeated opponent.

"What we have *is* a relationship. Why do you say it's one-sided?"

"Because you have all the money. And I have nothing."

"Is that what this is about? My money?"

"Partly."

"I don't understand. It bothers you that I have money? I thought you liked my money." He scrunched his face, looking perplexed.

"I guess I do like it, but I don't like feeling like a whore. It sucks for my self-esteem, and I know you deserve better. You should be with a woman more your class."

"Oh, Marley. Don't feel like that. When this first started, I thought it was kinda refreshing that you needed my money, and I needed you. It seemed like a win-win situation. Then I loved seeing how much you joy you got from me taking care of you. There is no shame in wanting to be pampered."

She pulled away. "Oh yes, there is. Maybe you don't know, because you've never been poor." She spit out the last word out as if it tasted sour on her tongue.

"Okay, that's fair. As for class, that's ridiculous. We don't have a class system in this country. Hell, if we did I wouldn't even belong in a lot of the places I go. You are every bit my equal, Marley doll. Why can't you just enjoy that I'm wealthy, and let me spoil you?"

"Because I have nothing I can give you back and you deserve more. You don't need to be with a prostitute," she sniffled.

"First of all, if it wasn't for that part of your life, I never would have met you. So I don't regret that. I'm sorry you had to sell yourself. You *are* better than that, but if you hadn't gone through that, we might never have met. And that would be a tragedy, my dear. Do you have any idea how amazing you are, Marley? How different you are from anyone I've ever known?"

She shook her head.

"Doll, for all the ugliness that you have seen, the hell that you have lived in your short life, you have a bigger love for life than anyone I've ever met. I have no idea how you do it, but you can make brushing your teeth seem like a trip to the amusement park. You always have a smile on your face. You find pleasure in the simplest things. As for what you can give me—you give me your submission. I treasure that. Something I take very seriously."

She eyed him skeptically. "But that's nothing compared to giving somebody a car."

"It depends on how you look at it. Marley, cars and clothes—those are just things. Things cannot share a life with me. Things cannot make me happy. And things will not give me companionship when I'm old and gray with a pot belly."

She smiled in spite of herself. "A pot belly?"

"It's been known to happen."

She touched a hand to his taut stomach. "I don't believe it," she said, a hint of flirtation creeping into her voice.

He cradled her hand with his. "Marley, there *is* something you could give me. Something that would mean the world to me. You may not be able to now, but I hope that someday you will."

"What is that?"

"Your love."

"My love?"

He grazed her brow with his lips. "Yes. I've been meaning to tell you, Marley, but I am not good at discussing my feelings. But yes, doll, I've fallen in love with you."

"You have?" She stood stock still, his words sinking in.

"Yes. I can't believe you didn't suspect." He chuckled.

"Well, I… no. I didn't. You never want to sleep with me. You always go to your own room after we play. I thought…"

"That's because I didn't want you to feel pressured. I asked you for an arrangement and I didn't want to be presumptuous, to ask more of you than you were comfortable with. I did enjoy that night you came into my room and stayed, but I assumed you only needed the satisfaction I'd denied you earlier."

"No, James. I wanted you. Not just an orgasm, but *you*. I love you, too."

He crushed her to him. "You do? Marley, my doll, you've made me incredibly happy."

She looked up into his brown eyes as his lips descended onto hers. A blissful surge of love filled her heart. She leaned into him, maintaining the soft, warm kiss until James broke away. His eyes shone with a new sparkle. "I almost forgot. I have some presents for you."

Marley's heart raced and she grinned from ear to ear. "Presents? But I didn't get you anything." She considered for a moment. "Except the three-way that I ran out on."

James went into his room and returned with two beautifully wrapped packages. "Let's just forget about that. From now on, it's just you and me in the bedroom. Deal?"

"Deal." They sealed their pact with a kiss, and he handed her the gifts.

"Will we sleep in the same bedroom?" she asked.

"If you like," he said.

"I would love that, Daddy. I get lonely sleeping all by myself." She pouted.

"Good to know." He tapped his chin. "When you are a good little girl, you may sleep in Daddy's room. And you will have to pay for running out on me. Don't think you're going to get away with that. But since it *is* Christmas, I'll give you a punishment holiday. You can make up for it later."

"Thank you, Daddy." Marley tossed the black ribbon aside and ripped into the cream-colored paper. Inside she found a small rectangular box.

Opening it, she discovered a black circular necklace. Fashioned of the most supple of leathers, it had a ring on one side and a small silver heart on the other. She looked at him quizzically.

"It's a collar."

"A collar?" She tried to remember what he'd said about collars.

"Yes. I'd like you to wear it. It will mean you are my little girl and that I am your daddy. In the BDSM world it's a symbol of commitment. It means you are mine."

Her heart leapt at the idea of belonging to him. There was nothing she wanted more. All the blood seemed to rush to her head and she experienced a tingle between her legs. Overcome with emotion, she didn't trust herself to speak, so she simply nodded her assent.

James fastened the collar around her neck and watched her open the other present. A pair of jet-black fishnet stockings. He laughed. "Okay. Those are really for me."

"I love them, Daddy. Super sexy." She raised an eyebrow. Then repeated how she wished she'd gotten him something.

"Hey, the last gift you got me caused us both a lot of trouble." He pinched her cheek. "I think you should leave the gift giving to Daddy."

She giggled.

"Anyway, the only gift I want from you is for you to give yourself to me every day, my love. That is all. And maybe wear those stockings every once in a while." A wolfish grin crossed his face.

"That I can do," she said, her heart full.

"You know what else I want to do for you?" he asked.

"What?"

"I want to get you a proper Christmas tree." He jerked his thumb at the pitiful fake tree on the coffee table.

"I'll bet you can get a great deal on one," she said, looking at her watch. It was half-past ten.

They laughed. "We might have an hour before the last ones are gone..." James traced the curve of her hip with his index finger.

"It *has* been a few days, Daddy." She looked at the ceiling. "And I *have* missed you."

"You've missed Daddy, have you?"

"Yes."

"You haven't been playing with my little pussy, have you?"

She opened her eyes wide and shook her head no.

"Good girl. Then go into *my* room and undress. Except for these stockings. Get into these. Then kneel on the floor, hands behind your back, and wait for me."

A tremor of pleasure travelled all the way to her toes and she answered saucily, "Yes, Sir, Daddy."

Her fingers touched the collar, snug beside her skin. He loved her. And she loved him.

She'd finally found the place she could call home. Wherever James was.

It's good to be home. Marley scooped up the stockings and skipped all the way to his room.

THE END

Daddy's Game
The Daddy's Girl Series, Book Two

Normandie Alleman

AUTHOR'S NOTE

    I would like to offer special thanks to the football players so close to my heart.
    First to Mr. Alleman, for sharing your experience and vast knowledge of the game. To say I could never have written this book without you would be an understatement.
And second to the born trash-talker in my life who would rather practice touchdown dances, one-handed catches, and flamboyant basketball dunks than anything else.

CHAPTER ONE

"The true object of all human life is play." – G. K. Chesterton

Carmen's stomach turned over, and she searched the office for a wastebasket in case she needed to throw up. The idea of people viewing her artwork made her queasy. She knew she was supposed to be proud of it, to want to show it off—but she didn't.

She was terrified.

What if it sucked? What if people hated it, laughed at it even? Then there was the possibility nobody would show up. The idea of that made her feel worse.

Knock! Knock!

That sinking feeling grew and she wondered who could be at the door. Carmen had barricaded herself in the office that belonged to Gustav, the gallery director. She'd slunk down on the floor, now practically hidden behind his desk.

Gustav had called for her to come out twice, but she'd refused, mumbling something about feeling sick. He must think she was nuts.

She sat on the cold tile floor, hugging her knees and ignoring the knock at the door, willing the interloper away. Eventually, whoever it was retreated.

Pretending to be invisible, Carmen listened for signs of how the event was going. The occasional laugh drifted over the walls, and the sound of glasses clinking together punctuated the dull hum of conversation. At least some people were here, but unfortunately, she had no way of knowing what their reactions were to her art, and clearly Gustav had given up on forcing her to be sociable.

Before tonight, her artwork had been private. She'd sold paintings to friends, given them as gifts, and this past year she'd even branched out to selling on Etsy, the online store for handmade items. Her New Year's resolution six months ago had been to take her passion for her artwork and turn it into a business. However, when she'd made that goal, she hadn't anticipated the terror she would feel when faced with showing her artwork to the public. The idea of strangers judging her made her feel naked and exposed; after all, her artwork was a piece of her. A ripple of nausea moved through her stomach and beads of perspiration formed along her hairline.

I will not be sick. I will not be sick.

Another knock at the door. "Carmen! Carmen, are you in there?" Gustav's voice was tight and high-pitched, as though he'd been pushed to his limit. "I have clients out here who would like to meet you. *Important* clients."

Oh, God, just what she needed. Having to smile and make nice while trying not to vomit on Gustav's VIP clients. She rose on shaky legs and smoothed back her unruly curls. Adjusting her crimson-colored dress, she strode over to the door. "Just a second."

Breathing deeply, she opened the door to find Gustav nervously holding court, a crowd gathered around him.

"Oh, I... I didn't realize..." Carmen gulped. She'd expected Gustav to have one client with him, perhaps a couple. The group of fifteen or more people intimidated her.

While there were over a dozen people in the crowd, Gustav introduced her to only one. "Carmen, this is Natron Dakers. Natron, this is Carmen Harris, our star of the evening."

Carmen shook hands with the tall black man. His hand swallowed hers, his grip firm but not painful. She was about to protest Gustav's labeling her a star, when it hit her—this was Natron Dakers. The famous wide receiver for the Dallas Vipers. Last season's MVP and spokesperson for more products than Carmen could count. The man had his own shoe line, his own cologne, even his own toothpaste. Her three younger brothers couldn't shut up about him.

"Like the red. Nice choice," Natron indicated her dress.

"Oh, thank you." Dark red, color of the Vipers. Of course he'd like it.

"Excuse me, I see someone I simply must say hello to," Gustav said before rushing off. Carmen stepped into the larger gallery space with Natron at her side. The rest of the group melted into the background and Carmen realized most of the hip-looking crowd were part of Natron's entourage.

"I really like your work." Natron scanned the large portraits that hung in the gallery before resting his eyes on her. "I'd like to cover my walls with your paintings."

"You would?"

He laughed. "Yeah, you seem surprised."

"I just, well... this is my first time showing my work. In public." She snatched a glass of champagne off the tray of a passing waiter for her dry mouth, forgetting her stomach troubles.

"Get out!" He nudged her playfully on the shoulder with his fist. "Girl, looks like you've been doing this all your life." His long, trademark dreads bounced when he moved and Carmen couldn't help but notice how handsome he was with his gleaming white teeth and kind, gorgeous brown eyes.

She found her lips relaxing into a grin. "No, this is all new to me." She leaned toward him conspiratorially. "I've been kinda nervous, if you must know the truth."

"Well, you've got no reason to be nervous." He gestured to the large group of patrons crammed into the gallery. "Apparently you're a hit."

She should have been offering up some fabulous sales pitch to him, but something about his warmth made her confide in him instead. "But who knows what they think? Maybe they hate it."

He raised a brow skeptically. "Girl, you gotta be kidding me. These are some happy people, look at 'em. They like it." He nodded, emphasizing his point. "I like it."

The tension in her shoulders lessened, and she could feel her upper arm muscles relax. "Are you a collector?" she asked in an attempt to shift the focus away from herself.

"Nah. But I've been thinking of investing in some art. My agent, he's friends with Gustav, so I thought I'd stop by, check it out."

She nodded. "What kind of art speaks to you?"

"Shoot, girl, I dunno, but I know it when I see it. My mamma took me to museums when I was comin' up, but I didn't pay any attention. She wouldn't let me bring my ball inside, so I was usually pouting and counting the minutes 'til I could get back to playin' ball."

"Really? You wanted to bring your ball?"

"Yeah. Guess they didn't want me breaking something in those fancy places so I always had to leave the ball outside."

"Ah, your football."

"Any kind of ball. Basketball was my first love. Dribbled everywhere I went. Mamma says I slept with my basketball from the time I was a year old." He paused and let his million-dollar grin spread from ear to ear. "Guess it worked out for me."

"I'll say," Carmen said. Natron was cocky, hovering close to arrogance. But hell, if she was as big a superstar as he was, who knew how she'd behave?

"You're pretty cute, ya know that?" Natron winked at her and suddenly she felt as though she were the only woman in the room.

Her heart fluttered in her chest and her cheeks must have flushed the color of her dress. He was flirting with her! Unable to keep the corners of her mouth from giving her away, she looked away, flustered.

He elbowed her lightly in the ribs. "Whatcha doin' afterwards?"

"Oh, I'm, uh, I have to help clean up," she stammered, wondering why she was lying.

"Me and my friends here, we're going out for dinner, maybe have a little fun. You're welcome to come with us."

"I couldn't, but thank you anyway." The idea of going out with Natron and his posse was overwhelming, surreal. His friends were chic and radiated an aura of nonchalant cool that Carmen had never been able to master. And while she couldn't see herself doing that, the invitation was flattering nonetheless.

"Suit yourself," he shrugged. "I'm goin' to talk to Gustav about gettin' some of your work, though."

"Please do," she said, hoping she didn't sound like she was begging.

Natron backed away from her. "I will. You're a talented girl, Carmen Harris. I'll be watching you." He made a box with his fingers, then blew them apart as if there'd been an explosion. "Breakout star right here." With another wink, he turned and gathered his crew.

CHAPTER TWO

The phone rang, jolting Carmen from her concentration. When she was in 'the zone,' the outside world seemed to disappear until something broke her concentration—like the phone. She puzzled over who it could be because she'd turned her cell to 'do not disturb.'

It rang again. Ah. It was her business phone, the one that didn't ring very often. Setting down her paintbrush, she crossed the room and picked up the receiver. "Hello. Carmen Harris' Studio. May I help you?" She hoped she sounded professional.

"Hello, Carmen. It's Gustav."

"Hi, Gustav."

"Do you have a minute?"

"Sure." She'd already been interrupted, might as well talk with him.

"How do you feel about commissions?"

"Commissions? I haven't really done any…"

"Well, I've got a customer, a big fish. If you'll agree to do a commission, I think he'll throw a good bit of work your way."

Most of Carmen's work combined realism with the abstract. Her paintings had been described as portraits infused with the influences of de Kooning and Georgia O'Keeffe. Up until now, her subjects had been people she'd observed at a park or in an airport—no one she knew and she'd never painted from a live model. The idea of being commissioned to paint a portrait was frightening, but after checking her bank balance that morning, she couldn't afford to be choosy. A job was a job.

"Sounds interesting."

"The client would like to meet with you tomorrow afternoon at his house. Will that work?"

"Sure."

"Good. I'll text the address to your cell, which you didn't answer, by the way."

"Because I was working," Carmen countered.

"That's what I like to hear. Let me know how it goes."

Carmen agreed and hung up.

She tried to calm the butterflies in her tummy. This year she'd vowed to grow her art business. Blowing her hair out of her face, she picked up her brush and got back to work.

• • • • • • • • • • • • • • •

The next day Carmen dressed in a casual pair of white slacks and a bohemian blouse, complete with embroidered flowers down the front. Donning a pair of gold sandals, she dashed out of her loft to the beat-up old Jetta she'd had since high school. She might not be new, but the old girl was reliable and got her where Carmen needed to go.

As she pulled onto the expressway, her heart sank at the traffic's pace. Waiting in traffic reminded her of trying to get the last drop of syrup from the bottle—irritatingly slow and a test of her patience. She made a mental note to allow extra time for delays when she had appointments.

She'd plugged the client's address into her GPS, and it directed her to an upscale part of Dallas. But before she could arrive at her destination, she had to stop at the guard house next to the entrance of a gated community.

Rolling down her window, she smiled at the wrinkly man in the security checkpoint. He looked way too old to stop any serious intruder, but maybe it made the wealthy residents sleep better to know they had someone watching out for them, no matter how ineffective.

"May I help you?" the man inquired.

Carmen nodded and told him the address. "I have a meeting, they're expecting me."

The man closed the window, picked up a phone, and spoke into it. The party on the other end must have confirmed her story because he waved to her and the gate magically opened.

It was a swanky neighborhood, reminding her of her friends' 'Dream House' boards on Pinterest. Colonials, English Tudors, French chateaus, and a modern glass number that didn't fit in at all, not that she was an expert on architecture—each one more posh than the last.

She took a right at the next stop sign and followed the GPS to the end of a cul-de-sac. "Arriving at destination" said the tinny female voice on her dashboard. Carmen looked up to see the biggest house on the block. The enormous Mediterranean had an almost flat barrel tile roof, and at least three wings. The lawn was immaculately groomed and tropical flora abounded; the hibiscus, sago palms, and climbing bougainvillea gave her the feeling she'd been transported into someone's luxury vacation villa.

She was here to sell her work, which was not her forte, and socializing with rich people made her nervous. Timidly, she rang the doorbell. If it wasn't for her impossibly low bank balance, she'd have stayed home.

When the door opened, she was surprised to see the famous smile belonging to Natron Dakers. In a pair of athletic shorts and a sleeveless t-shirt, he looked even more handsome than he had the other night. Her eyes couldn't decide whether to stare at his highly defined biceps or his gleaming smile.

"Natron?" She was perplexed. How had she not known she was meeting him? Either Gustav must not have mentioned it or somehow she had missed it. Apparently, she'd been too frazzled to realize she hadn't known the name of the person she was supposed to meet. Inside she was kicking herself, more notes to self...

"Yeah. What? You didn't know it was me?" He laughed and ushered her in.

"Oh, no, it's not that..." She stumbled over her words.

"Okay, then."

Ever since she'd met Natron, he'd been on her mind. Because she never expected to see him again, Carmen had allowed herself to fantasize about the man. She'd dreamed about what it would be like to kiss him, to rub her hands over that washboard stomach she'd seen in commercials, and even to sleep with him. She'd never dated anyone famous before. There was something so unlikely about being with him that it excited her. Imagining herself and Natron together seemed harmless fodder for a quick self-pleasuring session in the shower, but now she blushed, remembering her dirty thoughts as she stood here in his home.

They passed through the two-story foyer, complete with an indoor fountain that made her think of the Spanish explorer Ponce de Leon's quest for the fountain of youth. He led her back to a large living room filled with plush, comfortable-looking furniture in neutral colors. The back of the room was made up of custom-shaped windows, the natural light streaming in, highlighting an indoor aviary. A large stone fireplace served as a focal point, huge television screens flanked the room, and the accessories looked like they were from a magazine. Come to think of it, she *had* seen his home featured in *D* magazine.

When he offered her something to drink, she politely refused because her hands were so shaky she was certain she would spill it down the front of her blouse if she did. It was safer to decline.

"So you gonna take my commission?" he asked, literally on the edge of his seat. The man had the kind of energy that reminded her of an exuberant Labrador puppy.

"That depends. What are you looking for?"

Unable to keep still, he jumped up. "I want one of your big portraits—of me." He threw his arms out wide to illustrate the size.

"Okaaaay," she said; his enthusiasm was contagious. A painting as big as his ego, capturing his larger-than-life personality on canvas would be a challenge. But in her work, Carmen loved a challenge. Though it would be a big job, she believed she could do him justice. "What size were you thinking?"

"Ten by eight maybe. I'll leave it to you to decide the exact dimensions. I just want it big."

"Ten feet?"

He nodded and rubbed his hands together.

"I'll need you to model for a few sessions."

"That's fine. We're in the off season, I've got plenty of free time."

"Okay. And price…" Carmen squirmed in her seat. Asking for money to do what she loved made her uncomfortable, but it was a necessary evil.

"Hell, you can name your price. I'm just glad you've agreed to do it."

This was too good to be true. Name her price? "Um, fifteen thousand dollars," she said with a laugh in her voice.

"Done. You sure you don't want anything to drink? I'm dying for some iced tea." He started for the kitchen.

"Uh, sure. I'll have a glass." Sitting alone in his living room it began to sink in. She'd been kidding about the fifteen thousand dollars, stalling until she had the chance to add up her time and expenses in her head. The most she'd ever sold a painting for in the past was four thousand.

That he agreed to the outlandish figure shocked her. But she was starting to realize that nothing Natron did should surprise her. The man was full of surprises.

When he returned, he handed her a tall glass of iced tea with a wedge of lemon perched along the rim. "Now, I've just got to convince you to go out with me."

Definitely full of surprises.

CHAPTER THREE

Ever since Natron met Carmen the week before, he'd been trying to decide if he should pursue her or not. The girl had already rejected him flat out when he'd asked her to go out with him and his friends that evening after her show, but for some reason he couldn't get the curvy artist out of his mind. He'd tried to convince himself that she'd really had other plans after the show, that she wasn't making up an excuse. It had been *her show* after all; she must have had her own celebration to attend.

Yet it nagged at him that she'd said no. Women, as a rule, didn't turn him down. Natron Dakers was the toast of Dallas. Hell, he was the toast of the nation. His underwear-clad ass was plastered in Times Square, for God's sake.

With more money than he could spend and more fame than was good for any man, Natron never had any trouble keeping his bed warm. But the long parade of vacuous models and groupies had become lonely and unfulfilling. He longed to meet someone he could connect with, someone with interests that extended beyond commandeering his credit card.

And he longed for someone he could take care of. He'd long been a kinky devil, but he didn't dare show that side to any of the superficial Barbies with whom he dallied. The tabloids would have a field day with that information, and he had no intention of offering one of those bimbos a payday at his expense.

But when he'd met Carmen, bells went off in his head. Not alarm bells, but the 'ding ding' kind of bells that told him he'd won the jackpot. The way her golden brown curls framed her face reminded him of a grown-up Shirley Temple.

Carmen's innocence contradicted her not-so-innocent body. The girl was all curves, and he much preferred that to the anorexic look that was in fashion these days. He liked a woman he could grab a hold of, not a coat hanger.

Even though he prided himself on being a risk taker and putting it all on the line, it had taken him a while to gather the courage to contact Carmen, and even then he used her work to get an 'in' with her. Attempting to protect his wounded ego, he'd led with his interest in her artwork, justifying the manipulation by telling himself that, if nothing else, he'd wind up with an amazing portrait of himself. He truly appreciated her work, so if that was all he came away with, it wasn't a bad deal.

Now she sat here in his living room, and he wasn't sure how to move things along between them. He was afraid to come on too strong for fear the shy little dove would fly the coop, his instincts telling him he should take things slowly with her so as not to spook her. But unfortunately, his mouth got ahead of his brain and he'd blurted out that he wanted to take her out.

Carmen shifted her position on the couch where she sat, and he couldn't tell if she was pleased or trying to figure out how to let him down easily.

"I'd like that," she said, her blue-green eyes looking up at him through silky lashes.

"You would?" This wasn't the answer he expected.

She giggled. "Sure. Who wouldn't want to go out with Natron Dakers?"

He shrugged, thinking she hadn't that night at the gallery, but he ate up her flattery.

"My brothers would kill me if I passed up an opportunity like that."

"Oh, are they fans?"

"The biggest."

"They play ball?"

"All three of them."

"I'd better send them some gear, then."

"They would *love* that!" She clapped her hands together.

"I'll have my assistant take care of that. So where do you want to go?"

"Gee, I don't know. I thought you'd have that all figured out."

He paused. "Yeah. You know, going out, that can be kinda a madhouse. The paparazzi…"

"I'd just as soon stay in. Order a pizza or something, that's alright with me."

This was just the kind of girl he needed. Most of the women he dated wanted to go out, to be seen with him. They wanted their picture taken with him. Not Carmen; she seemed content spending time with him.

"Sounds good. Or I have a chef. We can get him to cook something for us…"

"Wow. That's so cool. I didn't realize that."

He nodded. "What kind of food do you like?"

"Pretty much anything. Italian, Mexican, Chinese…"

"My chef makes a mean lasagna."

"That sounds wonderful," she said, beaming.

He called his chef and then asked if she'd like to watch a movie.

"If you do," she said.

She was so easygoing that it made his heart sing. Carmen was a breath of fresh air, so different from the high-maintenance women he was used to.

"Maybe later. Tell me about you. Are you from Dallas?"

"Denton. How about you?"

"Pensacola, Florida. You said you have brothers, any sisters?"

"Nope, only brothers. They're all in high school. Trent is seventeen and the twins Robert and Jeff are fifteen. How about you?"

"Only child, I'm afraid."

She chuckled. "Why afraid?"

"My mamma doted on me, spoiled me rotten, probably ruined me for life." He slapped his knee.

"Oh, wow. So you're a mamma's boy?" she teased.

"Hey, now. That's not it. Let's just say I'm my mamma's favorite."

"The only child." She giggled. "You're her favorite, okay. What about your dad?"

"Never knew him."

"Oh. I'm sorry."

An awkwardness hung in the air until Carmen asked, "Tell me about football. When did you *know* you were going to be really good at it?"

"Good question. You know, I didn't even play football until I was a sophomore in high school. Before that I was a basketball player. I played soccer too, goalie. It's all about the hands," he said, holding up his giant palms.

"When I was eleven, I played goalie on my soccer team and after a game my mamma was talkin' to me about a difficult save I made, and I got to telling her how I saw it all going down, in my mind, before it happened. Like the ball, I could tell where it was going, and I visualized my hands catching it milliseconds before it got there. I'm not sure how else to describe it, but it's always been like that for me." He shrugged. "Easy to catch things."

"So how did you get into football?"

"Oh, well, both our school's wide receivers went down, one with mono and one with a broken wrist. They needed somebody and recruited me from the basketball team. Don't tell anybody," he said conspiratorially, "but at first I didn't like getting hit. I got used to it though, and then I played college ball at a small college in South Florida, then got drafted by the Vipers."

"And the rest, as they say, is history," she smiled.

He nodded, admiring the way her breasts peeked ever so slightly over the top of the neckline to her blouse. His cock twitched as he thought of the dirty things he'd like to do to her.

When their meal was ready, he showed her the way to the dining room. He let her go first, not only because he had good manners, but also so he could enjoy the view of her hips swaying in front of him, a slight shake to her plump, round ass.

Carmen gave him an appreciative smile when he pulled out her chair for her, and he took the seat next to her at the head of the table. Natron's chef came in and filled a goblet for each of them with red wine. Then he brought out their entrees, two plates of delicious-smelling meat lasagna.

They'd talked enough about him. Over dinner he wanted to learn more about her.

"So what about you? When did you first know you were an artist?"

She took a bite of her food and closed her eyes, savoring the flavor. Damn, she was sensual.

When she finished her bite she replied, "Mmm. That is delicious. Oh, you were asking me about my art. I don't know, really. I've been drawing all my life, used to get in trouble at school for doodling on all my schoolwork."

He pictured an adorable mini-Carmen being fussed at by the teacher for drawing all over her papers. She was a rebel in her own way, and that drew him to her. He appreciated that she had a little wild side.

"I won some awards too, some contests. By the time I got to middle school, people considered me 'that artist girl.' I was a geek, yeah, but most of the kids were impressed enough with my artwork that I didn't get picked on as much as you'd think."

He found himself feeling protective of her; it vexed him to think about anyone bullying her. "If anyone bothers you in the future, you send them to me. I'll have something to say about it."

She giggled. "Wow, I never had anybody like you stand up for me before."

"Well, now you do," he said with a wink. "I'll see to it nobody messes with you." He measured his words and kept his gaze steady on hers. The connection, the heat between them was palpable in the air and he hoped he could convince her to stay.

When the chef came in to take their plates, Natron was pleased to see that Carmen cleaned her plate. He found it refreshing after the carousel of girls who just picked at their food. She was no Barbie doll; she was a real flesh-and-blood woman with a passion for life that piqued his curiosity. Would he be the recipient of that passion if he kissed her? He could hardly wait to find out.

After they'd finished their lasagna, to be polite he offered her some dessert. She groaned, saying she was stuffed. Agreeing to skip the sweets, he led her into the adjoining foyer and slowly pushed her back against the wall.

Her eyes met his, then darted to his lips. Interpreting this as an invitation, he leaned in and touched his mouth to hers. Inhaling her, he slipped an arm around her waist and pulled her to him. She smelled of honeysuckle, the wild kind that grew on backyard fences. He felt her relax, her body melting against his, creating the perfect fit.

He let his tongue explore her waiting mouth. She responded with the fervor he'd hoped for, wrapping her arms around his neck and pressing her pelvis to his. Blood rushed to his cock, and he pressed his stiffness against her.

How he wanted to pick her up and carry her to his bedroom, the couch, wherever. But he stopped himself. There was so much potential with this girl, he hoped they could build something between them, and he knew not to rush. So instead they made out like teenagers in the hallway, losing track of time, caressing each other's skin, grinding their hips against each other. Until finally Natron pulled away.

"Can I give you a ride home?" he asked.

Her tousled hair made her look cuter than ever and she gazed up at him with lust-filled eyes. "Thanks, but I have my car."

"I'd ask you to stay, but…" His voice trailed off.

She began to straighten her blouse and tried to smooth back her unruly curls. "No, that's okay. I have to be going anyways."

Was that hurt on her face? The mood shifted from simpatico to uncomfortable.

"Okay. When can we get started on the painting?"

"Um," she said, looking around for her purse. "I have another project I need to finish up first. How about next week?"

"Works for me."

"Great. You can come by the studio, and we can get started. I'll text you the address."

"I'll be looking forward to it. Thanks for having dinner with me," he said and kissed her again.

This time it was she who pulled away first. "Thank you. It was lovely." She said goodbye and made a hasty exit.

He closed the door and leaned his back against it. Sinking down to the floor, he wondered what he'd done to screw things up with her already.

CHAPTER FOUR

Carmen yawned.

Sleep had eluded her the past week. Her sense of reason was in a battle with her love of fantasy for control of her heart.

She knew engaging in a fling with Natron Dakers was bound to end in heartbreak, resulting in her becoming just another one of his conquests. But she needed the money from his commission and if she screwed that up, she'd soon be dodging phone calls from creditors. And how could she pass up the opportunity to be with such an incredible guy? Even if it was only for the short timeframe, a one-night stand with him would be something she could remember forever. Maybe not exactly the kind of thing you share with your grandkids, but an experience she could treasure in any case.

Then there was the possibility he didn't want to be with her. When he'd asked her out, then kissed her after dinner, she'd thought he was attracted to her. But before anything more could transpire, he'd pulled away and basically sent her home. What the hell did that mean? Maybe he hadn't liked kissing her, and that was embarrassing, humiliating even.

Natron would be arriving at her studio any minute. Shoving her mixed feelings to the back of her mind, Carmen glanced in the mirror and applied lip gloss in a sheer coral color. She ran her fingers through her curly mop and turned to pick up some clothes she'd tossed on the floor. Not that Natron would come upstairs to her bedroom, but on the off chance...

Carmen's apartment consisted of a huge open space that took up most of the square footage, a tiny kitchenette to one side and a small living space upstairs. She ate at the bar of the mini kitchen and slept on a bed upstairs. She read so often that she didn't even own a television. If she wanted to watch a program or catch up on the news, she used her computer or tablet.

Her work space was cluttered and messy, but she was an artist, so organizational skills and tidiness were not her forte. She looked over at the kitchen sink, relieved at least that was clean and the dishes were put away.

He's coming over to have his portrait painted, not audition you for the job of wife.

Just then she heard a knock at the door, and her emotions did a tap dance in her abdomen. Her hands fluttered with excitement as she moved to let him in.

"Hey, babygirl," Natron said, leaning casually in the door frame, his smile lighting up the already sunny loft.

The flirty name caught her off guard, but she could feel her face strain with how hard she was smiling. So much for playing it cool.

"Hey." She ushered him in and offered him some bottled water.

Natron strutted through the door and looked around. "Man, this place is fly."

"Thanks," Carmen said, pulling two bottles from the refrigerator. Not exactly the luxury digs he was accustomed to, but it was perfect for her.

She noticed him searching for a chair. "Sorry, I don't entertain very often." She motioned to the bar stools at the kitchenette and made a note to create a small seating area downstairs with some of the money she would earn from this commission.

He straddled the stool and took a slug of water. "So tell me, how's this thing gonna go down?"

"Well, I was considering painting you from behind. I think that would make a statement."

The corners of his mouth curled up. "Oh, so you think I have a fine ass is what you're sayin'."

She slapped at his arm playfully. "Natron! I'm thinking artistically here."

"I know. That's what I'm sayin'."

Trying to hide her smile, she said, "Okay. We'll do it from the front. Just like everybody else."

He touched her chin and winked. "I'm just playin', babygirl. We'll do whatever you want. You're the artist."

"I know, but you're paying me, so it's important that you like it."

"I gotcha," he nodded and pulled his shirt over his head.

She couldn't help but stare at the chiseled muscles underneath. His skin was as smooth and dark as the finest chocolate. Unconsciously, she licked her lips, then took a sip of water.

"So... just the shorts?" she gulped. "You gonna leave on the shorts?"

"Yeah, don't worry. I'm not gonna strip naked on you," he laughed. "At least not right now."

She giggled. "Do you want to be holding a football or is that too... obvious? It's up to you."

"I think I need the ball. Without it, I'm just a guy."

"I'm not so sure about that."

He tried a few different poses, most of them giving her a prime view of his well-defined muscles. The way his back rippled with sinewy strength made her knees wobble. She didn't know a person could have so many different back muscles; the way the hard bumps contrasted with his silky black skin made her pussy cream.

She walked around him, snapping pictures with her phone. "I'll use these for reference. That way you won't have to stay in the same position for hours and hours at a time."

He lifted a brow lazily. "Girl, you tryin' to get rid of me?"

She shook her head. "Of course not." The man was like a sunshiny day; being around him lifted her spirits.

Finally he lighted on her stairs; legs apart, he leaned over, clutching the ball powerfully between his hands.

"That's it!" she exclaimed.

"What?"

"That's the pose right there. Don't move."

He stayed put as she circled him, taking pictures from every conceivable angle. After she'd determined that she'd gotten the shots she wanted, she moved to her sketchpad. "Next I'm going to make some gesture drawings. Be sure this is the pose we want. Try to act natural and tell me about one of your favorite plays. Feel free to walk around, use your arms. Use your body to tell me the story."

"Oh, I like that. You're good," he said, waggling a finger at her.

He began to talk, his movement as fluid and graceful as a dancer. He appeared to glide across the room, and a few times Carmen became so wrapped up in watching him that she almost forgot to draw.

"So it was the conference championship, biggest game of the year. And the ball wasn't even being thrown to me, but it was tipped so I went up for it anyway. Jumped as high as I could. The defender hit me in the thighs, upending me. I just remember thinking I had to focus on grabbing that ball. I felt it rather than saw it; my left hand reached out and grabbed it, pulled it in. After I flipped over, another guy hit me. I landed on the ground with both of them on top of me. When they all got up, no one could believe I had the ball. But I had it." He held his football up in the air to show her what he'd done at the end of the play. His eyes gleamed and Carmen found herself being drawn into his world; his passion for the game was infectious.

"That's amazing. I'd like to see that play."

"I prolly got it on my phone. I'll show ya later. You mentioned something about pizza the other night. What kind of pizza do you like? I'm starved."

"Pepperoni."

"Pepperoni it is." He turned and walked to the window for better cell reception and ordered them a pizza.

When it arrived, they were so hungry they ate more than talked during their meal. After they were finished, Carmen took their plates over to the sink to rinse them off.

"Can I help?" he asked, casually leaning against the wall.

Did he know how hot he looked just lounging in her tiny kitchen? Was he trying to distract her? Because he was totally succeeding. "I got it," she said.

"Oh, you got it alright." He gave her a long leisurely once-over. "I've been thinking about you, girl, haven't been able to get you off my mind."

She sensed his presence behind her before she felt his hands on her waist.

"I've been trying to be good, but you're so sexy. I can't resist you, babygirl."

A wave of desire thrilled through her as his hands skimmed over her belly and he started unbuttoning her jean shorts. Her knees almost buckled and she held onto his forearms for support.

"But…" was the only protest she could muster.

"But I think you have on too many clothes," he said, slipping her shorts down to her ankles.

Feeling dizzy, she turned to steady herself and found herself in his arms. When she lifted her face to his, he claimed her mouth, hungrily sliding his tongue between her lips. The electricity between them ramped up a notch, and for a moment she allowed herself the pleasure of letting go and relishing what it felt like to be in his arms. Things were happening so fast. It unnerved her, but it also excited her. She found her body responded to the aggressive way he acted on his desire for her.

He stepped back and lifted her t-shirt over her head.

Instinctively she covered herself with her hands. It made her uncomfortable to be half-naked in front of him. Like most plus-sized girls, Carmen believed men preferred a thinner woman, and she was self-conscious about her voluptuous figure. She weighed at least thirty pounds more than the models on the magazine covers she saw every week at the grocery store checkout line.

"What are you doing? Stop. I want to see you." He pulled her hands away, firmly placing them at her sides.

"I'm embarrassed." She felt the warmth rising in her cheeks. He smiled and shook his head. "Girl, you don't know how good you look, do you?"

"Well, I… I just need to lose a few pounds," she stammered.

"Lose a few pounds, my ass! You're beautiful. I love your curves. I don't need an anorexic woman. I want a girl who knows how to live, how to eat," he said, wrapping his arms around her again. "How to love."

He scooped her up like a bride about to cross the threshold and started climbing the stairs.

Panic rose in her throat. "Natron, you can't. Please! You'll drop me."

He merely chuckled. "You don't know how strong I am. I'm not gonna drop you."

"But Natron, what are you doing?"

"What do you think I'm doing? I'm taking you to bed."

"But, but… it's so fast." The alarm bells that had been going off in her head waned. His persuasive charms were quickly overriding her concerns, and she longed to give in to him, but how could she?

"When I see what I want, I have to have it. And right now what I want is you." He nuzzled her neck, nibbling his way around her earlobe.

The words 'right now' stuck in her head. Okay, so he wanted her now, but what about afterwards? Would he want her later, or would she be just another conquest for the big football star?

When he reached the top of the stairs, he tossed her on the bed and proceeded to take off the rest of his clothes. As he stood there in all his naked glory, Carmen drew a ragged breath. He was gorgeous.

Good lord, he must have to work out constantly to look like that and still be able to eat pizza. His body was rock hard, every muscle well-defined. He even had that sexy Apollo's belt that made that deep 'v' leading directly to his enormous cock. As impressive as the rest of him was, it was impossible for her not to stare at his erection jutting out proudly before him.

"Now it's your turn." He tugged at her panties.

"Natron, I don't know. Maybe this isn't such a good idea…"

He pursed his lips. "Alright then, let's play a game instead."

She closed her legs, eyeing him skeptically, feeling nervous and excited all at the same time. "What kind of game?"

"I call it 'Everything But,'" he said.

"What do you do?" The game sounded rather self-explanatory, but she was stalling for time.

"You get naked and we can do everything but have sex. No penetration. Just foolin' around." He sat on the bed next to her and reached behind her to unfasten her bra. "No harm in that, is there?"

He smelled so good, his skin felt so good against hers that she hardly noticed her better judgment melting away, seduced by his words. He was right. They were already both naked and if they weren't going to have sex, why not play around a little bit?

She lay back and allowed his hands to wander. He caressed her thighs with the palm of his hand, then travelled up her stomach to fondle her breast, whispering, "You're so beautiful."

Her breath caught in her throat and she rasped, "So are you."

After kneading her breast, his mouth enveloped its center and his tongue toyed with her nipple, sending a jolt of bliss through her veins.

She clutched him to her, embracing his attentions and praying they would continue for a long, long time. The broad expanse of his back and shoulders dwarfed her, and she loved how he made her feel small, more feminine.

The urgent nudging of his cock against her hip disclosed his need for her.

Wanting more, she raised her hips, trying to mold her skin to his.

"Now, that's a bad girl," he teased.

Normally she would have blushed, but Carmen was far beyond caring about propriety. She pulled him to her for a heated kiss, then said, "I don't care."

"Oh, okay. I see how it is." He bent his lips to hers and tasted her. His tongue moved with hers, each rolling over the other in a sensuous dance of passion.

He reached between her legs, stroking first her inner thigh, then moving deliciously closer to her core. Slowly, he traced her outer lips with his fingers, causing her to thrust her pelvis upward, betraying her wanton desires.

After much teasing, he finally dipped a finger inside her aching channel. She squirmed underneath him, a slight moan escaping her throat. He worked her pussy until it was drenched with wanting, needing to be filled.

He began tracing tiny little circles over her engorged clit.

"Oh, my God!" she shrieked, about to come.

He rolled away from her and ordered her in a hoarse voice, "Climb on top of me."

Usually Carmen was self-conscious about being on top; she didn't like giving her partner a full view of her ample figure. But Natron made her feel safe somehow. He could have any woman he wanted and it boosted her confidence that he wanted her.

She sat atop him, emboldened by the lust he'd inspired in her. Leaning over to kiss him, she ground her pelvis against his steel rod, which only served to increase the wetness at her core.

He brushed his lips over her erect nipples and she cried out in ecstasy, desire threatening to overtake her. Watching him suckle her, she was overcome by the beautiful contrast of his dark skin against her milky flesh. With a wanton disregard for the rules of the game, Carmen tilted back and forth until her opening hovered just over the head of his cock.

"Ah, ah, ah," he chided. "Everything but." He took her wrists and held them firmly.

She groaned. All this teasing was driving her insane; she wanted him inside her.

He lifted his pelvis so his cock rubbed against her swollen clit and then down to her throbbing pussy.

"That's not fair," she whimpered.

"Didn't say it was fair, but that's the game. The game you agreed to play." His eyes locked with hers and she saw her own lust and frustration mirrored in his eyes.

It wasn't much of a battle. Her brain told her to hold off, enjoy the foreplay... but her pussy had other ideas. Pulsing with a heartbeat all its own, her nether regions took charge, and her intrepid lust won the day. In a defiant move, she uncharacteristically challenged him. Though he held her arms, she shifted her crotch and impaled herself onto him.

Relief washed over her as she took him inside her. Slowly she rocked back, letting him fill her completely. The sensation was so welcome, tears began to form in her eyes.

He freed her wrists and she swiped at her eyes before laying her hands on either side of his chest to balance herself. Dropping her pelvis up and down, she fucked him at a languid pace, relishing every nuance of the movement. Her eyelids slowly fluttered shut as she embraced the delicious sensations that gripped her body. So it shocked her when she felt a sharp slap to her ass.

Her eyes flew open and she cried out.

"That's a naughty little girl, fucking Daddy when she was supposed to do everything *but* that."

His words stopped her cold. She wasn't sure if he was kidding or not.

He smacked her again on the other cheek. "Don't stop now. The only thing worse than a naughty girl who can't follow directions is a cock-tease."

She began gyrating her hips again hesitantly. The dirty way he talked to her made what she was doing seem all the more forbidden. The idea of being a 'naughty girl' had always turned her on. How had he known that?

Perhaps he'd sensed it, her longing to commit illicit acts, then be punished for them. In any case, she was in heaven here with him. He was fulfilling her in ways she hadn't known were possible outside her fantasies.

He swatted her again on the backside, his hand transmitting heat to her smarting buttocks, and with each smack she squealed. This seemed to egg him on, and he continued spanking her until she grew wobbly atop him.

At that point he scooped her up with one arm and flipped her over on her back, all the while remaining buried deep in her cunt. Flat on her back, Carmen sank down into the mattress and welcomed the hard fucking he gave her. When she no longer had the energy to hold onto his neck, her arms flopped over her head. Natron promptly took both wrists in one of his huge hands and held them above her head, restraining her movement.

She hooked one ankle over the other across his backside and held on for dear life. He pounded into her with the rapid power and speed that reminded her of a freight train. She'd never been with a man this athletic before; just experiencing the fervor with which he fucked her was a workout.

Within minutes the shimmering waves of one orgasm after another washed over her. He continued pumping into her for several strokes before pulling out and telling her to open her mouth. She complied as he placed a knee on either side of her head. He towered over her, controlling her weaker body with his stronger one. Carmen obediently held her tongue out to receive his salty essence. She captured the pearly droplets and swallowed.

"Suck it, babygirl, till Daddy's not hard anymore," he instructed her.

Closing her eyes, she took him in her mouth, gently sucking and gliding her tongue around his shaft until he was flaccid.

He pulled out and collapsed alongside her on the bed.

She rolled into him and he took her in his arms. "Good girl," he said.

She kissed his chest and answered, "Thank you, Daddy." The words spilled out of her mouth easily. Burrowing down into that cozy nook where his arm met his chest, she laid her arm across him and basked in the bliss of the moment.

● ● ● ● ● ● ● ● ● ● ● ● ● ● ● ●

Later that week, Natron asked Carmen out on a date. Not above wanting to impress her, he'd hired a driver to take them out for dinner and dancing.

Remembering how she liked to eat, he took her to one of his favorite restaurants, Matt's Tex Mex. It wasn't fancy, but the Mexican cuisine was out of this world. They slurped swirled frozen margaritas that came in a fishbowl glass the size of their heads, and Natron ordered beef fajitas while Carmen went with the cheese enchiladas.

They sat across from each other, nibbling tortilla chips, when Natron motioned Carmen to lean toward him. When she did, he laid a hand on her knee and whispered in her ear, "I want you to take your panties off."

She leaned back to look at him, eyes wide, lips pursed as she considered. She gulped. "Can I go to the bathroom?"

He grinned and shook his head. "Ah-ah-ah. Gotta stay here. Do it at the table." He was testing her, wanting to find out if she would play his games, how submissive she could be.

"But, how...?" she stammered, trying to figure out how she could possibly remove her underwear at the table. The table was covered with a tablecloth, but they were seated in the middle of the room. The restaurant was packed and there were people seated at tables all around them.

He shrugged. "Just do it." His eyes scanned the room. "Nobody's looking."

She snorted. "Really? The most famous football player in the world is here and nobody's looking? I doubt that!"

"Probably not the most famous 'in the world,'" he said with false modesty, teasing her.

She sighed heavily and started wriggling in her chair. He enjoyed watching her squirm as she tried to inch the elastic down little by little under her skirt.

Their food arrived while she was in the middle of her task, and she looked terribly uncomfortable as the waiter placed her food in front of her and asked if they'd like anything else. She gave him a plastered-on smile and shook her head.

Natron laughed and dug into his meal. A few minutes later, Carmen poked him. "Okay, they're off. Now what do you want me to do with them?"

"Hand them to me."

She pressed a handful of bunched-up fabric into his palm. He grinned and pocketed it. "Thank you. It pleases me that you did what I asked."

"You're welcome," she said, then started on her enchiladas.

After they consumed their meal, Natron asked, "How does it feel to be sitting there, in public, without any panties?"

"Kinda naughty," she said, scrunching up her shoulders as if she relished being a naughty girl.

Natron lifted his index finger. "Check, please," he told the waiter. While they waited, he and Carmen stared hungrily into each other's eyes. Under the table he laced his fingers through hers and stroked her palm with his thumb. He couldn't wait to get out of there so he could kiss her, hold her, fuck her.

Walking out to the car, he squeezed her ample bottom and she turned to face him. He grabbed her ass with both hands and planted a kiss on her lips. She melted into his arms, and he ruled her mouth with his. When she tilted her pelvis toward him, he broke away, saying, "Don't tell me you want to go dancing. Please say you don't still want to go dancing." Then he buried his mouth in the crook of her neck and ran his hands down the curve of her hips.

Her voice was breathy. "Maybe we could dance at your place," she whimpered in response to his kisses, "or mine."

He pulled her into the car and instructed the driver to take them home. The partition closed and they were alone in the backseat. Natron turned Carmen over his knee and started to raise her skirt.

"What are you doing?" she squeaked.

"Just an inspection. Don't move." He lifted her skirt to her waist, exposing her naked bottom.

"But the driver," she protested.

"He's not paying any attention to us. He's driving."

Natron hugged her torso with one arm and skimmed her magnificent round globes with the other. He investigated her pussy with his fingers. "Damn, you're wet, girl."

She made a whiny noise and wiggled in his grasp.

"I'm not sure you should be this aroused, little girl. You may need a spanking."

Her muffled cry indicated to him that she disagreed, but he took aim and swatted her lovely rear end anyway.

He entered her pussy with his finger. "Still wet. Better try again," he said, then smacked her hind end.

Carmen squirmed and protested, but he repeated the process several times until her ass cheeks were hot to the touch and her cunt was dripping with her juices.

When they arrived home, they didn't even make it to the bedroom. Once they got inside Natron's entry hall, he unbuckled his pants and let them slide to the floor. He picked her up and pressed her against the wall. "Lock your legs around my waist."

She encircled him with her thighs, and his erection pulsed hard against her mound. He re-adjusted, then in one swift move, sheathed his cock inside her slick welcoming walls. He pushed himself deep into her, captured her mouth, and they danced the dance he'd been fantasizing about all night.

CHAPTER FIVE

Natron fiddled with the cuffs of his sleeves.

He wore a navy, pin-striped Hugo Boss suit with a lavender shirt and a grey tie flecked with small blue squares. It wasn't often that he dressed up, but when he did, he made sure he was styled to the hilt. A four-carat diamond stud adorned his left ear and his dress shoes had been shined to perfection.

Butterflies zipped around in his stomach as his car pulled up to Carmen's loft. Being nervous before a game was normal; being nervous before a date was not. On the playing field, the nerves gave him an edge. He hoped they would benefit him in some way with Carmen, but he wasn't sure how; this was foreign territory for him.

Over the last couple of weeks he'd been on dates with several women besides Carmen and he'd been bored to tears. He found himself sitting across from a supermodel and missing most of what she said because his mind was on Carmen. He found himself wondering what she was doing, who she was out with, what she would think of the food he was eating…

Unable to get her off his mind, he'd made a decision. He would ask her to be his submissive. After all, what was the point of dating if not to find the right partner for yourself? Thinking he may have found that person in Carmen, he decided to ask her out for a special dinner. It was important he spoil her, show her the kind of life that would be possible if she were to agree to his proposal.

Walking up to her door, he wondered if he'd be able to follow through with it. He was great with the superficial bullshit, but opening himself up like this was more difficult.

He rapped on her door with heavy knuckles.

Carmen opened the door wearing a simple, but elegant blue dress. The hem came just above her knee, showing off her shapely legs to great advantage. Though the neckline was modest, he could still see the top of her cleavage poking out the top. She looked gorgeous, and he wondered how he'd make it through dinner. He'd hardened at the very sight of her.

"Hi," she said shyly.

"Hey, girl. You look great." he said, pulling her into a bear hug and inconspicuously readjusting his trousers so she wouldn't feel his excitement against her leg.

He opened the car door for her and her face beamed at the chivalrous gesture. On the way to the restaurant, they made small talk and discovered they liked the same type of music.

Natron had chosen a hot new steakhouse owned by one of the Food Network's celebrity chefs. The hostess recognized him and seated them quickly. He appreciated her avoiding the typical scene with autograph seekers and people wanting to take a selfie with him. Grateful for the opportunity to sit and enjoy a meal in public without too much distraction, he palmed the hostess a fifty for seating them in a secluded section of the restaurant.

Natron chose to sit with his back to the room, leaving Carmen to face the curious eyes of the other dining patrons.

He ordered a bottle of cabernet sauvignon, Jordan, which was one of his favorites, and they fell into a comfortable silence as they looked over their menus.

After a few minutes, Carmen said, "Natron, people are looking at us." She squirmed in her chair, clearly uncomfortable being part of a circus attraction.

"That's okay, baby. It's when they stop looking we should be worried," he chuckled.

She shifted in her chair, clearly uncomfortable. And while he didn't want her to be ill at ease, there was something about seeing her slightly undone that drove him mad with lust. He couldn't help but imagine her handcuffed to his headboard while he ran ice cubes over her naked body.

Shaking that arousing mental picture from his mind, he offered, "In a minute they'll go back to eating their meals. Ignore them. Look at me."

She focused her eyes on him and took a deep breath. Then she smiled at him and set her menu down on the table. "You're right."

"Of course I am. You know Daddy knows best, don't you?" He winked at her.

She nodded and crinkled her nose at him flirtatiously. That cute little nose of hers drove him wild, along with her eyes that, tonight, reflected the blue of her dress.

The waiter presented Natron with the bottle of wine, allowed him to take a taste sip, then poured them each a glass.

They each took a sip and agreed the wine was delicious, then Natron cleared his throat. "Carmen, I brought you out tonight because I wanted to talk with you about something important." Her eyes brimmed with curiosity. They were mesmerizing with their lovely sea-glass, ever-changing color.

He watched to make sure the waiter was out of earshot before he asked, "How would you feel about calling me Daddy?"

She pursed her lips and considered his question. "Okay, I guess."

"It doesn't bother you?"

The corners of her mouth lifted. "I've called you that before and I kinda like it. Why?"

The sip of wine he'd just drunk went down the wrong way and he choked on it.

"Are you okay?" she asked.

"Yeah. Sorry." He coughed again, trying to regain his composure. "Excuse me."

She drank her wine and waited for him to continue.

Keeping his voice low so they wouldn't be overheard, he asked, "Do you know what a submissive is?"

"You mean like in S&M?" she asked.

He was impressed. She seemed so innocent that he hadn't expected her to know much about his kinks. "Yeah, like that. The kind of relationship that turns me on the most is the kind with a daddy and his little girl. I like to be the daddy, and I wanted to find out if you'd be interested in being my little girl." A drop of sweat ran down his back. Damn, he was nervous.

"It's not like being a pedophile, is it?"

"Nothing like that. It's like a regular dominant and submissive relationship, except I'm more into spoiling and protecting my little girl than I am hurting her. The whole pain thing isn't really my thing."

"But there are punishments, right?"

"Yeah. When you do something wrong, definitely. But I'd never want to hurt you or push you past your limits. You'd have a safeword and we'd never do anything you weren't okay with."

"I'd like to give it a try," she said, and at that moment she looked like an angel to him with those cherubic lips and her halo of curls.

He'd thought she would have more questions, some objections maybe. But for her to say yes just like that—she truly was a natural submissive.

"Don't you have any questions, concerns, reservations?" he asked, wanting to be certain.

"If I do, I'm sure you'll answer them. Won't you?"

The trust she placed in him after knowing him such a short time was intoxicating. She made him feel like he could go anywhere, do anything with her. He wondered if she was the woman he'd been waiting for... He'd been living the life of a player because no one ever made him feel like settling down. Until now.

"Sure, babygirl." He winked. "I'll show you the ropes. All you really need to know is how to please Daddy, and I'll teach you how to do that."

She beamed. "When can we start?" she asked, her cheeks turning a lovely shade of pink.

"You're so pretty when you blush."

"Thanks," she said, fidgeting, clearly not used to being complimented.

"We can start now, tonight, if you like."

"I would like that."

Natron ate fast normally, but tonight he finished his steak in record time. He knew it wasn't the best manners to shovel his food, but he couldn't wait to get Carmen home.

He noticed she barely picked at her food. "Is it okay?" He indicated the lobster tail and vegetables on her plate.

"It's fine. My appetite is… I don't know." She struggled to explain, but he knew exactly what she was feeling. Excitement, arousal, perhaps even some trepidation. He felt it too. The sparks between them electrified the air. In short order Natron asked for the check and a to-go box. Then he paid and ushered her to his waiting car, ignoring the prying eyes that followed them through the restaurant.

He opened the car door for her and bent to kiss her. Tilting her heart-shaped face to his, he captured those velvet lips of hers into a long, sensuous kiss. As he explored her mouth, she met his ardor with a passion of her own. When they finally pulled apart, they were both breathless. Carmen slid into the passenger seat and Natron hurried around to drive them to his place as quickly as possible.

They fought to control themselves on the way home. Natron held her hand on his thigh, conscious not to let things go any farther until they got to his house. The last thing he needed was a sexually induced car accident. Once he'd parked the car in the garage, he practically pulled her out of the car and inside the house. Most of the lights were off, and he flicked a few hallway switches to illuminate their path to his bedroom.

Carmen had never been in this part of his house. She looked around curiously.

"Well, what do you think?" he asked. He'd hired fancy, big-name designers to decorate the place, and though he loved it, he realized he wanted her to like it too.

"It's beautiful," she gushed.

"Thanks. Now, I think it's time to get down to business." He could feel the adrenaline rushing through his veins already. His cock had joined the party, but his own pleasure would have to wait. Right now he needed to do some training to break in his new sub.

They stood in the middle of the bedroom between his massive mahogany four-poster bed and the fireplace with a big screen television mounted above it. Two oversized chairs were positioned behind them, and Natron settled himself in one of them to watch. "Take off your clothes," he said.

"Right here?" she squeaked.

"Right here," he said, relishing her discomfort.

"I'll need help with my zipper, okay?"

"Sure. Come here."

She walked toward him, turned and bent down so that he could reach the top of her dress.

He unzipped her dress and pushed the straps off her shoulders so that the garment fell to the floor. She stepped out of it and bent to pick it up.

"Leave it. Now the bra."

Her back was to him as she unfastened the lacy pink bra and dropped it on the floor.

"Panties," he said, his breath becoming slightly more labored.

She pulled them down to the floor and stood awkwardly, shifting her weight from her left foot to her right, then back again.

"Turn around."

Though he hated to lose the view of her juicy ass and curvaceous hips, he was deeply rewarded when he saw her bountiful breasts, nipples hard, jutting toward him and the small strip of brown fuzz hovering just above her pussy.

"Lovely."

"Thank you," she said, still fidgeting.

"Try to be still. You don't need to be nervous. You look beautiful," he said, doing his best to reassure her. "When we play tonight, I'm going to explain some things. Instead of giving you a bunch of lectures, I'm just gonna talk as we go."

She nodded.

"When you wanna talk to me, you should call me Daddy. If that's too weird at first, you can say 'sir.' Make sense?"

"Yes, sir."

"Good. You can have a safeword. Do you know what that is?"

"Yes, sir."

"Okay, what's your safeword going to be?"

"I don't know." He could tell by the way she chewed on her bottom lip that she was nervous. It would be strange if she wasn't.

"Alright. What about 'safeword' for now until you come up with something you like better?"

"That sounds fine."

He pulled her to him and kissed her belly. "Do you trust me, babygirl?"

She played with his dreads with trembling fingers. "I do. I know it might sound strange, but I do."

"It doesn't actually. I trust you."

"You do?"

"Of course. I wouldn't be sharing this side of myself with just anyone. Hell, my lawyers would have me makin' you sign shit, nondisclosures and all that."

"Do you want me to?"

"Nah. Fuck that, I just want to be with you."

"That's what I want too." She might be scared, but she was willing to do what he asked anyway. The realization made his chest tighten.

"Good girl. Now I want you to come to the end of the bed. Stand with your legs apart, bend over and hold the end of the bed."

The bed had an elaborately carved pattern of leaves and scrolls. Carmen found a place to hold with each hand and leaned over like he asked.

"Stay there," he instructed, giving her bottom a smack as he walked past her to his closet.

The closet, which was the size of most people's guest rooms, housed several drawers specifically for toys of the adult variety.

Hmm. What to choose. Looking over the various options, he chose a long black leather flogger. Being that this was the first time he would be doing this with Carmen, he opted for one with a lighter sting. His intention was not to blister her, but to introduce her to the idea of submission. Picking it up, he appreciated the feel of the leather and the weight of it in his hand. He would enjoy flogging her with it.

When he came back into the bedroom, her eyes flew to the leather whip in his hand and its mini tails.

"I'm going to flog you for two reasons. First, because it will introduce you to what it's like to submit to my will. I know it might be scary, but I will not hurt you. If you feel like it's hurting too badly, you may use your safeword. Second, because it will bring the blood to the surface of your skin and potentially increase your arousal by raising your endorphin levels, which can make things more pleasurable."

"Okay," she said with a determined stare.

Good. He liked a girl with gumption, and he needed one with staying power.

With the flip of his wrist he brought the first strike down on the alabaster skin of her back. The leather made a soft thudding sound as it made contact with her flesh.

She flinched, but otherwise seemed intact.

He let fly another stroke of the whip. And another until he developed a pattern that ran from her buttocks up her torso, up one side then down the other. The smell of leather wafted through the air as he pulled his arm back to prepare for the next blow, and the welcome sound of pleasure rose from her lips.

"You like that, babygirl?" he crooned.

"I do. It doesn't really hurt. More like a little sting, but it feels good."

"That's it, baby. Go with it."

"Yes, sir."

He raked the tails across her backside until her skin began to pinken. At that point he set the flogger down and stood behind her.

"Now back up a step and lean over and grab your ankles."

This flustered her. "What?" she asked, clearly stalling.

"I'm going to inspect you."

"For what?" she asked, leaning over hesitantly.

"My pleasure."

"I'm not sure I can grab my ankles. I'm not very flexible."

"Hmm. You might want to work on some daily stretches then. But for now grab your legs as low as you can go."

"Yes, sir," she said and grabbed her lower calves.

He cupped her sex with his hand, and he could feel the heat coming from her most intimate region. Smacking her pussy a few times elicited a small cry from Carmen, and he could tell it was the first time anyone had ever done that to her.

Breaking in a virgin to BDSM was an intoxicating experience. No one would need drugs or alcohol when an experience like this was available.

She had the most delectable ass with such pretty pink folds blushing against her creamy pale skin. Her beauty made his heart lurch, and he caressed her ass, her warm globes feeling heavenly under his touch. When he spread her cheeks to inspect her asshole, her whole body tensed.

"Relax," he said.

"That's easy for you to say," she muttered.

He laughed. "The point is for you to trust me, become comfortable with me exploring your body."

"It's embarrassing," she whined.

"It shouldn't be. I want your body to belong to me. Everything about it is beautiful. Allow me to enjoy it. Do you think you can do that?"

"I guess so."

"Did you mean to say 'Yes, sir'?" he prodded.

"Yes, sir," she said, sounding like a chastised schoolgirl.

"That's more like it," he said, spanking her ass before wetting his thumb between his lips, then slowly inserting it into her rear entry. She flinched, but remained silent.

"Good girl. Relax and it will start to feel good."

He found her lips with his other fingers and worked them in and out of the womanly folds between her legs. Dipping in and out of her ass and her pussy at the same time had begun to arouse her. Her hips shifted slightly to meet his attentions and she coated his hand with her sweet nectar.

"Be still," he commanded and he felt her struggle to control her urges to ride his hand.

His middle finger sought the center of her lust, and he flicked back and forth over her clit until he felt her muscles tightening more and more. Just when she was about to tumble over the edge, he withdrew.

"Stand up."

She obeyed, her legs wobbly.

"Turn and face me."

She whirled around and he saw the confused look in her eye. The look that said, why?

With the pitifulness of a baby harp seal, she looked up at him. "Daddy, I was about to come. Why did you stop?"

His big dom heart almost stopped. She was too adorable, too perfect for him. How could he deny her?

Clearing his throat, he said, "Because your orgasms are mine. I tell you when you can come and sometimes you will have to wait until I tell you it's okay to come."

She frowned. "So it's a control thing?"

"You could say that. But don't worry. I'm going to let you come. Sometimes Daddy just wants to drag it out because then it will feel even better."

She sighed.

"Now I want you to get on your knees and suck Daddy's cock."

In a beautiful show of compliance, she dropped to her knees.

The proximity of her face to his crotch brought the blood rushing to his dick. He unzipped his pants and took down his boxer shorts, his shaft hard as steel.

She reached her delicate hands to touch him, but he caught them in his. "Place your hands behind your back, use only your mouth."

Her brow furrowed, but she obediently clasped her hands behind her back.

She tilted her head forward and the pink tip of her tongue traveled up and down the length of him. Once she'd wet his shaft completely, she took him between her plump, splayed lips. Closing her eyes, she bobbed her head up and down, stimulating the large dark vein on the underside of his cock.

"Open your eyes. Keep them on me, babygirl."

Her lashes fluttered and her gorgeous greenish-blue eyes gazed up at him, sleepy with lust. His heart raced as he acknowledged the connection between them, so transparent in their locked gaze.

"That's it. You feel so good to Daddy," he said, encouraging her.

She nodded imperceptibly and blinked hard.

He tried not to gag her. As much as he would have liked ramming himself down her throat, he tried to remain focused on teaching her what he liked. It was his job to determine what made the delicate flower that was his babygirl open up her petals and shiver with satisfaction. So far he was pleased with his discoveries. Not only was Carmen compliant and a natural submissive, but she was also responsive to his attentions and that turned him on.

While most men were as simple as a wind-up toy in the complexity of their needs—give them a wet hole and they were satisfied—women were a different story. Each one was like an exotic flower with different instructions for how to make them grow and blossom. It was important that he learned what she liked, what made her hot, what made her come.

His balls contracted when she purred under his touch, and his toes wanted to curl every time he made her squirm beneath him.

Her jaw began to tremble and he used all his willpower to withdraw from her face. "Get up on the bed. I'm going to fuck you senseless now."

Her expression was one of relief mixed with passion and she stumbled to get up and climb on the bed.

Offering her a hand, he helped her up. "You're being a very good girl."

"Thank you, Daddy."

His chest tightened at the sight of her sitting on the bed, hair tousled, her eyes bright with desire. He'd only just begun to know her, and yet he loved everything about her. Her talent, her passion for her work, the way her eyes changed colors like some ethereal enchantress.

"Lie back," he told her. "Now spread your legs for me, babygirl."

She fell back on the bed and parted her legs.

"Wider," he growled.

Though she opened them a bit more, he forced her legs apart as wide as they would go. "That's what I'm talkin' about, girl."

After another trip to the closet, he brought back a set of pink leather wrist restraints. "Give me your arm," he said, indicating her right one.

She offered her wrist and he fastened the leather snugly against her skin. He repeated the process with her other arm, then picked her up in his arms like a child and repositioned her in the middle of the bed. Reaching back behind the bed, he brought back a strap with two hooks, which he clipped to each of the leather bracelets that now held her hands above her head, attached to the bed.

He could hear her breath quicken, and he grazed her earlobe with his teeth, whispering, "You're mine now. To do with as I like."

He watched as a shiver ran through her body, and she tried to remain calm.

Grabbing a condom from a drawer in his nightstand, he knelt on the bed and rolled it onto his erection. "Remember, you have a safeword."

She nodded.

"What was that? I couldn't hear you."

"Yes, sir," she said, her lower lip quivering.

He took pity on her. Hell, he didn't want to scare the crap out of her. He'd hoped this would be a pleasant experience for her. Maybe the bondage wasn't her thing…

"Tell me what you're feeling right now," he said.

"I'm not sure."

"Are you scared? Excited? Nervous? What?"

"All of those things and maybe a little cold."

"Cold? Yeah, with the air conditioning, no covers... It is chilly in here."

He stroked her inner thigh, relief washing over him. "That's alright. I'll warm you up. Keep those legs spread just like that."

Kneeling between her legs, he teased her, pressing the head of his cock against her pussy, rubbing it just around her opening, but never entering her.

When she began to lift her hips and arch her back, he chastised her. "Uh-uh-uh. Daddy gets to decide when to stick it in. You have to be a good girl and lie back."

She grimaced with frustration, but stilled.

Then in one long stroke he entered her. Her body quivered with pleasure as he filled her needing cunt. "Then when Daddy does give you what you want, you will be a very grateful girl."

"Yes, sir," she groaned.

He thrust in and out of her warm, wet pussy, saying, "You've been a good girl. You can move your hips now."

She tugged at her restraints over her head. He kissed her full on the mouth, invading her with his searching tongue and muffling the tiny moans forming in her throat.

He rocked into her, giving her all the passion he had until her muscles took over, contracting around him as her orgasm shook her to her very core, wringing a climax from him at the same time. Spent, he stayed inside her; propping his body onto his elbows, he asked, "So what do you think?"

"Where do I sign up?" She beamed up at him.

● ● ● ● ● ● ● ● ● ● ● ● ● ● ●

Several months later, Carmen stood in her studio putting the finishing touches on her portrait of Natron. She was proud of this piece. Her love for the man came through in the painting and she knew it.

Natron gazed back at her from the massive canvas in front of her. She was having it photographed this week before giving it to Natron. She considered how far their relationship had come. At first she had worried about being a mere notch on Natron's bedpost, but it turned out she needn't have been. She and Natron had a unique chemistry all their own, he was always coming up with games for them to play, and Carmen adored those 'sessions.'

She'd never had multiple orgasms before, but with him she experienced them almost every time they were together. Whether it was *him*, the way he fucked her so hard and with such stamina, or how aroused she became from the way he talked to her and his games—she wasn't certain, but she'd become addicted to him and the special brand of love they shared.

While she loved his fancy lifestyle, it was Natron himself that she was drawn to. How had he known how well she would fit with his kinky side? Hell, she surprised herself how much she liked being submissive to him. It fit not only her personality, but also her fantasies. She'd always wanted a take-charge kind of man who would take her hard and ravish her.

But she hadn't expected to be excited by him ordering her around. When he'd told her to spread her legs, she thought the butterflies in her stomach might just take off and fly her right out of the room. And even though she was an independent, grown woman, whenever he called her babygirl, she melted into a puddle of goo at his feet.

In her heart she believed that Natron was a good man and that she could trust him. And because she knew he had her back, she agreed to play his quirky games. No matter what he did, she felt he had her best interests at heart, that he wanted to nurture and protect her as well as please her. That made her want to serve him, to give to him more than he gave to her. But even as she luxuriated in the love they shared, she wondered if there might come a time when he wanted more than she'd be able to give.

CHAPTER SIX

Football season had begun and Carmen and Natron had been together for months. Being the girlfriend of a big football star was fun and while she missed him when he was on the road, she'd grown accustomed to the lifestyle.

The Vipers had Natron practicing most of the time he was in Dallas, which didn't leave much time for her. To keep her from being at such loose ends, Natron arranged for her to meet with a group of girls he thought she might like.

Apparently his financial advisor, Mason Dubreaux, had a Daddy/little girl relationship with his girlfriend, Nellie, and Nellie had a group of friends who all liked being a Daddy's girl. They even called their group the Daddy's Little Girls Club. Natron had put Carmen in touch with Nellie, who told her that the girls had decided to meet in Fort Worth for a night of bull riding at the rodeo.

Carmen was nervous about meeting the girls for the first time, but she looked forward to it. She arrived at the stockyard early. She and Nellie planned to meet outside the Cowtown Coliseum. She got there first and since she didn't see Nellie, Carmen leaned up against a post and played a candy game on her phone while she waited.

"Carmen!"

Hearing her name, Carmen turned to find a cute blonde with big hair coming toward her, high heels clicking against the pavement. The girl had the poise and presence of a pageant queen, and she held her arms out, intent on giving Carmen a hug.

"Nellie?" Carmen asked as she was swallowed up into a cloud of Chloe perfume.

"Yes, and you must be Carmen." Carmen nodded and Nellie embraced her, giving Carmen a firm squeeze before releasing her.

Carmen nodded. She couldn't help but stare at the girl. Nellie's flawless makeup and ultra-smooth skin made her seem more like a doll than real. Nellie wore a red western-style blouse with shiny red pearl snaps up the front and painted-on jeans. Her hair reminded Carmen of a Dolly Parton wig, but she had a feeling it was Nellie's actual hair under all that hairspray.

"So you're Natron's little girl?" Nellie's blue eyes sparkled.

Carmen nodded, "And your boyfriend is his financial advisor?"

Nellie beamed. "Mason. I'm so glad he told me about you. I can't wait for you to meet the other girls. They're going to be tickled pink." She linked arms with Carmen and they went into the arena.

Apparently Kimberly, who was the leader of the group, had arranged for tickets and Nellie led them to their seats. Once there, she introduced Carmen to the other girls. First there was Kimberly, a striking brunette with coffee-colored eyes. "Welcome to the group, Carmen. We're so happy you could join us."

Sloane stood on the other side of Kimberly. She was a tall, thin girl with a long, sleek curtain of blond hair. Her eyes were so dark they were almost black, and she reminded Carmen of Cher, only with white-blond hair. "Nice to meet you," Sloane said in a no-nonsense voice.

At the far end of the row was Lucinda. Carmen had read about her in the arts section of the Dallas Morning News. A child prodigy, Lucinda Lake was one of the most famous concert pianists of their generation. Lucinda Lake had a daddy? That got her curiosity bubbling, and Carmen couldn't wait to learn more about that. Lucinda waved, and Carmen waved back trying not to act too star-struck. She'd never heard Lucinda play, but she'd always wanted to.

"Where is Charmaine?" Nellie asked.

Sloane scowled. "Late as always. I should give that girl a watch for her birthday, not that it would do any good."

"Maybe somebody should show her how to set an alarm on her phone," Kimberly said.

"She knows how to do that, she just chooses not to," Sloane huffed. "She's consistently disrespectful of other people's time."

"She's on island time," Lucinda offered.

"Yeah, that's her," Nellie agreed.

They all stood for 'The Star-Spangled Banner.' Looking around, Carmen saw most people covering their hearts with their hands so she did the same. She'd never been to the rodeo before, which was strange because she hadn't grown up too far from here, but her family had never been into that sort of stuff.

It was exciting, the lights, the sounds, the announcer on the loudspeaker, and yes, the sexy cowboys waiting their turn to ride one of the top bulls in the nation. The place smelled of livestock, more like the smell of a barn freshly stocked with hay than of manure. It reminded Carmen of the country and visiting her grandparents' farm.

Just as the bull-riding contest was about to start, a girl walked up the stands like she owned the place. She was gorgeous, with blond-and-brown striped hair, shocking blue eyes, and a sexy little figure. She wore skinny black jeans, stylish cowboy boots, and a beige suede jacket with fringe swaying from it.

It only took a minute for Carmen to recognize her. Charmaine Bainbridge was the talk of Dallas. She was what you might call a celebutante—a debutante with a great deal of celebrity. Her father was the wealthiest man in Texas, and when he'd divorced her mother when she was six years old, the local media had dubbed her 'the poor little rich girl' and documented her every move since. Charmaine turned into a wild child, her name in the headlines sold newspapers, and she became a household name in the Lone Star state.

Once she got to their row, she had to push past several people to get to the empty seat next to Carmen. Just as she plopped down into it, flashbulbs went off. A couple of paparazzi had followed her into the coliseum and were standing just a few rows down, trying to get her picture.

Charmaine stood up and shot them her middle finger. "Screw you, hey, let these people enjoy their rodeo!" she yelled at them and sat back down. Reluctantly the men lowered their cameras and slinked away.

While Charmaine's reputation as a diva preceded her, Carmen was glad to find Charmaine was just as interesting as advertised. "Hi, I'm Carmen," Carmen said and held out her hand.

Charmaine took it and gave it a good shake. "Hi, Carmen. Natron's girl, right?"

Carmen nodded.

"I'm Charmaine," she said and waved to the other girls seated on Carmen's other side.

"I know who you are," Carmen said, feeling her cheeks warm.

"It's about time you showed up," Sloane griped.

"That old saw again? You should really find something more original to bitch about, Sloane," Charmaine said.

"I told her you were on island time," Lucinda said.

"What does that even mean?" Sloane asked.

"It's like when you go on vacation to the islands and nobody keeps track of time. It's all laid back, nobody rushes. Island time," Lucinda explained.

Charmaine sat back and crossed her legs. "Yeah, island time. You should really listen to Lucy Lu over there. Has the beer guy come by?"

Sloane let loose an exasperated sigh and Kimberly patted her arm while Lucinda signaled a beer vendor from a few sections over. They all ordered a large beer, except Charmaine who purchased the huge one that came in the container they called 'yard.'

"You're gonna get so hammered," Sloane complained.

"That's the plan," Charmaine shrugged, then added, "I have a driver."

The girls sipped their beers as they watched the spectacle unfold in front of them. The biggest, baddest bulls on the rodeo circuit were competing tonight and tomorrow night. The bull riders competed as well. The anticipation in the coliseum was palpable with each new rider, especially in those last moments when the rider tightened his grip on the ropes just before the gate swung open and the bull exploded out of the chute.

The bulls bucked like mad, throwing the riders around like ragdolls. Carmen loved seeing all the differences in the bulls; some were red, some black, and some spotted. Some had horns, some had no horns to speak of or horns that had been filed down, and it interested her that you couldn't tell by looking at the bull how fierce he would be or how difficult a ride he would give his rider.

According to the announcer, the baddest bull of the night was Stranger Danger. The announcer stated that Stranger Danger had only been ridden twice during his entire five-year career. Carmen gulped, glad to see his rider tonight wore a protective helmet.

"I wish they wouldn't wear those helmets. The guys who wear the cowboy hats are much hotter," Charmaine said, taking a slug of her beer.

"That's just stupid, Charmaine, that's like saying guys in motorcycle helmets aren't as hot—so ignorant," Sloane chided.

"I think this cowboy made a smart move, wearing it with this bull," Carmen said.

Charmaine shrugged.

The chute opened and Stranger Danger bolted out of the chute. The 1,500-pound red bull flew through the air; as he bucked, he moved more vertically than forward. First his head was in the air, horns slashing, then fast as lightning his tail launched into the air, and he was quick, like a fish flopping out of water. But a fish flopped frantically without purpose; not Stranger Danger. He knew what he was doing, you could almost see the calculations as he whirled around doing a 360-degree turn in mid-air, rearing up on his back legs, then hurling himself into the air again, kicking up a cloud of dirt behind him.

After two seconds, the bull tossed the rider into the air. The poor fellow landed on his rear end only a couple of feet away from the still-kicking bull. The rodeo clowns approached Stranger Danger waving their long, colorful scarves in his face while the bull rider hopped up and climbed over the wall to safety. The consummate professional, Stranger Danger ignored the rodeo clowns, turned and trotted through the open path back to the holding pens.

"Did you see the balls on that animal?" Charmaine whispered, nudging Carmen. She looked to see that they were enormous, and stifled a giggle.

Leave it to Charmaine to point that out.

The next rider came out wearing a cowboy hat, reddish-tan chaps, and a blue shirt that showed his muscular physique underneath. "Now that's more like it," Charmaine said.

"Have you ever dated a bull rider?" Carmen asked her.

Charmaine nodded. "They work out too much. If they're any good, they don't have time for fun. Hot to look at though."

The handsome rider in the blue shirt was one of the few to stay aboard the bull for eight seconds and wound up with the highest score of the evening.

After the rodeo, the girls headed over to Billy Bob's for some barbecue. They sat around a table eating ribs, drinking beer, and telling stories.

"So how did you and Natron meet?" Charmaine asked.

Carmen told the girls the story of meeting Natron at her art opening and then painting his portrait.

"Oh, you paint portraits? I'm sure Mason would love to have a portrait painted of me," Nellie said.

"Really?" Carmen said, feeling uncomfortable with being put on the spot.

Nellie nodded and Carmen was thrilled when Sloane changed the subject. "So what kind of daddy is Natron?" she asked.

This caught Carmen off guard. "I'm not sure what you mean," she responded.

"Like is he into punishment? Does he make you stand in the corner or is he into more pain or humiliation stuff, what?"

"Oh, games. He likes to play games," Carmen said.

"Oh, I love this guy," Charmaine clapped her hands. "What kind of games?"

"Like the first time we were together we played 'Everything But...' where we did everything but have sex, I mean intercourse." She snickered. "It didn't really work out that way, but that was the goal anyway."

The girls laughed.

"So what's your favorite thing about having a daddy and being his little girl?" Carmen asked them.

"My daddy keeping me in line. I wouldn't be where I am if he weren't so strict with me," Lucinda said.

"I don't have one right now, but I love when they make you get on your knees and worship their cock," Sloane said with a dreamy smile.

"I don't have one either, but when I did, I loved when he tied me up, pulled my pigtails, and rode me hard while he smacked my ass," Charmaine said. "Mmm."

"That is hot," Carmen said.

"Okay, I have something that Charles did the other night that was super hot," Kimberly said.

"Oh good. It's been so long for me I have to live vicariously through y'all," Sloane groaned, leaning in so she wouldn't miss a detail.

"Well, I was sleeping, dreaming actually, and I felt this body press up against mine from behind. This hard cock poking me in the small of my back, against my ass. Then he pulled my nightgown up and pulled my legs apart. I sleep on my stomach and usually without underwear so he already had easy access, but I was totally asleep.

"I was dreaming about Russian spies or something; I was a spy, and there was some sort of espionage going on. I almost thought, as I woke up a little, that the person behind me about to fuck me was a spy and I had to go along with it or I would blow my cover. That made it super hot. I started wiggling my ass, moaning a little, encouraging him. He spread me wide and entered me. I swear I don't think I've ever been so ready for it, and it was amazing because I was halfway in my dream world and halfway in the real world—in bed with my fiancé.

Then he fucked me so hard, so relentlessly. It was super hot not only because it felt so damned good, but also because there was almost a questionable consent—I love that he just woke up in the night and took what was his."

"Damn, that's sexy," Nellie said, fanning herself.

"So you weren't irritated? I might have been if I had an early day the next morning," Lucinda said.

"No. Maybe because I was having a sexy dream already, I'm not sure. But he would have stopped had I asked him to," Kimberly said.

"Really?" Carmen asked.

"Of course, that's what being a submissive means. You do what Daddy says, what he wants, unless you don't want to and then you just say no. No always means no, even when you're submissive to your partner. That's why we have safewords. I think that's one of the things people who don't have relationships like that don't understand. Your submission is a gift, one that can always be revoked."

That made sense. Carmen enjoyed the rest of the meal, getting to know the girls better. It pleased her to have new friends she could talk to about her relationship with Natron. Her other girlfriends would have thought she'd lost her mind. They were all about equality and not letting the man get the upper hand. These girls understood you could give the man the upper hand because you could trust him to take care of you, and that deepened the relationship.

The party soon broke up with Lucinda and Sloane leaving first, each citing an early morning the next day. Then Kimberly and Nellie stood up. "Are you ready, Carmen?" Nellie asked.

"I think I'll stick around for a little while with Charmaine if that's okay."

"Sure, y'all have fun. We're exhausted. Let's go shopping one day soon, alright?" Nellie asked.

Carmen nodded, waved them goodbye and went back to her conversation with Charmaine.

"You think she's an airhead, don't you?" Charmaine asked, referring to Nellie.

"Well, I... no," Carmen stammered.

"Liar."

"She's not?"

"No. She is a pageant queen, that's obvious, and she can be annoying. She's quite a princess and all, but her heart is pure gold. She might come across superficial, but she is someone you want in your corner."

"I see. Do you mind if I ask... what's up with Sloane? She seemed really mad that you were late."

Charmaine brushed a hand in front of her face. "Sloane's as much of a sister to me as any of my half-sisters. She and I have known each other for years, and our relationship is complicated. We fight, but we're close. Like sisters."

They talked for another half hour before they paid their tab.

On the way out, Carmen bought two posters of Stranger Danger from a vendor just outside, one for herself and one for Charmaine. She handed it to Charmaine, who winked at her. "For my wall," Charmaine said. "Awesome, do you need a ride home?"

"No, I'm good, but thanks. I didn't drink that much," Carmen said.

"Suit yourself," Charmaine said, getting into her black SUV limousine.

Carmen practically floated to her car. Normally she was shy and didn't like meeting new people, but meeting these girls—it felt like opening the door to a whole new world for her. She decided to drive to Natron's place rather than hers. Who knew? Maybe he might wake her up in the middle of the night and they could play Russian Spies...

CHAPTER SEVEN

Summer had arrived, and with it Carmen had found new success with her paintings. Her portrait of Natron had been accepted in a prestigious show and she traveled to New York for the opening ceremony.

Upon entering her hotel room, Carmen stopped short; the perfume of roses hung in the air so thick it overpowered her senses. Everywhere she looked was another vase filled with roses, baby's breath, and eucalyptus; she counted seven bouquets in all. The swath of yellow filled the room with sunshine, even though outside the day was rainy and grey. Carmen didn't need to read the card to know they were from Natron, but she wanted to read the message anyway. The bouquet on the desk had a large note attached to it.

Congratulations on your big show! I'm so proud of you, babygirl.
Now for a game of Hide and Seek. Within one of these bouquets you will find a surprise.
Find it before the opening and wear it close to your heart, the next best thing to me being there.
Love,
Natron

Hmm. Natron frequently played little games with her. Usually they were sex games, but this could be fun too. She moved around the room, inspecting each of the arrangements, the yellow rose petals soft as satin under her fingertips. Where had he hidden it, and what could it be?

She rolled her luggage into a corner and sat on the queen-sized bed. Her day had started at the crack of dawn in Dallas and would most likely end with her calling for some room service and turning in early.

The flight to New York had been something out of a dream. Since Natron was at training camp and he'd had to miss her at her first big show, he'd pulled out all the stops and chartered a private plane to take her to the Big Apple. She had been the only passenger aboard and had been treated to a delicious chicken salad sandwich, cheese, fruit, and a bottomless glass of champagne. Any entertainment she'd required had been available to her—movies, Internet, TV shows—but Carmen had used the flight as an opportunity to catch up on the latest romance novel she'd been reading.

Natron had arranged a private car to take her to the Plaza, where she checked into her room and was greeted by his latest romantic gesture. Not only had she never seen so many flowers in her life outside a florist's shop, but she was also impressed he remembered that yellow roses were her favorite flower. She knew it was kinda corny, considering the whole 'Yellow Rose of Texas' cliché and all, but she loved them nonetheless.

She looked through the packet of information from the art show and mapped out her activities for the following day. Tomorrow night was the opening for the National Portrait Society's Annual Awards, and she would be attending as a prizewinner. With Natron's blessing, she'd entered his portrait in the competition and was flabbergasted when she won the 'Stroke of Brilliance' award in the painting category.

The festivities would begin with a cocktail party reception at five o'clock at the Guggenheim, followed by a dinner for the winners at Tavern on the Green. She lay back against the plethora of pillows and tried to soak it all in. The whole experience was more than she'd ever dreamed of. The only thing Carmen had ever wanted to do was her art. As far back as she could remember, she had been creating art, from doodles along the margins of her notebook to paintings in art class and countless creations from her markers and crayons at home.

She'd never exactly planned a career for herself in art, but it was never a question of what she should do with her life either. Art simply was her life. She lived it, breathed it, and she used it to communicate.

When she was seven years old, something had happened to her on the school bus. She'd come home crying and her mother asked Carmen to tell her what was wrong. Unable to stop crying, Carmen grabbed some paper and managed, "I'll draw it," through her tears. Then she proceeded to create an elaborate picture illustrating a bully hitting a little girl in the head. The girl's wide eyes displayed the terror she must have felt, and the bully's satisfaction was evidenced by his evil grin. That drawing was only the beginning of Carmen capturing emotions on paper. She was aware she'd been granted a gift and spent most days trying to improve it.

Lost in her thoughts, Carmen snapped back to the present when something in one of the vases caught her eye. There was something in the vase atop the armoire, something yellow yet too small to be a rose. She climbed off the bed to investigate. Pulling several roses out of the water, she found what she was looking for. Taped around the middle of one of the roses' stem was a yellow index card. She ripped the tape away and unfurled the message.

Look in the bottom inside zipper pocket of your luggage.

Her heart fluttered in her chest as she set up the luggage stand and hoisted her case atop it. She unzipped the red Brighton suitcase, flung open the top, and tossed a sweater and some panties onto the bed, trying to get to the pocket. Inside was a blue jeweler's box. She opened it and gasped when she found an ivory and onyx cameo with a black velvet cord to tie around her neck. She had seen that very necklace when she had gone shopping with her girlfriends Nellie and Marley for her dress for the opening.

Nellie must have told Natron how much Carmen had liked it. Enamored of his fame, Nellie was always sucking up to Natron. Nellie had been a well-known beauty queen several years ago and had never quite adjusted to life outside the limelight. Carmen shook her head. Fame meant nothing to her except the occasional inconvenience when the paparazzi followed Natron. She knew famous people were just like anybody else, with hopes, dreams, and problems like everybody else.

Carmen walked into the bathroom and held up the necklace. It was beautiful against the curve of her neck. She took a selfie with her phone and sent it to Natron with a big thanks and a happy face. She hugged herself, thinking how lucky she was to have a daddy who spoiled her rotten and made her feel so loved and cherished.

• • • • • • • • • • • • • • •

The next day Carmen did some sightseeing at the Empire State Building before getting dressed for the opening. When she returned from her outing, she stopped downstairs at the Todd English Food Hall and had lobster hush-puppies for lunch.

After showering and trying to tame her curly mop, she put on her new, chic black pantsuit and tied the cameo around her neck. The style was very becoming on her and reflected her personality to a tee. She was tempted to take another selfie to send to Natron, but didn't want to come across vain so she resisted the impulse.

On the cab ride to the museum, she checked her phone again. Nothing from Natron. She hadn't heard from him since she'd sent him the thank-you text the day before. An emptiness skittered through her and she took a deep breath as she prepared to face the biggest moment of her career alone.

CHAPTER EIGHT

Natron closed his locker, high-fived some of the guys, then strolled out to the parking lot. Practice had been a killer today. Coach had really pushed them throughout this training camp and there was a significant amount of pressure for Natron to rise to the occasion. His coaches, his agent, hell, even his mamma were all expecting him to keep up the incredible play that had landed him MVP the previous season.

The league's Most Valuable Player award was an honor usually reserved for quarterbacks and running backs. But his 2,000+ yards of receiving had catapulted him over the rest of the field, and in one stellar season he'd become a media darling and the most popular receiver since Jerry Rice.

For Natron the whole experience had been surreal, especially since he hadn't grown up wanting to be a football player. The fact that he'd never stepped onto a football field until he was sixteen years old made his story all the more impressive.

Natron's first love was basketball. His mother loved to tell how he'd slept with a basketball from the time he was old enough to haul it into the crib with him. Growing up, Natron dribbled his basketball wherever he went, and by the time he was in middle school, his ball-handling skills were out of this world.

When he got to high school, Natron was the best basketball player in the region, the sport coming easily to him. Though he'd never had to work as hard as the other kids, he was significantly better than they were, thanks to his talent.

The season of his junior year, a new coach took over the team. The new guy and Natron went round and round over his work ethic, or lack thereof.

Near the end of football season that fall, his school's football team lost both of their wide receivers. Desperate for some additional bodies to fill that position, the football coach attempted to recruit some of the basketball players to help them finish out the season. Sick of his coach's nagging, Natron agreed to play wide receiver for the last three games.

To everyone's amazement, Natron caught every ball thrown within ten feet of him. He played both sports that year, but when his senior year rolled around, he realized he needed to make a decision about where to focus his efforts. To be able to attend college, he would need an athletic scholarship and to get one, he needed to choose a sport.

Playing professional basketball was a possibility, but Natron knew it was a reach for all but the most elite athletes. Football, on the other hand, recruited more players and offered more opportunities for a football player at the professional level. Once he learned to take a hit, Natron found playing the position of wide receiver to be easier than basketball, so ultimately he chose football. He earned a full-ride scholarship to a small Florida college where he received a good education and earned a reputation as one of the best wide receivers in the country.

On draft day the following year, Natron Dakers was chosen as the Dallas Vipers' first round pick, the fifth draft pick overall. His mother had wept on national television as he'd signed a multi-million-dollar deal with the Vipers, then packed his bags and moved to Dallas.

Last season had been his third season with the Vipers and they had gone all the way to the Conference Championship game, where they lost by two points. This year anything short of a trip to the Super Bowl would be considered a failure by management, the players, and most important, the fans.

The Vipers held their training camp in Orlando, Florida, which was eight hours from Natron's hometown and five hours from where he'd played college ball. Natron had only been there a week, but to see the throng of fans that showed up every day to see him, one would think the camp was taking place in Natron's hometown.

Everywhere he went, reporters stuck a microphone in his face, asking him all kinds of questions—from the inane to the insane. They wanted to know everything about his life, from how he worked out to what he ate, and they particularly wanted to know who he fucked.

Natron and Carmen had been together for over a year, and for the most part, he shielded her from the spotlight. He'd been trying for months to get her to move in with him, but she always refused, saying she was more comfortable at her place where she could paint whenever the muse called her.

His grueling work schedule kept them apart a fair amount of time, so it didn't seem fair to push her to move into his place when he would go on the road for days at a time. So instead of pressing the issue, he started bringing his things over to her place. Occasionally, it struck him funny that with all his millions, he basically lived out of a few drawers in a loft apartment. But then he'd think of Carmen and realize how lucky he was to have found her. He'd do whatever it took to keep her in his life.

Carmen had everything he wanted in a woman. She was talented, beautiful, kind, and she embraced his kinks in the bedroom. It was such a blessing to have found a little girl he could take care of, one who would submit to his every desire in the bedroom. She gave her body to him unconditionally. They'd developed a trust and a rapport that made him comfortable acting out all his dominant fantasies with her. She trusted him not to hurt her, and he trusted her not to go running to the media with stories of his perversions.

This weekend she'd flown to Orlando to see him, and he couldn't wait to spend time with her. Getting into his black Lamborghini Veneno, he donned a pair of sunglasses and drove to Don's, the fancy seafood restaurant where he'd reserved a private back room so that he and Carmen could eat dinner without it becoming a circus. After working his ass off all week, he needed a babygirl fix and he needed it bad.

He parked at the back of the lot and went inside. Once his eyes adjusted to the dark, he glanced around, taking in the romantic atmosphere, flickering candles, and soft music adding to the ambiance. Pulling back a curtain, the maître d' showed him into a hidden dining area at the back of the building.

Upon entering, he saw Carmen sitting at the table. Her beauty never ceased to affect him. When she stood up to greet him, he noticed her silky, sapphire-blue dress hugged her curves in all the right places. In an almost imperceptible exchange, he palmed the maître d' a fifty before crossing the room to Carmen.

She opened her arms to him, and as he embraced her, a significant amount of his stress evaporated. She felt insanely good. He'd missed the way her body melded perfectly to his and they shared a long, sexy 'I've-missed-you-so-much' kiss before settling back into their seats.

They both ordered salads and the Dover sole. They declined cocktails; Natron because he was in training, and Carmen for solidarity. Carmen chattered away about her trip to New York. She had only been back for a couple of days and they'd barely had a chance to talk with the intense practices he'd been attending every day.

Carmen's portrait of him was currently on display in New York at the Guggenheim. After a month-long engagement there, the portrait would join the other award winners on tour around the United States.

"Natron, I feel like I've 'arrived' as an artist. You should have seen all the important people I met, and the other artists were amazing, so talented. I was in incredible company."

"I'm so proud of you, babygirl. I always knew you were the best."

She blushed prettily. "Ever since that big show in Dallas, I've been getting requests for more and more commissions." She opened her eyes wide. "I'm not sure if I'll be able to keep up."

"Now that's the kind of problem we like to have." Natron lifted his glass of icy water to hers. He'd always known she had a gift, but it thrilled him that others now recognized her talents.

A tuxedoed waiter placed their dishes before them.

"Do you want me to cut your meat for you?" he asked, only half-teasing.

She giggled. "No, thanks, Daddy. This fish is super flaky. Not like a steak or anything." She wrinkled her nose at him.

"All right. Just takin' care of my girl."

"Thank you, Daddy."

It had taken him awhile to explain the Daddy/little girl relationship he craved to Carmen. He'd started off slow, spanking her for infractions to 'rules' he laid down. Some of them were arbitrary, an excuse to spank her lovely bottom. He adored reddening her ass.

But he also wanted to take care of her. That was more difficult because like most women these days, Carmen was independent. At first she bristled at the idea of a man taking care of her, and money was a big part of the problem. She didn't want to take his money, so he respected her feelings and found other ways to spoil her. Since she wouldn't live in his mansion, he improved her place with some upgraded furniture, citing his need for a more comfortable place to sit when he came over. He'd also convinced her it was unsafe for her to drive around in her broken-down old car, and she'd allowed him to buy her a new one.

Once she understood what a submissive was, Carmen had taken to it like a cat to meowing. It was in her nature to please people, and she wanted to please him. But he needed more than that; he had a deep burning need to make her his, to nurture and protect her. To his satisfaction, she was becoming more and more comfortable with their dynamic all the time.

"So tell me more about your trip," he said.

"The opening was incredible. I met so many wonderful people: other artists, patrons, important art gallery owners, even a stuffy old art critic. The food was great, the hotel was lovely."

"How 'bout the plane ride?" he winked.

"Wonderful. But you don't need to spoil me like that. I can take a regular flight. Bump me up to first class if you must, but you don't need to charter a jet like that!"

She waved away his grand gesture with protest, but he could see by the way her cheeks flushed with pleasure that she enjoyed the five-star treatment.

"Fine. We'll save that for special occasions, but *this* was a special occasion. It made me sad I couldn't be there with you, babygirl, so I had to do *something* extra for you."

She placed a hand over his. "The seven humongous bouquets of roses would have been more than enough."

"Did you count how many there were?"

"Of course. Eighty-seven, just like your number. I texted you but I wasn't sure if you got it."

He ran a hand over his head and shook his dreads. "Girl, I'm sorry. I haven't had the chance to check. Been so busy. Coach is really putting us through our paces this year, and the pressure is *on*."

"I was afraid of that. I know you want to be good, but don't kill yourself over it," she said, worry wrinkling her forehead.

"Don't you worry about that. Now that I've got my girl here, it's time for some R&R." He touched her knee under the table and lowered his voice. "You wearing underwear?"

She looked around and saw they were alone in the room. "No. You asked me not to, Daddy."

"Good, because Daddy wants to play a game."

Her eyes twinkled, telling him she loved playing Daddy's games. "What is it?"

"It's called 'How Wet Can She Get?'"

Her lips parted as if she were going to speak, but she remained silent.

"Let's get started. I want you to go into the bathroom and finger yourself with two fingers while you count to fifty. Then I want you to make little circles on your little clit while you count to fifty. Do it three times, the whole thing. Then come back and we'll see how well you've done."

"Yes, sir," she said and pushed her chair back.

He knew his instructions would get her juices flowing. Her half-closed eyelids and slowed breathing gave her away. His cock twitched at the image he conjured in his mind of her perched in a bathroom stall playing with herself exactly as he'd ordered her to.

While she was gone, he paid the bill and left the waiter a sizable tip. When she entered the private room, he beckoned to her.

Lifting her hands to his nose, he gave her a disapproving look. "These hands don't smell like they've been in your pussy. Have you been a bad girl? Did you do what Daddy asked you to?"

She tugged to get her hands back, but he held on, gripping them tighter.

"I washed them, Daddy! You didn't say I shouldn't."

"True. So that's why they smell of lavender instead of your delicious little cunt."

She nodded. "I did what you asked," she hissed, looking around to be sure they were still alone.

"I'll be the judge of that."

Ever so slowly, he ran a hand up under that tantalizing blue dress. With no panties to impede his progress, he felt her arousal present on her thighs and inserted a digit into her churned-up channel. She was wet. Ready for whatever he wanted to do to her.

Not only did her dampness bring his cock to life, but her obedience gave him great satisfaction. It was a heady experience to have such an enchanting and accomplished woman do his bidding, and he tilted his head in approval.

He removed his finger, now coated in her slick fluid.

"Lick this off for Daddy," he rasped.

She wrinkled her nose, but opened her luscious pink lips, took his finger into her mouth, and ran her velvet tongue around it.

He plucked his finger from her mouth. "That's right, babygirl. I like to see you getting wet for Daddy."

He could see by the twinkle in her eyes that she took pleasure in his words. He stood, put his Tom Ford sunglasses back on, and ushered her outside, his hand resting on the small of her back protectively.

Outside, he nodded to the driver he'd hired to bring Carmen to the restaurant. He and Carmen climbed into the back of the town car, and he gave the driver an address, then pressed a button that closed the privacy glass. He'd have someone pick up his car later.

"Pull that dress up to your waist," he growled.

A glimmer of excitement crossed her face as she gathered the hem and hiked it up. The movement was awkward from her seated position, and he liked watching her have to struggle slightly to obey.

"Open your legs and let Daddy see what you've got for me."

He moved to the seat across from her for a better view of the show.

Tentatively she parted her knees.

"More."

She splayed her legs.

"Wider."

She complied, spreading her thighs as wide as she could. "Natron…" she pleaded.

"Yes?"

"This is embarrassing," she squeaked.

"But it pleases me. And you want to please me, don't you?"

She nodded.

"Words. Use words," he chided.

"Yes, sir," she said, bowing her head.

"Good girl. Now, I want to see you play with that pussy. What were my instructions for you in the bathroom earlier?"

"Finger myself fifty times, then make circles on my clit for fifty counts. And to do it three times."

"Good. Do it again."

He settled back into his seat, fighting the urge to unzip his fly and relieve the pressure of his hardening cock.

She closed her eyes and brought her fingers down to her pussy. She needed to hunch over slightly to be able to fuck herself with them, and his cock pulsed as she dipped her hand in and out, soaking her fingers with her own juices.

When she'd finished the first round of ministrations, he commanded, "Taste yourself."

Humiliation clouded her face. He knew this made her uncomfortable and seeing her squirm aroused him all the more.

She inserted her fingers into her mouth, sucking, then removing them in a quick gesture.

"Not so fast. I want you to enjoy it. What do you taste like?"

"I don't know, Natron. Tangy. It's kinda gross."

"You're going to learn to like it," he assured her. "Continue."

He held back a self-satisfied smirk, watching her pleasure herself. When she reached fifty, he said, "Now taste yourself again. This time I want you to enjoy it."

She lifted her fingers to her mouth and made a face.

He ignored her show of distaste. "That's it. Suckle on them. I want you to think about my cock, pretend you're sucking on me."

That appeared to help, because her face took on a wanton expression and she licked and suckled her fingers with a fresh passion.

"Good girl. Now think about my face between your legs. Think about me licking, nipping, tormenting your sweet little pussy."

She moaned.

"Yeah, you like that?"

She nodded.

"You taste delicious to me. Why would I ask you to taste yourself if I didn't think your juices were yummy, babygirl? Think about how much I like to devour you."

Her other hand traveled south and began stroking her clit.

"Uh uh uh. No, you don't. Now it's Daddy's turn."

Dropping on the limo floor on his knees, he closed the distance between them.

"Take your hands and lace them behind your head."

She complied, the arch of her back another indicator of her arousal.

"Time to see how wet you are for Daddy," he said, then bent his head between her legs.

He started by running his tongue along the outside of her inner thighs. Her hips bucked and she groaned, spreading her legs even farther apart.

He inserted a finger and lapped up her copious juices. She tasted truly delicious to him. In any case, he would train her to love her own unique flavor.

Her delicate folds called to him and he used his tongue to torture them. Tugging with his lips and teeth, pressing hard with the point of his tongue, he elicited an almost constant barrage of cries from her sweet throat.

He knew it was all she could do not to grab his shoulders and pull him into her, but he'd stopped that by instructing her to hold her hands behind her head.

"Oh, please lick me, Daddy."

He leaned back and slapped her inner thigh, causing her to jump. "Hush, babygirl. You don't do the bossin' here. You need to sit still and trust your daddy. I'll take care of you, don't you worry."

Sitting back on his heels, he took her in. His darling girl was open like a book, hot and ready, dripping with lust for him. Her blue eyes, normally edged with green, took on deeper peacock tones when she was aroused.

These were the moments he craved, why he needed to dominate her. For nothing turned him on as much as her arousal. Seeing her in the throes of passion made him feel in control, made him feel whole. Made him love her.

Grinning, he went back to work plunging into her with his fingers. He reached inside and tickled her g-spot—softly at first, then with more ferocity. She eagerly scooted down into the leather seat, giving him better access.

With the palm of his other hand, he pressed down on her lower abdomen, his fingers meeting each other on either side of her vaginal wall. She wiggled underneath him and her moans became screams.

"Now we're really gonna see how wet you can get, little girl."

"Daddy!" she shrieked. "Oh, my God, Daddy!"

His powerful hands served him in many capacities. In addition to giving him a dream job, they also allowed him to please his woman in a way he wasn't sure other men could. He moved his hand rapidly in and out of her dripping pussy.

Her whole body tensed and, knowing she was close, he ramped up the speed and power with which he fucked her, all the while curling his fingers back toward himself, massaging her g-spot from both sides. Then the liquid started flowing out like a dam had burst. Copious amounts of silken liquid girl-cum gushed from her cunt and pooled onto the leather seat and covered his hand.

"Such a good girl," he said as he removed his hand from her sopping womanhood. "That's pretty wet." He slid onto the seat next to her and unlocked her hands from behind her head, bringing one hand to his lips. He kissed it, saying, "You're good at this game."

Carmen flopped onto his shoulder, spent. "May I pull my dress down now, Daddy?"

"Yes, you can," he said.

As she was arranging herself, the glass partition rolled down. "Mr. Dakers, we've arrived at your destination."

CHAPTER NINE

Carmen tried to keep pace with Natron as they entered the condominium, but his strides were larger than hers even when her gait was not shaky from just having experienced a mind-blowing orgasm. She tugged at his hand to slow his speed.

"Sorry, babe," he said, slowing down. "I'm just excited to get you inside."

Her head was spinning the way it often did when she got swept up in her relationship with Natron. He was the best lover she'd ever had. Sometimes he made her come more often than she'd ever imagined possible, and something told her tonight was going to be another one of those nights. Another perk to being with an athlete, she smiled to herself.

The moment they walked through the door, he started unzipping her dress.

She unbuttoned his pants and reached in and wrapped her fingers around him. His cock pulsed in her hand and she tugged the sensitive skin until he stepped back and pulled his shirt over his head. No matter how many times she saw his incredibly defined abs, they made her breath catch in her throat. And she licked her lips in anticipation as she eyed that v-shaped valley that led directly to his crotch.

In seconds, they were naked standing in the entryway of the building Natron had rented for the duration of training camp. She'd get a tour later, for it was obvious he had other things on his agenda first.

He drew her to him, their mouths finding each other, eager to reconnect after the last few weeks apart. Their tongues collided, awkwardly at first, then finding the familiar rhythm exclusive to them.

"C'mon, babygirl. You think you were wet before… just wait to see what Daddy has in store for you now."

Her stomach did a flip. What could he possibly mean? She couldn't remember getting as turned on as he had her during that limo ride. How could she get wetter? Damn, she needed to hydrate.

"You stay right here. I'll be right back," he said.

"Yes, sir. Can I get some water?"

"Of course," he said as he strode into the other room, the site of his gloriously round ass cheeks igniting another fire between her legs.

She opened the refrigerator and took out a bottle of water. Taking a sip, she looked around the room. The accommodations were first-rate, somewhere between Natron's luxury abode and her serviceable apartment. The furniture was high-end contemporary, with *avant garde* lighting and sliding glass doors that opened up to a screened-in pool.

She hugged herself. Maybe Natron meant they were going swimming. The thought of skinny-dipping with him, their naked bodies pressed against each other in the slippery water, made her pussy thrum with desire.

"Carmen, come here," Natron called from the other room.

She followed his voice into a hallway and heard the sound of water running.

The sound came from a beautiful bathroom; inside were two sinks and a massive tub in addition to the large shower that Natron stood outside in all his naked glory.

He held out his hand and gave her a ladies-first gesture as he ushered her into the shower. Taking a step inside the marble tiled enclosure, she was enveloped by the hot steam. Natron liked to shower with incredibly hot water, and she'd gotten used to the scorching water's soothing properties by now.

He came up behind her, pressing his erection against the cleft of her bottom. Reaching around the front, he took up a bar of soap and lathered it in front of her. "You're such a dirty girl. I thought you needed to get really wet tonight. Now it's time to get you really clean."

His soaped-up hands fondled her breasts, pinching her nipples, twisting them. She threw her head back and found his lips for an over-the-shoulder kiss. Reaching behind her, she found his cock and milked it with her palm.

"See? I knew you were a dirty girl. And filthy little girls need a good scrubbing."

Bathing her in soapy-slick caresses, he nibbled her neck and slowly made his way down her legs. One by one he lifted each of her feet, massaging and cleaning it at the same time. Tingles of pleasure ran up her leg when he flossed between each of her little piggies with his magic fingers.

Cupping his hand, he poured shampoo into it before washing her hair ever so thoroughly. As his fingertips rubbed her scalp, she relaxed and reveled in the amazing sensations of his strong hands massaging her head. Without meaning to, she backed her ass up against his rod, wanting that connection, needing him inside her.

She wondered what would happen if she leaned over and gave him easy access to her wanting cunt. While she'd probably earn a smack, she might also get a good, hard fucking. Before she could act on that thought, he soaped up her pussy, exploring all her girl folds and crevices.

"Such a filthy little brat. Gotta clean you up," he said as he rubbed a finger over her plumped-up clit.

"Ooooh, Natron. Please, Daddy."

"Please what?" he teased.

"Please fuck me," she whimpered, about to explode from desire.

"You know I like it when you beg," he all but snarled.

"Please, Daddy! Please fuck me so good."

"Get on your knees and ask."

She turned and dropped to her knees, hot water pelting her back. Placing her hands behind her back, she bowed her head. "Please fuck me, Daddy."

She closed her eyes so the water from the shower wouldn't wash away her contact lenses, but she didn't need to open her eyes to know what gently smacked the side of her cheek. She turned to take him in her mouth, but he reprimanded her. "Uh-un-un. Wait until I say, you greedy little girl."

His thick meaty cock thumped along the side of her face, then went to work on her other cheek. Something about being dick-slapped made her horny as hell, perhaps the humiliation of it. Wrong or not, being objectified by the man she loved got her juices flowing.

"Worship my cock," he ordered, sliding it into her willing mouth past her teeth all the way to the back of her throat.

She mumbled her agreement around his cock. While she was sure he couldn't understand her, he would know what she meant, that she loved pleasing him and would do whatever he asked of her.

He pumped his hips in and out for several minutes before he exited her mouth and pulled her to a standing position. Grabbing her buttocks, he hauled her up and shoved her against the slippery shower wall.

Inside, she panicked, her gut clenching, and she frantically tried to set her feet on the tiles. The cold marble jolted her skin, a strong contrast to the hot water that struck her lower extremities. She was heavy, and she was petrified Natron couldn't hold her. What if he slipped? One of them would probably crack their head open...

Sensing her concern, Natron crooned, "Carmen, I got you, babygirl." With that, he thrust inside her aching hole, filling her and pushing his cock in and out, the friction of the movement exactly what she'd been craving for weeks.

She wrapped her ankles around his waist and clutched his broad shoulders for dear life. The welcome sensation of him inside her washed over her and she tried to crush her fear of him dropping her.

He drove into her hard and fast, like a man possessed. She didn't blame him; there had been enough teasing for tonight. It had been difficult enough for her and she'd had one orgasm already. She couldn't imagine how he'd endured it so long without giving in to his desires. But Natron was that way, he controlled his needs while he dominated her, allowing his passion to build over time. When he finally gave in to it, he loved her with wild abandon.

As he pulsed inside her, she was forced to let go of her worries about falling. He fucked all thought from her mind and she merely clung to him, letting the tides of bliss wash over her again and again. Multiple orgasms ebbed and flowed through her from the tips of her toes to the ends of her fingertips, each one piercing her with an exquisite ecstasy that transported her to another place.

When her quivering ceased, he thrust a final time, jetting his seed deep inside her.

She slowly unwrapped her rubbery legs and stood up. He held her up, covering her face with soft, sweet kisses. "Such a good girl."

"Thank you, Daddy."

He turned off the water, stepped out of the shower, and grabbed a towel. Inside the warm shower he dried her off slowly, lovingly.

She considered him through sleepy lids. "You take such good care of me, Daddy."

Bundling her up in a sumptuous white bathrobe, he took her by the shoulders and directed her to the master bedroom. "Daddy always takes care of his girl. I've missed you, baby."

"Me too. I love you, Daddy," she said, pulling back the covers of the bed.

"Me too," he said tucking her in. His lips on her forehead were the last thing she remembered before drifting off to sleep.

They spent the weekend holed up at Natron's rental house, cooking, swimming, and fucking each other's brains out. It wasn't until they were reunited that Carmen realized how much she'd grown accustomed to her life with Natron. Back in Dallas he practically lived at her apartment and she saw him every day.

During last year's football season, their relationship was new and it wasn't *that* terrible when he went on the road. But they had grown closer during the off-season and she'd become spoiled by the extra time Natron spent with her. Rather than let herself get down, Carmen vowed to do her best to focus on the positives. She wouldn't let the time apart dampen her spirits or become an issue between them.

But there was no denying the upcoming season would be more difficult. Besides the time apart, Natron was under more pressure after his breakout season the year before. The expectation now was for him to be brilliant on the field, whereas before his successes were an unexpected boon to him and his team.

This year, nothing short of excellence was expected of him, and she could see the pressure of these lofty expectations was already taking a toll on him. His nerves seemed frayed, he was jumpier than usual, and he looked exhausted.

Seeing how tired he looked, Carmen let him sleep fifteen hours or more each day during the weekend. She'd learned that an athlete's body required significantly more sleep than 'normal' people did. Their bodies worked harder and needed the extra sleep for its recuperative effects on the muscular system.

His excessive sleeping didn't bother her. She loved curling up next to him with a good book and occasionally glancing over to marvel at the incredibly attractive man who lay next to her in the bed. The whistling of his snores provided the perfect backdrop for reading.

Things were going well with her and Natron, but this season was bound to have its difficulties. Not only would they be apart more, but she knew he would be more focused on football once the season started. She hoped their sex life wouldn't come to a standstill. She deliberately shoved her concerns aside and opened her book again, determined to lose herself in its pages.

CHAPTER TEN

Carmen took a sip of her beer. Champagne flowed freely in the suite, but Carmen had always had simpler, more plebian tastes. Time around some of her more well-to-do friends had taught her it was classier to pour her beer into a glass rather than carry around a can. Natron wouldn't have cared, but it was a nice touch that made Carmen feel more at home in the company of millionaires.

It had been a month since she and Natron had spent time together in Florida. After a couple of weeks, she had to come home to meet some deadlines for clients.

This pre-season, Natron had worked like a beast, determined as he was to be the best wide receiver in the history of the game. Carmen knew he had a history of 'just getting by' in his younger days, and she could see he was a different man now. His work ethic had never been better and he pushed himself like a fiend. Most days, Carmen only saw him when he fell into bed at night.

If Natron had been a well-known football player when they'd met, he was now a mega star. After a last minute circus catch made by Natron helped the Vipers get to the Conference Championship the year before, he'd become the media's darling. In the off-season, Natron had signed twenty-two endorsement deals, making him the most famous football player in the world.

Today marked the Vipers' home opener, and Carmen's friends, Marley and James, had invited her and the rest of the girls from the 'Daddy's Girls' club to watch the game in her boyfriend James' box suite. Marley had joined their group soon after Carmen did. Her daddy, James, knew several of the girls. His mother had been Lucinda's first piano teacher, and he had gone to college with Sloane and Charles, Kimberly's daddy. Now they were all friends and Carmen considered herself fortunate to have such a great group of people in her life.

She'd much rather watch Natron's games with her friends than with the other 'football wives.' Those women acted like they were the stars of a reality show, catty and bratty—that's how Natron referred to them. Mean girls all grown up with wealthy husbands or boyfriends to foot the bill for their wild shopping sprees and outrageous snobbishness.

The football wives constantly compared notes on how much money they spent on cars, houses, jewelry, and clothes. Oh, the clothes! They were always trying to out-dress each other. Carmen couldn't relate. She liked to wear simple clothes that she could launder in the washing machine, and Natron appreciated her casual style. Impressing people wasn't on Carmen's agenda. If the garment needed dry-cleaning, she had no place for it in her closet. Her life was too practical and busy for all that.

Working as an artist, Carmen needed clothes that could handle a little mess. No matter how hard she tried, she usually had a smudge of paint somewhere on her—even with her paint smocks. Natron liked to find one, then tease her by licking it off, whether on her neck, her cheek, her forearm…

The thought sent chills running through her.

It still amazed her that Natron Dakers was her man.

She wasn't famous, rich, or wildly successful. She wasn't even beautiful in the traditional sense. Chunky by today's beauty standards, she liked to think of herself as pleasingly plump. Natron said he loved her curves.

Across the room, Charmaine waved to her. Carmen waved back and smiled to herself, thinking Charmaine would eat the football wives for lunch. She imagined turning Charmaine loose on the snobby women and pictured Charmaine cutting them down to size in less time than it takes a lion to take down a zebra. The heiress was dressed to the nines as always in a chic black and white dress and she was flirting mercilessly with one of James' executives. Poor guy; by the end of the day he'd be in love with Charmaine and she'd cast him aside as she did countless others.

Marley came over and gave her a hug. "Come sit with me, Carmen. Are you all set for drinks?"

"Yes. Thanks so much for having us."

Marley looked at her as if she had sprouted another head. "Well, of course, Carmen. You're the guest of honor. We're all so excited to watch Natron play," she said, squeezing Carmen's hand.

They found seats near the front, and Carmen peered out the glass picture window just in time to see the Dallas Vipers' offense take the field. She scanned the Astroturf for Natron and found him, lining up left of the line. Her daddy, number eighty-seven.

Natron crouched forward, his muscles tensed, and he stood like a statue waiting for the ball to be snapped.

At the snap, the quarterback, Clay Davis, handed the ball off to the running back. Natron blocked the cornerback, tying him up while the running back ran the ball ahead five yards.

Carmen watched, but for her, the rest of the game, including the location of the ball, was peripheral. During each play, her eyes stayed locked on Natron. He moved with the grace of an angel, displaying an athleticism that was rarely seen, even in professional football. She sighed a contented sigh. He was beautiful and she could watch him all day.

The Vipers continued to move the ball on the ground. Running the ball effectively not only got them closer to the goal-line, it also ground down the defense and opened up the passing game.

On the next play, Davis dropped back in the shotgun, ducked to his right to avoid an oncoming defensive end, and let the ball fly. Carmen followed the ball with an eagle's intensity. Sprinting toward the end zone, number eighty-seven launched himself into the air, elevating at least a foot over the defender. Laying his body flat in the air, Natron reached for the ball. His hands curled around the swirling bomb and pulled in into his chest. The defender at his hip fell helplessly beside him and Natron landed in the end zone. Touchdown Vipers.

Cries of "Oh, my God!" and "Did you see that catch?" echoed throughout the suite. Hoots and hollers were accompanied by high-fives and fist bumps all around. Marley gave Carmen a little squeeze on the shoulder.

"He's amazing." Marley shook her head. "How does he do that?"

Carmen giggled. "I have no idea. But I love it when he does."

Marley laughed. "So do millions of Viper fans."

Natron stood up and started his trademark touchdown dance. Rolling his hips, he twirled his arm in the air as if throwing an imaginary lasso, then jerked it back. The movement was a cross between a disco dance and the crack of a whip. Carmen felt her face redden at the image in her mind of a naked Natron wielding a whip.

Natron ran toward the cheering fans and jumped into the stands. He handed a kid the ball as the fans embraced him. He was their hero, and anyone could see he loved every second of it.

Carmen frowned. He'd be fined for giving the ball away; it was against the rules. He was supposed to give the ball to the referee, but Natron didn't care much for rules. He loved the spotlight and the brighter it shone, the happier he was. On the field, he strode along the sidelines, chest bumping and high-fiving his fellow players, basking in all the attention.

With the Vipers' defense about to take the field, Carmen joined Kimberly on a trip to the ladies' room. Last year, when Carmen still had questions about the Daddy/little girl dynamics between her and Natron, Kimberly had been especially helpful. Kimberly had been in a Daddy/little girl relationship for several years and she helped Carmen navigate some of the newness of it.

Kimberly and Carmen walked down a hallway to a large, well-appointed ladies' room complete with a seating area plush with leather couches and a plethora of fresh floral arrangements.

After they took care of business, she and Kimberly reapplied their lipstick.

"How was the New York show?" Kimberly asked. "I can't believe I haven't seen you since then."

"I know, it was great, thanks." Carmen looked at her friend in the mirror and whispered, "I've gotten so many jobs from that, I've been so busy…"

Kimberly winked at her. "You are so talented, girl. I'm so happy for you and Natron. Your stars are really rising, and at the same time. That's so rare for couples."

Carmen agreed. "Dare I ask how the wedding planning is going?" Kimberly and her fiancé Charles had been engaged for almost two years and they'd had one setback after another, many of them caused by roadblocks put in place by his ex-wife.

Kimberly waved a hand in front of her face. "No, do not. You don't want to know."

The two girls walked out of the restroom and started back down the hallway to James' box.

"At this point we're thinking about going to Vegas one weekend and just doing it."

"Really?" Carmen was surprised. It had been Kimberly's dream all along to have an elaborate wedding with all of their friends and family there.

"I don't know," Kimberly sighed. "I hear you can get hitched in a gondola at the Venetian."

Just as they were about to reach the door, Marley opened it from the inside and clutched Carmen's forearm.

"What?" Carmen said, knowing instantly by the way Marley touched her that something was wrong.

Marley's face was paler than usual against her black hair. "Come inside."

Carmen felt the blood drain from her own face. What had happened? A terrorist attack? Kimberly's fiancé Charles, a former ranger in the Army, was always worrying about things like that happening. "What is it?" Marley's pitying look made her wonder if this was something more personal.

"It's Natron," Marley said, dragging her inside and helping her into a comfortable chair.

Carmen gazed up at the television monitors, unaware that her friends and well-meaning bystanders were gathering around her.

On the screen she saw Natron lying on the ground surrounded by coaches and trainers. It appeared he wasn't able to get up. He tried to sit up, but his face morphed into a mask of agony.

Carmen's stomach churned with nausea. She'd never seen Natron in pain, not like this, and he actively worked on increasing his pain tolerance. It was something he and Charles talked about all the time.

The air in the box had grown thin and the silence was interspersed with a few whispers. Then James picked up a remote control and turned up the volume so they could hear the announcers who were calling the game.

"Matt, it looks like a knee. See how the knee appears to buckle here."

Then they ran a tape in slow motion that showed Natron stretching out to catch the ball in the air, then pulling into his chest. As he came down with the ball, his hips rotated as he prepared to make the cut toward the end zone, and at that very instant a defender came in and tackled him hard at the knee. As they showed the grisly replay over and over again, it was easy to see Natron's left knee bend in a way that knees are not supposed to bend.

Several people gasped and groans were heard over the broadcast.

"That's gotta hurt, Steve. You hate to see that happen," the broadcaster said.

"You're right, Matt. First game back, the defending Conference Champions, he's got one touchdown on the day and they may be about to lose Natron Dakers."

"And that's going to hurt them."

The tape of the injury played over and over again until Carmen finally had to look away. Swallowing hard, she walked over to the window to see what was happening on the field and a sinking feeling overtook her as she watched Natron leave the field on a cart.

CHAPTER ELEVEN

Natron stretched his arms out in front of him, his fingers clasped the football, and he pulled it in. His cleats pressed into the turf, planting his left leg and he turned toward the end zone, all of it happening in a nanosecond. But before he could make the cut, the opposing team's cornerback ploughed into him and buckled his knee sideways.

Natron heard a snap and felt his knee go in a direction that was foreign to him. A stabbing pain gripped his left leg and he fell to the ground. Crumpled on the field, he tried to catch his breath. He rolled around, holding his knee at a ninety-degree ankle, but every time he changed position, a shooting pain exploded in his leg.

Right away the Vipers' training staff surrounded him, forming a circle with him at the center, shielding him from the voyeuristic cameras of the media. After answering a number of their questions and trying various movements, Natron realized he was unable to stand. Once that was ascertained, the training staff sent for the cart, a stretcher on wheels.

Dazed, Natron replayed what had just happened over and over again in his mind. Had he torn his ACL? Was that what he'd heard breaking? Whatever it was, it was something bad. Healthy most of his career, Natron had never had an injury sideline him before. At most he'd dealt with cramps and the occasional pulled muscle. But everything about this situation told him this injury would prove to be more serious.

While waiting for the cart to take him to the locker room, he started telling himself he'd only pulled a tendon. With a few ice packs and rehabbing, he could be back in time for their game against the Lions in two weeks.

The trainers tried to get him to straighten his leg, but each time he did, it caused him excruciating pain. Normally he would have had more of an awareness of the cameras and tried to control his reactions, but he was in such misery that he didn't care.

He winced when they helped him onto the cart. One of the trainers rode in the back with him to stabilize his throbbing leg. Reminding himself to be tough, Natron bit back the profanity that threatened to spew from his lips. Instead, he waved and smiled at the fans through gritted teeth. Rising to their feet, the crowd responded with a rousing cheer and he inhaled their adulation and support.

Upon entering the tunnel, Natron attempted to bend his leg, but the trainer stopped him, saying, "Keep it like this for now. We'll have an x-ray in a minute and an MRI at the hospital if necessary."

Natron nodded and closed his eyes, reliving the play over and over again. His leg had been extended and, with his cleat planted in the turf like it had been, his knee had been in a vulnerable position right when he'd been hit.

The stadium housed a special section dedicated to medical care, which was where the team doctor and trainers set up the x-ray machine and took pictures of the injured leg from several angles. While Natron waited for the results, the staff flipped on a monitor so he could watch the game being played on the field. As he watched he thought of how cocky he'd been on the field earlier. He'd taunted the defender covering him, his own words now coming back to haunt him. "You can't cover me, son. Ain't nobody can cover me!"

Natron let out a deep breath, wishing he could take back those words. They made him feel foolish now. Only moments ago he'd felt invincible. But Zeus had fallen off Mount Olympus, and it was more than his knee that was injured. His pride had taken a hit as well.

He made himself focus on the game. The Vipers were beating the Cougars 13-7 at the end of the second quarter. At least they were winning.

After what seemed like an hour, the team doctor came back in the room.

"So, Doc, when can I get back out there?" Natron asked, flashing his money grin.

"Natron, I'm sorry to tell you this… It looks like your season's over, son."

"What?" Natron's throat began to close and his heart threatened to come out of his chest, it was beating so hard. He hung onto the sides of the examination table because the room seemed to be spinning. Surely it couldn't be as bad as all that. "I don't understand. It's feeling better already," Natron said, full of false bravado.

"That's because you aren't moving it." He held up the x-ray for Natron to see. "Here's your tibia, the lower leg. And here's the ball socket that holds your knee in place."

Natron tried to focus on what he was seeing on the cloudy black and white film as the walls around him were still moving.

"The bone is broken off here," the doctor pointed with a pen. "Right down the center of the ball socket."

The information shocked to his system. This couldn't be happening to him.

"So I have a broken knee?"

"Essentially. You can't bear weight on it, and you'll need surgery to repair it."

"When?"

"The sooner the better. Preferably before it gets any more inflamed. We're calling the orthopedic surgeon now. Don't worry, Dr. Whitaker's the best there is and Buddy keeps him on payroll."

The doctor clapped him on the shoulder. "Sorry to see this happen. You okay? Got any questions?"

Natron's mind was whirring a hundred miles an hour and for once he was speechless. All he could do was shake his head.

"Alright. The ambulance will be here shortly. We'll get you on over to the hospital where you'll meet Dr. Whitaker. He'll be able to answer your questions better than I can as he'll be the one doing the surgery. Anyone you'd like me to call?"

Carmen. She was watching the game with James and their friends. His poor girl must be worried about him. He quickly gave the doctor her number and downed a few anti-inflammatory pills handed to him by one of the medical staff.

Lying back on the bed, he watched in disgust as the Los Angeles Cougars come from behind and won the game 21-13.

CHAPTER TWELVE

Carmen rushed through to the parking lot and was opening her car door when her phone rang. It was the team doctor telling her which hospital Natron was being taken to and that was about it. When she'd asked about his condition, he'd clammed up, mumbling something about confidentiality.

She climbed into the new Jetta Natron had bought her and drove toward UT Southwestern Medical Center. As she drove, her phone made continual 'bing' noises as dozens of text messages were delivered. While she knew it was a bad idea to check them while driving, her eyes darted to her phone once and a message from James was displayed on the screen.

Broken knee. Wow. Tough luck. Tell Natron we're all behind him.

Carmen's eyes widened. A broken knee? How did James know Natron's knee was broken and she didn't have a clue? She'd tried to get the information out of the doctor and failed. She wondered if it was true, and if it was, why she seemed to be the last to know.

She'd been left out of the loop, and all of a sudden she felt like a child with her nose pressed against the glass watching other children play at a party she wasn't invited to. Natron was her man, and she wished she'd been there with him, that she'd found out when he did. She wanted to be there to comfort him, help him, to be a part of his life. An icy shiver ran over her skin, but she kept driving.

Once Carmen arrived at the hospital, she had a difficult time finding Natron. Once the staff had learned she wasn't technically 'family,' they became tight-lipped after that and all she could get out of them was the runaround. Apparently being a patient's girlfriend gave you zero clout, especially when your boyfriend was a major celebrity.

She finally gave up and went to the vending machine, dropped in some coins, and comforted herself with a chocolate bar and a coke. Sitting down in the emergency room waiting room, she picked up a well-worn three-month-old issue of *People* magazine and flipped through it while she ate.

When she'd consumed the whole magazine and her snack, she sighed and settled in to watching some show about prospectors looking for aquamarines on the Weather Channel. Just as she was about to give up and go home, a nurse appeared and called her name. Jumping up, Carmen crossed the room in record time and practically accosted the woman.

"Carmen Harris?" the tiny blond nurse wearing peach-colored scrubs asked.

Carmen nodded. "Yes, that's me."

"I'll need to see some ID," the nurse said, and Carmen realized this woman was a petite little bulldog the hospital had assigned to keep Natron's fans and the paparazzi at bay.

Digging through her purse, Carmen retrieved her driver's license and handed it to the woman with a begrudging amount of respect.

"Alrighty then, if you'll just come back with me."

The nurse opened the door and led her into a room where Natron lay on a hospital bed, dressed in a white hospital gown flecked with blue stars. Whether it was the gown or the setting, she wasn't sure, but something had made her usually larger-than-life daddy appear small.

When he opened his mouth, she could tell he'd been taking some sort of pain medicine. His words looped and floated around in the air. "Carmen! Come here, babygirl. I'm glad you're here."

She smiled wanly. "Where else would I be, Natron?" she asked and bent to kiss him.

His eyes were glassy and he was calmer than she expected. "Broke my ball socket," he said, the corners of his mouth pulling back toward his ears.

"That's awful. What are they going to do?"

"Surgery. Tomorrow."

"So soon?"

"Yeah. Gotta fix me up so I can get back on the field." He paused. "You gotta see this x-ray. It's wicked bad, this break."

"Okay," she said, sitting down in a chair next to his bed. "Can I get you anything? Are you hungry or thirsty?"

"Nah, thanks, babe." He motioned to a large cup filled with ice water. "They're takin' real good care of me."

Carmen had been worried Natron would be upset about the injury, but it appeared the morphine drip had quashed his concerns for the moment, which was a relief. She waited until he fell asleep before even considering going home. The nurse in the peach scrubs came in and showed Carmen the x-rays, went over his treatment plan, and gave her instructions for coming back for the surgery the next day. Though Carmen considered spending the night, she decided to go home so she could pack a bag for Natron and herself. He'd be in the hospital for at least one night and she'd stay with him then to make sure he got everything he needed.

Leaving the hospital, she walked down the deserted fluorescent-lit hallway. The click of her heels against the laminate floor echoed through the hallways and she was reminded why hospitals always seemed eerie late at night. When she opened the exit door, she took a deep breath of the midnight air, and despite a phone full of messages from friends, Carmen felt completely alone.

The next morning at 6, Carmen opened the door to Natron's room to find a dark-haired woman standing beside him holding his hand. The woman was clucking over him and he seemed to know her.

Natron lit up when he saw Carmen and waved to her. "Hey, babygirl."

The woman turned and pasted on a fake smile. "Hello. You must be Carmen." Even at this ungodly hour of the morning, the woman was as put together as a model about to walk the runway. Her hair was curled so perfectly that Carmen wondered if it was a wig. Her creamy *café au lait* skin reminded Carmen of a frothy drink one could order at Starbucks, and she wore a well-cut beige pantsuit that set off her flashing amber eyes.

"Yes," Carmen stammered, confused.

"I'm Veronique, Natron's mamma."

"Oh!" Cutting her eyes at Natron, Carmen smiled sweetly. "He didn't tell me you were coming."

"Sorry, babe. I was a bit out of it last night." Natron gave her his most pitiful puppy-dog eyes.

"That's fine," Carmen said, feeling out of place.

"Well, of course I'm here. My baby's having surgery, I had to come take care of him." Veronique said, pinching Natron's cheek.

Great, Carmen thought. *Then what am I supposed to do?*

Carmen took a deep breath and reminded herself that this was not about *her*. It was Natron who was injured and having surgery. She needed to focus on him, helping him as best she could.

"So when are they coming to take you to surgery?" Carmen asked.

"Any minute now," his mother answered.

"Do you need anything?" Carmen asked.

"I'm really thirsty, but they told me I can't have anything to drink," Natron replied.

"Carmen, why don't you go to the nurse's station and see if he could have just a few ice chips?" Veronique asked.

Carmen agreed and walked down to the nurse's station. She found a nurse who agreed he could have a couple of ice chips and gave her a small paper cup half-filled with tiny ice pellets from the kitchen.

By the time she walked back to Natron's room, it was empty. Natron was gone and apparently his mother had gone with him.

"Ugh!" Carmen muttered under her breath and went to find him. Of course she ran into the same trouble she had the night before, not being 'family.' She finally gave up and asked directions to the surgery waiting room.

When she got there, she found Natron's mother sitting there smugly reading a magazine.

"Hey," Carmen said.

Peering over the top of her *Vogue*, Veronique said, "There you are. I had no idea where you'd run off to."

Carmen thought her head might explode. "I-I-I went to get him some ice chips, as you requested."

There it was, the fake smile again. "Well, I don't know where you went to get them. We looked everywhere for you… He's in surgery now."

Carmen just stood there staring.

"It should take a few hours. If you like, I'll give you a call once it's over."

Planting herself in the seat across from Natron's mother, Carmen said, "Oh, no, I'm fine, Veronique. I'll wait." Then she opened her phone and began checking emails.

"Suit yourself," Veronique said dismissively.

Carmen had heard Natron talk about his mother. Veronique had raised him as a single mother, the two of them against the world. Clearly his mother didn't relish an outsider disrupting their little dyad. Carmen wished she could talk to Natron about his mother, but this wasn't the time for him to worry about his mother being jealous of his girlfriend.

When the doctor came out to discuss the surgery, Veronique practically shoved Carmen out of the way, then did most of the talking. Fortunately, Dr. Whitaker made a point of including Carmen in the conversation as he explained that he installed a stainless steel plate along the outside of Natron's tibia, stretching up along the curve of the ball joint. The plate along with the screws used to secure it would become a permanent part of him and would serve as a sort of internal cast so an external plaster cast would not be necessary.

He showed the women an x-ray of the plate now implanted in Natron's leg, complete with the eight screws that went through the plate into the bone to hold it in place. Dr. Whitaker told them, "The stability of the knee is of utmost importance for an athlete like Natron, and the plate in his knee will give him the extra support he will need when putting the kind of pressure on it he does on a regular basis. Keeping that in mind, I did everything I could to save as much of the cartilage around the knee as possible. I had to cut the lateral meniscus in order to install the plate, so he will have to recuperate from that as well."

"What's the meniscus?" Veronique asked.

"The cartilage around the knee."

"Oh." Veronique's brows knitted together.

"It's too early to tell how much overall cartilage and ligament damage has been done. The first thing we have to do is heal the bone. That's the biggest injury, and while he's healing from that, the cartilage and ligaments should heal up as well, especially since he's young and in such good condition."

"Will he be able to play football again?" Carmen asked.

"With the ball socket being broken the way it was, there are bound to be cartilage issues, so I can't make any guarantees his knee will ever get to where it was before, but I hope it will. We won't be able to really assess the situation until he's able to bear weight on it again and that will take a few months."

Veronique and Carmen thanked him and he gave them his card and told them to call him if they had any questions or if Natron had any problems. Natron would stay in the hospital for two days to be sure there were no complications, and Carmen had to hold back a chuckle when Dr. Whitaker said Natron would be going home in a wheelchair. He was *not* going to like that.

For the first two and a half months, Natron wasn't allowed to put any pressure on his injured knee. After that, he'd be allowed to put fifty pounds of weight on the knee and slowly work his way back to standing on it. It sounded like they had a long road ahead of them, but Carmen vowed to be by Natron's side. They could do this together, and it would probably bring them closer.

Carmen and Veronique waited another hour before being told which room Natron had been moved to. Carmen went to her car to retrieve the bags she'd packed for Natron and herself. She knew Natron well enough to bring his laptop, his headphones, and his favorite sneakers for his trip home. All of that made his bag super heavy and she was out of breath by the time she found his room and walked through the door.

Setting the bags down with a thud, she noticed Natron was sleeping in the hospital bed.

Veronique shushed her and sweetly asked Carmen to "run to the cafeteria and bring us a salad, would you, dear?"

Carmen nodded; she'd resigned herself to her role as Veronique's errand girl. But she did stop to kiss Natron on the head before making her way to the cafeteria. He stirred, saying, "Love you, babygirl." Even though he was asleep, he knew she was there. His words gave her strength and during the elevator ride back from the cafeteria, she promised herself to be more patient with his mother. After all, Natron *was* her only child.

Upon entering the room, Carmen found Veronique filling out a bunch of paperwork. The night before, Carmen had been told by a nurse that she would be asked to fill out paperwork to get Natron a set of crutches and a walker for the first few days and that could be used in the shower.

Apparently now Veronique was filling out those papers.

Handing Veronique a salad, Carmen sat down on the small couch and pulled out her knitting, determined not to feel useless.

Veronique turned the television to soap operas and watched them in silence, every now and then getting up to fuss over her sleeping son.

When dinnertime came, the hospital staff rolled in a tray for not only Natron but also for Veronique.

"How did you get a tray?" Carmen asked.

"I was here when they asked. I guess this morning before you arrived."

"Oh," Carmen said flatly, her stomach grumbling. "Guess I'll go down to the cafeteria and get something."

"You can go on home, dear. We'll see you tomorrow."

"I was planning to stay the night with him," Carmen protested. "I brought my bag and everything." She gestured to her suitcase.

"So did I," Veronique said, a challenge in her voice. "I'm his mother, dear. You just run along and come back tomorrow when he's awake. There's really not much you can do here now."

Carmen frowned at her sleeping boyfriend. Veronique was right. There was nothing she could do here while Natron slept, except feel her presence was unwanted. "Alright."

She kissed Natron on the cheek, picked up her bag, and wished Veronique a nice evening.

Walking down the hall, she fought the dreadful churning in her stomach that told her this injury was slowly squeezing her out of Natron's life.

CHAPTER THIRTEEN

From the moment Natron got hurt, Carmen had envisioned herself taking care of him, nursing him back to health. He was such a caring daddy, always meeting her needs and doing things for her. This would be the perfect opportunity to pay him back for all the wonderful things he had done for her. Her turn to care for him.

But it had been a week since Natron had been released from the hospital and today Veronique was tending to him. Carmen had been invited to Charmaine's place for brunch and she was looking forward to seeing her girlfriends. The other 'Daddy's Girls' would be there and Carmen was looking forward to catching up with her friends. The other girls either had a daddy and were in a dominant/submissive relationship with him, or were between daddies like Charmaine and Sloane.

Come to think of it, Carmen had never known Charmaine to have a daddy. The girl was too wild and always had several guys on the chain, but Charmaine talked about wanting a daddy. Though she was way too intimidated by Charmaine to tell her this, Carmen thought her friend could really use a daddy to keep her in line.

Sloane, on the other hand, had been hung up on a dom named Rocco for as long as Carmen could remember. A workaholic, Sloane spent most of her time designing clothes, and Carmen wondered if she used work as a distraction from her unrequited love.

Carmen pulled the Jetta to a stop at the front of Charmaine's building and handed the keys to the valet. Would she ever get used to the opulent lifestyle Charmaine, James, and Natron led? Her lower middle-class upbringing consisted of clipped coupons, a one-story ranch house, and hand-me-downs from her cousins, so having servants, doormen, and stylists took some getting used to.

After a quick trip up the elevator, Carmen barely had a chance to knock before Charmaine threw open the door and enveloped her in a bear hug. "Come in, come in, girl. The champagne's flowing. How *are* you? How's Natron?"

Charmaine was striking as usual in a low-cut black jumpsuit trimmed in leopard, her sun-striped mane spilling out in every direction, looking every ounce the sparkling golden Leo that she was.

"I'm good. He's doing well," Carmen responded.

She must have been the last one to arrive because all the other girls were lounging in the living room sipping Cristal from crystal flutes—Sloane, Lucinda, Marley, Nellie, and Kimberly. They all rose to greet her and hugs were exchanged all around.

Kimberly, the mother hen of the group, fixed her big brown eyes on Carmen and whispered, "How are you *really* doing?"

Carmen smiled. "I'm fine," she said, shaking off the truth. She didn't want to fall apart within three minutes of walking through the door.

Perching on the arm of a white suede couch, Carmen accepted Marley's offer of a glass of bubbly. She hadn't seen Marley since the day of Natron's injury, though they'd texted and spoken on the phone almost every day. Carmen had always felt close to Marley because they were both new to the opulent world of money and fame. When she and Marley hung out, it felt like she was spending time with a friend from high school.

"Tell us about Natron's injury. I want to hear all the gory details," Sloane pressed.

"Eww, Sloane. Not that gory, feel free to leave that part out." Kimberly made a face.

Carmen filled them in about the surgery. Then, wanting to change the subject, she turned to Lucinda.

"Long time no see, Lucy. How've you been?" Carmen asked.

Lucinda and Colin, a former conductor, had a daddy/little girl relationship both in and out of the bedroom. Lucinda had told the girls many times that she credited Colin for her success with all his prodding her to practice and study. With her hectic travel and performance schedule, it was unusual for Lucinda to be in town when the girls had one of their get-togethers. The last time they'd met, she was in Norway giving a private concert for the royal family.

"Exhausted," Lucinda sighed. "I just got back from Prague last night. But I had to come by to see how you were, and hear about Natron."

"Thanks, Lucinda. You're sweet, but we're fine," Carmen said.

"Then how's work going?" Lucinda asked. "I saw your portrait of Natron at the portrait show at the Guggenheim Museum. I stopped by and saw it when I was in New York a couple of weeks ago. Impressive."

"Aw, thanks. I haven't had much of a chance to paint lately. Fortunately the woman whose portrait I'm doing right now is a socialite, and apparently she's so tickled to have her name linked with Natron's that she didn't mind pushing back the completion date on her portrait. She called me the other day and grilled me about Natron. I think she wants to brag to her friends that she's in the know." Carmen giggled. "That's good, I guess."

Sloane nodded. "She's all about the drama. When will he be able to play again?"

"The doctors aren't sure. We won't know much about that until he can start to put weight on his leg, and that won't be for another three months."

A chorus of groans rose from the group.

"I know. It sucks," Carmen said.

"What's going to happen to his endorsements?" asked Nellie, the former beauty queen whose currency of choice was fame.

"Nellie!" Kimberly hissed.

"What? Don't tell me y'all weren't thinking it," Nellie pouted.

"No, that's okay. I don't know. I haven't heard anything…" Carmen's voice trailed off.

"What kind of patient is he?" Kimberly asked.

"A crappy one, I'm sure. Men can be such babies." Charmaine rolled her eyes.

"Actually, I don't really know," Carmen said sheepishly.

"What? How can you not know?" Marley asked.

"Well, his mother is the one taking care of him," Carmen said.

"Shut up!" Nellie said. "You mean his mamma has taken over?"

"Pretty much," Carmen said with a shrug.

"What about you?" Marley asked.

"Have you seen him?" Kimberly asked.

"I go see him just about every day, but she's always hanging around. We have no privacy, and it's super awkward," Carmen said.

"I'll bet," Sloane said.

"How did that happen?" Marley asked.

"I don't know. He called her when he got hurt and she drove all night to get here. Once she arrived, I was kinda shoved out of the picture."

"That sucks," Marley frowned.

"Yeah," Carmen nodded. "I don't know what to do about it. I had this mental picture of me taking care of him, you know—me and Natron facing adversity together, but that is *not* what is happening."

She had pictured him on a pull-out sofa at her loft, watching her work while she prepared him yummy meals and catered to his every whim. Their daddy/little girl relationship would have the chance to blossom with all the extra time they'd be able to spend together, and with her nursing Daddy back to health. But her fantasy would remain just that, thanks to Veronique. Natron's mother had ensconced herself in his mansion and appointed herself head nurse and caregiver, while Carmen was relegated to a supporting role.

The visits were awkward; with his mother hovering around, she and Natron had no privacy and the closeness they'd once shared seemed to have evaporated. She felt like a stranger in his life now, an intruder almost. To make matters worse, she felt guilty even having these feelings. This was a time where she should be focused on Natron and his recovery, not on her petty jealousies of his mother.

"Have you talked to him about it?" Kimberly asked, always the sensible one.

Carmen shook her head.

"Well, you need to. Communication is key," Lucinda piped up.

"But I don't want to make this about me and my insecurities. She's a single mom, he's her only child. They have this bond, and I'm afraid if I make a big deal of it, he'll see me as too demanding and I'll lose out," Carmen said.

Some of the girls nodded their heads in understanding.

Charmaine disagreed. "Fuck that. He's your man. You should be the one taking care of him if that's what you want. Personally I'd be happy to let someone else do it, but I'm not much of a nurse."

"At least talk to him. Let him know you're feeling pushed aside," Kimberly encouraged.

"You think?" Carmen wavered.

"Yes! At least tell him you miss the sex," Nellie said.

"But what if that makes him feel bad he can't do it right now?" Carmen asked.

Sloane snorted. "Seriously? From what you've told us, I'm pretty sure Natron could find a way."

Carmen hadn't thought of that. Natron was rather creative in the bedroom. "Okay. I'll talk to him."

"That's all you can do," Lucinda said.

Carmen nodded, grateful for her friends. She considered what separated these girls from her other friends. The biggest thing was they all liked to be dominated in the bedroom. They liked a take-charge kind of man who would also take care of them and protect them. At first Carmen had thought some of Natron's 'Daddy' requests were a little odd, but she'd grown accustomed to them. Now she even craved some of them, like a good spanking when she was bad.

"Ting!" A timer went off. Nellie popped up and told them the food was ready. They all went over and chose a seat at Charmaine's elaborately carved dining table. The chairs were upholstered in the finest silk, each one boasted an elaborate blue and gold pattern that was unique yet complemented the others. The china was edged in sapphire and the flatware and crystal goblets dripped with gold. A mass of pink peonies nestled in a wide vase of robin's-egg blue served as a centerpiece. The girls didn't always dine in so much splendor, but Charmaine was known for setting a fine table.

They drank more champagne, and ate the frittata and little mini quiches Nellie had baked to go with a variety of homemade breads and a colorful fruit salad swimming in poppy-seed dressing.

"God, I'm going to have to spend an extra hour at the gym because of you," Charmaine grumbled at Nellie.

Nellie was the best cook in the bunch, though Kimberly was a close second, and the two of them had been teaching Marley a thing or two. Sloane and Lucinda existed purely off takeout and reservations. Charmaine usually had a chef on the payroll, but they never lasted long. Carmen's cooking prowess fell somewhere in the middle. She loved the ease of takeout when she was working, but her mom had taught her how to make a few yummy dishes.

The girls talked of Lucinda's recent adventures in Prague, Nellie's latest decorating project, and Charmaine's father's latest marital fiasco. The man had been married six times and the marriage license office in Las Vegas recently told him that seven marriages was the legal limit, so he put the brakes on his latest planned wedding and his new girlfriend was in a tizzy that she might not become the seventh and final Mrs. Bainbridge.

Charmaine had a boatload of siblings from each of her father's marriages. She was the oldest and her mother had only had one child with Quintin Bainbridge. Charmaine stayed a cold arm's length away from her half-siblings, and the only familial connections she kept strong were those she had with her father's banker and his lawyer.

After they'd stuffed themselves, the girls agreed to meet next month for a dinner party. Carmen hugged everyone and said her good-byes. In the elevator, bolstered by a couple of glasses of liquid courage, Carmen decided it was time to tell Natron how set aside she'd been feeling, and she sent him a text as she handed her ticket to the valet.

CHAPTER FOURTEEN

Veronique opened Natron's front door looking as chic as a fashion model and greeted Carmen. "Hello, dear. Won't you come in."

Carmen gulped and managed a smile as she followed Veronique down the corridor to Natron's bedroom, Veronique's wide hips swaying gracefully in front of her. Cringing, it suddenly occurred to Carmen the reason Natron might appreciate her full figure was because it resembled his mamma's.

Turning the doorknob, Veronique's voice dripped with honeyed sweetness as she said, "I just gave him his pain pill so he'll probably doze off in a few minutes."

Carmen rolled her eyes. *Of course you did.*

"Babygirl!" Natron said, sounding loopy but excited. He looked fine, but he was missing some of his usual animation. He seemed weaker than she was used to, which made perfect sense.

She crossed the room and pulled him to her, cradling his head against her bosom. "Hey, baby. I missed you."

Veronique loitered in the doorway until Natron said, "Thanks, Mamma. Can you close the door behind you?"

Veronique sniffed disapprovingly but she exited, closing the door behind her. Carmen was certain Veronique was outside with her ear pressed up against the door.

Whispering in his ear, Carmen said, "Do you think you could get her to go somewhere, run an errand or something?"

"Why? And why are you whispering?" Natron asked.

Raising her eyebrows, Carmen whispered, "Privacy."

A wolfish grin spread across his face. "Oh, I get ya now. Babygirl's been missing her daddy. Okay, I see." He laughed and picked up his phone.

Carmen sat on the edge of the bed, careful not to disturb his knee or the ice packs balancing atop it.

When he was finished texting, he looked up at Carmen. "That will keep her out of our hair for a while."

"What did you say?"

"That I wanted some of these special pita chips, but that you had to go across town to the Fresh Market to get them."

"And she bought that?"

"Sure. I used a smiley face. Mamma wants her baby boy to have whatever he wants."

Carmen felt her forehead wrinkle. "So does *your* babygirl," she said in a tone that was more sullen than she'd intended.

He took her hand. "Hey, what's wrong? You seem mad."

"It's nothing. Hey, I don't know how to ask you this, but…"

"Just ask."

"Okay. Your mom, her skin is so much lighter than yours…"

"Yeah, that's because her mamma, my grandma is white."

"Oh, so because your grandmother was white, does that make it easier to date a white girl like me?"

"Girl, what has gotten into your head?" He frowned. "I don't know. I just like you; the color of your skin doesn't matter to me."

"What about how curvy your mom is? Is that what makes you like me even though I'm overweight?"

"Baby, I think you're beautiful. I love your curves, but not because I'm in love with my mamma or some other weird shit. What's gotten into you?" He shook his head.

"I don't know. Sometimes I wonder what you see in me. I mean, you're this big superstar. You could have any woman you want." She twisted one of her errant curls.

"Carmen, I don't know what makes people fall for each other, but I fell for you. Babygirl, I'm crazy about you. You're the perfect girl for me."

She crinkled her nose. "Do you think she's gone?"

"Yeah. I heard her car leaving just now. What's going on between you and Mamma anyway?"

Taking a deep breath, Carmen launched into a diatribe. "Ever since your mother has been here, actually ever since you were injured, I haven't had any time with you."

He listened and nodded his head encouragingly. "You're right. Go on."

"And I feel selfish even mentioning this because you're all laid up, unable to walk, your career's on hold… I mean, you have more problems right now than this. But I just feel squeezed out, like I don't matter."

He held his arms out to her and she laid her head against his chest. "I'm sorry, baby. I should have realized. Guess I got so wrapped up in all this stuff with my leg that I… I'm sorry."

"It's okay."

"No, it's not. You know, I wouldn't have thought you'd have wanted to be all in the middle of all this… mess. I like to be able to take care of you, not the other way around." He kissed the top of her head.

"Natron, of course I want to take care of you. You're my daddy, and I want to make things better for you, the way you have for me. But there's no room in all this for me. Your mom has pretty much taken over."

He nodded. "She likes to feel needed. You know she doesn't have anybody else."

Carmen snorted. "She needs a boyfriend."

"Hey, that's not a bad idea."

"See if you can get her on an online dating service."

He laughed. "You're really ready to get rid of her, aren't you?"

"It's just that I thought it was going to be you and me. And instead it's you and her."

"I'm sorry, baby. I'll see what I can do to fix that. You want to move in for a while?" he asked hopefully.

He'd been trying to get her to move in with him for months and the idea was becoming more appealing, but Carmen wasn't ready to give up her place or her freedom. "Not yet," she hedged.

"Then I'm going to need my mom around to help me until I can get around better by myself."

She grimaced. "Don't you have servants for that?"

"You are *not* yourself, girl. I think you're jealous," he teased.

She pounded a fist on the bed and whined, "Yes, I am jealous. It all just sucks."

"True that. Look, I'll talk to Mamma and get her to take some days off to go do other things. I'll send her shopping. She'll love that. And you can come over and spend the days with me. How does that sound?"

"Good. That would be great, actually."

"All right. Then we'll work up to some nights." He winked at her.

"You know, Daddy, it doesn't have to be night…" she said innocently.

"Oh, I see. Now I know what my girl's been needin'. Go lock that door and take your clothes off."

Her concern about his mother returning was overshadowed by her desire to obey him, so she pressed in the lock button on the door handle and disrobed.

"First, I think you need a spanking for not telling me about your feelings earlier," Natron said.

"But…" she began to protest.

"But nothin'." He raised himself to a more seated position, propped up by a slew of pillows. "Come here and lie over my lap."

She was tentative in her movements. "I'm afraid I'm going to hurt you."

"I'm tougher than I look," he said. "You're not going to lie on my knee.

I'll be fine."

"If you say so," she said, draping herself across his crotch. "If I hurt you, please tell me."

"Girl, for someone who's about to get a spanking, you sure are talking a lot. I'll be fine, now hush."

Carmen pursed her lips together. It had been a long time since she'd had a spanking. The delicious anticipation rising inside her made her realize she'd missed it.

She heard him rustling papers and shifting slightly underneath her, but instead of turning to look, she closed her eyes and waited. To her surprise, something bulky and slick came down on her ass.

He hit her with it again. It smarted, and this time she turned to see what he was using.

In his hand he wielded a rolled-up *Sports Illustrated* magazine. She made a face. He was essentially hitting her with a rolled-up newspaper—like a dog that had peed in the wrong spot.

With the next swat she let out a groan, as much protesting as she would do. Hell, if she complained he'd just do it longer. Or harder.

She tried not to wiggle, not only because it would increase her punishment, but also because she didn't want to accidentally bump his knee. He smacked her ass until she thought she might explode, and she had to remind herself to breathe.

Underneath her, his cock grew harder and she could feel it throbbing against her pelvis. The more he struck her, the more firm and swollen he became. The thought of taking him in her mouth made her salivate and she bit her lip in frustration.

Heat had begun to rise on her posterior. Just when it felt like flames might erupt from her skin, he stopped and rubbed his cool palm across her fleshy globes.

"Mmm, I've missed this ass, all cherry-red and hot like this," he crooned.

"Mmmhmm," she responded.

After caressing her skin for a few minutes, he went back to swatting.

She let go of all the tension she'd felt over the situation with his mother and a peace began to wash over her with each thwack of the magazine.

When he was finished, she said, "Thank you, Daddy."

"You're welcome, love. I have missed you. Now climb on top of Daddy and fuck my brains out."

Carmen giggled. "Really? I'm scared I'll hurt you," she said, though she *had* been craving skin-on-skin contact with him.

Natron lifted his shirt over his head and gingerly pulled down his shorts, revealing his huge, pulsing erection. "I'm not gonna tell you to do anything that will hurt me. Now hop on and get busy."

Slowly, she set one thigh on either side of his hips, careful not to bump his knee. Lowering her hips, she rubbed her aching pussy against the length of his hardened shaft. Relief flooded her consciousness, and the experience of being with him again overwhelmed her. She felt like she'd been deprived of water for days and was finally now able to drink.

He reached up and fondled her breasts as they swung in front of his face. She moaned when he pinched and twisted her nipples just the way she liked. Leaning over, she touched her lips to his. He smelled of Irish Spring soap and his favorite deodorant as he captured her tongue hungrily between his lips and sucked on it.

Their hips gyrated against each other, desperately increasing the need building inside her. Unable to wait any longer, Carmen sat up and buried his cock inside her slick, wet channel. After luxuriating in the joy of being filled, she began to move up and down, and the friction between their bodies kicked her senses into high gear.

Soon the look on Natron's face changed from that of bliss to one of discomfort.

"Daddy, what's wrong, am I hurting you?" Carmen fretted.

"It's this angle. And it's hard not to want to pump into you from underneath, but that hurts my knee too much. Let's try something else."

She dismounted and sat beside him on the bed, concerned. "Maybe we just stop."

He shook his head vehemently. "No way you're getting me this worked up and we're not finishing this. Here, I'm going to lie flat and you climb on top of me 69 style. Suck my cock, girl, and drop your pussy over my face."

She hesitated, feeling incredibly self-conscious about having her pussy hovering over his face. It made her feel terribly exposed and vulnerable, and she had managed to avoid doing that with Natron. Until now.

It didn't bother her when she was lying on her back and he went down on her. Perhaps this felt too dominant. Whatever it was she didn't like it. But she wanted to please him, and it had been so long since they'd been together. Disobeying him now wasn't an option.

Awkwardly, she positioned her body over his as he'd requested, her desire was replaced by anxiety. Going to her elbows, she used one hand to jerk his cock and she ran her tongue around the head. She'd kept her ass high in the air, but Natron wasn't having that. He slapped her buttocks and dragged her pussy toward his eager mouth.

Carmen moaned and forced his cock to the back of her throat. Her mouth slid up and down, as she rolled her tongue along his shaft, then pushed it back as far as she could take him. Natron's hips pressed into her, but then he stilled and his tongue entered her pussy.

Modesty told her to resist, but her arousal disavowed any ideas of propriety she might have entertained. His lips sucked in her outer lips, then he moved on to her plumped clit. Licking all around it, he teased her before flicking his tongue across the swollen center of her sex. He fucked her with his fingers, all the while licking her from perineum to her throbbing hot button.

The more excited she became, the more zealously she sucked his cock. They'd established a rhythm of oral pleasuring, a dance of lustful abandon with their mouths that spun Carmen into a frenzy of spasms. Every one of the zillions of nerve endings in her clit felt like it exploded in ecstasy.

As she climaxed, he shot his load down her throat. She shook with her ongoing orgasm and continued to suckle him until the waves subsided for both of them. Swallowing the last droplets of his cum, she fell over to the empty side of the bed.

There was a knock at the door.

"Natron? Natron, why is this door locked?" Veronique's irritated voice came from the other side.

Carmen jumped up like she'd been stung, and flew off the bed to retrieve her clothes.

Natron chuckled, "Hang on, Mom," and pulled up his shorts.

"I feel like we're in high school," Carmen hissed as she dressed.

"I know, right?" he said, amused by the whole thing.

"It's not funny. She's going to think badly about me," Carmen said.

Natron waved his hand as if to say, "Who cares?"

Carmen shot him a dirty look and straightened her shirt before opening the door. "Veronique, we didn't hear you come in."

Veronique raised a disapproving perfectly penciled eyebrow at Carmen and breezed past her. "Natron, honey, I hope these are the ones you wanted. They had two different kinds. I texted you, but you didn't answer me," she said, handing him a bag of chips.

Natron turned on the charm. "Oh, I'm sorry, Mamma. Carmen and I got to visitin' and I must not have heard it."

"Uh-huh," Veronique responded, clearly not buying it. "Well, I'm going to see that dinner is on schedule. Can I get you anything? Do you need another ice pack?"

"No, thanks," Natron said, tearing into the bag of pita chips.

"Do you need any help with anything, Veronique?" Carmen asked.

"No, thanks, dear. Just don't tire Natron out. He's supposed to be resting, you know, keeping his knee *immobilized*." With that, she marched off, leaving the door wide open.

Once she was out of earshot, Carmen said in a low voice, "I really don't think your mom likes me."

"That's not true. She's just being protective. Don't take it personally, babygirl," Natron said.

"If you say so," Carmen said, completely unconvinced. Something told her it would be a long time before things got back to the way they used to be with Natron. If that was even possible.

Natron threw the *Sports Illustrated* across the room.

Everything was turning to shit.

It had only been a couple of hours since Carmen had left, and he missed her already. He hated not spending time at her loft watching her work. That was his down time. The time for the two of them. But since he broke his knee he hadn't wanted to be a burden to her.

He hated not being able to fuck his girl this afternoon. How sad was that? Of course that was temporary, but telling himself that didn't make it better. His relationship with Carmen was suffering, and his mamma was driving him insane—always hovering over him, treating him like a baby.

But dammit, he needed someone to bring him things, carry things for him, and empty the plastic urinal next to his bed. He took a deep breath and tried to ease his intensifying anxiety. When he'd seen Carmen, he had purposely not told her what a setback this injury was to his career.

The Vipers had put him on injured reserve, which basically meant he was off the team until he was healed and ready to play. There were only a handful of players who had kept in touch with him after he'd been deactivated, and one of them was his fellow wide receiver Marvin Stalcup.

For the past two weeks, Natron had watched Marvin light up the opposing defense and rise to the top of the leader list in yards returned. His friendship with Marvin had always been characterized by good-natured ribbing and friendly competition. Having Marvin on his team made him a better player, and vice versa.

To save face, Natron pretended to be happy for Marvin's success, but in reality he was envious as hell. It ate him up inside that Marvin's success had come at his expense. That him being out for the season cleared the way for his friend to basically replace him on the Vipers' team.

Isolated from his team, unable to compete, reduced to an invalid, and now his wallet was being affected. He hadn't told Carmen that his endorsements had all but dried up since news broke that he'd be out for the year. According to his agent, most of the companies had put their deal 'on hold,' while a few had unceremoniously dumped him as their spokesman.

The toothpaste deal was the only one still in play, at least his agent had confirmation of that. His salary with the Vipers ought to cover his bills, but he was taking a hit from this injury on every front.

Rummaging on the bedside table, he found a pain pill, popped it in his mouth, and swallowed.

CHAPTER FIFTEEN

Carmen turned the key in her front door, and opened it to find Natron leaning on his crutches with a 'you-caught-me-with-my-hand-in-the-cookie-jar' look on his face.

It had been a month and a half since his surgery and though he still wasn't able to put weight on his bad leg, he got around amazingly well on his crutches. Only an athlete like him could maneuver crutches in a way that helped him move faster than he did when he was able-bodied. In fact, he wore out the rubber tips of them every other day. They'd cleaned out every drugstore in the Greater Dallas–Fort Worth area, and they were about to have to start ordering the tips online.

"Hey, Natron, what are you up to?" Carmen greeted him. She hadn't expected him to be at her place, but it was a nice surprise. He was able to drive now, and spent more time with her these days, much to his mother's dismay.

"I've got a new game for us to play," he said with a wink.

"You do, huh?" She set her bags from the drugstore down on the counter.

"I do." He hopped over to her and hugged her to him. His new way of moving was to basically hop on one leg and use the crutches as a supportive aid as he catapulted himself forward. It was truly amazing to watch. Most people Carmen had seen using crutches sort of hobbled around, while Natron practically flew.

"That sounds fun. Should I pour us a beer first?"

"Oh, you're definitely going to want a beer for this one."

She knit her brows together. What was he up to now?

Sidling over to the refrigerator, she opened two bottles of light beer. She drank light because of the lower calories, and Natron wasn't usually picky.

Handing him the bottle, she said, "Okay. Tell me about this game you've come up with."

He had already maneuvered himself into one of the comfortable chairs he'd bought for her place. "Alright, but you're gonna want to sit down for this one."

She sat on the chair opposite him.

"Have you ever heard of pony play?" he asked, barely containing the excitement in his voice.

She considered this. "Yes, but I'm not sure I really know what it is."

"Well, I've been researching it. Gonna show you some pics on my phone."

She nodded, unsure what to say.

"Apparently some people do this without the sex, like they have their partner dress up like a horse and pull them around in a cart," he explained, looking perplexed. "I can't really see doin' it without the sex, but then everything about you makes me think of sex, so…"

Carmen eyed him skeptically. "Let me see these pictures." Natron had always been adventurous when it came to sex, but this was beyond anything he'd ever talked with her about before. Was this a long-held fantasy of his?

Natron pulled out his phone, opened a window, and handed it to her. "You can scroll through and see what I'm talkin' about."

The first picture showed a sexy-looking girl with a head-gear on that had ears and what looked like blinders on the side. She was naked except for a leather harness with some straps (none of which covered her naughty bits) and a pair of boots. One of her heels was kicked back so you could see that the bottom of the footwear was made in a horseshoe pattern.

Scrolling to the next picture, this one showed a sub with a black bit in her mouth. Her hands were bound above her head and her dom was swatting her with a riding crop. Carmen felt a bit of heat surge to her crotch.

The next picture showed a guy with an erection about to fuck a girl who was on all fours, her front arms sheathed in black leather 'legs' of some sort. The girl was wearing a butt plug with a tail hanging from it similar to a horse's, and a black hood covered her head. While she didn't care for the hood, the rest of the scene seemed kinda hot. Weird, but hot.

Carmen's eyes met Natron's. "Really?" she asked.

"Yeah, babygirl. It's just fun. I want you to be my little fuck-pony. I got all the stuff."

"You what? What stuff?" Her heart beat faster, and she reminded herself it was good to get out of her comfort zone sometimes. She could always say 'safeword' if she needed to.

"In the bag over there," he pointed, and she got up to retrieve a large black duffel bag he'd brought.

She unzipped the bag and the first thing she pulled out was a stainless steel butt plug with a dark tail that felt stiff like horsehair, similar to the one in the picture. Then she found some cuffs with chains attached to them, the use of which was unclear. The bag also contained a short, purple, glittery crop, a leather headpiece, and a rubber bit.

Natron looked tremendously pleased with himself. He could scarcely sit still, he was so excited. "What do you think?"

"Um, I think that I love you and I'll try anything once," she said, forcing a smile.

"Aww, babygirl. Tell you what. I promise Daddy's gonna make it worth your while if you let me dress you up like a pony and fuck the shit out of you."

Her smile began to feel more real. Even if it wasn't her kink, she could at least try it for him. He was her dominant, after all. That meant not only that she should obey him, but also that he often knew what was best for her.

"Can you do whatever you have planned with your knee?" she asked. Until now they had mostly been having sex in the missionary position. He managed it by supporting all his weight on his good knee. It took a lot of strength to do it that way, and he always worked up a sweat, but he claimed it was a great way for him to be able to get some cardio work in.

"Pppshh! Don't you worry 'bout my knee, girl. You're gonna have enough to worry about. Go ahead on up those stairs and get naked. I'll be right behind you."

Carmen downed the rest of her beer. "I'll bring the bag."

"That's a good girl," he said, finishing his.

Natron scooted up the stairs on his butt the way kids do when they're playing. He immobilized his bad knee as he bumped up the stairs holding onto his crutches, a move he'd perfected in the last couple of weeks. He laid the crutches on the floor and sat on the edge of the bed. "Bring me that bag," he said in a hoarse voice.

She did, and he spent a few minutes attaching the rubber bit to the leather head-piece. Then he handed it to her and told her to go put in on in front of a mirror and come back for him to buckle it.

In the bathroom, Carmen took off her clothes, put on the head-piece, and stood before the mirror. She was surprised at how attractive she looked in the thing. A leather strap dipped to a pleasing 'v' shape upon her forehead. She slid the bit into her mouth and admired the interesting angles of the blinders on each side. Overall, she looked quite fetching, even to her own mind.

When she reappeared, Natron made an exuberant horsey, "Neigh!"

Carmen giggled. "It is cuter than I expected."

"See? My girl is one hot filly!" He winked at her. "Now put these on, around your biceps." He handed her the cuffs with the chains.

Slipping them on, a light switch went off in her brain and she realized what the chains were for.

"Get up on the bed."

She complied, and he fastened the headgear behind her head. Then he caught a nipple in his mouth. A ripple of pleasure pulsed through her as he licked and sucked her until the flesh hardened into a tight knot of arousal. He moved to the other one and she moaned with ecstasy. Her breasts felt super sensitive today and his attentions made her swoon.

He opened his mouth, releasing her and commanded, "On all fours."

She dropped her hands to the comforter and faced him at the edge of the bed.

He ran his fingers to the end of a chain attached to the cuff on her right arm. "Hold still," he said.

Cold metal touched her right nipple right before a zip of pain shot up her breast into her brain like a flash of hot lightning. She heard herself gurgle her discomfort, but before she had a chance to vocalize a protest, the same sensation gripped her left nipple.

She heard rather than saw his wicked grin as he ordered her, "Crawl."

With a whimper she slowly moved her right arm forward, followed by her left knee. As she moved her arm, the chain yanked on her nipple, stretching it; the feeling was a delicious, dark combination of pleasure and pain.

"That's it, pony." His voice was smooth as liquid chocolate, and she continued circling the bed on her hands and knees slowly, sensuously, her bottom on display for his pleasure.

So lost in the world of her own sensations she hadn't seen him get out the crop. The sound of its flat head meeting her ass cheek startled her. It took her brain a second to acknowledge the blow. It felt like more of a slap, almost like being hit by a strong flyswatter.

As she crawled around receiving smacks to her rear, she began to feel more like an animal, somehow less human. Rather than disturbing her, there was a part of the experience that was enjoyable. Giving up one's 'personhood' to become more of an object came with an element of freedom not unlike the freedom she felt when bound by her daddy. Surrendering control was a heady experience, and though she felt slightly silly acting like a pony, there was a certain aspect of it that appealed to her.

"Stop," Natron said, and she did. "Now I'm going to redden that ass of yours, pony girl."

Carmen made a strange noise, a cross between a whimper and a pony's snicker.

Short, staccato strikes lit up her behind as he worked her entire backside over with the crop. The pain was bearable, almost welcome and she could tell by how thoroughly he spanked her that the crop was quickly becoming a favorite tool of his.

The hot little bursts on her tender derriere ignited a lust inside her and she prayed he would soon decide to mount his little pony. The thwacks of the crop now resulted in breathy, wanton moans escaping her throat, and she couldn't help but say, "Ride me, Daddy. Please ride me."

He laughed. "Oh, you like being a pony, do you, girl?"

She nodded, the harness around her head jangling.

"I didn't hear you," he chastised.

"Yes, sir. I love being your pony."

"That's a good thing," he said and landed a few blows along the backs of her thighs for good measure.

Suddenly something cold slid into her bottom hole. His finger, slick with lube, moved in and out, softening the tight ring of muscle that gripped him so tightly. What started out as discomfort began to feel good and when he withdrew his finger, she wished for more of the unfamiliar sensation.

As if reading her thoughts, an object she could only guess was the horsehair butt plug entered her tiny hole. She clenched her muscles down around it and Natron told her to relax. Taking a deep breath, she tried to loosen up and release the tension back there. After a moment or two, her ass accepted the intrusion and she smiled as Natron swished the horsey tail across the backs of her thighs.

"Now this is something special. I've never fucked a girl with a tail before." He laughed and the bed heaved as he climbed on behind her, his weight on his good knee.

He curled his body over the top of her back and he clipped what looked like black leather dog leashes onto the sides of her harness. Oh, dear God, reins. He truly was going to ride her.

She felt the pressure at the back of the sides of her mouth as the bit pulled at the corners of her jaw. Damn, he wasn't kidding with this thing. The more firmly he held her reins, the more she had to hold her head high, or in whatever position he wanted.

His erect cock pressed insistently against her dripping pussy and it was all she could do not to lean back and rub her throbbing cunt into him. He dragged his hips across hers a few times, teasing a frustrated groan from her lips.

"Damn, that's a horny pony. Frisky. I think that's what I'll call you, pony girl—Frisky."

Carmen gurgled a response, not bothering to form words. Another freeing aspect of pony play—she wasn't expected to form coherent sentences. Grunts and squeaks worked just as well in her current condition.

He moved her tail to the side and slapped her pussy with his rock-hard cock, quick strikes in rapid succession. The beating of his flesh on her swollen clit was almost enough to make her come. Just when she was about to, he drove inside her welcoming cunt.

She was so wet that he was able to bury himself inside her completely with the first thrust. Having both her holes filled was a new and intense sensation. She felt as though she might burst with ecstasy. Her vaginal walls clenched him tightly, and with the next pulse of his cock, her muscles reverberated with a climax. Ignoring her shaking body, Natron pulled back her reins and continued to fuck her, her pussy quivering with a prolonged orgasm.

Dazed, Carmen tried her best to remain on all fours as he plundered her pussy all the while holding her head up. The position was less than comfortable, but the pleasure ripping through her made up for the awkward posture she was forced to hold.

The bit in her mouth held it open so much that she realized she had drooled all over the bedspread. While it was slightly embarrassing, at the same time there was nothing she could do about it, so she surrendered herself to the experience. She was being taken like an animal, and she loved it. Reduced to carnal, animal urges and instead of being mortified, she wanted more.

Natron dropped her reins and without warning plucked the butt plug from her ass and tossed it on the floor. "Damn thing's in the way," he growled, grabbing her hips and slamming harder into her cunt. She dropped her head as he picked up the pace and braced herself for the hardcore fucking. The more his balls smashed against her clit, the closer she came, until finally the world exploded again into another climax. She groaned a loud guttural noise as the insanely divine feeling started in her pussy and radiated out into the rest of her body, leaving a bliss-filled tingle in its path.

Her vaginal muscles clenched around his cock, but to her surprise he pulled out. Reaching onto the floor for something, Natron picked up a shallow bowl and jacked his load into it.

Exhausted, Carmen collapsed onto the bed.

"Frisky, did I say you could do that?"

Too tired to make a sound, she shook her head.

He unbuckled her harness and removed the bit.

Instinctively she wiped her arm across her mouth to dry her wet mouth, forgetting that her arm was attached to her nipple. She screeched in pain, and she could tell Natron was trying not to laugh.

"Here, let me unclip you," he said sympathetically. As he unclipped each one, the blood rushing back into her nipples made her yowl in pain.

"Aaaaggg! Daddy, that's the worst part."

"I know, I know." He patted her head and set the bowl of cum on the bed in front of her. "Now, Frisky, drink this up for Daddy."

She felt her eyes widen. "Are you serious?"

The look on his face said it all. "Hands behind your back, pony girl. I want to see you lap it all up."

She clasped her hands behind her back and he held the dish up to her face. Tilting her head down, she stuck out her tongue and touched it to the viscous white pool at the bottom of the dish.

"Good girl," he said, stroking her hair.

His praise washed over her like a verbal embrace, pulling her heart closer to his and she reached her tongue in for more.

"Such a good pony," he crooned as she dipped her head enthusiastically and lapped up the rest.

CHAPTER SIXTEEN

A month after Natron's surgery, the site where his staples had been healed up and Natron's trainer, Jack Thomas, put him to work swimming laps. When he started it was awkward, dragging his broken leg and kicking with the other one. But it allowed him to keep up his cardiovascular workouts. Natron was surprised at how out of shape he was when he first started swimming in his pool. Jack told him his stamina would be the first thing to drop off, and that it would do so significantly. As much as he hated to admit it, Jack had been right.

Jack turned out to be right with regards to everything involving training and athletics. He was the most highly regarded personal trainer in the business for helping athletes come back from an injury. Hell, this was the guy that helped running back Deshawn Thomas come back in nine months after a blown-out knee. That was enough testimony for Natron, and he'd hired Jack as soon as he woke up from surgery.

At the beginning Jack gave him instructions via Skype and e-mail, because he was based in California, but now that Natron was able to do more, he'd moved into Natron's place where he could take an active role in the training on a daily basis.

Today Natron floated in the pool, the water heated to a comfortable eighty-six degrees, while Jack barked instructions at him.

Stopping in chest-high water, Natron switched from swimming to jogging in place. It was important to keep his running motion going and if he did it underwater, he wouldn't be putting any pressure on the bad knee. At the same time he could work his range of motion in both legs.

While Natron ran in place, Jack walked around the pool and threw the football to him. Natron was supposed to catch it in one hand.

"Natron," Jack was saying as he tossed him the ball, "if you want to come back from this injury this season, you're going to have to prepare yourself for several things."

Natron snatched the wet, slippery ball out of the air with his palm, his fingers curling onto it and gripping it tightly. "What's that?" Natron asked good-naturedly.

"When you first come back, you won't have that top-end speed you used to have, and you won't have that burst of speed that usually allows you to break away from the defenders."

"If I can't break away from the defenders, then what good am I on the field?" Natron scoffed.

"Well, if you're lacking in elite speed, you're going to have to make up with it in other areas."

"What other areas?" Natron slowed his jogging.

"You're going to have to change the way you play wide receiver." Jack said with a burst of enthusiasm.

Natron slapped the water, splashing Jack's legs. "Come on, dog. I can't be learnin' a new way to play the game."

"Then you're gonna get beat. You're gonna slide down that slippery slope into mediocrity and in a couple of years no one will remember your name." Jack crossed his arms over his chest.

"Damn, Jack, you're killin' me. What do I gotta do?" Natron hated change, but he hated the idea of falling into obscurity more.

"We're gonna have to counter your lack of speed, lack of explosiveness with good old-fashioned brute force. You know how I've been pushing you to work your upper body, your core? That's because when you've got more strength in your chest, in your arms, in your center, you'll be able to outmuscle most of the defenders," Jack said as he tossed another ball two feet over Natron's head.

Rising out of the water, Natron pulled it in and threw it back.

Jack continued. "We're gonna make those arms and shoulders like hydraulic cylinders that can't be moved off their location. You'll have to get used to defenders playing tight coverage on you. That means pulling on your arms when you go up to catch a ball. That means getting bumped around much more than you're accustomed to. There will be times when you and the defensive back will both have your hands on the ball. You're gonna have to out-muscle them to come down with it. And with more strength, you'll be able to do that. You are gonna have to fight them for the ball on every single catch."

"Dog, that sounds depressing." Natron said, his energy level sinking.

"Don't let it depress you. Let it motivate you. Envision yourself being successful."

Natron shrugged, unconvinced.

Jack moved on. "You will also have to work on your catching ability. Your hands."

Natron bared his set of million dollar choppers. "Whatchu talkin' bout, Jack? You know I got elite hands. Nobody in the business has got better hands than me."

"Elite, yes. But you're going to have to be better than elite. You've got to be invincible, Natron. That's what I'm talkin' about. Invincible!"

Natron chilled. "Okay, I like invincible."

"You'll have to catch passes that aren't put in great positions. Passes the defender might catch first, and you're gonna have to somehow find a way to take the ball away from him. In other words, if you want Clay Davis to throw that ball to you, he's gonna have to throw it out of the reach of the defender in most cases. So you're gonna have to show him that you can make catches that are impossible to catch. And you have to make them every time. No matter what!"

Jack was asking him to do the impossible. Natron nodded. Umhmm. Now that was something to strive for. "Whatchu doin' just jawin' then, Jack? Let's get to work."

Jack started throwing the ball to Natron while he swam freestyle without a foot planted on any surface of the pool. When Natron missed some of the first few balls, he complained. "This is stupid, Jack. Why would anyone practice like this? You're nuts, man."

Jack just smiled. "Keep after it, Natron. You'll get it."

Natron sucked it up and pushed himself. Soon he and Jack progressed to where he swam laps and he was able to pull the ball out of the air as soon as Jack yelled 'ball.' Natron had developed the core strength and honed his coordination to where he could catch the football mid-stride without having to push off on anything in the pool to make the elevation necessary. He also had to turn his head with ultra-quick speed and locate the fast-approaching ball.

Sometimes to make the catch, he had to reach his arms up out of the water using his core strength to twist and contort his body like never before to leap for that football. Then he had to find a way to catch that slippery sucker with one hand.

To say it was a challenge would be an understatement, but it was a challenge Natron accepted, reminding himself that if anyone could get him back to playing shape this year, it was Jack; the man was a fifteen-year veteran of the NFL and the best trainer in the biz. He'd put himself in Jack's hands and he trusted him.

Natron was just finishing up his post-workout stretches when Veronique walked out toward the pool. Jack excused himself and headed inside to go check on their lunch. He'd gotten Natron's chef preparing only healthy foods.

I'd kill for a pizza right now, Natron thought as he waved to his mother. She was frowning at Jack's retreating form.

Veronique and Jack didn't see eye to eye on most things, and not only was the house getting too crowded, but the daily conflict was hardly conducive to his recuperation. It was time he and his mamma had a talk.

Veronique brought him a Powerade and a pitcher full of iced water. "I brought you something to drink, baby. Gotta stay hydrated, you know."

"Oh, I know, Mamma. Thanks."

She rested fists on her hips. "What are you doing in there? You know the doctor said you weren't supposed to be putting any weight on that leg!"

"I'm not, Mamma."

"Well, that's not what it looks like to me," she huffed.

"It's fine. The water gives me the resistance I need, but it also keeps the leg floating, with no pressure on it, like a zero gravity thing."

"This is all Jack's idea, isn't it?" Her mouth pinched up at the word 'Jack.'

"Mamma, I don't know why you are so down on him. He's trying to help me get back to playing football."

"Too fast. He's reckless. He's not worried about you like I am. That man only wants a paycheck."

"Mamma, that's not fair."

"Hmph!"

"Mamma, sit down. We gotta talk."

Frowning, she pulled one of the chaise lounges closer to the pool and sat down. "What do you mean, Natron? What's wrong?"

"Mamma, I appreciate everything you have been doing for me. You've been great, and I love you from the bottom of my heart."

She crossed her arms over her ample bosom. "But?" she said, an 'oh-no-you-did-not' look on her face.

"But soon it will be time for you to go back home."

"What?"

"Yeah, at the end of the week I'm going in for my next x-ray and if they let me put weight on it like I'm hoping, then Jack and I are going to be hitting the rehab hard. I'll be able to walk pretty soon after that and I won't need you to be here anymore."

"Well, that's a fine thank you. You won't need me anymore," she snorted.

He looked at her with as much love as a boy can have for his mamma. "I love you, and I am grateful for all your help, but I'm a grown man and it won't do for me to be seen as a mamma's boy. I have to stand on my own two feet… As soon as they tell me I can stand."

Veronique was quiet for a while, then brushed a tear from her cheek. "I'm sorry, Natron. I've clearly outstayed my welcome."

"It's not that, but you're making things harder on the people around me. You haven't been very accepting of Carmen, and now you're fighting with everything Jack says. All that makes the environment very stressful. And what I need right now is peace and support."

She sighed. "You're right. I'm not doing too well with all these other people in your life. I feel like I'm being squeezed out."

"That's exactly what Carmen said."

"She did?" Veronique seemed surprised.

"Yes, Mamma. She's my girl. Probably the future mother of my future children, and you've treated us like high-schoolers. She's here to stay, so you're just going to have to accept that."

"Well, I didn't know you were serious about her." Veronique touched her hand to her chest defensively. "I thought she was just another gold-digger."

"She's the opposite of a gold-digger. Carmen is down to earth. She has her own career. And if she only loved me for what I could do for her, why would she be standing by me now?"

Veronique shrugged. "I don't know, Natron. I didn't realize…"

"It's okay."

"Well, I'll pack my things and leave whenever you want me to."

"Hey, not right away. I just want you to start thinking about it, because once that doc gives me the go-ahead, I'm going to be getting really busy around here prepping to get back out there on that field."

"Alright," Veronique smiled wanly and reached down to pat his cheek. "Sometimes I guess I forget you're not my little boy anymore. You're all grown up now."

"I know, Mamma. I know."

Ten days later, Dr. Whitaker informed Natron that his bones had healed well enough for him to be able to put light pressure, fifty pounds worth, on his leg. The news that his bones had healed so rapidly increased Natron's belief that he would be back to playing football *this* season. After all, he was almost a month ahead of schedule for his recovery.

The doctor's instructions launched Natron on a strenuous daily exercise regimen with the team trainers in addition to the workouts he already did twice a day with Jack. The Vipers' facility had a machine that could determine exactly how much pressure he was putting on his knee while he worked it. It was important he not put more than the fifty pounds on it or the bone could split again at a weak point. And while Natron knew better than to push how much weight he bore on his left leg, he had no intention on training lightly in any of the other areas.

He'd been working his core so hard that he had an eight-pack. Not only did it make Carmen even hotter for him, but it helped him stay in shape so it would be easier coming back to football. In fact, his core was not the only area in which he'd improved. Because he'd been so limited in his weightlifting ability with his legs the past two months, he had drastically improved his upper body strength. Before his injury he was bench pressing 365. Now he could bench a solid 415.

Once Carmen had teased him about bulking up his upper body, saying he was overcompensating. He agreed that was exactly what he was doing, and he explained that more upper arm strength would help him be able to push away defenders when they tried to jam him up off the line, allowing him to run his route unencumbered. He would also be in a better position to pull the ball away from a defender. Another player might be able to get their hands on the ball, but with the strength he had now, he'd be the one coming down with it.

Two weeks later, an x-ray showed that Natron was ready to put 100% pressure on his leg and go full bore into massive rehab. His left leg had suffered a fair amount of muscle atrophy even with the electroshock therapy. He launched into a daily three-hour workout with the Vipers' team trainers in addition to the two-hour workouts he did with Jack for his upper body and his good leg. They also added another hour to work his weak leg.

One morning Natron was preparing to head over to the team facility for his daily workout with team trainers, when he caught the reporters on ESPN talking about Marvin Stalcup.

"They are just as good a team with Stalcup as they were with Dakers," a heavyset commentator said.

"You mean to say, you think Stalcup's as good as Dakers was last year when he was MVP?" The other commentator was Hall of Fame wide receiver Jerry Rice.

"I'm not saying he's as good, I'm just saying they don't seem to be missing Dakers. Stalcup has replaced him on the team. The guy is second in the league right now in total receiving yards, Jerry. You can't argue with that."

Natron clicked the television off. What the hell did they know? If Stalcup had 800 yards, Natron would have had 1,000 yards by this point had he been playing.

Angrily, he kicked a football that lay on the floor before storming out the door.

In the car, he made a point to listen to music instead of more jackasses with an opinion. He cranked up some hardcore rap tunes and lost himself in the heavy beat.

When he entered the facility, Stalcup was the first person he saw.

"Hey, man." Stalcup raised a hand and Natron took it, giving him a bro handshake. "What's up? Good to see you back."

Natron nodded. "'Sup?"

"Not much. Killin' it out there on the field. Can't wait to get you back out there. Two of us? We'll be unstoppable." Stalcup raised his chin and tilted his head back, camaraderie laced with arrogance.

"Yeah, dog. That's it." Natron said, cognizant it wasn't Marvin's fault they were in this situation. If Natron were in his shoes, he'd take advantage of the opportunity too.

"Aaiight. See ya then," Marvin said, then sauntered out of the building with the confidence Natron realized he no longer had. Anxiety gripped him and his blood ran cold as if fear had just pinched him in the shoulder.

You can do this. Hell, you're going to come back better than ever.

Natron waltzed into the workout room and spied Bill, the trainer assigned to him. They acknowledged each other, Natron lay down on the table, and Bill began working on his knee, stretching it, straightening it, warming it up for the workout to come.

"So, Bill, whatchu think about me comin' back so soon?" Natron said in a relaxed tone. This was the easiest part of his physical therapy.

Bill gave him a puzzled stare.

"What? I'm a month ahead of schedule, dog. I'll be back on that field catching balls in the playoffs."

Bill sputtered, shaking his head.

"What? You don't believe me?" Natron's fingers twitched with agitation.

"It's not that, Natron. It's just... well, it's a long way from the doctor telling you that you can walk on your leg again to getting back into the kind of condition you need to be in to play."

"I've been staying in shape, Bill. My cardio's not that off. I've been swimming, keeping it up, ya know?" Natron heard the pleading note in his voice and it made him nauseous.

"Yeah, but stamina isn't the biggest issue. It's going to be the knee, making those cuts. How much cartilage damage that's been done." Bill set Natron's leg on the table and leveled a serious look at him. "Don't overdo it, Natron, and give yourself a break. No one expects you to be back this season."

A rough breath escaped Natron's lungs. "You mean 'cause Stalcup is tearing it up."

Bill shrugged. "I mean because you're human."

Then he helped Natron onto the treadmill and they got down to business.

After his training session, Natron's mood had gone from irritable to foul. Instead of going home for a healthy lunch made by his chef, he called up an old buddy of his, Clarence, and they hit a local strip joint.

Natron had stopped hanging around with Clarence once he and Carmen had become a couple, but in his stormy frame of mind, knocking back a few drinks with a friend who wouldn't judge him seemed just the thing he needed.

Thrilled to hear from Natron, Clarence made a big show of getting them a VIP table up front.

Natron could not have cared less about the women. They looked great, but sex was the last thing on his mind. He would have gone to a sports bar, but he knew it would only depress him further to look up and see Marvin on the big screen, the commentators talking about how great he was. What did Marvin have that he didn't? When he was healthy... He'd been quicker, more explosive, and hell, he'd had endorsements coming out of his ears. Not to mention a gorgeous, talented woman by his side supporting him all the way. Now *that* was something Marvin didn't have.

Ordering a whiskey sour, he gave the scantily clad waitress his credit card and told her to open a tab. Clarence succeeded in cheering him up, regaling him with some crazy guys-night-out stories.

Clarence worked as a security guard for a bank now, but he and Natron had met when he was working for the Vipers organization. He told Natron a story about a guy who had robbed their bank recently. The guy had written the note telling the clerk to hand over the money. The funny part was he'd written it on a pad of paper from the hotel he was staying at half-a-mile away, making it almost too easy for the cops to pick him up an hour later at the hotel.

"Man, that guy's too dumb to be walkin' around," Natron said and they laughed until their sides hurt.

After a few rounds, some of the girls had recognized Natron and were beginning to get a little too friendly.

"Come back and I'll give you a lap dance you'll never forget," promised a blonde with a pixie haircut and small tits.

"See me after and I'll take you to paradise, brown sugar," a buxom brunette said, touching a well-manicured fingertip to his lips.

Natron didn't mind the attention and he appreciated beautiful, naked women, but he wasn't in the mood. The last thing he needed was another person with their hand out wondering what good ole Natron could do for them. He had nothing left to give today. His chest tightened and it felt like a crowd of people were standing on him, making it impossible to breathe.

Then a gorgeous chocolate Nubian princess came out and did her gyrating right in front of him. At the end of her dance she taunted him. "C'mon, big boy. Let Mamma treat you right," she said, smashing her jugs together and making a lewd movement with her tongue. When that didn't get the response she was looking for, she turned around and bent over, giving him a view of her goodies that left nothing to the imagination.

The 'Mamma' reference was bad enough with all he'd been dealing with regarding his own mother, but the blatant pussy in the face was more than he was looking for. The situation was escalating and he didn't want to be a part of it getting worse. He loved Carmen, and cheap sex wasn't going to do anything to solve his problems. It would probably only add to them.

"I need some fresh air. Let's get out of here," Natron said.

"You got it, chief. We may need a ride. Want me to call a cab?" Clarence asked, standing up to get their waitress so they could cash out.

"Naw. I'll call Carmen to come get us."

"Carmen? You sure? She might not like it that you're here."

Natron waved his concern away. "Babygirl's cool. She won't care." He stood up and walked outside to make the call.

CHAPTER SEVENTEEN

"You're where?"

Carmen had stepped out of the shower to find she'd missed two calls from Natron. She'd giggled. He always had this kind of naked radar and called when she was undressed.

Her towel fell to the floor and she looked at the phone. *The Booby Trap*? What the hell?

"Sure, I'll come get you," she said through gritted teeth and hung up.

She shook her head and threw on a pair of jeans and a t-shirt, then hurried out to her car.

Hands gripping the steering wheel, she wondered why Natron felt the need to go to a strip club. Wasn't their sex life satisfactory? Hell, she thought it was great, beyond great. Beyond anything she could have imagined prior to meeting him.

Perhaps he didn't feel the same way. Or he was getting bored with her. Was that it? He was looking for someone new?

She shook off these notions. A strip club wasn't where Natron would pick up women. Being a professional athlete, he'd be too scared of gold-diggers, those kind of women who held semen in their mouths so they could later spit it in a cup and try to get themselves pregnant by an athlete—the biggest payoff they were likely to see. Plus, if he was cheating, she doubted he'd ask her to pick him up from the scene of the crime.

There had to be some other explanation. Maybe one of his buddies wanted to go, was getting married or something. Now that was a scenario that made sense. Come to think of it, Natron's voice had sounded a bit slurred over the phone.

A bright pink and purple neon sign of a naked girl served as an easy landmark, and she pulled into the parking lot.

Natron and Clarence appeared out of the shadows. Natron gave her a quick kiss through the window and asked Carmen if she could give Clarence a ride home.

She agreed and the ride to Clarence's was a quiet one. When he got out of the car, Clarence made a big point to tell Natron to stay in touch. "Don't be such a stranger." Natron agreed and clapped him on the shoulder.

Once they were alone, Carmen inquired, "Where do you want me to take you?"

Natron's gaze was fixed on his phone. "Oh, crap. Jack's been looking for me."

"Do you need to go home and work out with Jack?" He reeked of booze and seemed to have had several drinks. It didn't seem the best time to work out to her, but her experience with working out was limited to going up and down the stairs in her loft, so she kept quiet. Let the professionals figure that one out.

"I was supposed to," he sighed, the smell of booze assaulting her nostrils.

"What happened?" she asked, purposely leaving her question open-ended.

"Had a rough day is all," he grumbled.

"So you went out and got drunk? Anyway, I need to know where I'm taking you."

"Your place."

"You want to go to my place? What about Jack?"

"Jack can go fuck himself."

She took a right at the next light, pointing her vehicle in the direction of her loft. "So Jack's who's got you in this mood?"

"No. I just texted him back anyway. We can get back on schedule tomorrow. I mean, I'm payin' the guy regardless if we work out today."

She nodded, hoping he would tell her what was wrong once he felt like it. Natron sat silent for the remainder of the ride home.

Carmen looked over once and he'd closed his eyes. Her temples throbbed and she could almost feel the hangover he would soon be getting.

They arrived at her apartment and she offered him some coffee. When he declined, she fixed him a glass of ice water and urged him to drink it.

He downed half of it and sent her upstairs, ordering her to get naked.

She stripped off her clothes, leaving them in a pile on the floor. Tidiness was the last thing on her mind. Something in her gut told her tonight was going to be anything but tidy. No, tonight had messy written all over it.

Grunts and heavy breathing echoed up the stairs, giving away the fact that it was hard for him to climb the stairs in his current physical state.

After he'd hauled himself up the stairs on basically one leg, he limped into her closet, winded.

He returned with one of her belts. It was leather with a heavy gold buckle. He turned it over in his hands, examining the leather, considering how he would use it on her.

Terror coursed through her blood. "Please, don't use the buckle, Daddy," she pleaded.

"Shut up and lie down on the bed," he growled. "On your stomach."

He won't use the buckle. He wouldn't do that, she told herself as she lay down.

"Spread your legs more," he said and gave the belt a test shot on her upper thigh.

"Eeek! Daddy!" she hollered.

"Okay, I'll stick to your ass," he grumbled.

Remembering to breathe was going to be the only way she could do this. She inhaled purposefully.

This time he didn't caress her bottom cheeks or take care with her. This time she felt his anger. It puzzled her because she hadn't done anything to him, and it wasn't like Natron to take out his rage on her. It wasn't like him to be full of rage.

What had happened that day? She wondered, then forgot as the next blow striped her ass with a red ribbon of pain.

He covered both of her ass cheeks well with whipping motions, the leather licking her flesh as it grew more tender with each blow.

Something had made him feel helpless, and she could tell he needed to express his power over her. *He needs me to be his, to control me when the rest of his world is out of control,* she realized and vowed not to use her safeword unless absolutely necessary.

Each lash of the leather sent a searing sensation to her sore skin, but after a few minutes she relaxed and drifted away.

The spanking continued until Natron told her that her ass was red as a cherry.

Without preamble he climbed on top of her from behind, his erection poking hard against her asshole.

For a minute she held her breath, praying he wouldn't take her ass. Her heart raced. There had been no butt plug, no stretching, and she thought she might die of agony if he did it without lube. Her butthole was tiny, and anal sex was sometimes more painful than fun even when they prepped her beforehand.

To her relief his cock drifted lower and pushed inside her pussy.

It was slow going at first, since she'd been more concerned than aroused by the beating with the belt. But after he moved in and out a few times, the old, familiar lust surfaced and wet her walls.

Once he sensed her arousal, he increased his speed, pounding hard into her.

Tilting his hips, he ground against her g-spot, causing her to squeal with pleasure.

"Hush, my girl," he snarled and inserted a thumb into her mouth.

Her lips curled around his big finger and she suckled and tried not to wiggle too much beneath him. This was one of those times when she needed to let Daddy fuck her the way he wanted. It was her job to do as he said and take whatever he gave her.

His cock smashed into her g-spot with an unrelenting fury. The room, the bed, everything seemed to fall away as she felt the welcome gush leave her pussy. Her insides contracted again and again as she floated on wave after wave of pink, silken girly cum.

Natron covered her body with his own, stretching out atop her until she wasn't sure she could breathe. But he left her just enough room as he bucked into her at a frenzied speed. His skin slapped against hers and she was slightly relieved when he pushed into her one last time, then collapsed beside her.

They lay silently in each other's arms as their heart rates returned to normal.

Natron almost always fell asleep after sex, but in his alcohol-induced state, she knew it would only be a matter of seconds before he dozed off. Perhaps their romp had taken the edge off. She tried again to get at what was bothering him.

"Daddy, what happened today?"

Half-asleep, he threw an arm across her body, mumbling. "They don't think I'll make it back this year."

"Who? Who doesn't think you'll make it back?" she pressed.

Her question was met with light snoring noises. She dared to poke him gently in the ribs, but he didn't stir.

So that's what the problem was. She knew Natron thought he'd be back playing football by the playoffs. Someone—maybe Jack, one of the other players, or even one of the coaches disagreed. What did they know? Her daddy knew his own body better than anyone else did. Natron was certainly not *normal*, by anyone's assessment.

She curled herself around his sleeping form and stroked his long dreads. "I believe in you, Daddy," she whispered, "I believe in you."

He mumbled something in his sleep, and she wasn't sure whether or not he heard her.

CHAPTER EIGHTEEN

After that day, Natron felt like crap. He apologized to Jack for blowing him off and to Carmen for exorcising his demons on her, and he committed himself once again to his comeback.

Fuck those bastards who don't believe in me. I'll show them.

Every day he worked out with Jack in the morning, then went to the Vipers' training facility for his workout with the trainers, and later he and Jack worked out again in the evenings.

By December he resumed light jogging. Almost daily he experienced swelling around the knee, but he fought it with lots of icing and massage therapy. He hoped by January he'd be ready to attend a team practice.

When the regular season drew to a close, the Dallas Vipers had claimed a spot in a Wildcard game. The game would be held in January in New England, and though Natron would have given anything to be able to play in that game, he comforted himself with the knowledge that if you had to miss a playoff game, the one held in New England in the dead of winter was the one to miss.

So Natron watched the game at home with Jack and Carmen. It was a nasty battle, played outdoors in negative ten degrees temperature with a wind chill factor of negative forty. Natron shivered just thinking about playing in that kind of weather.

"I can't imagine being in the stands, much less playing in that type of weather," Carmen said, snuggling up to Natron.

"Yeah, it's bad enough being that cold, but trying to catch the ball in that…" Natron's voice trailed off.

"What do you mean?" Carmen asked.

"Well, like here in Dallas where it's warm and humid for most of the football season, balls are easy to catch in that weather," Natron said.

"Why is that?" she asked.

"The ball has a lot of give to it," Jack explained. "Up there, in that kind of weather," he pointed at the television screen, "the ball is frozen."

"So?"

"So, it's like catching a solid block of ice coming at you at sixty miles per hour when you can barely feel your fingertips—now that's a challenge." Natron laughed. "Probably not the best game to make a comeback."

"Yeah," Carmen agreed.

They watched and crossed their fingers the Vipers would advance and give Natron a chance to play.

Without much of a passing game due to the weather, the Vipers ground out over 300 yards running in a physical defensive game and beat the Commodores 10-3. The Vipers advanced and were slated to play the Los Angeles Cougars the following week, and that game would take place in Dallas.

That Sunday night after the game, Natron got the call he'd been waiting for. He was to report to practice on Monday.

Natron showed up early for practice, his fingers twitching as he itched to get out on that field and catch the ball.

After warm-ups, Natron worked with the receivers coach. He ran sprints, then moved on to agility drills. He weaved in and out of the cones, then the tires, to get his footwork back. As he worked, he noticed the other receivers running routes and working with the backup quarterback.

That night he called their starting quarterback, Clay Davis, and asked if he could stay after practice one day so they could work together. He and Clay used to have incredible chemistry, which was probably why Clay agreed. The two of them recruited Benji Youngblood, a cornerback and the team's emotional leader, to help them out.

Fortunately, the chemistry between Clay and Natron only took a few throws to get back. They connected on nine balls out of ten the quarterback threw, and Natron was pleased to see his elevation sent him half a foot over Youngblood when they both went up for the ball.

Benji noticed Natron's improved strength when they simulated lining up and Natron pushed the big man aside. "Nice work, Dakers. Packing on some muscle while you've been out. Guess I'm really gonna have to try this time," Benji joked on the next play.

"Yeah, good luck with that, Gramps," Natron retorted. Youngblood was one of the more senior members of the team, but he played with the intensity of a guy in his prime.

The one thing that became more and more apparent as the session progressed was that Natron's cuts were slow. He had trouble running the correct route. The flexibility of his knee simply hadn't developed to the level where he'd been previously. Clay and Benji knew it, but they had the decency not to make an issue of it.

After one failed route, Benji slapped him on the shoulder. "Take it easy on yourself, bro. Takes time. Hell, you broke your fuckin' knee. No one expects you to come out here like Superman."

"I do," Natron said with more honesty than he usually displayed. Natron had made a career of parading his bravado out front, and keeping his insecurities hidden. His mamma said he'd been a trash talker ever since he played his first basketball game.

"You'll be back before you know it," Clay said, slapping his rear.

Clay's was the first voice of confidence Natron had actually heard from anyone on the Vipers' organization, but he didn't know whether Clay was blowing smoke up his ass or if he truly meant it.

In the end it didn't matter what Clay thought. On Thursday Natron saw that he had been added back to the team's fifty-three–man roster, but he was listed as inactive.

There would be no playoff game for him that weekend.

CHAPTER NINETEEN

The day had started out with a new game—how many times can Daddy make you come. Natron had woken Carmen up by fingering her pussy and rubbing her clit until she came. Then he fucked her good and made her come again. Now it was late morning and Natron asked her to help him with a hair-trimming project in the bathroom.

"You're sure you want me to do this?" Carmen asked, her features scrunched with worry.

"Yeah, babygirl, I do. Time for a change. A new look for the new and improved Natron Dakers. Take a picture with your phone. Like a 'before.'"

Carmen picked up her phone, aimed, and clicked. "Maybe you should do it like a selfie."

"Great idea." He took a few with his own phone and tweeted one out with a 'before' caption.

"Daddy, you love your dreads. I love your dreads," Carmen whined as she held the shears up to one of his beautiful locks.

"Do it, Carmen, or I'm gonna spank you, girl, and you won't sit down for a week," he ordered, waggling a finger at her.

"Fine, Daddy. I'll do it." She inched her fingers together and a two-foot-long lock of hair fell to the floor.

It had taken him years to get his hair like that. He sighed, then urged her to continue. The swishing sound of the scissors was followed by another lock hitting the bathroom floor.

"Tell me again why you're doing this."

"Hey, I'm showing that I'm not Samson. I don't need my hair to make me strong and powerful."

Carmen's hand flew over her mouth. "Oh, my God, Daddy, what if it does sap your strength? Cutting off all your hair…" she teased.

"Girl, I'm goin' wear you out when we get through."

She giggled. "Promise?"

"Oh, yeah. Now keep cuttin'."

It took over an hour to cut all of his hair off. At the end he was left with a crazy, nappy-looking mess. Carmen took the scissors and ran them as close to his head as she could and then they took out the electric clippers.

"I'm going to do this part, but I may need you to do the back," he said.

Carmen nodded, staring at him.

"What? You're making me feel self-conscious," he snapped.

"No, Daddy. It's fine. It's just so different. That's all."

He wasn't sure if she was just trying to make him feel better or if she meant it.

Once he'd gotten the hair as short as the clippers would take it, he turned to Carmen. "Okay, lather me up, baby."

Her eyes lit up and she sprayed some shaving gel onto his head. She then took a soft-bristled shaving brush and worked it into a foamy white layer all over his head.

Picking up the new razor, he shaved one long strip from his forehead to the back of his neck.

"What do you think?" he asked.

"The stripe makes you look like a reverse skunk."

He laughed. "You are askin' for it, girl." He swatted her ass playfully.

She nodded and grabbed a towel for him.

He finished the rest of the job carefully, then rinsed his head in the sink. It wasn't perfectly smooth yet, but he'd heard not to overdo it the first time you shave your head bald.

His reflection in the mirror looked foreign to him. Like he was trying on someone else's look. Hell, he'd get used to it.

He turned to Carmen. "Alright. What do you think for real?"

A slow smile spread across her face. "I am going to miss the dreads, but you're as handsome as ever, Daddy." She ran a hand over his round dome. "I like it. Feels sexy."

"Oh, yeah?" he asked and playfully snapped his towel at her legs.

"Eeek! Don't, Daddy. Don't!" She took off into the bedroom.

He chased her down and tossed her on the bed onto her stomach. She pretended to protest, but stopped wiggling when he pulled her pants down around her ankles.

"Time to pay you back for teasing Daddy."

"But I was helpful, Daddy."

His palm crashed down onto her rear. "That's true. I'll keep that in mind," he said, bouncing his hand off her ass again.

The slapping of his hand was followed by the cute little noises Carmen made. They started out as indignant squeaks, then as the spanking continued morphed into breathy moans. He knew the punishment aroused her.

Which, in turn, aroused him. The sight of her pink cheeks filled him with lust and longing to be inside her, and he impatiently decided to make the spanking quick. When his hand met her bottom the last time, the warmth of her round tush spread up into him, cementing the connection between them.

He loved this woman. Loved how she played his silly games. Loved how she stood by him and supported him through his injury and everything that had accompanied it. Some women would have been concerned about the drop in his income, the dried-up endorsements, but Carmen never mentioned it. She loved him for who he was, not what he could do for her.

And that made her the most precious person in the world to him.

He slid his hand over her tender flesh, softly rubbing and kneading.

"Umm, thank you, Daddy," she purred.

"No need to thank me yet. I'm not near done with you," he growled and rolled her over onto her side.

Carmen squealed. "Oh, no? What are you going to do to me now, Daddy?" she asked with a coy smile.

"I'm gonna fuck you sideways, the way you like it. Fuck you until you beg me to stop."

Her eyes lit up with a combination of desire and mock horror.

She settled back onto her side and rested one arm under her head and planted the other one in front of her on the bed. She curled her bottom leg back on the bed and Natron lifted her top leg and hooked it around his waist.

Carmen curled her fingers around his cock and moved her fist back and forth over his shaft, which was quickly becoming engorged. He covered her hand with his, encouraging her. "Um, good job, babygirl. You know what Daddy likes."

He could see her eyeing his cock and licking her lips. "You want Daddy to fuck your mouth first, baby?"

She nodded.

"Use your words," he said, slapping her ass as a reminder.

"Yes, Daddy, please may I suck your cock?"

"Yes, you may." He repositioned himself on his still-tender knee as well as his good one so that he was closer to her adorable face and forced his erection into her welcoming little mouth. Her tongue swirled around the underside of his shaft, sending waves of pleasure through him each time he pushed in and out of her lips.

Once he was well-lubricated by her saliva, he thrust deep, as far as he could go. The sensation of filling her completely, hitting the back of her throat until she couldn't take him anymore made him want to burst. But since he didn't want to come yet, he pulled out and maneuvered back to the end of the bed. Carmen still lay on her side and he took her top leg and hooked it around his waist.

He rubbed the tip of his cock over her lower lips, stroking her in all her most sensitive areas until he felt her hips begin to jerk. Satisfaction washed over him. He loved nothing better than to make her want him. To make her want him so much that she would beg for him to take her.

"I can feel you bucking those hips, girl. Is there something you want?" he smirked.

"Daddy," she breathed heavily. "I want you, Daddy."

"What? No magic word?"

"Please, Daddy, please fuck me like the naughty little slut I am."

He loved it when she talked dirty. He knew she did it to please him, and it worked. Rubbing the head of his cock against her opening, he surrendered and plunged deep into her tight, wet pussy. She let out a groan as he filled her, which fueled his passion and he drove hard into her repeatedly.

"Ooh, Daddy. With your bald head, it's so weird. Like getting fucked by a stranger."

He smacked her on the butt. "You better not be fucking a stranger."

She laughed and stroked his arm. "Nobody but you, Daddy."

Her reassurance made his heart soar. He wanted to be her everything. "Damned straight. Daddy wants to make it so good for you, babygirl, that you never need anybody else."

She pulled him to her and kissed him deeply. "You do, Daddy. You make me so happy."

Rising up, he buried himself deep inside her, grazing her g-spot with the head of his penis. He liked this position because he could reach everything. He grabbed a handful of her hair and tugged. With his other hand he tweaked and twisted her plump nipples until she cried out with pleasure.

As he pounded away at her, he remembered that Carmen liked this position because he could play with her clit while he fucked her. He bent to kiss her breast, then let go of her hair and started stroking that sensitive little button at her very core.

He traced the tiniest of circles with his large index finger, changing up the pattern and direction every so often so she didn't become desensitized to it. Her body grew more and more rigid and she bit down on her lip hard.

He felt the swell of her orgasm as her muscles clamped down on him. All of his problems disappeared and the rest of the world melted away. His cock pulsed and jerked with pleasure as she milked him to completion. The sweetest feeling in all the world had to be emptying yourself into the woman you loved.

Bathed in sweat, their bodies stopped quivering after a few moments and he lay beside her, folding her in his arms. "I'm going to give you a minute, then I'm gonna eat that little pussy of yours for lunch."

"Daddy!"

"Told you this was 'how many times can Daddy make you come' day. How many so far?"

"Three," she answered breathlessly. "But we've been fucking all day. At least let me take a shower first." She held her hands over her crotch protectively.

"You think a little cum and pussy juice is gonna scare me off?"

Her face screwed up, clearly uncomfortable.

Natron went to the bathroom and returned with a wet rag. "If it will make you feel better, babygirl, Daddy will give your little kitty a bath first." He spread her legs wide and wiped her luscious mound with the damp warm washcloth, taking care to clean off any leftover semen. Then he laughed. "Now for a tongue bath."

He began by licking her outside lips, his tongue traveling up and down from her opening to her clitoris. Making his tongue flat, he caressed her languidly, developing a sensuous pattern as he buried his face between her legs. "Damn, you taste good, girl."

"Daddy!" she protested as if she didn't believe him.

"You do. You are one hot and sexy girl," he insisted. "I love to taste the nectar from your sweet honeypot."

He must have said the right thing because she gripped his newly bald head and held him to her.

Sucking her clit into his mouth, he flicked his tongue back and forth over it in a dirty little oral tango. Carmen's moans grew louder as he persisted in pleasuring her magic spot. She grabbed for his vanished locks but came up empty. Instead, she began to stroke his head feverishly between both hands. Her body tensed, then shook uncontrollably as he worked her pussy with his mouth.

Her orgasm seemed to go on and on in waves. Giving his tired jaw a break, he continued manipulating her clit with one finger as he stimulated her hardened nipple with the other hand.

After convulsing for almost ten minutes, Carmen's body slowly returned to normal.

"That felt like a lot. How many times do you think you came that time?"

Dazed, Carmen responded, "I don't know. Three or four. Maybe five." She wiped her brow.

"Let's go with four. Aren't you glad you're multi-orgasmic?" he asked.

"Only with you. I've never been like that before."

Natron nodded, pleased with himself. "That's because Daddy prides himself on pleasing you. That's my job, and I want to be better at *that* job than anything else I do."

She chuckled. "Better than playing wide receiver?"

"Yeah, better than that. Anyone can play wide receiver. Haven't you seen that fool Stalcup killin' it out there on the field lately?"

She shook her head. "Sure, but he's not just anyone."

"Whatever. Shoot. He can do that, but nobody else can do what I do to you. Nobody." He scooted up next to her and pressed his lips to her neck. "I want you to be so happy with me that you're never tempted by any other man. Because you know that nobody can satisfy you the way I can."

"Aww, Daddy, that's so sweet. I already know that."

He clasped her to him, feeling her heart beating against his chest. "Just don't you forget it. Nobody can take care of you like your daddy."

She snuggled further into his embrace. "That's right, Daddy. You're the only one for me."

They lay quietly for a while, and Carmen dozed off. Natron was tempted to fall asleep too, but instead he got up, threw on a robe, and padded barefoot into the kitchen. He'd ask chef to fix them a nice lunch, maybe some chicken salad with fruit.

He may have given her seven orgasms already today, but if he was going to make it to his goal of a dozen he was going to need some sustenance.

CHAPTER TWENTY

A couple of days later, Natron conducted the big reveal of his new haircut, or rather lack of hair, on television. That Thursday he invited Joanne Mills, the sexy blond *Entertainment Nightly* reporter to his home. With the Super Bowl coming up in less than a month, the media was more focused than ever on professional football players, and Natron meant to capitalize on it.

The *EN* staff had rearranged his living room to provide the optimal backdrop for the interview. Mini-microphones were clipped to his shirt and the hairdressers gave Joanne's coif a last minute fluff-up.

"3-2-1… And we're rolling," the cameraman warned.

Joanne came to life, blossoming under the harsh lights that had been set up in front of the seating area. "Good evening. I'm here in Dallas with last year's MVP, Natron Dakers. As you might know, Natron suffered a broken knee during the first game of the year this season."

Turning her attention to him, she asked, "Natron, how's your rehab coming?"

"It's going well, Joanne. Thanks. I'm at least a month ahead of schedule and expect to be back on the field before the end of this season."

"Wow. Already? You know your team has to win its next game in order for you to do that…"

"Joanne, I have every confidence that the Vipers will continue their playoff run all the way to the Super Bowl."

"You sound rather convinced. Now everyone is going to be asking about the hair. For a man who's known for his wild dreadlocks, what made you decide to shave your head?"

"Joanne, it was time for a change. I'm a different person since my injury and I thought my appearance should reflect that."

"Well, it's a pretty drastic transition, from lots of hair to none at all. How have you changed and are you making a statement with your new look?"

"You could say that. Since I've been injured I've had a chance to pause, reflect, think about what's really important in life. And while I love a good touchdown dance, I've realized there's more to life than football."

"What, specifically is at the top of your priority list then, instead of football?"

"It's not that football isn't a priority, I have dedicated myself wholeheartedly to coming back, but I think now I realize how important family is to me."

"I've heard your mother came to stay with you and take care of you during your recuperation. I know the two of you are close. She raised you as a single mom... Did her being here help bring you closer together?"

"Yeah. My mom is great and she helped me a lot. But my girlfriend, she really supported me too. I couldn't ask for a better partner than her."

"Your girlfriend Carmen Harris, the local artist?"

"Yeah. She's a super talented girl." He flashed a grin at the camera.

"So you've gotten closer. I've heard rumors that you and she might be getting engaged. Any truth to those rumors?"

Natron managed a look that was both sly and coy at the same time. "Now, I wasn't expecting you to ask me that."

"C'mon, Natron. You're an eligible guy. The ladies want to know if you're going off the market."

"To be honest, Joanne, I have to say I can't imagine life without her. When I look into her eyes, I see my future children."

Joanne giggled. "Okay, now you've given me goose bumps. That Carmen is one lucky girl. How does she feel about your new look?"

"Well, she helped me do it, actually. She likes it, but she says it is taking some time to get used to."

"I'll bet. Now, back to football. This year your good friend and Dallas Vipers wide receiver Marvin Stalcup is having an impressive season. He's second in the league in receiving yards and his numbers are close to what yours were last year. What do you say to the critics who say that it's the system and not the individual that makes Vipers receivers so successful?"

"Well, for one thing I don't think Marvin would agree with that any more than I do. Marvin is a talented football player and I'm pleased to see him following in my footsteps. When I get back out there, defenses better look out. We'll be the biggest double threat in football."

Joanne nodded. "Will you be in Philly this weekend for the playoffs?"

"I'm not sure, but wherever I am I'll be doing everything I can to get back on that field."

"Thanks for sitting down with us, and good luck with your comeback."

"Thank you, Joanne."

Friday morning, a phone alarm jingled in Carmen's bedroom. Upon hearing it, Carmen rolled over and hid her head under the pillow. Natron turned it off and threw his arm around her. Carmen snuggled closer to him. Having missed him for the past few days, she wound her legs around his and began kissing his smooth neck. Nibbling on his ear, she settled in for a sweet cuddle session.

But Daddy had other plans.

Under the covers she realized that his hand had been on his morning wood. He growled and moved her hand over his erection. "Baby, I've been missing you."

She felt a slight throb in her head but ignored it. "Me too, Daddy." She curled her hand around his shaft and stroked it. Her fingers deftly worked their magic, bringing him to the height of arousal.

The alarm went off again. "Just a minute," he said and hit the snooze button. "I almost want to call in to work, tell them I'll be late and have you ride me this morning." He wore a devilish grin.

"Natron, you can't do that! You have to go in."

"Naaah. I'll be late this morning. You and that little pussy of yours are too tempting. Climb up on top of Daddy."

She sighed. Really, what she wanted to do was sleep, but she crawled out of bed and peeled off her pajamas and warm socks. Jeez, it was cold. Normally she slept naked, but when it was cold out like last night, she wore her flannel pajamas. Forget being sexy, she needed comfort when she was freezing.

As she stood on the side of the bed, her head pinged with the beginning of a headache. She shook it off, laughing to herself at the idea of a headache stopping her from performing her duties as a sub.

If Daddy wanted her body, she would submit to him and do as he asked. Of course she always had the option of saying no, they both knew that. But what she had found over time was that even when she didn't feel like being sexual with Daddy at first, she still took great pleasure in pleasing him and along the way she usually enjoyed herself too. Daddy prided himself in making her feel good. Hell, the endorphins might make her headache go away.

Naked, she got back in the bed and draped her body on top of his. Grinding her pussy over his cock brought her little excitement at first. She was dry and sleepy, but her body woke up and lubed itself as she impaled herself and rode him like a pogo stick.

"Mmm," she purred.

Fondling her nipples, he kissed her deeply, his lips claiming hers, inviting her into an intimate dance that could match no other. Then he captured her hands and held her over him in a seated position, and thrust into her at a rapid pace. She loved being his captive, atop him, on display for him as he rammed up into her so hard and fast that she could only try to hold onto his hands as tightly as she could.

Her body began to jerk as she climaxed, her pleasure increased by the way he held her so securely in his arms, yet controlled her movements as though she were restrained. His cock pulsed several more times inside her before he came with a shudder.

When he released her arms, Carmen drowsily curled into the crook of his arm and they fell asleep.

The alarm went off again. "Oh, my God. I want you again."

"Tonight. Daddy, you need to go to work," she yawned.

He slipped his leg between hers. "I want to take you from behind."

"Seriously?"

"Yes. Spread your legs for me."

Really? She knew he should be going to work, but it wasn't her place to push him. Or to refuse him.

"C'mon, babygirl."

Those words made her melt every time. Whenever he called her that, she was his to command. Her legs parted and she lifted her ass to give him easier access.

Still coated with his cum, his cock slid in easily. He liked to fuck her deep, driving all the way to the cervix, pounding her hard, then angling back to hit her g-spot.

Pinned underneath him, she felt like his prisoner and he knew it. It was part of the game. "You can't get away," he taunted. "No matter how much you struggle, no matter what you do, you aren't going anywhere. You just have to lie here and take it."

She wiggled underneath him to test out his theory. Sure enough, he was too heavy on her. She wasn't getting out of this, not that she'd want to. Having him fuck her was one of her greatest joys, but the idea that she was at his mercy increased her pleasure immensely.

Reaching around her head, he held her chin in one hand and her forehead in the other, stabilizing her head as he fucked her hard. Shoving a thumb into her mouth for her to suck simultaneously made her feel completely controlled and immobilized. That turned her on even more and she moaned in ecstasy as she suckled on his finger. Her body felt as if she were on fire, the helplessness of her position bringing her arousal to new heights. When he shifted his weight so that he was fucking her g-spot at a fast and furious pace, she cried into the thumb gag and her consciousness was wracked with an earth-moving orgasm. Giving up everything she had to him, she felt her cunt release her girly fluid as she came all over his exploding cock.

CHAPTER TWENTY-ONE

An hour later, Natron's mood took a nosedive when the offensive coordinator cussed him out for showing up late. Part of him didn't give a crap. Why the hell did he need to come to the meeting anyway? It was about the upcoming game this weekend. The one they weren't going to let him play in.

The other part of him cringed at his selfish, immature behavior. He knew he needed to show the coaches his best, and that included being on time for meetings, practices, everything.

His heart rate increased every time the coaching staff talked about the plays drawn up for Marvin. Natron could feel the jealousy eating away at him. The frustration that he couldn't yet play rose up in his throat like bile. He had been the MVP last year. It should be him, not Marvin, they were designing plays for.

Patience had never been his strong suit, but he had done his best in his current situation and now it looked like all his work, all his training, and all his sacrifice would be for nothing. The team thought he'd be ready to play by March, a month after the Super Bowl, which did him absolutely no good. He desperately wanted to play in the playoffs and as reality set in, so did depression.

When the day's meetings finished, Natron found himself walking out to the parking lot the same time as Marvin. Natron rolled his eyes. He'd hoped to avoid talking to Marvin altogether.

"Hey!" Marvin called to him. "Heard you were throwin' the ball around with Clay this week."

Damn! Did everything get back to this guy?

"You'll get it back, bro." Marvin offered him a handshake.

Natron saw the glimmer of pity in Marvin's eye and his throat began to close. He reached out tentatively, curled his hand in Marvin's and made the appropriate handshake gestures.

Natron forced a smile. "Aww yeah, you know it. Better look out next year," he said and left the building feeling lower than an alligator's belly.

The team plane would be leaving for Philly the next day and he wouldn't be on it. It was a Friday night and wanting nothing more than to forget his life and let off a little steam, he dialed Clarence's number.

That night Carmen turned on the television to see Natron's *EN* interview. Sitting on her sofa, alone in her apartment, watching him talk about her on TV was surreal. She didn't usually watch entertainment gossip shows.

She should have been pleased that Natron talked about settling down with her, but something about the interview seemed calculated, staged. And when he told her about the interview, he didn't mention that he practically said he was going to marry her.

He'd shaved his head to draw the media attention back to him. Was he doing the same thing by talking about getting engaged to her? That must be it, because he'd never mentioned anything about their future to her and it made her feel like a pawn.

It sucked feeling like you were the last one to know, especially about her own relationship. It reminded her of when she'd been the last one to learn that Natron had broken his knee. Hell, everyone who had a television found out before her and she'd had to find out in a text from James.

The whole thing made her wonder if Natron was even considering proposing to her at all…

CHAPTER TWENTY-TWO

If Natron hadn't just told a reporter that he was practically engaged, the media shitstorm that ensued might not have been so bad, but when Carmen woke up Saturday morning, a small army of reporters were camped outside her apartment ready to get her reaction to the latest celebrity scandal.

Originally she'd been on the way to her car to fetch a sweatshirt she'd left there, but she forgot all about that when several microphones were shoved in her face and sharp, staccato voices shouted questions at her.

"Did you know Natron was cheating on you?"

"Is it true she's going to have his love child?"

"Have you ever met Inya Burkheart?"

Carmen's face tightened and her lips clamped shut. What the hell were these people talking about? Without thought, she rushed back inside and locked the door behind her.

Those reporters were animals, rabid for some sort of reaction from her. About what? She had no idea what were they talking about. Her first reaction was to call Natron and ask him. But something inside her, something mistrusting, told her to check the Internet first.

If those vultures outside were talking about it, it had to be on the Internet. She opened her laptop and searched for 'Natron Dakers + Inya Burkheart'— however you spelled the bitch's name. She already hated the mystery woman for encroaching upon her life.

The first result was from *The Daily Poop*—a trendy gossip website that traded in embarrassing photos of celebs and breaking news of stars' breakups. The headline read, 'Breaking His Leg or Breaking Hearts?'

Carmen clicked on it and a giant boob appeared on the screen. The tip of it had a black circle covering it so no nipple was obvious in the picture. The breast looked like it was pressed right into Natron's face. Dread gripped her entire body. *No, no, no, no, no!* her brain shouted. A chill swam through her body and she hugged her arms to her, hoping it would stop the shaking.

She examined the picture more closely. A smiling Natron was pressed up against the breast of a half-naked woman. The proximity of one of her breasts to his mouth was dangerously close. It looked like she was shimmying in front of him and he was about to take it in his mouth.

Wait, was it in his mouth? Not exactly. You could tell he was smiling... could he have her body part in his mouth and smile at the same time?

Her head spun with the implications. Was he cheating on her? Was this a one-night fling or something more substantial? Maybe there was an explanation, or perhaps it was possible that it wasn't as bad as it looked...

She wanted to slap herself for that last thought. Instead, she went to the bathroom and splashed some cold water on her face. She needed to calm down so she could think, but her phone started dinging with incoming text messages.

Several of her friends had texted "*WTF?*" and Charmaine's message read, "*On my way over. Bringing provisions.*"

She'd talk it out with Charmaine before she called Natron, but there had to be an explanation, didn't there? She climbed the stairs and threw herself on the bed. Tears threatened to fall, but she held them back. Trying to make her body as still as possible, she willed Charmaine to hurry.

Finally she heard a loud knock.

Flying downstairs, Carmen opened the door for her friend. Charmaine waved and blew kisses to the reporters. Carmen rolled her eyes. Leave it to Charmaine to take advantage of a media opportunity.

"What are you doing?" Carmen snapped as she pulled Charmaine in the door.

Charmaine shrugged, setting down several grocery bags, a chinchilla coat rolling down her arms onto one of the sofas. "Honey, you have to be nice to them. If they hate you, it makes everything worse."

If anyone knew about the paparazzi and the media, it was Charmaine. She'd been in the spotlight ever since her parents' divorce. Her mother had tried to keep her out of the spotlight, but Charmaine seemed to draw attention everywhere she went. In the end, her mother failed and the press documented all of her milestones and screw-ups. She was, after all, the daughter of the richest and most infamous man in a state where rich and infamous men were as commonplace as hand sanitizer in a hospital.

"Have you talked to Natron?" Charmaine asked.

"No. I thought maybe he'd call me, or... I don't know."

"Well, there's not really much he can say, is there? The asshole's cheating on you." Charmaine strolled into the kitchen and began making mimosas.

"We don't know that for sure, do we?" Carmen squeaked.

Charmaine stopped what she was doing, planted hands on hips and said evenly, "Really? Really, Carmen? You are living in a fantasy world, babe."

The dread that had settled in her stomach gnawed away at her insides. "Maybe the photo was doctored..."

"Ha! Fat chance. Carmen, you know women are always trying to sink their claws into him. Big superstar and all. This bitch just made it work. Clearly, you can't trust him."

A lone tear rolled down Carmen's cheek.

"Aww, I didn't mean to make you cry," Charmaine said. "Here, have a drink. Charmaine will make it all better." She handed Carmen a flute of champagne mixed with orange juice and held up her glass.

"Men are bastards. I've always known it." Charmaine said and clinked her glass with Carmen's.

"I guess so," Carmen said and downed her glass in one gulp.

Charmaine refilled her glass. "That's the spirit."

Over the next couple of hours they got nice and drunk, and eventually the reporters gave up and went home. Carmen made some sandwiches for lunch, and while they were eating Charmaine devised a plan.

"Does Natron keep a lot of his stuff here?"

"A few things."

Charmaine's already glassy eyes gleamed with inspiration. "Let's get rid of them."

Carmen perked up. She was upset Natron hadn't even texted or called her to apologize or see how she was doing after his betrayal. The bastard. "Yeah, throw them in the yard."

"Burn them!" Charmaine rubbed her hands together like a cartoon villain.

Carmen giggled. "Burn them, seriously?"

"Oh, yeah. That fool has done you wrong, girl. That's the *least* you should do!" She got up and looked around. "Where's his stuff?"

"Mostly upstairs," Carmen said and followed Charmaine, who was already bounding up the stairs.

Carmen pointed out a drawer of Natron's things and Charmaine started throwing them over the side of the half-wall down into the living area below.

Heading for the closet, Carmen pulled shirts off hangers and grabbed a handful of Natron's underwear. *This is kinda fun*, she thought, throwing the clothes over the railing as Charmaine had.

Charmaine turned to her. "What else?"

They went to the bathroom, gathered up his toothbrush, deodorant, and razor and ran down the stairs.

"I'll check outside to be sure the buzzards are all gone," Charmaine said and peeped out the door. "All clear."

The girls carried everything out to the middle of the lawn on tipsy legs.

"Now what?" Carmen asked, hearing the alcohol-induced slur to her words.

"Oh! I've got just the thing," Charmaine said and ran inside in a zig-zag type pattern. Carmen laughed, thinking she'd heard that was how you were supposed to run if someone had a gun pointed at you. Zig-zag, rather than straight, so they might miss. Of course, Charmaine wasn't running from a bullet, she was just hammered.

The beauty came back outside with a long slim lighter with a handle, the kind of lighter people used when igniting the barbecue grill.

Carmen chewed on a fingernail. "Are you sure we should? I don't know… Hey, where did you get that anyway?"

Ignoring her, Charmaine held a pair of Natron's boxer briefs just above the flame she'd just ignited with the click of a button.

Carmen squealed. She couldn't believe Charmaine had lit his shorts on fire. A mixture of glee and trepidation swirled inside her, and a foreign demon took over her body as she urged her friend on. "Do it."

Charmaine tossed the half-burning underwear into the pile of clothes. Instead of going up in flames, the spark petered out slowly and with it their spirits.

"Well, that sucks," Charmaine said, the corners of her mouth falling.

"Yeah," Carmen sighed.

"Hey, I know. Wait right here." Charmaine disappeared into the apartment, returning a few moments later with a bottle of rubbing alcohol.

"Found this in your bathroom," she said and doused the pile.

Before Carmen could protest, Charmaine lit the whole thing on fire.

The flames exploded, sending the girls backwards.

"Ouch!" Charmaine cried. "I may have singed my eyelashes off."

"Oh, my God, for real?" Carmen asked.

"Yes, come look. Damn, that's what I get for paying for eyelash extensions." She groaned. "And it takes so long to get them done."

Carmen had only used mascara on her lashes and had no idea what Carmen was talking about. She knew Charmaine had hair extensions, nail extensions, and now eyelash extensions. Sometimes she thought Charmaine must *live* at a salon.

When she got close, Carmen could see the edges of Charmaine's jet-black lashes were charred, a funny yellowish color. And they smelled kinda funny, like burnt hair. "Eww, Charmaine, they are!"

"Oh, fuck me!" Charmaine cursed then started laughing. "Oh, dear, imagine what my eyelash lady is going to say when I show her these."

Carmen got tickled and they both busted out laughing. The kind of laugh when you know it's really not appropriate to laugh, but you just can't help it, like when you're in church. They fell to the ground and sat with their arms around each other giggling and watching Natron's stuff burn.

As their hysterics began winding down, Carmen realized the pain was still there, and she had the feeling it was going to become her constant embittered companion.

About that time, Natron's car pulled up in front of the building. Seeing the fire in the yard, he screeched to a stop, jumped out of the car, and sprinted over to Carmen.

Natron fell to his knees and lunged forward to embrace her. "Carmen, are you okay?"

Charmaine inserted herself between them and pushed his shoulder. "You stay away from her, Natron. How could you do this to her, you jackass?"

The reality of the situation dawned in his eyes and he turned to the flaming pyre. "What's all that?"

Tears stung in Carmen's eyes. "Your stuff," she answered dully.

He sat back and pulled her to him. "No, baby. You don't understand. It's not what it looks like, really it's not."

Charmaine snorted and was about to say something when the whirring of sirens bore down on them. A fire truck barreled down the street toward them and stopped behind Natron's car. Red and white lights flashed and two firemen dressed in full gear rushed out of the truck toward the bonfire next to them.

One of the firefighters doused the flames with a large fire extinguisher while the other one approached the group. "What's going on here?" He spoke in a firm, almost harsh voice.

Charmaine popped up and said to Carmen and Natron, "I'll handle this." They watched her take a few wobbly steps away and the fireman followed. It was a Bainbridge trait; people followed them.

Natron started to speak, but Carmen shushed him. The firemen's arrival on the scene had sobered her up and she wanted to hear what Charmaine told the fireman.

"Ma'am, what is going on here? A neighbor called in a fire, is this the only one?"

"Yes, occifer. Should I call you oddifer?" she asked twirling her wildly colored hair around a perfectly manicured nail. "I mean officer," she said, correcting herself.

"That's fine. What happened here?" The man was all business. He appeared oblivious to not only Charmaine's charms, but also to who she was.

"What's your name, officer?" she trilled, plastering a winning smile across her face.

Carmen rolled her eyes.

"Baldwin. Sergeant Hunter Baldwin. Now what started this fire?"

Charmaine bit her lip. "I guess I did."

"Why?"

She kicked at the grass. "Well, you see, my friend found out her boyfriend was cheating on her, so we threw his stuff in the yard, and well, I thought it would be a good idea to burn it."

"That, ma'am, is most assuredly not a good idea. In fact it's against the law, did you know that?"

Charmaine's eyes widened. "No! I had no idea. I'm so sorry."

"Not to mention that you or someone else might be injured in the process. I could issue you a citation…"

"Oh, no, officer! That won't be necessary. I promise I won't do it again."

"If the surrounding area caught fire, the blaze might spread and you'd be booked for arson. Do you realize that?"

"No, I had no idea." She hung her head and looked up prettily through her charred lashes. "I'm so sorry, officer. I was all caught up in the moment and just did something stupid. It will never happen again."

"It better not. Fire is not for playing around with. It's serious business."

Carmen felt the urge to clap at Charmaine's performance, but she refrained and instead piped in, "We're really sorry, officer. It won't happen again. We promise."

Sgt. Baldwin glanced over at her and Natron. His handsome face showed no recognition he was in the presence of last year's MVP or the star of dozens of commercials. "I guess I could issue you girls a warning."

"Oh, thank you, sir," Charmaine enthused.

Hunter narrowed his eyes at her. "But I don't want to ever hear of you burning someone's belongings again, do you hear?"

Charmaine nodded vigorously. "Yes, sir. I promise." And she crossed her heart to prove it to him.

Hunter's gaze met Natron's. "This isn't your stuff, is it?" he asked, pointing at the smoldering pile that was now covered with a white foamy substance from the fire extinguisher.

"'Fraid so," Natron replied.

Hunter shook his head and looked from Carmen to Charmaine, then back to Natron. "Good luck to you, man. Be sure y'all clean this up once it's cooled down."

"Sure will, bro. Thanks." Natron shook his hand and Sgt. Baldwin walked back to his truck and he and his crew drove away.

"Whew!" Charmaine laughed. "I thought he would never leave."

Natron gave her a sharp look. "Charmaine, what are you thinking?"

Crossing her arms over her chest, she sneered. "I could ask you the same question."

Natron turned to Carmen. "Baby, can we please talk?"

Feeling her lip begin to quiver, Carmen answered, "I don't think so. Not right now."

Charmaine draped an arm over Carmen's shoulder and walked her back inside, leaving Natron to deal with the charred remains of his possessions.

CHAPTER TWENTY-THREE

The grey cloud that seemed permanently fixed over his head was firmly in place when Natron reported for practice Monday morning. The day before, Natron had watched the Vipers' game with little more than a passing interest. No matter how much Jack had tried to snap him out of it, he was devastated about the situation with Carmen. She wouldn't respond to his text messages or his phone calls. He'd finally sent her an e-mail explaining what had happened, but had received no response.

The Vipers had won their game on Sunday, which meant that they were heading to the National Football Conference Championship this next weekend. They were set to play the Portland Explorers, a team known for their high-flying offense with one or two superstars on defense.

Natron had only been in the Vipers' building for two minutes before three different people told him Coach Morrison was looking for him. Nerves tickled the inside of his stomach. Maybe Coach was going to tell him he could play in the game this weekend. Natron balled his fists and walked faster.

When he got to Coach's office, the man waved him in and motioned for him to take a seat in a chair across from his large mahogany desk. Coach Morrison was on his cellphone, listening to the speaker on the other end. He closed the door behind him, told the caller he had to go, pressed a button and sat behind his desk.

Coach leaned back in his chair and laced his hands behind his head. "Hey, Natron. How ya doin'?"

"Fine, Coach. How're you?"

Coach ignored his question. "I mean, how's the knee comin'?"

"It's comin' along good. I'm ready to go."

Coach nodded thoughtfully. "Ready to go, huh, son?"

Natron flashed one of his money grins. "Sure, Coach. Been workin' hard. Gettin' back in shape. Killin' it in the weight room. Know what I'm sayin'?"

"Oh, I know what you're sayin'." He paused, then leaned forward in his chair. "You know, Natron, you've always been an asset to this team, an important part of our success last year."

Natron nodded. "Uh-huh. Thank you, sir."

Coach set his elbows on the desk, steepling his fingers pensively. "So tell me, Natron, why've you got to go and be such a fuck-up?"

The question caught Natron by surprise. "What do you mean?"

"I mean that I can't stop the phones in here from ringing. I've got two PR people on this nonsense with you and this hooker, but that's all the press wants to talk about."

Natron's jaw dropped. He had no idea that picture would trickle up to becoming a problem for the team. Sure, it looked bad, but… and this was the first he'd heard about the girl being a hooker. Great, when it rained, it fucking poured. "Coach, I'm sorry. I just…"

"You just can't keep it in your pants. I know. But dammit, Natron, if you're going to do that, don't do it on camera. And don't do it two days after you tell a reporter you're madly in love and about to propose to your girlfriend, and for fuck's sake don't do it the week before the championship game!" As his tone became more heated, he rose in his chair so that by the time he was finished, he was towering over the seated Natron, his voice growing louder and louder until Natron cringed at the decibel level.

Coach sat back in his chair, lifted his reading glasses to his face, and began shuffling some papers. After he'd regained his composure he said, "You are to resume practice as usual, but this weekend you will be riding the bench."

Then he stared Natron down. "You will get your house in order, son, if you want to play on my team."

Stunned, Natron mumbled, "Yes, sir," before getting up and slinking out the door.

In the hallway, he had to fight to hold it together. He wasn't going to play, and all because of some stupid whore trying to get her fifteen minutes of fame.

Everything he had, everything he loved was slipping away.

He stumbled toward the practice field, steeling himself for the jokes, the bullshit he'd take from the other players. With great effort, he put on his game face, cocky and confident as ever on the outside.

Only he knew that cloud over his head had just turned from grey to black.

CHAPTER TWENTY-FOUR

Carmen arrived at Gustav's gallery a few minutes early. She had recently signed a deal to work with the popular local photographer, Niho, creating portraits for high-end clients.

Today she was supposed to meet Niho to go over some of their new clients' proposals. The marriage of their two businesses could possibly double Carmen's commissions, and she'd also be able to charge more based on the wealth of most of Niho's clients. Soon she'd be hobnobbing with the wealthy on her own, and she wouldn't have to rely on Natron for those kinds of contacts.

Carmen wasn't sure where things stood with Natron. He'd sent her a long e-mail in which he insisted that he'd never had anything to do with the woman in the photograph. He swore that he was at a party with Clarence and some of Clarence's friends, minding his own business, in a hot tub, when that girl took off her top and slid against him.

His story was that he said, "Excuse me" to her and that was the end of it. He said he didn't remember seeing any photos being taken, but these days when everyone had a phone with a camera on it, pictures could be snapped anytime, anywhere.

The whole thing sounded farfetched and Carmen thought she'd be a fool to believe him, setting herself up for the whole thing to happen again. She needed to accept that he was a cheater. Most professional athletes were; the temptations were too great and too numerous.

But her heart ached. She loved Natron Dakers with everything she had. He'd opened her heart and shown her a love she hadn't known was possible. He cared for her so sincerely, so tenderly, so completely… that it broke her to know he'd never be hers and hers alone.

The sound of her name being called jarred her from her thoughts and she looked up to find Niho approaching.

"Niho! Good to see you," she said, trying not to breathe as he hugged her tightly. The man refused to wear deodorant, and it always amazed Carmen that his fancy clients never seemed to notice the putrid stench that surrounded him. It was as though his eccentricities made him more exotic and therefore his portraits became even more of a status symbol.

She frowned, hoping her jeans and t-shirt look wasn't going to stop his clientele from commissioning her. Compared to Niho, dressed in a sapphire-blue velvet suit with purple suede cowboy boots, she looked like a conservative teenager. Hmm. Note to self—jazz up the wardrobe a bit. She could always get Charmaine to take her shopping. Or Nellie. Those two were always shopping.

Niho took her hands in his. "*Cherie*, before we get down to business I must tell you how sorry I am to hear of all this trouble with Natron." He pursed his lips in a funky-looking pout.

She brushed a hand in front of her face. "Oh, it's nothing."

"*Cher*, you do not fool me. I know how attached you are to zee football player."

Niho's concern made her uncomfortable, like he was overstepping. She and Niho socialized sometimes, but she wouldn't say he was a close friend who knew her intimate business. Yet, somehow, whenever you were talking about celebrities, people tended to insert themselves. She'd learned that with Charmaine as well as Natron.

People wanted a piece of their fame, even if it was a distant piece. It didn't make sense to Carmen. Fame had never been important to her, but she'd learned that it was a tendency of most people to chase fame. Or famous people.

"Yes, well, can we get down to business?" Carmen asked, exuding a cheerfulness she did not feel.

"But of course, but first I have some news for you." The little man was so excited it looked like he might bust the shiny blue buttons off his suit.

"You do? What news?"

He drew close to her and whispered in a conspiratorial tone, "I know who took the picture."

She nodded. In Carmen's mind they had moved on to portraits, pictures of wealthy socialites and politicians willing to put groceries in her cupboard.

He turned his protruding eyes to hers. "*The* picture." When she still didn't seem to get it, he nudged her with his elbow. "Of Natron with the hooker."

Carmen felt the blood rush from her face and she found the nearest chair and slumped down into it.

"Oh, dear," Niho cried, hovering over her. "Are you okay? Let me get you some water, *Cher*."

Carmen nodded. Why did this have to happen? She'd been hoping to escape her personal problems and focus on work today.

Moments later Niho returned with a bottle of water and Gustav, who brought several pieces of paper which he fanned her with.

"Are you okay, Carmen? You don't look so good," Gustav said, fussing over her.

"I'm fine. I just don't want to talk about the thing with Natron. That's all."

"Oh, but honey, you do. You need to meet with this man who took the picture. He was there." Niho patted her on the shoulder.

"Why do I need to talk to him?"

"Because it's not what it looks like." Niho shook his head.

"How do you know? Who is this guy?"

"Let's just say he's a friend of mine. Going through a divorce, poor guy. He goes to some of the same meetings I go to."

"Meetings?"

"Yeah, you know, honey, the confidential kind." Niho gestured himself tipping a bottle to his mouth, and Carmen realized he meant Alcoholics Anonymous meetings.

"So… what do you know?" she asked.

"I don't know the whole story, but he said he sold the photo to the tabloids for some money to get a place to live, and that he feels bad because he knows it didn't really represent the true situation."

Carmen forgot all about her work. "How can I get in touch with him?"

Niho handed her his bedazzled cellphone. "His name is Nicholas Marinovich."

Seeing the number, she pressed the call button.

The Vipers won their game against the Portland Explorers. Monday morning Natron showed up for practice thirty minutes early. His team was going to the Super Bowl and he planned on doing everything possible to play in that game. This was his last chance and he was going to do everything in his power to show everyone that he was back.

Later in the week, he had a meeting with the team doctor who would either approve him to play or leave him benched. But between now and then Natron would be working overtime with Jack to get him in the best shape possible for his potential return.

Practice that day went well, the coaches integrating him in with the other receivers. When he'd first come back, he'd been given the newest additions to the playbook during the time he'd been gone. He'd made sure to learn every detail of every play and now he was showing it on the practice field.

His abilities to juke around the defender and make quick cuts were still not where they used to be, but he had improved in other areas. His quarterback even commented on it. "Damn, Natron. You've bulked up. What the hell have you been doing in rehab? Maybe I need to get hurt, see if I can come back with guns like that."

"Hell, no, Clay. I don't recommend it. Don't you be doin' nothin' to get hurt. I've been working too hard and too long to get back so you can toss me that ball."

They laughed and clapped each other on the back as they headed into the locker room.

"Really, Natron. I'm hoping you get to play," Clay said.

"From your lips to Coach's ears," Natron said.

"I know I can count on you in certain situations. Stalcup is good, but he's not you."

Natron beamed. "Thanks, man."

CHAPTER TWENTY-FIVE

Carmen had arranged to meet the photographer at a diner. It seemed like the kind of place people met private eyes in movies, and that was as close as she could get to these strange circumstances she found herself in.

Sitting in the booth, she knew Marinovich from the moment he walked in. He looked every bit the part of the down-on-his-luck guy who'd been kicked to the curb by his wife and was trying to make sense of the cruelties life often doles out to the already downtrodden.

The five o' clock shadow that covered the lower half of his face had turned into more of a two a.m. last-call kind of shadow. His eyes were bloodshot, and he had the lethargic air about him of a man who had given up.

He scanned the handful of customers in the restaurant before his eyes rested on her. Carmen lifted a hand in greeting and he approached her table.

"Hi. Mr. Marinovich?" Carmen asked extending her hand.

He took it, offering the limpest of handshakes.

"Have a seat," Carmen offered.

"Alright," he said.

"Thank you so much for meeting me. Niho said you know the real story behind that photograph of Natron Dakers."

Before he could speak, the waitress came over and they each ordered a cup of coffee. Carmen felt like she might jump out of her chair and strangle the woman for interrupting them. But since the woman was only doing her job, she refrained.

The instant the waitress was out of earshot, Carmen leaned across the table. "Tell me, what happened? The real story."

"Miss Harris, I'm real sorry about that picture getting out. When I saw it on my camera I couldn't believe my good fortune. I knew the papers would pay big money for it. And I needed the money something fierce. You see, my wife..."

"Mr. Marinovich, I understand that you're in a bad place financially. I realize you have regrets, but the photograph looked like there could not be any other explanation other than Natron was being, ahem," she cleared her throat, "inappropriate, with that woman."

"I agree. But you see, Miss Harris, that was not the case."

"What do you mean?"

"Okay, I was at the party and once I saw that Natron was there I went to the car and got my camera. I know it was horrible, but when he got into the hot tub in his shorts, I thought I could maybe get a money shot, you know? Because he's got that awesome physique women love and the Internet guys will pay for pictures of that. That was my only intention, to get a shot of him in his shorts."

"Go on," Carmen encouraged.

"Except there was this woman there, she was kinda tipsy and she kept hitting on him. He wasn't interested. She practically followed him around the party and when he got in the hot tub, she followed. When that didn't get her anywhere with him, she took off her top."

"Eeew!" Carmen couldn't help herself. What a skank.

"Well, most of the guys were excited and paying her lots of attention, as you can imagine. But Natron, he was trying to avoid her."

"Okay." So far it didn't sound so bad.

"Then she tried to kinda sit in his lap or something. I'm not sure because I was back behind some bushes, so nobody would notice my camera and kick me out. Next thing I know he started helping her out of the hot tub. She was so drunk she kinda stumbled and well, judging by my pictures—her boob kinda hit him in the face."

Carmen grimaced.

"Yeah. I think it grazed him. Sorry, but he just laughed it off and some other guy gave her a towel and went inside with her. I didn't see her again."

"So... he didn't hook up with her?"

The waitress ambled over with their cups of coffee. "Anything else?"

"I think that will do it," Carmen said shortly.

Marinovich poured two packages of creamer into his coffee and took a sip. "Not that I saw. From what I could tell he's used to dealing with a lot of attention. It looked like he could tell she was trouble and he was trying to steer clear of her. He was nice about it too. When she started falling down he helped her, like a gentleman. That's why I felt so bad that my picture made him out to be a cheating bastard."

She frowned. "Yeah. Having to deal with paparazzi sucks."

He shrugged. "Hey, I gotta make a living. If I hadn't taken that picture, somebody with their Smart phone might have. Being a celebrity is a tradeoff. You get the money and the fame, but you pay for it by losing your privacy.

The public thinks they own celebrities, and in a way, they do."

"One hell of a tradeoff."

"Like I said, I'm sorry it made Natron come off like a bad guy. He's not, at least as far as I could tell."

Carmen bit her lip thoughtfully. "So you're sure he didn't hook up with her? That nothing was going on?"

He shook his head. "Nothing I saw."

She nodded. "Thank you for meeting with me. You have helped put my mind at ease."

"Sure," he said, taking another sip of his coffee. "So can I come to the wedding?"

"Don't push it," she replied, leaving a ten-dollar bill on the table.

"Leaving so soon? I thought maybe we could at least have a piece of pie."

She tossed another ten on the table. "Knock yourself out. I've got someone I need to see."

CHAPTER TWENTY-SIX

That afternoon while Natron was lifting with Jack, a text came through to his phone. His spirits lifted when he saw it was from Carmen.

"Can you come by tonight?"
"Sure. What time?" he texted back.

They agreed on eight and he rushed to finish the rest of his workout.

Certain that she was still mad at him, he stopped at the store and picked up some flowers on his way over. His mamma had taught him that it was never a bad thing to show up bearing some sort of gift, so he picked out a bouquet filled with yellow roses.

Carmen let him in, kissed him on the cheek, and thanked him for the flowers. She set them on the kitchen counter and asked him to sit down.

"Babygirl, I know you're still mad at me…" he began.

"Not really," she interjected.

"Wait, you're not?" He'd been devastated by the rift between them. The only way he'd been able to deal with it was by putting the situation out of his mind and focusing on football.

Carmen told him about her conversation with Marinovich.

"You gotta be kiddin' me. So that's how that picture got taken. That's nuts." He shook his head. "Damn, I can't go anywhere."

"Apparently not. Especially places where there are half-naked women." She frowned.

"Hey, babe, I didn't know women would be takin' their tops off. I was doin' my best to stay away from that tramp."

"Alright. Well, maybe you should steer clear from Clarence. Every time you two get together, naked women seem to be involved," she said, crossing her arms over her chest.

"That's probably not a bad idea. He's a good guy, but…"

"And what is this about you proposing to me that I saw on *Entertainment Nightly*? Don't you think you might want to mention that to me first?"

"Baby, now don't be mad about that. Why would that make you mad?" he asked, perplexed. Being proposed to, isn't that what women wanted? Hell, he'd never understand women.

"Because first of all it sounded like a publicity stunt, since you've never even talked to me about our future. And second of all because if you did mean it, well, it sucks always being the last to know."

"What do you mean always being the last to know?"

Her eyes began to well up with tears. "It's like when you were hurt and I was at the bottom of the list. Everyone in America with a TV knew you'd broken your knee before I did. And then, when they wouldn't let me see you…"

He got up and sat beside her. Draping an arm around her, he said, "I'm sorry. You're right. I wasn't thinking. That reporter started asking me about you and I just told her what was in my heart. I'm sorry that upset you."

He hugged her close. She felt so good in his arms. He'd missed holding her. What he'd said in that interview was true. She meant the world to him.

"Will you forgive me?"

"For what?" she asked.

"For being stupid."

She giggled. "Sure, I can forgive you for that."

"I really do see a future with you, babygirl."

"And I can't imagine a future without you, Daddy."

"I'm not sure what kind of future it will be," he said.

"What do you mean?" Carmen asked, twisting her lips in confusion.

"Just that I don't know what's going to happen with my career, Carmen. I just don't know," he said, rubbing a hand over his bald head.

"Daddy, you are going to make it back from this. You've worked so hard, and you're so talented."

He shook his head. "That may not be enough…"

"You've got to get all that negativity out of your head, Daddy. I believe in you. You can do anything you put your mind to."

She turned her face to his and he bent to kiss her. She believed in him. With her, all his hopes and dreams seemed possible, and this fueled his passion for her. He needed her, not just as his sexual plaything, but as his partner, the woman he wanted by his side always.

He pressed his lips against hers. She opened to him, invited his exploration of her mouth. Her arms encircled him and she gently scratched his back through his shirt. Damn, it felt incredible to hold her.

He pulled back and gave her a sharp look. "There is another matter we need to discuss."

She raised a brow quizzically.

"You and Charmaine burning my stuff."

Her shoulders slumped and she chewed on her bottom lip. "Yeah, sorry about that, Daddy."

"You should be. Not only was that impulsive, but that fireman was right. You girls could have caused a real fire and hurt somebody."

"You're right. I'm sorry about your things…"

"Shit, I can buy new things, Carmen. You know, if I'm not supposed to hang out with Clarence, maybe you shouldn't hang out with Charmaine. That girl's a menace."

"Now Daddy, that's not fair. Charmaine was looking out for me. She just doesn't want anyone to hurt me, she's protective."

"She's also nuts."

"She is not. You just don't like her because you and she are too much alike. That's all," she said, massaging his shoulder.

"I don't know. Maybe you're right."

"I know I am." She winked.

"But that doesn't excuse your behavior, does it, babygirl?"

Her eyes grew wide. "No, sir."

"I think somebody needs a spanking."

Carmen gritted her teeth.

"C'mon. Down with the panties. Over the knee."

She stood up and slipped her panties down to her ankles, then kicked them aside.

Obediently, she draped herself over his lap and held his leg. He loved how she liked to hold his leg during a punishment. He could tell how much it hurt by how tightly she gripped him. And he could tell when she let herself float away under the magic stream of endorphins.

"How many do you think you've earned?"

"Ten," she answered meekly.

"Ten? Girl, you burned my shit! Try again."

"Twenty?"

"Twenty-five," he said firmly.

"Yes, sir."

He started out with a light hand covering every inch of her ass cheeks with his huge palm. The resounding thwacking sounds reverberated through the room alongside Carmen's little grunts and groans. After fifteen strokes, her cheeks were hot to the touch and as pink as cotton candy. He rubbed her rear to ease the pain, and Carmen purred under his gentle touch.

"Ten more," he said, striking her backside again. This time the noise that arose from her was not so pleasant.

Her muscles tensed and he reprimanded, "You know it's only going to hurt worse if you do that. Relax."

She slowly seemed to give herself over to the process, the tension easing out of her muscles with each blow.

"Good girl. We're almost done."

She mumbled that she was sorry for burning his clothes.

"I know, baby," he said with a final swat to her hindquarters, which were a brilliant red now. "All done, and you've been such a good girl, Daddy's going to make you come."

She wriggled underneath him.

"Be still," he commanded and inserted a finger into her slick, wet channel.

She moaned and pressed her pussy against his hand. Normally he would have fussed at her, but tonight was about patching things up, not causing more conflict.

He added another finger and fucked her with them, hard and insistently. Her vaginal muscles clenched around him and her hips bucked, indicating her hunger for deeper thrusts.

Giving her what he knew she wanted, he increased the speed and curled his fingers to where they hit her sensitive g-spot. This brought a howl from her throat. He responded by flicking her clit with his thumb. He thrummed that spot with each thrust and within minutes he felt her convulse across his lap, her orgasm overtaking her.

He continued his ministrations until her body stilled and she brushed his hand away. He knew sometimes she could get so sensitive down there that it almost hurt if he kept fiddling with her.

Hoisting her up, he switched her to a seated position on her lap. Her face bore the glorious blush of being freshly loved. Disheveled and adorable as hell, she asked him, "Daddy, aren't you going to fuck me?"

He smiled wanly. "No, babygirl, not tonight."

"Why not?"

"I'm exhausted. Had a tough practice today, then Jack and I lifted, worked on some more footwork. And I can't stay." He kissed her on top of the head. "I'm sorry, but I gotta go home. Have to be at practice early tomorrow." He was tired. In fact, tired didn't even begin to describe it.

"No more being late to work in the morning?" she giggled.

"No. Coach chewed my ass out for that. I'm on thin ice anyway with all the negative publicity. It'll be a miracle if he lets me play in the game."

"Really?"

"Yeah. Babe, my career is in shambles," he said, placing a hand on her knee.

"That's not true."

"Yeah, it is. My endorsements have all dried up. I can't move the way I used to be able to, and I'm probably not going to play in the Super Bowl even though I've practically killed myself to be able to come back this year."

"Daddy, I had no idea about your endorsements. Why didn't you tell me?"

A mask of concern covered her face.

"Didn't want you to worry."

"But Daddy, we're partners. I'm here for you. No matter what."

"I don't want you to see me like this," he said, his emotions threatening to get the best of him.

"Like what?"

"Floundering. Out of control. Baby, how can I be a good daddy for you if I can't even control my body or my own career?"

"Control? Control is an illusion. Nobody has control. Natron, you are an incredible athlete, an amazing man, but you're human." She touched his bald head lovingly. "Just remember that. You're human, not Superman."

He heard what she was saying, but he didn't agree. People *expected* him to be Superman. He was Natron Dakers. He wasn't supposed to fail.

"Whatever happens," Carmen said, "I'll be here, right by your side."

"Thanks, baby," he said and held her tight, needing her now more than ever.

CHAPTER TWENTY-SEVEN

On Thursday, the team doctor cleared Natron to play. The team would be leaving for New Orleans on Saturday. The following week would involve practices, a few sightseeing tours and events, in addition to media day.

Friday morning Coach Morrison asked to see Natron in his office.

The grumpy look on Coach's face reminded Natron of a bear who'd missed his last meal and was eager to find some poor suspecting creature to pay for it.

"Hello, Natron, how's it going?"

"Going well, Coach."

"Working out those personal issues like I told you? I don't want any of those distractions following us to New Orleans," Coach said as he glared at Natron.

"All taken care of, Coach. Just a misunderstanding."

"I hope that's the truth. You've got a wonderful girl there, I'd hate to see you fuck that up."

"I agree."

"Okay, if I have your word there won't be any shenanigans, we're taking you with us to New Orleans. Doc cleared you, you can go."

"Thank you, Coach!"

"I'm keeping you on injured reserve for now. I can't promise you'll play. Probably won't start."

"Alright, I just want the chance to get out on that field, Coach."

Coach scratched his head. "I know, Natron, and truth is I know you've been working really hard. You are a valuable member of this team and I hope you'll be back in the lineup like before. But we'll just have to see. That was a big injury, son, and it may take the off-season to get back 100% from it."

"A chance, Coach. That's all I'm askin' for is a chance."

"I hear you. Keep working and keep your nose clean. Got it?'

"Got it."

With his relationship with Carmen on the mend, Natron made arrangements for her to attend the big game with their friends James and Marley. It meant everything to him that Carmen would be in the stands watching the game.

Natron had also gotten tickets for his mother and her new boyfriend. She'd followed his advice and met a guy online. While Natron wasn't sure he wanted to meet the guy right away, he was glad his mamma had found someone to spend time with.

Now he just needed to have a chance to play. As difficult as it was to push his thoughts of Carmen to the side even for a short period of time, he had to focus on his performance in the Super Bowl.

The week leading up to the game was packed full of meetings, events, and plenty of film study. On media day he plastered on his most charming smile and answered questions about his injury:

"No, I'm not sure if I'll be able to play."

"It depends on if Coach thinks I'm ready."

"Yes, I've been cleared by the doc, but I'm still not 100% yet."

The Vipers' head coach had made it clear that he wasn't going to make a public decision about whether or not Natron would play until the last possible minute. The hope was that the Raptors would think he was still hurt so they wouldn't prepare for Natron to be on the field. Whether or not the tactic would work, they'd find out soon enough.

Team activities kept him busy most of the time, but he found time to text Carmen several times a day. She was supportive as always, but if he couldn't play he wouldn't feel whole, and he wondered what kind of man he would be for her.

He reminded himself that Carmen had faith in him before putting all thoughts of her out of his mind in order to focus on the game. He put on his headphones and tuned out everything else. That night instead of counting sheep, he pictured himself catching touchdowns in the end zone, one after another.

Natron had played in big games before. He knew what it was to be a champion.

But today, standing in the Superdome, his hand on his heart, listening to the national anthem play, things were different. *He* was different.

Last year he was still a reckless kid with nothing to lose. This season he had dealt with adversity, and it was time to see how what kind of man he was. To see if he would rise to the challenge or buckle under the pressure.

Natron watched as the Vipers' offense ran out onto the field for the first possession without him. Coach had said he might not start, but hearing that and experiencing it were two different things. A hollow pit formed in his stomach and he paced the sidelines trying to walk off his anxiety and disappointment. He turned his energy to pumping up his teammates and tried to have faith that he would get his chance. On the field, the Vipers were held to three plays and were forced to punt.

The Raptors struck when their mammoth running back launched himself over the pile of bodies lined up along the goal line, the culmination of a thirteen-play drive led by their quarterback. The extra point put them up over the Vipers 7-0.

To Natron's surprise, one of the coaches waved him into the game for the Vipers' next offensive series. His pulse thumped loudly in his ears as he snapped on his chinstrap and took the field.

A roar arose from the crowd. Normally, Natron would have acknowledged the fans, waved, maybe even taken a bow. But not today; today he'd have to earn the cheers of the fans, and it wasn't going to be easy.

The first couple of plays, his job was to block for other players, and he executed the task well. He felt a difference in his strength, just as Jack had told him he would and that gave his confidence a boost.

On third down with fourteen yards to go, he ran a fade route to the outside. Clay Davis sent the ball flying in his direction, and the ball soared two feet above his head. Somehow he mis-timed his jump and while he got a fingertip on the football, he wasn't able to come down with it. As he got up off the ground, he kicked at the turf in frustration. He knew it was only his first game back, but it totally sucked being so rusty.

Clay came over and patted Natron's rear. "My bad, man."

Natron nodded as they ran off the field and the punt team came on.

On the next possession, the Vipers' defense held the Raptors to almost no gain and the Vipers got the ball back quickly.

Back in the game, Natron found he was having trouble with the cornerback jamming him up at the line of scrimmage. Out in the flats, the press coverage was also giving him fits. His legs weren't as explosive as before, so the defender was able to jam him up for the first five yards, which slowed him down and impeded his route running. All that was throwing off the timing he and Clay had been working so hard on for the past few weeks.

After another few times getting beaten one on one, he was sent to the bench. He tried to console himself by thinking of Carmen and her support for him. Rather than distracting him, her belief in him calmed him and boosted his confidence enough to help him focus. Fortunately, the Vipers' running game was beginning to roll and they scored a touchdown on a fifty-two-yard run up the middle, tying the game.

Right after that the Raptors got the ball and marched down the field to score another touchdown, making the score 14-7. And with that, all the momentum that had belonged to the Vipers shifted back to the Raptors.

During the next possession, Natron was back on the field. By now he had made some much-needed adjustments, and he knew he needed to use his newfound strength if he wanted to break open on a route. In the past he'd had such explosiveness that he'd accelerate to top speed much quicker than the defender and he easily ran past the defensive backs.

But his explosiveness disappeared when he was injured. Without it, he was slower coming out of his cuts and less crisp than he wasn't accustomed to. His own body behaved like a foreign entity. In the past he'd always been able to create separation between himself and the defender, but not now. He remembered Jack telling him he'd have to use his strength, he'd have to be aggressive and fight the defender for the ball.

The Raptor's cornerback, Rick Isaac, was one of the best in the league, and his job for the day was to make sure Natron was not a factor in the game. Isaac ran stride for stride with him after every jam, every cut, and every play. Hell, it felt like the guy was super-glued to him.

After several series in which the ball didn't come his way, Natron approached Clay. "Man, you can throw me the ball. I know I missed that first one, but I'll catch it. Promise you I'll catch it."

"Isaac's got you jammed up at the line, and then he is covering you stride for stride. You're not beating him." Clay shook his head.

"That's cuz my cuts aren't what they used to be. I'm not able to accelerate like I used to, but if you throw the ball up, I will come down with it. Trust me, man."

Clay nodded, but he didn't look convinced.

Natron slapped Clay's shoulder pad and found a cup of Gatorade. Drinking it in one gulp, he took a seat on the bench.

The game unfolded in front of Natron, but he barely paid attention. His mind puzzled over a solution to the problems he was having on the field, and everything Jack had told him came back to him.

When they'd worked together, Natron only half-listened to the personal trainer. Honestly, he'd expected Jack to be wrong. It was inconceivable to Natron that he might not be quick and explosive once he regained his health. He'd always figured Jack was 'over-correcting' and he hadn't expected to need it. While Natron had done everything Jack asked of him physically, but he hadn't paid enough attention to what Jack said.

Jack wanted to talk about all the things Natron would no longer be able to do this season and Natron's brain had been unwilling to absorb the man's advice. Now, sitting on the sidelines, he recalled Jack's advice.

You'll have to use brute force. That had been the message. He'd have to do this thing old school, take it to 'em. As he sat on the sidelines, his heart began to beat faster, and adrenaline pulsed through his veins. He needed to do this. For himself, for his team, for Carmen.

He watched as the Raptors score another touchdown. Damn, those fuckers made it look easy. What was happening with our defense? Natron banged his helmet on the turf, then checked himself. He had no business blaming the defense when he'd done little himself to contribute. With the team down 21-7, Natron knew they'd have to pass the ball if they wanted to catch up. He wanted to get back on the field so badly that his hands itched to feel the ball between them.

Instead, the Vipers' return man caught the ball at the two-yard line and ran it back 98 yards for the touchdown, eluding the entire opposing team. The Vipers bench went wild, and the stadium erupted in a cacophony of cheers. Being that New Orleans was closer to Dallas than Baltimore, there appeared to be more Vipers fans represented in the stands. Not exactly a home crowd for the Vipers, but close.

Even though the score brought them closer to the Raptors, Natron was still nervous, his leg shaking like it had its own motor as he waited impatiently for the Vipers' next possession. The player next to him placed a firm hand on Natron's thigh. "Chill, dog. You're shakin' the whole bench!"

Natron got up and trolled the sidelines, trying to calm himself. Fortunately, the Vipers' defense held the Raptors to a three and out. The place went wild again and the momentum had clearly shifted in the Vipers' favor.

There were only two minutes left in the first half and the Vipers desperately wanted to tie up the game before halftime. Natron and the rest of the offense took the field and went to work. A completed pass to Stalcup was followed by two long runs, resulting in the Vipers having the ball past mid-field at the forty-yard line. Then an eight-yard run set up a second down with two yards to go. On the next play, Clay threw the ball to Stalcup. The ball was tipped and fell to the ground, bringing up a third and two.

Natron released the breath he'd been holding. They'd been lucky the ball hadn't been intercepted. He crouched down at the line of scrimmage, waiting for the ball to be snapped. Every nerve ending in his body came alive as he poised himself for the battle in front of him.

When Isaac came to jam him, Natron's hands came up and blocked Isaac's attack so hard that it looked like he'd been struck by an upper cut from Mike Tyson. Isaac stumbled backwards, off-balance.

That was all the opening Natron needed. He ran the seam route down the middle of the field between two other defenders. Just as he turned and leapt for the ball, one of the safeties also went up for it. Both players' hands locked onto the ball at the same time. In that split second, Natron summoned all his strength, all his power, all his will and ripped the ball out of the safety's hands.

As Natron came down with the ball securely tucked high and tight, he rotated at his hips and turned his shoulders upfield. Since the safety had gone for the ball and missed, he fell to the ground, unable to stop Natron.

Out of the corner of his eye, Natron saw the other safety coming at him. Timing it perfectly, he extended his free arm like shooting off a cannon. He hit the defender in the chest with a punishing stiff arm, forcing him off balance. Able to get a step on him, Natron took off and ran the ball all the way into the end zone for a thirty-two–yard touchdown.

A few of the other Viper players ran into the end zone to chest-bump Natron in congratulations, and for the first time since his injury Natron felt like himself again. The elation that came with scoring a touchdown, the feeling of accomplishment that came with beating a defender and doing your job successfully—these were things he'd missed when he was fighting the uphill battle of recovery.

On the sidelines, one of the younger receivers came up to congratulate Natron. After a fist bump, he asked Natron, "No touchdown dance? I was looking forward to that." Natron just smiled and clapped the kid on the helmet. Triumphant in his personal victory, he hadn't thought to do a celebration dance in the end zone. In the past he'd loved to showboat and the touchdown dance had been as important as the play, but today Natron was a more humble man and the score itself was enough.

Natron slugged down some water while the Vipers kicked the extra point, knotting it up at 21-21 as both teams entered the locker room for halftime.

CHAPTER TWENTY-EIGHT

During halftime, Coach Morrison jumped all over his defense and made some key changes to a few of their defensive schemes. Concern and nervous laughter permeated the locker room. Natron was pleased with his own performance and the adjustments he'd made. He would love to have seen Carmen's face when he scored that touchdown. He imagined her look of pride she'd be wearing about now and it made him feel even more confident.

While Carmen's support lifted him up, something else had him concerned. Though he wouldn't say it out loud, Natron was worried about what must be happening in the Raptors' locker room at that very moment.

The Raptors' head coach, Mark Billings, was famous for making key adjustments at half-time. He knew how to size up the opposing team's weakness and exploit them for his team's gain. The Raptors had come from behind to win more times this year than any other team in the league, and even if the Vipers weren't talking about it, Natron knew his teammates were thinking about it.

The Raptors' offense would get the ball to start the second half, and walking back out onto the field, Natron prayed Coach Morrison's defensive adjustments would help hold the explosive Raptors' offense. Natron sat on the bench and tapped his cleats impatiently; only thirty minutes left in the game.

The kickoff went out of bounds behind the end zone so the Raptors' offense would start at their own twenty-yard line. Coach Morrison's adjustments appeared to work. The Vipers' defense came with a variety of exotic coverages and disguised blitz packages, which made the Raptors' quarterback hold the ball a few more seconds during each play. This allowed the Vipers' pass rushers to get to him. It was one of their outside linebackers who came in on a delayed blitz, which blindsided the quarterback and gave the Vipers their first sack of the game.

The Vipers' new defensive looks confused the Raptors and they were only able to advance seven yards before they were forced to punt. This fired up the entire Vipers team, and high-fives and fist pumps ruled the sidelines.

Adrenaline zipped through him as Natron inserted his mouth guard and ran out onto the field. The first play was a pass play and Natron didn't like what he saw. The Raptors' defense was showing a two high safety zone look, with man coverage underneath. Not a traditional double team, but it still meant that Natron would be fighting not only the cornerback Isaac, but the safety as well.

After one unsuccessful play, Isaac bumped into Natron's shoulder and hissed under his breath, "All day long, sucka. All day long."

The old Natron would have taken the bait and started jawing right back at Isaac, but instead Natron took a deep breath and ignored him. He had enough to focus on without letting Isaac into his head.

As the series progressed, Natron couldn't help but notice the strong safety shadowing his every move. Even when he beat Isaac, the safety was right there playing him deep. Between the two defenders and with him being unable to make sharp cuts, Natron just couldn't get open. To make things worse, Clay was unable to get the ball to any of the other receivers. On third down with ten yards to go, Clay was sacked and the Vipers were forced to punt. Walking toward the sidelines, Natron could feel his frustration mounting.

The third quarter had become a defensive battle, with both teams stopping the opposing team's offense on each possession. Natron and the passing game had been shut down completely and the team had to find some answers. When the Vipers were on offense, the only thing they could do was run the ball. Time to play smash mouth football. Near the middle of the third quarter, the Vipers' running game marched the ball down the field and scored a touchdown, making the score 28-21.

The Vipers' defense had been able to keep the Raptors' offensive line off balance with their new looks, but on the last possession of the quarter, the Raptors kicked a field goal, ending the third quarter with the score Vipers 28, Raptors 24.

The final quarter of the Super Bowl began with the Raptors kicking off to the Vipers. With the Vipers unable to move the ball, they had to turn around and punt it back to the Raptors. On the next play, the Raptors' best receiver got a step on the defender covering him. The receiver caught the ball and made a sharp cut, causing his defender to slip, and he was off to the races. No other defenders were anywhere close, and the Raptors' receiver ran sixty-seven yards all the way to the end zone. With momentum on their side, the Raptors made a two-point conversion, putting the Raptors ahead 32-28 early in the fourth quarter.

As they watched the Raptors' sidelines erupt, the Vipers team felt the air being let out of their tires. Natron's heart sank, but he jumped up and lifted his knees to his chest one at a time. He had to keep stretching out his knees, keep them warmed up. This was no time to give up, gotta keep fighting. *Always keep fighting.*

The game continued to play out as a defensive standoff between the two teams. Natron had noticed that since the Vipers were relying so heavily on their running game, the safety who had been double-teaming Stalcup had moved up closer to the linebackers to help stop the run. This might bode well for their passing game and soon the Vipers' offense began to come alive.

Now that Marvin Stalcup was in single coverage, he started to gain a step on his defender. Clay recognized this and let the ball fly Stalcup's way. Stalcup scooped it out of the air and made a gorgeous catch, netting the Vipers a fifteen-yard gain and a first down.

On his side of the field Natron was still double covered, but Stalcup made another catch, this time for twenty yards. Frustration welled up inside Natron's chest. He wished he were more of a team player, and he was happy to see their team moving the ball down the field, but he couldn't help but wish *he* had the chance to make a big play.

With less than two minutes to go, the Vipers were down by four points 28 to 34, and the clock was running. The Vipers needed a touchdown to win. A field goal wasn't going to help them. The fans were on the edge of their seats, and Natron imagined Carmen nervously biting her nails.

A play action pass from Clay to the tight end brought the ball to the eighteen-yard line, and with twenty seconds left, Coach Morrison took his last time out.

On the sidelines, Coach was laying out a pass play designed for Stalcup, but on the last two plays, Stalcup's man had beaten him with perfect coverage.

"Coach, if Clay throws that ball up high, I can go get it and I promise you I will come down with it."

Coach Morrison gave Natron a dismissive glance and continued drawing up the play.

Clay interjected, "He can, Coach. I've seen him. He's much stronger than before."

Coach shrugged and grumbled, "Fine. We're running a three receiver set with two extra tackles at the tight end positions for maximum protection. They are going to blitz. Natron, Stalcup, you run a crossing pattern." He showed them on the board what he wanted. Natron and Marvin locked eyes, and Natron knew his own gaze held the same intensity that he saw mirrored in Marvin's eyes. They both wanted to go old school, the toughest man wins.

Wiping everything else from his mind, the frustration, his envy of Marvin's success this season, his doubts about his own ability—Natron erased them all as he strode purposefully back out onto the field. All he could do now was his job. And he would do it to the best of his ability.

The ball was snapped and Natron pounded down the field. He and Stalcup were to run a deep crossing route at the five-yard line. As he ran to the spot where they were to cross, he saw Stalcup and the safety who had been double covering Natron collide. Both players went down, but Natron stayed on course.

Out of the corner of his eye he could see the cornerback who'd been covering Stalcup. The guy was coming for him, and he sensed Isaac's presence with him step for step. As he reached the end zone, he saw Clay's pass spiraling hard toward him. Clay had thrown a bullet in order to try to fit the pass into such a tight window. Natron knew the third receiver would have trouble shaking his defender and with Marvin going down, the only real option the quarterback had was to throw it hard into double coverage and pray Natron would catch it.

As his feet left the ground, Natron visualized where the ball was heading and he knew he would catch it. What he hadn't counted on were the hands of two other players also getting in the mix.

With the focus of a surgeon, he plucked the incoming football out of the air with both hands and willed himself to hold on. He felt the hands of the other cornerback batting at the ball trying to knock it away, but he held on. Then Isaac ripped at the ball as he bumped the lower half of Natron's body out from under him, trying desperately to knock the ball loose. Natron flipped backwards and as he rotated in the air, he brought the football into his chest and held on with everything he had.

The next thing he knew he was at the bottom of a pile-up. The referees stood watching as they pulled the two bodies off of him. When Isaac got up, the world could see Natron, lying on his back at the bottom of the pile in the end zone, ball tucked tight against his chest. The referee lifted his arms high in the air, signaling touchdown.

Natron smiled the biggest and most heartfelt smile of his life. He handed the ball to the ref and welcomed the barrage of Vipers who ran over and piled up on top of him. Underneath the pile, he laughed and whooped with his teammates. When they finally all got up, the Vipers kicked an extra point, which put them up over the Raptors 34-32.

With only seconds left on the clock, the kickoff was not returned and the Vipers defensive line shut down the Raptors on the next play as the clock ran out. Red, black, and white confetti fell from the sky as the Vipers ran onto the field, leaping and embracing each other, slapping each other on the back with congratulations. Players hugged, and Coach Morrison was doused in a green Gatorade bath.

As he headed for the sidelines, a group of reporters approached Natron. Before he could reach them, none other than Marvin Stalcup broke through the crowd and wrapped an arm around Natron's neck. "We did it, bro!"

Marvin exclaimed. "Super Bowl champs!"

Natron hugged Stalcup back. "Yep, we killed it out there."

Stalcup shook his head. "I knew when you came back, man... I knew we'd be unstoppable."

"Thanks, man." Natron bumped his fist against Stalcup's and walked toward the cameras and reporters motioning for him. Somebody handed him a 'Vipers Super Bowl Champions' hat, which he plopped on top of his head.

"We're not used to seeing you without all the hair," one of the reporters said.

"Hey, I'm not used to it yet either. This hat feels sort of funny without it, but I'm not givin' it back!" Natron joked with one of the cameramen.

"Natron, when you were going up for that last catch in the end zone, what was going through your mind?" another reporter asked.

Natron pursed his lips, considering his answer. "Nothing except doing my job. My job is to catch that ball and that's what I did."

"But coming back from that injury, I mean, this is your first game back. How did you do it?"

Natron sighed. "I gotta tell you—it was difficult. It's been harder than anything I've ever done in my life. Nobody thought I could do it... Well, nobody except maybe my girl, she kept me goin'."

"Your girl? So Natron, are you and Carmen back together? Even after the tabloid reports that you were cheating?" a short, slimy-looking reporter asked.

Natron waved the question away. "Y'all don't believe everything you read. Next question."

After a few more questions, Natron was escorted by security into the locker room where champagne was flowing freely, mostly all over the players. Handshakes and hell-yeahs were exchanged all around and Natron felt like he was on top of the world.

As he opened his locker to change, he checked his phone. There was a single text message from Carmen.

Congratulations, Daddy. I knew you could do it.

Tears sprung up in his eyes and he brushed them back, but he took a moment to stare into his locker and take in the emotion that welled up inside him. In his entire life he'd never felt so full, so complete, so proud.

Natron had gone from being a great football player to being a person who'd lost everything. Over the course of the season he'd lost his health, and with that his autonomy, the majority of his income, and the girl he loved. He'd gone from the top of his game to being out of the game. Now he stood at the pinnacle of football, and he'd done it all with hard work and fortitude, things that were foreign to him only months before. In the past Natron let things come easily to him. He'd never had to work for his success, not really. But this injury had taught him how to dig deep and find the strength within himself to succeed.

One of the coaches tapped him on the shoulder, interrupting his reverie.

"Yo, man, whassup?" Natron folded the shorter man in a bear hug and lifted him up off the floor. "We're the champs!"

"That's right, and you're the MVP. C'mon. The owner of the team and the commissioner are waiting for you."

CHAPTER TWENTY-NINE

Carmen arrived at Gustav's gallery at six o'clock on the nose, just as the gallery owner had asked her to. She glanced at her phone and saw that she was on time, but the place looked closed. Perhaps she had gotten the date wrong. Gustav had told her that he wanted her to attend a special opening, something about it being a good move for her future. Carmen had agreed. Gustav had done so much for her career—she wouldn't deny him any request within reason.

A light flipped on inside the gallery so she knocked on the door. Someone was there, now if she could only get their attention.

To her surprise, the person who came to the door was Natron. She'd thought he was still on his Super Bowl MVP media tour. It had been less than a week since the Vipers' big win and he'd been asked to guest everywhere from the *Late Show* to the *Today Show* to *Saturday Night Live*. He wasn't due to be back until next week, but here he was looking dapper in a grey pinstripe suit and a pink tie. What was going on? Natron rarely got so gussied up.

Natron used a key to open the glass front doors of the gallery. "Hey, babygirl. I've missed you." He ushered her into the gallery, then into his arms.

His masculine cologne tickled her nose and she immediately felt a wanton throbbing between her legs, her brain associating his scent with her own arousal. She pulled him closer, reveling in the pure joy she felt just being in his arms.

A moment later she pulled away. "What is all this? I thought Gustav was having an opening, and I thought you were in New York."

His million-dollar teeth flashed as he arched a brow. "Girl, that's what I wanted you to think."

"So what's going on?"

He took her hand and led her to the back of the gallery and away from the windows. There, in one of the side galleries stood a beautiful table set with gorgeous china and a silver candelabra resting inside an elaborate centerpiece of pink and yellow roses. "I thought we needed a special night just the two of us."

"Natron, it's lovely. But I'm not really following. I mean, couldn't we go out to dinner or something? I don't understand why you had to bring me here, why all the subterfuge? Gustav was in on this, wasn't he?"

Natron nodded his head in affirmation and held her chair for her as she sat down before taking a seat across from her. As if by magic, a waiter popped out from the back and poured them each a glass of champagne.

"Let's celebrate." He raised his glass to her.

Carmen clinked her glass against his. "Okay," she said and took a sip, the bubbles tickling her tongue. "What are we celebrating, your Super Bowl victory? MVP?"

"Nah, we did that in New Orleans. Tonight is about us. I've planned a nice catered dinner. I was going to hire a musician or two, I was thinking about the piano player you like, but we can do that another time. I wanted tonight to be very intimate—just you and me without a lot of distractions."

They did have a lot of distractions in their life, especially recently. And now that Natron's star was bright again, that wasn't liable to change any time soon. How thoughtful of him to plan a private dinner for her.

She grinned at him. "Thanks, Daddy. This was sweet of you."

"You know, I was going to wait until after dinner to do this, but I can't hold out that long." Natron fidgeted in his chair.

Carmen narrowed her eyes. "What are you talking about?"

Natron took her hand in his. "Carmen, do you know why I did all this, tricking you into coming here—to this gallery?"

She shook her head.

"Babygirl, this is where we first met." He smiled tenderly at her. "The first time I ever saw you, you were hiding in Gustav's office."

She rolled her eyes, slightly embarrassed remembering how shy she'd been, how green. It blew her mind to think about how far she'd come since then. Now she was established in her career, her own star was rising, and she was miles more confident than she had been the first night she met Natron. She attributed some of that to Natron's belief in her and her talent.

"But you impressed me. Your talent blew me away and there was something about you that made me know that I needed you in my life. We've been through a lot, you and me, and when I broke my knee I couldn't have asked for any more support and love than you gave me."

He chuckled. "Now I know I didn't make it easy on you. With my mamma driving you crazy, the stupid tabloid fiasco... but baby, you stuck by me through all that, and I know it couldn't have been easy."

Natron shifted in his chair and suddenly he was on the floor next to her. Kneeling. Her heart beat loud and fast in her throat and a little thrill danced up her spine.

"Carmen, my beloved babygirl, would you do me the great honor of marrying me?" He slipped a box out of his coat pocket and opened it to display the most beautiful ring she'd ever seen.

"Oh, Natron, it's lovely!" she said, covering her mouth with her hand.

"Try it on then." He inched the platinum band onto the ring finger of her left hand and she gazed at the enormous, cushion-cut diamond, its brilliance sparkling up at her.

"It's perfect," she said, the corners of her mouth strained, she was smiling so big.

Natron pretended to be offended. "Would you expect anything less?" he teased.

"No, Daddy, I wouldn't."

He kissed the top of her hand, then stood up and whisked her into his arms. "Now are you going to give me and answer or are you just gonna leave me hanging?"

"Yes!" she said, throwing her arms around his neck and touching her lips to his.

He kissed her back with as much passion as she'd ever felt from him. He claimed her with his mouth the way she knew he'd claim her body later, and the mixture of love and desire she felt for him made her feel unsteady on her feet. He clutched her to him and she knew she could trust him not to let her fall.

She and Natron fit perfectly together, not only their bodies, but also their personalities, and their hopes and dreams. Carmen had never dreamed she'd have a connection like this with anyone, but she had found it with him. And while she had resisted him when he'd asked her to live with him in the past, now it felt right to move forward together.

He released her and motioned for her to sit down. "We do have some delicious food coming out; sorry I just couldn't wait. I was gonna be too nervous to eat."

"Nervous?" Carmen asked.

"Yeah, girl. What if you'd have said no?"

She giggled. "Not likely. I love you, Natron, and I want to spend the rest of my life with you."

He returned to his seat. "You know, my first instinct was to ask you on television, after we won the Super Bowl, or on late night TV. That's what I would have done, but see… Daddy's been listening. I knew you wouldn't like that, making our relationship all public; you'd think it was a publicity stunt. I'd have to tell other people and they'd know before you." He sighed. "And you'd hate that. This way the only person who knew anything before you was Gustav and I had to tell him to be able to surprise you, I hope you can forgive that."

Her heart lurched. He *had* been listening, and he'd created a proposal specifically for her, even though it was him who loved the limelight and all the attention, not her. But in this instance he put her above himself and his desires. "Wow, Daddy. I'm impressed. You know, you've really changed."

He straightened the lapels of his jacket. "Thank you for noticing, babygirl. Now we can start talkin' 'bout the basketball team."

She sputtered as a sip of water went down the wrong pipe. When she'd regained her composure, she asked, "Basketball team?"

"Yeah, you know—five little Natrons running around." He looked around as if someone else might hear. "You know basketball's my favorite sport, but don't tell nobody."

Carmen just shook her head. It was better than eleven little Natrons running around, which was the number it took to field a football team. She pressed two fingers against her temple. "Let's not get ahead of ourselves," she said, though she did like the idea of a mini-Natron.

He threw his hands in the air. "Okay, I'm just teasin' you. The only thing I need is you. You've made me the happiest man in the world tonight. I'm looking forward to spending the rest of my life with you, babygirl."

The waiter came back out with a plate of appetizers. Natron fed Carmen a jumbo shrimp dipped in the mouth-watering sauce that accompanied it, and she was struck by the fact that her life with Natron was just beginning. A peace she'd never felt before settled over her. There was a palpable contentedness she felt, confident in the knowledge that she would belong to her daddy forever.

Filled with unadulterated happiness, she reached across the table and squeezed his hand.

THE END

Poor Little Daddy's Girl
The Daddy's Girl Series, Book Three

Normandie Alleman

CHAPTER ONE

Lawrence Wellington rolled off Charmaine with a huff and landed heavily beside her on the bed. She stared at the ceiling. It was covered with that white popcorn texture that had always baffled her. Sure, such a treatment was a hassle to remove, but a flat ceiling was certainly worth the trouble.

Lawrence patted her thigh then turned and faced the wall. "I've got an early day tomorrow. Hope you understand, I've got to get some shut-eye."

Sighing, Charmaine responded, "Oh, that was *more* than enough." Her voice dripped with a sarcasm she expected to be lost on him, but she was wrong.

He turned to face her, his caterpillar-like brows furrowing to meet in the middle. "What do you mean?"

She shrugged. "Just that I had expected so much more, you know."

By this time he'd sat up, defensively covering his lower half with the bed sheet. "No, I don't know!"

Charmaine fiddled with a lock of her long hair, twisting it between her fingers, continuing to gaze absently at the ceiling. "I had higher hopes for you, for us."

"Are you serious?" His incredulity told her he wasn't an advocate for honesty at all costs.

Undeterred, she scrunched up her face and continued. "Yeah."

Standing up, Lawrence pulled the sheet around his waist, leaving her naked and exposed on the bed. "I think you need to leave."

She snorted. "Why? Did I insult your manhood?" The slur in her voice was unmistakable and she wished she could make it go away. Apparently she'd already had a significant amount to drink, yet she suddenly wanted another one. "Hey, do you have anything to drink?"

"I just told you I have to get up early tomorrow!"

She could almost see smoke coming out his ears. This made her giggle, which proceeded to make him even angrier.

"Charmaine, some of us have to go to work for a living. It's time for you to go." He bent over and hunted for her clothes which were strewn all over the room. Once he had an armful, he tossed them at her. "Here, get dressed."

She gave him an exaggerated eye roll before saying, "Fine. God, you're such a party pooper."

As he ran a hand through his hair, he began to tug on it in frustration. "Me? I'm a party pooper? That's rich."

Charmaine snickered. "Okay, chill player." She drawled out the word "player" then snickered. Lawrence was anything but a ladies' man, and if the performance she'd just been treated to was any indication, she knew why. She stood up and started fumbling to put her clothes on.

Once she'd put on her skirt and blouse she felt Lawrence's hand on the middle of her back guiding her to the door.

"Okay, okay, you don't have to be so rushy rushy," she whined.

"Here," he said, placing her Birkin handbag and Louboutin shoes in her hands and opening the door to his apartment.

Charmaine drew herself up to her full five foot six inches and tried to steady herself. "Wait, I have one more thing to say."

He shook his head in a way that said, "You always have one more things to say," but she ignored that.

She placed a hand on his forearm and leaned into him as if she were going to tell him a secret.

"What?" he asked impatiently.

"It's not your fault. I'm sure you're perfectly good at doing other things," she whispered and patted his arm.

With a grunt of disgust, he pushed her into the hallway and slammed the door in her face.

Charmaine exhaled then said loudly, "Some people are too damned sensitive." She leaned against the wall for support as she put on her five-inch heels. Then she slung her bag over her shoulder and weaved her way down the sad, bare hallway of Lawrence's apartment building.

The elevator took forever, but it finally arrived and she toppled into it. Pressing "1" she rummaged in her bag for her cell phone. She texted her driver, Rollins, that she needed a ride.

Within seconds she received a text back saying he would be outside in five minutes.

She opened the door to the street and a wall of Dallas heat and humidity hit her in the face even though it was past two in the morning. Blech! God how she hated summer and it was only June. She had been planning to sit on the curb and wait, but she was afraid the asphalt would burn her behind so she found a column to lean against instead.

Lawrence. She'd had such high hopes for the man. After years of running around with pool boys, baseball players, and even the occasional European club owner, Charmaine had tried to do the right thing, the mature thing, by dating Lawrence. He was an upstanding citizen, an attorney who worked for a non-profit organization. She thought he even went to church. Unfortunately, she'd just found out that he was as dull in the sack as he was out of it.

Like most men, he'd been attracted to her. She knew men were drawn to her beauty, her wildness, her fame. The fact that she was one of the wealthiest girls in Dallas probably didn't hurt either, she grinned wryly to herself.

She checked her phone. 2:33 a.m. Rollins should be here…

She and Lawrence were clearly mismatched. He couldn't have been more boring, and she could tell he was beginning to grow weary of her high maintenance personality. But in the past couple of years, she'd come to feel something was missing in her life. Dammit, she was lonely. That was the only reason she bothered with guys like Lawrence.

Good riddance, she thought as a Lincoln Navigator pulled to a stop at the curb. Rollins exited the driver's seat and wordlessly opened the door for her. She appreciated that he didn't ask any questions. Rollins never gave her the third degree, never asked her why she was somewhere, never mentioned the wobble in her walk when she'd had too much to drink. Hell, he'd even had to pull over to the side of the road for her to barf a few times. But he did not interfere and thank God for that.

Sliding onto the leather bench seat she relaxed. It felt good to sit down. She lay down, pressing her cheek against the cool leather, grateful at least she had Rollins to take care of her. No one else did. Not the revolving door of men in her life, or her family, or even the housekeepers who passed through her life. Nope, Rollins was a constant.

She must have fallen asleep because the next thing she remembered was Rollins helping her into the lobby. She stumbled to the elevator.

Lifting her eyebrows she told Rollins, "You don't have to see me all the way up. I can get there myself."

"It's alright, Miss Charmaine. I don't mind a bit."

She sniffed, but secretly appreciated the extra care he took with her. Through her alcohol-induced haze she contemplated Rollins. He stood well over six feet tall, had a slim build and always wore starched dress shirts, slacks, and a tie. His children were grown, and his wife had passed away a few years ago, breast cancer or something. The main job he had was tending to Charmaine, or at least taking her where she needed to go. These days he shopped for her too. It hadn't originally been in his job description, but she hated going to the market, one day he offered, and now it was a habit.

When the elevator arrived at the top floor, she exited and Rollins followed. With a wave of her hand she indicated he should go back downstairs. "Thanks, I'm good."

He took a step back into the elevator and held the door open with the palm of his hand. "I'll just wait until you get inside," he said.

She fished in her bag for her key, muttering under her breath. "Ugh!" Losing her keys was a common occurrence, and as helpful as Rollins was, it irked her that he suspected she might not find the blasted thing.

The keys jangled as she pulled them from her purse with the flourish of a magician. "Voila," she said holding them up by their silver spoon handled keychain.

Rollins removed his hand and allowed the elevator doors to close. "Goodnight, Miss." For a brief second she felt alone. A sense of sadness threatened to settle upon her, but she pushed it aside.

The key wobbled in her unsteady hand and it took several tries before she could insert it into the lock. Whew! She really had tied one on, hadn't she? Click! The deadbolt turned and she pushed open the heavy door.

Her white leather sofa looked so tempting, but a loud growl from her stomach made her head for the kitchen instead. She opened the refrigerator, then the freezer and stood there letting the cold air wash over her. The cool air on her skin felt divine. She closed her eyes, inhaled the frigid air, and almost forgot what she was doing. With a start she opened them again. Hmm. What looked good?

The SubZero was stocked even better than she expected, and she narrowed down her choices to ice cream or jalapeno poppers. The craving for grease outweighed her desire for sweets so she removed the package of frozen poppers. She turned on the oven to preheat it and read the directions from the back of the box. She rarely cooked, and the words on the back were so blurry that she had to squint to see them. *Looks like I can heat them up on the cooktop.* She rummaged around until she found a skillet. Turning on a burner she went in search of some cooking oil. Surely, you needed oil to fry these things.

She found some on the high shelf of a cabinet and doused the skillet with it. She set the skillet down on the hot burner then her phone beeped alerting her she had a text message.

Her eyes scanned the kitchen for the phone, but it sounded like it was coming from the living room. She found it beeping in her purse, which she had thrown on the luxurious couch. She read the text. A coupon code from one of her favorite retailers. Figures, she sighed and tossed the phone on the floor.

The lure of the cozy cushions won her over and she stretched out on the couch and grabbed the remote control. She turned on the television and flipped through a few channels stopping on an infomercial for a hair styling tool that appeared to turn wild, unruly hair into sleek, gorgeous up-do's with the flick of a wrist. With each hairstyle makeover they showed, she became more entranced. Eyes glued to the 50" curved HD screen, she reached for the alpaca blanket draped over the back of the sofa and snuggled down beneath it…

• • • • • • • • • • • • • • • •

Charmaine was awakened by the loudest alarm she'd ever heard.
BEEEP! BEEEP! BEEEP! BEEEEP!

What was that. God-awful sound? She covered her ears. Where was it coming from? Her brain was foggy, and it took longer than usual to process the information.

She opened her eyes slowly, and a spike of pain shot through her head. The incessant beeping was not what she needed with the hangover she now had. Gathering her bearings she realized she was in her own bed. How did she get here? Hadn't she been with Lawrence last night? She tried to remember how she'd gotten home, what she had done… but the alarm was going off at a disturbing decibel level which made it difficult to think.

Reaching for her phone to turn off the alarm, she sat straight up in bed. Sunlight was barely beginning to stream through the window but it was enough for her to see her phone wasn't on the nightstand in its usual place.

And something smelled funny, like something was burning. Oh dear Lord, that is not my alarm! Bolting out of bed, her head pounded as she ran toward the noise. When she reached the kitchen she froze.

Flames engulfed the room, the whole kitchen was ablaze. Her eyes darted to her favorite couch where she'd fallen asleep last night, flames licking all around it, threatening to turn it into a puddle of soot.

The heat from the fire warmed the room to an unbearable temperature and she felt pangs of nausea in her stomach. Panic rose in her throat as she registered that her path to the front door was blocked by flames.

Then she noticed her phone on the floor.

When the phone started melting, she began to scream.

CHAPTER TWO

The alarm bell boomed, rousing Hunter from one of the best night's sleep he'd had in months. His body immediately transitioned into alert mode, and he jumped out of bed and threw on his gear in quick, fluid movements like he'd done thousands of times. By now he'd mastered the process.

Helmet in hand, he climbed aboard the big, red fire truck with the rest of the crew and the rig pulled out onto the crowded Dallas streets. The chief radioed him with the 411 on the early morning call—a penthouse fire.

A few groans were uttered when he passed the information along to his men. A fire in a high rise could cause numerous complications, the first being that stairs must be used once the power to the elevators was cut, which was probably already the case. Some of the less physically fit firefighters would struggle climbing more than twenty flights of stairs, much less climbing to the seventieth floor with all that gear on their backs.

"You and I'll go, make an assessment," Hunter said to Mitch, the other lieutenant and his best friend.

"Ten-four," Mitch nodded. Mitch was almost as much of a fitness nut as Hunter. Mitch preferred wild endurance courses, the kind that had participants crawling through mud pits under barbed wire, while Hunter was more of a lift-weights-at-the-gym kind of person. They ran together sometimes and had both recently competed in a half marathon. They would be the best prepared team for the challenge.

As the engine pulled up to the building, lights flashing, sirens blaring, Hunter glanced up at the high rise and shook his head. This was going to be a bitch, no doubt about it. His own negativity sent off an alarm bell in his brain and he immediately pushed the thought aside. There was no room for any unconstructive thoughts when he went to work. It was essential he focus on the task at hand and forget everything else.

The building manager ran toward him and informed him that the fire was on the top floor, in the penthouse. Emergency fire hoses were located on the floor below, and as expected, the elevators had been shut down.

"Show me the stairs, and give a blueprint of the building to him," he said pointing to another firefighter. He gestured to Mitch, "Let's go."

He and Mitch jogged up the stairs. Not only were the stairs plentiful, but they were also steep, with short steps their big feet kept slipping off. Once when his foot slipped off a step he groaned.

Mitch half-laughed, "Man, these stairs suck."

Hunter nodded in agreement, and they pressed on.

When they reached the fiftieth floor they slowed down at the landing to catch their breath, then pressed on. Hunter's calves screamed at him and each breath was punctuated by a sharp pain. The faint taste of vinegar lingered at the back of his throat due to his lack of oxygen and damn, his chest burned.

At times like these, Hunter had to dig deep to find the resources to cope with the situation. "Whatever it takes," he told himself. He would do whatever it took to come to the aid of whomever was in that fire at the top of this building. It was his job. It was what he did.

When they reached the sixty-eighth floor the two men's adrenaline kicked in. "Almost there," Mitch wheezed, and Hunter nodded. He didn't think he had enough breath left to speak.

The manager had given them a key to the small hallway outside the only apartment on the seventieth floor and one to the penthouse apartment itself. When they finally topped the stairs, they used the key and burst into the hallway dragging the fire hose from the hallway below and a couple of fire extinguishers along with their regular gear.

They looked for evidence of the fire but saw nothing suspicious. Mitch felt the door to the penthouse and signaled it was hot. Hunter banged on the door first. When there was no answer he tried the key, but it wouldn't budge in the lock.

Upscale apartment or not, they'd have to break the door down. He motioned to Mitch who swung his axe and soon brought the door down. From the doorway he could see the kitchen was in flames and the fire was spreading through the apartment. He motioned for Mitch to turn on the hose while he radioed down for more backup. Then he sprayed one of the fire extinguishers, then another. At least this stopped the fire from creeping any farther.

It was then he heard the screaming. He entered the apartment, ran down a hallway toward the noise, and quickly located a girl crying in the corner of a bedroom. Even through the haze of the fire, Hunter noticed the pure luxury of the apartment. The silver gilt bed frame looked as if it belonged at Versailles, the craftsmanship was so detailed and over the top.

"Fire department," he said identifying himself. "Are you alright?" He took the girl by the arm.

She looked up at him with arresting blue eyes. "I think so."

"Good, let's get you out of here. Anyone else here?" he asked guiding her back to the door where Mitch was controlling the inferno with the fire-hose.

She shook her head no. "Just me," she said, a startling loneliness shining in her eyes. He shook it off. He must be imagining things.

Mitch waved them past, "Anybody else?"

Hunter shook his head, "Negative. She's the only one."

"Take her down. I got Johnston and Pulaski on their way up. We got this."

Hunter gave Mitch a thumbs up, put his arm around the girl's waist and led her into the stairwell.

He took the stairs two at a time and she tried to keep pace with him. Once they reached the first landing, he turned to make sure she was following. She had no apparent injuries, except for possible smoke inhalation, but she was ambulatory, no need for him to carry her.

Taking her in he realized for the first time how beautiful she was. Her wild hair stuck out every which way. The unruly locks consisted of several different colors and it looked more like a mane than any hair he'd ever seen; she reminded him of a lion. Her blue eyes pierced his soul and mesmerized him at the same time. It was an unsettling combination. "Are you sure you're not injured?" he asked.

"No, I'm okay," she gazed up at him pitifully. "But my head hurts. Do you think they'll ever turn off that freaking alarm?" She rubbed her temples.

"Once the fire is out," he said.

"Crap! Can't you make it sooner?" she pleaded.

He held out a hand to her and started down the next flight of stairs. "It's not my job to see that it's turned off. Somebody who works in the building will have to do it. Come on."

She stalled on the top step, put her hands on her hips and stuck out a luscious bottom lip. "Can't you carry me?"

He couldn't have been more shocked if she'd slapped him. Carry her? Down sixty-something flights of stairs. Who did this bitch think she was, the Queen of England? Some people he'd rescued lost their mind in times of crisis and this girl was definitely one of them if she thought he was going to do that.

Remembering his position helped him control his urge to tell her where to stick it. He'd been passed up for captain once already due to his impulsive behavior in the field. The last thing he needed was the little rich girl making trouble for him. "You're fine, you can walk," he said calmly and began walking down the stairs.

She remained on the top step kicking it with her pretty foot, her toenails perfectly manicured with hot pink nail polish. "But my head hurts," she whined.

"No," he said firmly. "Now come on."

"But if I were burned you'd have to carry me down, right?"

"Yes, but you're not burned, are you?"

She scowled at him.

"Come on," he ordered her testily.

But rather than complying with his request she sat down on the top step, crossed her arms and rested her forehead on them.

"You've gotta be kidding me! Ma'am, there is a fire up there. It is my job to see you to safety. Now let's go!" His blood began to churn, and he struggled to keep his temper in check.

She didn't budge.

Exasperated, he climbed the short flight of stairs to her. When he reached her he picked her up, flung her over his shoulder like a sack of potatoes, and started back down the stairs.

"What are you doing?" she asked, wriggling in his arms. She wasn't specifically fighting him, but she wasn't making it any easier to carry her either.

"My job," he answered her through clenched teeth.

She tussled with him, but he held her tightly and she was no match for his strength. Frustrated little sounds bubbled up from her throat, but he kept going, determined to get her downstairs to safety.

After descending about ten flights of stairs she yelled, "Put me down!" and started kicking at him.

"No," he answered, afraid her gyrations would send them both tumbling down the stairs.

"But this is hurting my head. All the blood is rushing to my head, plus that noise, it's killing me."

"Hold still or I will have to give you a spanking!"

He felt her stiffen. "You can't be serious."

"Oh, I'm deadly serious. If you don't co-operate you're going to hurt yourself or both of us."

Bent over his shoulder, she squealed as she beat on his back with tiny fists.

She wasn't going to behave. This was a woman who liked to play games, and he had little patience for people like that.

She wore a skirt and he knew he should leave her skirt down, but a need deep inside him got the better of him and he pulled it up to reveal two round, tanned globes interrupted by a thin strip of yellow fabric that served as underwear. His breath caught in his chest for a second as he admired her ass.

He knew better. The higher-ups and the paper pushers would try to take his shield if they ever found out about this. But they didn't know. They wouldn't last a day in the field and he smiled to himself picturing some of them trying to get this entitled brat down from her ivory tower. It would never happen.

Allowing his frustration to take over he gave her cheeks a smack, and then another. To his surprise his victim didn't scream or cry out. In fact, he thought he heard her moan, though it was difficult to be sure over the ear-splitting alarm that still rang through the building.

Realizing she could take it, he struck her harder and harder until he felt her tense up and clutch his coat with a whimper. His cock twitched with arousal and he swatted her again with the same velocity. He'd transformed her bottom into juicy reddish-pink globes and realized they would be nice and warm by now.

He paused and removed one of his heavy gloves. The moment his skin touched hers the electricity in the air became palpable. Her smooth, baby-soft skin felt like velvet as he touched it with his fingertips. Then he grazed her bottom with his palm, wishing he were somewhere else doing this under different circumstances.

Remembering himself, he pulled down her skirt and delicately set her on the stairs, her blue eyes wide, her lips slightly parted.

She was speechless.

He had unnerved her, the lovely penthouse-dweller, and he liked it. This chick was probably used to ordering everyone around, always getting her way. Maybe his spanking would wake her up, teach her a thing or two. He stared at her evenly. "Now, you are going to walk the rest of the way down and you are not going to give me any more trouble. Do we understand each other?"

Her lips curled up slightly at the corners and she managed, "Yes, sir."

"Good, you go on ahead." He was afraid if he left her behind she'd sit down again. This way he could monitor her progress.

She descended the stairs ahead, and he followed. A few firefighters ran up the stairs past them, and he could tell from the radio chatter they had gotten the fire under control. Someone mentioned the fire looked to have started in the kitchen.

"So what happened? Were you cooking something, and it got away from you?" he asked.

"Oh, I don't know. I was asleep," she peered over her shoulder at him then kept walking down the stairs.

"Asleep?" he asked. The nonchalant way she said it touched a nerve. When he carried her, he'd smelled alcohol. What she meant was that she'd passed out, probably after leaving a burner on and setting something flammable next to it. He'd seen enough house fires to know that was one of the more common ones. Passing out while smoking was another one that happened all the time.

She shrugged, offering no explanation.

Hunter took a deep breath. They witnessed several deaths each year from people killing themselves by accidentally setting fires when they were high or intoxicated. The senselessness of it weighed heavy on him, and this little twit acted like she didn't have a care in the world. She'd just burned her house down, or at least the majority of it, and all she seemed worried about was getting an aspirin.

When they got to the next landing he put a hand on her shoulder and turned her to face him. "You passed out, didn't you? Didn't realize you started the fire…"

"Maybe, I dunno," she said coolly.

As he studied her, something about her face struck him. She looked familiar all of a sudden, but he couldn't place her. Before he could figure out where he'd seen her before she wrenched her shoulder from his grasp and continued down the stairs.

"Unbelievable," he said, disgust dripping from his voice.

"What's your problem?" she snarked.

"People like you."

"Whatever. You're just doing your job. You're not paid to give your opinions about my misfortune." She straightened her shoulders and trudged down more stairs.

"Yeah? Well I'm not paid to keep them to myself either." This was not exactly a lie, but he knew the brass wouldn't approve of him spouting his mouth off either. Everything was about political correctness these days, not rocking the boat. It didn't stop him from speaking his mind.

"I don't see what you're so fussy about. It's my apartment that's ruined. My things that are burned to a crisp!" she trilled, her voice growing more high pitched.

"You're right. I'm sorry about your apartment. But you need to take this seriously. You realize other *people* could have been hurt?" The last thing he needed was for her to get hysterical on him, but she seemed oblivious. "Do you have anyone you can stay with?"

She nodded, her chest heaving.

"That's good. Okay, let's take a break, catch our breath."

She looked relieved and plopped down on the next step.

"Hey, you do that and you'd better get back up," he said, half-serious, half-teasing.

Her smile dazzled him. Even disheveled with a streak of black soot across her cheek the woman was gorgeous. He wasn't sure he'd ever seen a more gorgeous woman.

Hunter set his watch two minutes. They sat silently, each breathing heavily until the watch beeped and Hunter offered her his hand. She took it and he helped her to her feet. "I'm Hunter, by the way. Hunter Baldwin."

"Charmaine Bainbridge," she said.

The name didn't mean anything to him, but her face did. Where had he seen her before? He shook his head. Unless he was imagining it, it would come to him.

As they journeyed down the never-ending steps Charmaine asked, "How long have you been a firefighter?"

"Ten years."

"Did you always know you wanted to be a firefighter?"

"Yeah, ever since I was a kid."

"That must be nice, to know what you want to do and then do it."

"I guess. How about you? What do you do?"

"Not much."

"Oh, right." The penthouse. She must live a life of leisure, coveted by most but he knew he'd go crazy with nothing to do all day, no purpose.

"Well, what did you want to be when you grew up when you were a kid?" he asked.

"An architect."

"For real?" Hadn't seen that one coming.

"Yeah. I love buildings. When the other kids were drawing stick-people and their pets, I was drawing buildings."

"What sort of buildings?"

"Anything really—houses, skyscrapers, museums, even treehouses."

"What happened? I mean why didn't you become an architect?"

"When I was a teenager my father took me for career assessment. I took all sorts of tests, two long days of testing. In the end when they gave us the results it turned out I was horribly unfit to be an architect."

"What?" Even though he'd just met this infuriating girl, for some reason it irked him for someone to squash a young girl's dreams like that. "Unfit how?"

"Well, during one of the tests I took, the examiner took a piece of paper and folded it. He punched a hole in it and asked me to show him on another piece of paper where the holes would be if he unfolded the paper. When it was folded once or twice I could do it, but then he started folding it all different ways, numerous times. I was lost. I had no idea where the holes would be when he unfolded it—none. Turned out that test determines your aptitude for three-dimensional thinking, and I flat out failed it. I was in the 20% percentile for three-dimensional thinking, which is far too low for what you need to be an architect."

"That sucks." He liked to believe that people could do anything they wanted to do, but he did have to acknowledge that some people were more suited in life for certain jobs. That's just the way it was.

"Yeah," she said and walked a little faster. "It's okay. My life is fine, great actually."

"Uh huh." Who was she trying to convince—him or herself?

A sign on the wall indicated they had reached the second floor. Finally.

As they started down the last flight of stairs he said, "When we get outside there will be paramedics waiting. I will take you to them. They need to check you out, and they'll probably let you go, though you may have to go to the hospital if they're worried about smoke inhalation."

"I may need to go to the hospital after walking down all these stairs!" she huffed.

He laughed. For some reason he found it hard to stay mad at her. It couldn't be the fact that she had super-model looks complete with a magnificent ass. "Well, I hope you don't."

When they reached the bottom he had the strangest urge not to take her outside, but to trap her against the wall and press his lips hard to hers. Invade that sassy little mouth with his tongue and squeeze her breast hard enough to make her flinch. His breathing slowed down even more and he realized he'd actually enjoyed talking with her.

With great effort he redirected his thoughts and pushed open the door to the outside. Sunlight shot them in the face, and they squinted against the brightness. Someone came and draped a blanket over Charmaine's shoulders even though it was already over eighty degrees and muggy out. Hunter wrapped a protective arm around Charmaine and led her to the waiting ambulance. A flash of lights blinded him for a moment. Was that a camera?

"Take good care of her," he said, handing Charmaine over to the paramedic.

"You know it," the paramedic responded and helped Charmaine lay back on a gurney. Then she placed an oxygen mask over Charmaine's nose and mouth.

Hunter gazed into her big blue eyes. "No more playing with matches, little girl. I don't want to have to come back here." Oh what a lie that was.

He touched her chin briefly then went to report to his commanding officer.

CHAPTER THREE

The wooden gate squeaked when Charmaine opened it and strode into the vine-hidden retreat in Kimberly and Charles's backyard. The rest of the girls were already assembled on the back deck, and they waved to her as she approached.

An unfamiliar feeling of warmth washed over her as she walked up the stairs of the new deck and handed Kimberly a bottle of Skinny Minnie tequila and hugged her friend. Kimberly squeezed her shoulders hard. "You okay?" she asked Charmaine.

Charmaine brushed aside Kimberly's concern with a flick of her hand. "Of course, a little fire can't keep me down, you know that," she said with as much bravado as she could muster. These girls were more of a family to her than the bio-jerks nature had given her to, and since the fire she'd been feeling displaced. This evening had been the highlight on her full social calendar this week. A meeting of Kimberly's bridesmaids to talk about her upcoming wedding would serve to distract her from her own dismal life.

She hugged Carmen and Marley, both were dressed casually. Carmen was an artist who cultivated a rather Bohemian appearance, wearing a colorful peasant blouse, huge dangly earrings and linen pants. A student, Marley looked the part in her white T-shirt and jeans. In fact she looked stunning, and Charmaine's mind flashed briefly to the night Marley had invited her to join her and her daddy dom, James, for a threesome. It had been fun, though the trouble that followed had been epic.

"Would you like a margarita?" Nellie asked, jarring Charmaine from her reverie and handing her a frothy concoction, salt glazing the rim of the glass.

"Sure," Charmaine said and half-heartedly returned Nellie's European greeting with kisses on both cheeks. Some people found Nellie pretentious, but Charmaine knew Nellie had a great heart and uncharacteristically cut the girl some slack. Years ago, Nellie had proven herself a true friend and she had a special place in her heart for the former beauty queen.

Sloane looked up at Charmaine then back at her phone before offering her the cold smile meant to serve as a greeting.

"Hey, Sloane, good to see you too," Charmaine cooed. Sloane was forever bitching at her for being late or a number of other things. Charmaine ignored Sloane's withering gaze as she sat down at the outdoor table, mostly because she knew it drove the fashion designer insane that Charmaine had given up openly fighting with her.

"Lucinda on tour?" Charmaine asked no one in particular then took a sip of the margarita. It was delicious, the perfect amount of tart and sweet with a kick.

"She is," Kimberly answered. "I'll be lucky if she even makes it to the wedding, she's in such demand these days."

"Surely she can take one day off to attend your wedding," Nellie said and the rest of the girls agreed.

A rare breeze in the night air provided a slight reprieve from the unbearable heat outdoors. Charles had been working on the deck for weeks, and it looked like it had been done professionally. Seeing Kimberly and Charles so happy filled a place in Charmaine's heart. They had been through so much, and they deserved a happy ending. She felt a little catch in her throat as she realized how much she loved vicariously experiencing a piece of their domestic bliss. *Stop feeling sorry for yourself, Charmaine.* Self-pity was for the weak, and she was not weak.

"There will be plenty of time to talk about the wedding later. I want to hear more about the fire!" Kimberly said to Charmaine.

Charmaine inhaled deeply, and shooed away a mosquito. "Not much to tell. My kitchen caught on fire. About thirty percent of the apartment was damaged so I've moved out so they can fix it back up. Major hassle."

Sloan furrowed her brow. "How did it start?"

Charmaine glossed past the accusation in Sloane's voice. "I guess I left a burner on. An accident, could have happened to anybody," she said lightly.

Sloane made a face.

"I'm so glad you're okay," Carmen said and the rest of the girls nodded.

Charmaine looked at the concern on her friends' faces. They cared about her, this group of girls. They had come together for their love of kink and daddy doms, but they stayed friends because they truly loved each other.

"I'm fine," she reassured them. She had no intention of telling them she'd been passed out when the fire started. That was better left her little secret.

"So where are you staying?" Nellie asked. "You know you can always stay with me and Mason if you need to."

"Thanks, Nellie, but I'm staying at my mom's."

"I didn't know your mom had a place in Dallas." Marley sounded surprised.

"It's more of a landing pad than anything else," Charmaine said. "A place where she can stop off between flights. It's a bit like camping out, but it will do."

"I didn't know you and your mom were getting along," Sloane said.

"Oh, we're not. I haven't told her," Charmaine said with a mischievous smile. "She's off at some Santa Fe retreat. Haven't talked to her in ages. She'll never know."

"But won't she be worried about you?" Carmen asked.

Charmaine shook her head. "I don't think that woman ever worried about me." She took a long sip of her drink. "Now my father, that's a different story. He's super pissed. Blames me for setting the fire, destroying everything, doesn't understand accidents happen. Hey, I'm human," she said with a shrug. "Shit happens."

Sloane glared at her, clearly in agreement with her father. Screw you, Charmaine thought and turned her body slightly so that she faced her other, more sympathetic friends.

"Well, when it happened were you scared? I mean, what was it like, were there flames everywhere?" Kimberly asked.

"Did you think of anything special to take with you to save?" Carmen asked. "People always ask you what you'd save in a fire."

A hollowness engulfed Charmaine. It hadn't occurred to her to save anything, not for a second. She had an entire penthouse full of expensive objects, yet none of them meant anything to her. There was no treasured childhood toy, no special gift from a parent, no irreplaceable love letter. Her stomach clenched with loneliness, and it made things worse that she could feel so alone even when surrounded by her best friends. How depressing, maybe she needed medication.

"Yeah, it was scary, but the fireman who came to rescue me was hot," she laughed, trying to lighten her mood.

"Wait, what?" Marley giggled. "A hot fireman? You've been holding out on us. Spill!"

Charmaine tapped her chin. "Well, he was gorgeous, all blue eyes and chiseled cheekbones."

"Oh my God! Firefighters are so hot. They totally have that hero thing going for them. What happened?" Kimberly asked. It was no surprise to hear her sing the praises of a heroic alpha male since she was about to marry one.

"I couldn't really tell much about his hair or body as much because of his suit and his helmet but he's strong. He carried me down a few flights of stairs and it didn't seem to faze him."

"Wow, so did he have to climb all those stairs to your apartment?" Nellie asked, dropping her jaw. "That's like, what, almost seventy flights?"

Charmaine nodded. "And he was barely winded by it. Isn't that insane? He must be in great shape."

"I'd say," Carmen said. "Wait until I tell Natron. He'll probably want to start running your stairs Charmaine."

"He will," she agreed. "Plus I made the guy mad, and he spanked me," she said realizing she'd captured the girls' full attention and they were going to love this story.

"He *spanked* you?" Sloane echoed.

"Sure did. He asked me to go down the stairs and I wouldn't. I sat at the top of the stairs being a brat so he threw me over his shoulder and hauled me down the stairs. I loved it until the blood started rushing to my head. I was already hung-over, and the fire alarm kept going off. Ugh, I thought my head might explode. It was awful." She cringed, recalling the agony. "So I finally begged him to set me down, but he told me he needed to teach me a lesson first and so he spanked me, to get me to cooperate."

"And did you?" Sloane asked, scrutinizing Charmaine.

Charmaine twisted her mouth. "Yes."

"Sounds like the man for you," Sloane said.

Charmaine sniffed. "I doubt I'll ever see him again."

"How was the spanking?" Nellie asked, an anticipatory glimmer in her eye.

Charmaine sighed. It had been awhile since she'd been given a spanking. Too long. "It was hot. He even lifted my skirt up, did it on my bare ass."

The girls erupted into shrieks and giggles.

"You weren't wearing underwear?" Sloane's nose wrinkled with distaste.

"Thong." Charmaine shrugged.

"You need to call that fire department and get him back over," Marley said. "Tell them your cat is stuck in a tree or something."

They laughed and the talk soon turned to Kimberly's wedding plans. "I'm going to let each of you choose your dress. I'd just like it to be a pastel color, and maybe don't duplicate each other's color choices."

"I want mint green," Nellie shrieked.

"Yellow," Marley called out.

"I want blue," Sloane said.

"I'll take whatever's left," Charmaine said before excusing herself to go inside and use the restroom. When she came out she found Kimberly fiddling around in the kitchen. Charmaine walked over and placed a hand on Kimberly's. "You just tell me what color, and I'll wear it," she said with a wink.

"Thanks, Char," Kimberly said in a low voice.

"So, the big day is less than a month away," Charmaine smiled tenderly at Kimberly. She and Charles had been trying to get married for the past several years but a difficult situation with his ex-wife had made their road a tumultuous one. Last month they'd finally decided on a destination wedding and in a matter of weeks they would fly to Mexico with around twenty of their closest friends and Charles's son Benji to finally become man and wife.

"I know, I can hardly believe it," Kimberly said and gave Charmaine a hug.

With Kimberly's arms around her, Charmaine fought back tears. Why was life so fucking bittersweet? At the same time she was so happy for Kimberly and Charles, a voice in the back of her head reminded her that she would probably spend the rest of her life alone.

They untangled themselves and Charmaine blinked several times hoping to rid herself of the unshed tears. "What can I do to help?" If there was one thing her mother had given her was impeccable manners which held fast through life's ups and downs.

Kimberly gave her a tray of chips and guacamole to take to the girls outside. As Charmaine opened the door she heard her name, instinct kicked in and she froze in her tracks to listen.

"Are you sure she can even *be* submissive?" Carmen asked.

"Yeah, I can't really picture her like that," Marley said.

"That's because you never saw her with Preston," Sloane said.

"Who?" Carmen asked.

"He was Charmaine's daddy," Sloane said through a clenched jaw.

"What happened to him?" Marley asked.

Nellie wrung her hands, and Sloane looked at the ground.

Unwilling to let the party go that direction Charmaine called too loudly, "Hey, girls! I've brought sustenance."

Marley and Carmen looked at each other, still puzzled. Sloane plastered a fake smile on her face and Nellie said, "Yay! I'm famished, aren't y'all?"

The rest of the girls agreed and the conversation moved back to the bridesmaid's dresses and travel plans. Thank God for the wedding to distract them. The last thing in the world Charmaine wanted to think about was Preston Harris.

CHAPTER FOUR

It had been a long day. Hunter and Mitch were coming off a grueling three-day shift and they'd stopped off at Lulu's, their favorite watering hole, on the way home. When a few of their fellow firefighters challenged them to a game of pool, Hunter and Mitch wiped the floor with them.

"We want a re-match," one of the guys on the losing team said.

"Maybe. First, I'm getting another pitcher," Hunter said and headed to the bar with the empty pitcher. He handed it to the bartender and waited for him to fill it. A baseball game played on the overhead screen. The game had developed into a one-sided affair and therefore didn't hold his attention, so he leisurely scanned the room. Being vigilant was a habit he'd developed as a first responder.

It was then that he saw her—the girl he'd brought down the stairs when her penthouse caught on fire. His heart skipped a beat, and his gut tightened. She sat at a table with another girl with long, sleek blonde hair, and the two appeared to be engaged in an animated conversation.

What was her name? He tried to remember. She didn't see him so he felt safe to watch her unobserved. Her hair was wild—long, curly and a plethora of colors. Blondes mixed with coppers and streaks of chestnut—it looked like the sort of hair a rock-star would have, and she pulled it off. He remembered thinking she resembled a lion with that outrageous, golden mane. She wore a skimpy little aqua sundress, the thin straps showing off her tanned, creamy skin.

Lost in her beauty he forgot he was staring until suddenly she looked up and her eyes met his. Slow recognition ignited in her eyes and the corners of her mouth were beginning to turn up when he looked away. Fortunately, the bartender had just set the full pitcher of beer in front of him. Hunter fished some bills out of his wallet and handed them to the man. "Keep the change." The bartender gave him an appreciative nod and moved on to another customer.

Hunter carried the brimming pitcher back to the corner of the bar with the billiard table and set it on the small table where Mitch and the others were.

"Thanks, man," Mitch said.

"Hey, you know that girl whose penthouse we went to last week?" Hunter asked Mitch.

"Charmaine Bainbridge."

"How do you know her name?" Hunter shook his head.

"How do you not? The chick's famous, Hunter. Open a newspaper, man," Mitch punched him lightly on the arm.

Hunter rolled his eyes. "Nobody reads newspapers anymore," and punched him back.

"You know what I mean. You gotta get out more, get to know your community, go online."

"What is there to know? We see enough bad news every day, I don't feel the need to read about more when I'm off duty. You're a glutton for punishment." Hunter filled his empty mug with beer from the pitcher.

"Nah, I'm a man who is interested in the world around him. You should try it sometime. At least I'm thinking about something besides working out."

"Shut up," Hunter said, but he knew Mitch had a point. He spent his off-time lifting weights and cardio training. If there was more to life than working out, he wasn't concerned with it. "So what do you know about the girl, Charmaine? She's over there." He jerked his head in her direction, but didn't look over at her.

Mitch craned his neck to see Charmaine then he looked back at Hunter. "Yeah, now she's looking at you," he laughed.

"I'm gonna kill you. That's the last thing we need is that spoiled little rich girl coming over here to bother us." Hunter had been mixed up with a wealthy woman before, and the experience had been a disaster. He had no interest in a repeat of that debacle.

"Bother? Man, what's wrong with you? Have you *seen* her? I mean they don't make 'em any sexier. Plus she's got more money than God. What more could you want in a woman? Okay, okay, a nymphomaniac who owns a liquor store, but she could buy a liquor store with one phone call. I wonder if she could be a nymphomaniac…"

"Enough. What do you really know about her?" Hunter asked trying to rein him in.

"Just that she's been in the news since she was a kid. Her father's the richest man in Texas, and that's pretty rich. Apparently her parents divorced when she was little and her father's been married a bunch of times since then, like Elizabeth Taylor, six or seven times. The press loves her. She's quite the party girl, always getting her picture in the paper with celebrities, occasionally getting into trouble, saying the wrong thing. She's our home-town version of Paris Hilton, only without the jail time or the sex tape. Wait, maybe there's a sex tape. Let me google it." Mitch got out his phone and started typing.

"Slow down. So what you're saying is that she's just a wealthy, spoiled brat who gets into trouble and is only famous for being famous?"

"Pretty much," Mitch said taking a drink.

"Figures, bet that's why Chief showed me that picture of us in the paper the other day."

"What picture?"

"There was a picture of me handing her over to the paramedics. It was in the papers. Chief called me in to tell me good job, guess it made us look good or something."

"Yeah. Do you know how many guys would love to be able to tell people they pulled Charmaine Bainbridge from a burning building? And to have their picture in the paper doing it? You're halfway to having your own reality show," Mitch teased.

"Shut up. People like that, they make me sick. You know she started that fire with her carelessness. She was drunk and passed out with a burner on."

Mitch shook his head. "Yeah, but we respond to lots of calls like that. What's with the judgment?"

Hunter ignored his question and continued. "Thanks to her we had to climb all those freaking stairs, she destroyed a perfectly good luxury apartment and didn't even seem to care. Why should she worry? Someone else will come along to clean up her mess. God, I hate rich people." He slammed his mug down on the table, beer sloshing from the top.

"Well chill because she's heading this way," Mitch said, his eyes widening.

Like a lovely gust of wind, Charmaine sashayed up to the table. Hunter was determined not to smile at her.

"Hi. When I saw you boys over here I thought it would be horribly rude of me not to offer to buy you heroes a drink. I mean, you did save my life and all, Hunter Baldwin."

Damn, she'd remembered his name. "We can buy our own drinks," Hunter said.

"Hunter!" Mitch rebuked him then turned to Charmaine, "That's awfully sweet of you. Don't mind him. He was born grumpy."

"I've noticed," Charmaine said conspiratorially and linked her arm with Mitch's. "What are y'all drinkin', beer?"

Mitch nodded, and Charmaine searched for the cocktail waitress making the rounds. Mitch got up and offered Charmaine his seat. "Is that your friend over there? I'll go get her."

Charmaine sat down and took a sip from Mitch's beer mug. Unbelievable. This girl thought the world belong to her. She looked up at him sweetly. "Who peed in your Cheerios?"

"I beg your pardon?" Hunter said icily.

She let out an exaggerated sigh. "What is the matter with you? I'm just trying to be nice. Polite. Grateful. And you can't even lower yourself to be polite back? What an ass."

"Why thank you," he said, his voice dripping with sarcasm. "Started any fires lately?"

"No, I haven't, thanks for asking. How about you? Put out any?"

"More than one," he said smugly.

She wrinkled up her nose. "Good for you. I'll bet you're real proud of yourself."

He shrugged and took a long draw on his beer. "Hey, I've got a question for you."

"Shoot," she said, crossing her arms and resting them on the table.

"When we tried to open the door to your apartment, the key the management gave us didn't work. Why was that?"

"I changed the locks."

"But weren't you supposed to give them another key when you did that?"

"I guess, but that's why I changed them."

He stared at her quizzically.

"I don't want them having a key to my apartment!" she said indignantly.

"But what if we hadn't been able to get in? What if someone needed to get in, for safety reasons, and that key didn't work?"

She shrugged. "But you did get in."

"That's not the point." he said, rubbing his chin.

"I think it is."

"You just don't get it," he said, taking a deep breath.

"You know you're about a much fun as a colonoscopy with no drugs."

"Have you ever even had a colonoscopy?"

"No, but I should because my mother died of colon cancer last year."

"I'm sorry," he said thinking maybe he shouldn't have been so hard on her. But then something made him ask, "Wait, is that true?"

"No."

He shook his head angrily. "You are some piece of work, you know that?"

She nodded her head, "You bet your ass I am, and I'm getting sick of hanging around with you and your shitty attitude. I'm going outside to smoke."

"You smoke too?" he asked incredulously. "Why am I not surprised?" He felt his blood pressure go through the roof. The woman was insufferable, he thought as he watched her slink toward the back door, her ample hips swaying as she walked. Damn, he'd love to grab those hips from behind, hold her down, and... He stopped his thoughts right there. Charmaine Bainbridge infuriated him. He had no business fantasizing about her. But as he watched her go she was every bit as tempting to him as Eve had been to Adam, and just as much trouble.

After she'd left, he looked over to see Mitch in deep conversation with Charmaine's blonde girlfriend. There was only a half a glass of beer left so he quickly chugged it and stood up to go to the bathroom. He was tired, all the hard work he'd been doing the past few days had caught up with him. Tomorrow he hoped to sleep most of the day.

The bathroom was one small room with a toilet in the corner behind a short partitioned wall. A long cabinet with a Formica counter held a sink and a mirror hung above it. Across from the sink was a urinal that he stepped up to and relieved himself.

He washed his hands and noticing there were no paper towels, he shook them dry. As soon as he opened the door and stepped into the hallway he saw Charmaine coming in from the door at the back. The hem of her dress danced sensuously over her shapely bronzed legs and he instantly grasped how stupid it was for her to be hanging outside in the poorly lit alley even if it was only for a few minutes to smoke. Those were the kind of places women frequently got attacked. As frustrating as she was, she didn't deserve for something like that to happen to her. He should have gone with her.

"You should know better than to smoke," he said.

"Why do you care?" she said walking right up to him. She stood so close that he could smell her expensive perfume. It was exotic, like her. He couldn't name the scent, but it captivated him like the song of a siren. She placed her index finger on his chest and swirled an imaginary circle on his shirt.

They were alone in the hallway. He closed his fingers around hers and pressed her up against the wood paneled wall next to the restroom, his hips touching hers. He wanted to stop himself, to leave her alone, but he couldn't. "You need someone to keep you in line, little girl."

She laughed, her eyes mocking him. "What? Someone like you?" He expected her to protest, but she stood still waiting for his next move.

Encircling her waist with one arm and propping himself against the wall with the other, he leaned down, his lips almost touching hers. The heat from her breath warmed his face and his cock nudged against his jeans. Hungrily, he claimed her mouth with his, and she responded with a fervor that surprised him. He moved his hand lower, cupping her ass and pulling her in tighter. Her tongue brushed against his and she wrapped her arms around his neck drawing him closer.

He wanted this girl, wanted to take her in so many different ways. He knew she was trouble, but he ignored his own counsel, telling himself he liked a challenge. Perhaps once he'd had her, he could get her out of his system.

He traced her shape with one hand and then pressed open the door to the men's room with the other, and they practically fell inside. Once she realized what he was up to, her eyes lit up with mischief. Damn, she was ready for anything. Locking the door behind him, he picked her up and she hooked her legs around his waist. He set her on the counter and ground his erection against her pussy. She let out a groan he interpreted as desire. If they could just get rid of these clothes. As if she read his mind, Charmaine's fingers nimbly pulled up his shirt and the velvety softness of her tongue glided up the mid-line of his torso.

His balls clenched, and a shiver ran up his spine. Holy crap, she made him feel like a teenage boy checking out his first dirty magazine. She was as stunning as any centerfold he'd ever seen. "You think you can handle me, do you?" she purred flirtatiously.

"I do," he answered confidently, kissing the hollow of her throat.

"What makes you think that?" she asked, also sounding confident. He knew she probably ate men for lunch and spit them out, but she was playing with the big boys now. Reaching into his front pocket, he found what he was looking for.

Diving into another kiss, he distracted her with his mouth as he captured both her wrists behind her in his left hand. Her hands were so much smaller than his that he was able to hold them both in one hand. With his free hand, he pulled the zip ties from his pocket and secured her wrists together with them.

When she realized what he had done she leaned back, tried to free her hands and failed. A flash of distrust crossed her face. "What did you do?"

He released her arms and let his hand travel over the curve of her hips, her waist, then against the pleasing weight of her breast. "I agree you're a handful, girl. Now I know I can control you."

He half-expected her to pitch a fit. If she did he could easily cut away her bonds, but he might be in trouble if she decided to start screaming. To his relief, she only whimpered, closed her eyes and parted her lips. Inviting another kiss?

As he covered her mouth with his, the answer revealed itself immediately. She kissed him back with an enthusiasm that took his breath away and he could feel her body wriggling toward him. She wanted him as much as he wanted her, and she was willing to let him bind her to do it. His dick grew harder, and he was about to take down his pants when there was a knock at the door.

"Charmaine, are you in there?"

CHAPTER FIVE

Charmaine's body froze. Hunter stepped back, and she answered, "Yes, I'm in here."

"Can I talk to you a minute?" Sloane's voice came through the door.

"Er, yeah, just a minute."

Hunter pointed to her bound wrists and mouthed, "Should I cut them off?"

She grinned at him wickedly. "Just help me get down and crack the door so I can talk to her."

He gave a quick nod and hoisted her down off the counter then opened the door several inches, which put her face to face with her friend.

"What are you even doing in the men's room?" Sloane asked in an exasperated tone. "Or do I even need to ask?"

Charmaine tried to look innocent. "I don't know. What's up?"

Sloane shifted her weight from one foot to the other. "I'm tired. Mitch says he's been working a two day shift and offered to give me a ride home. Is that alright with you?" She tried to peer around the door at Hunter, but the small opening prevented it.

"Sure. I'm fine. I can always call Rollins if I need a ride. You're good. Go on home, and thanks for coming out with me."

"No problem. If you're sure it's okay." Sloane's brow creased, sending Charmaine the message that if she was in trouble this was the time to tell her about it.

But Charmaine just laughed. "No, I'm fine, really. I'll text you tomorrow."

Sloane nodded and Charmaine closed the door with her hip. Turning around to face Hunter she giggled. "Let's go."

"Yeah, that kinda killed the mood. Are you sure you don't want me to unbind you?"

She lifted her eyebrows. "Maybe later, but I kinda like being your prisoner." Normally, she wouldn't trust a man to bind her so quickly, but this was Hunter Baldwin, Mr. Perfect. He was a fireman, and they were even more trustworthy than policemen in her book. The way he played the role of dominant intrigued her, and she wanted to know more about this kinky firefighter.

He shook his head. "You're a wild one, you know that?"

She winked at him. "You have no idea."

He grabbed her bound wrists and turned her around. She wondered if he would march her through the bar with her hands tied behind her back, and she was slightly disappointed when he muscled her out the back door without anyone seeing her. Not quite as fun, but still hot. She'd been pleasantly surprised when he'd pushed her into the bathroom and bound her wrists. Bondage aroused her more than any other aspect of BDSM. It made her weak-kneed and her pussy wet. Whatever else he had in store for her, the night was off to a good start.

Hunter opened the door to a beat-up Honda Civic and helped her in, bottom first then shielding her head the way police shove suspects into the back of patrol cars. She'd had enough to drink that it didn't hurt, and she liked the way he was manhandling her. It made her feel feminine and somehow cared for with him controlling her body.

As he walked around to the other side of the car, she had a chance to observe him. He moved like an athlete, a boxer—strong, yet light on his feet. He wore a skin-tight Under Armour shirt with his jeans, which highlighted the perfect triangle of his frame that started with his broad shoulders and tapered down to a trim waist and those drool-worthy abs she'd gotten a peek of before he'd captured her hands behind her back. A shiver of lust ran through her belly as she thought of being naked in bed with him.

He slid into the car and glanced over at her. "You are a beautiful little captive." He buckled the seat belt around her and stroked her hair back the way one pets a cat. For some reason it made her feel warm inside and she twitched with the desire to touch him back, run her hands through his sandy brown hair, but since her hands were immobilized, she reached over with her mouth and kissed him instead. He covered her mouth with his, his tongue darting between her lips, invading her in a way she craved. She ached to feel him inside her, and it had been a long time since anyone had gotten her this worked up.

Admiringly he said, "You know, you're full of surprises."

"Thanks." She grinned.

He backed up the car and headed down a main thoroughfare. "You know I can untie you during the ride. That doesn't look too comfortable."

"No, I'm good." He had no idea how much she loved being bound and helpless. "Where are you taking me?"

"My place if that's okay."

"Purrrfect," she said feeling silly and buzzed, though she couldn't be sure if the effects were from the booze or the lust growing inside her.

She could hardly wait for him to put his hands on her again and hoped that he lived close. Nuzzling closer to him she whispered seductively, "If you undid your pants for me I could show you how grateful I am to you for saving my life."

He glanced at her, and shook his head like he'd never met anyone like her before. Typical male reaction. At the next red light he took her chin in his hand and turned her face toward his. "You don't owe me anything. I was just doing my job."

She pouted. "I know, but I still want to."

"That's not safe. I'm sure you're very good at showing your appreciation, but you might cause me to have an accident." The traffic light turned green and he released her, put his hands back on the steering wheel, and pressed the accelerator. "You know you really are a naughty girl."

"The naughtiest," she said quietly, then stayed silent for the rest of the ride.

When they arrived at their destination he parked at an older building that looked more like an old warehouse than an apartment building. It certainly wasn't the sort of fine accommodations she was used to, but he was a public servant, so she hadn't expected the Four Seasons. Charmaine didn't discriminate. She'd dated men from a variety of socio-economic statuses. Come to think of it, cabana boys were some of her favorite companions.

He helped her climb out of the car. "Here we are." He hauled her toward an old freight elevator and they climbed on. The gate clamored shut and the rickety contraption began to ascend.

"Are you sure this thing is safe?" she asked, biting her lip.

"Yeah," he chuckled. "I've only gotten stuck in here a few times."

She stared at him open-mouthed. "You're kidding. A few times?" The elevator jerked and they swayed from side to side, causing anxiety to replace the butterflies in her stomach.

"Nope. But we've got our cell phones."

"Crap, I left mine in my purse, and I think I left it at the bar."

"For real? You left your purse?" he looked at her with disappointment.

She nodded. "Well, you threw me off in the bathroom…with the…" her voice trailed off. Dammit, they'd been getting along so well and now he'd have another reason to fuss at her. Not to mention she'd have to spend the next couple of days figuring out how to cancel all her credit and debit cards. Ugh. She needed to hire an assistant to help her deal with crap like that.

Before they were out of the elevator, Hunter called the bar. While he waited for them to pick up he asked her to describe her purse.

"Baby blue Birkin," she said.

"Baby blue Birkin," he said into the phone with a puzzled look on his face. She giggled. When he said it, it sounded like a tongue twister. Clearly he'd never heard of the most expensive handbags in the world. But why would he have? More than likely it was a good thing he didn't know that she'd left a thirty thousand dollar bag behind. He'd kill her. Hell, he probably hadn't made that much money all of last year. Yeah, better he didn't know.

He ended the call and the elevator stopped. He opened the gate for her, and she stepped out into the open space of his apartment. The furnishings were spare, but mostly of decent quality—an easy chair, a leather club chair, what looked to be a comfortable sofa, and a distressed wood coffee table outfitted the main room. A few items looked as if they might have come from a flea market, but for the most part she was impressed. The place was neat and tidy, which told her he was proud of his domain.

"You're in luck. They found your bag and the manager already put it in the back. You can go by tomorrow and pick it up."

"I'll send Rollins," she said.

"Who's Rollins? And you're welcome by the way," he said.

She reached her lips up to kiss him on the cheek. "Thank you. He's my driver."

"You have a driver?" he looked at her like the idea was absurd. "What are you, Miss Daisy? Who needs a driver?"

She tilted her chin primly. "I do."

"What in the world for, don't you know how to drive?" He stared at her as if she were nuts, and inside she felt a twinge of delight. She loved to push people's buttons.

"If you must know, I'm a terrible driver for one, and for two, I like to enjoy a cocktail from time to time. You wouldn't want me behind the wheel inebriated would you?"

He considered this. "I guess not. Here." He pulled a knife from his back pocket and showed it to her. "I'm going to cut you loose."

"Are you sure you can trust me?" she laughed.

With one quick pass he sliced the thick plastic bands and they fell to the floor. "Trust you to do what?"

She shook her arms. As much as she'd enjoyed their little game, it did feel good to have that freedom of movement back. "Not to run away," she teased.

He folded up the knife and placed it back in his pocket before taking her in his arms. "Oh, I'm not worried about that. You're not going anywhere." His lips descended upon hers and she let herself fall against him. The butterflies in her stomach fluttered, churning up a deep, ripe lust.

His hand dipped down, and he reached under her skirt, gliding a hand across her skin, over her hips and ass. Suddenly, she remembered the last time his hands had been all over her ass, spanking her cheeks then rubbing them with his comforting touch once he'd soundly spanked them. Was he thinking about that right now the way she was?

Without preamble, he lifted her dress over her head and tossed it on the floor. She stood there in her expensive cream-colored bra and panties with light blue accents. Stretching her arms above her head she asked, "Should we adjourn to the bedroom now?"

He chuckled and shook his head no. "You'd like that wouldn't you?" He circled her slowly. "You're quite a tiger. But you've come to the wrong place if you think you're going to call the shots with me. Go stand behind that chair," he said pointing to an easy chair in the middle of the room that faced a big screen TV.

It had been a while since she'd been around a man who had the confidence to order her around. Had Preston been the last? Possibly, she thought, and walked over to his chair, wishing he'd chosen the leather. This one was so ugly it should be illegal. She stared at the oversized monstrosity hoping it wasn't velour.

"Put your elbows on the back of the chair, lean over and stick your ass out."

His words alone were enough to get her wet, and she forgot all about her misgivings about the chair. She did as he asked, feeling a thrill as she realized he'd be able to see her arousal from behind her. Her tiny panties wouldn't hide that.

He inched his body behind hers so he almost touched her. His scent, pine and cedar mixed with a manly musk, drifted under her nostrils and she breathed it in and wanted more.

As if sensing her need, he pressed his legs against hers. With one arm around her waist he pulled her rear back against him, and fondled her breast with his free hand. Her nipples strained against the soft fabric of her bra, nerve endings coming alive, relishing his touch. He nuzzled the sensitive spot behind her ear and nibbled her earlobe. "Damn, you're too attractive for your own good," he growled into her ear. A quiver of excitement danced down her spine, and she ached for him to touch her pussy.

"So are you," she said, nudging her ass back against him. She could feel his erection straining at his jeans, and she wanted it, didn't have the patience to wait.

He kissed her neck then stood up and backed away from her. "Must you have a response for everything?" he asked testily.

"It's called having a conversation," she said smartly.

"Well, do you want to have a conversation or do you want to get fucked?" he growled.

"Excuse me?" she pretended to be offended.

Suddenly he grabbed her hair at the nape of her neck and tugged. The energy coming from him was palpable. "Listen here, little girl. I thought you wanted this. If you don't, then say the word now. I can tell you've been around the merry-go-round before. What's your safeword?"

"Red," she said meekly. She'd always been afraid she'd forget anything fancier.

"Fine, then say it if you want. Say it now and leave. Call Robbin or whatever his name is to come get you because I don't play games, and I'm not interested in playing them with you."

Her heart beat loud in her chest. "No, I'm sorry. I'm just chatty, but I'll be quiet. I promise," she pleaded. Whether he was really irritated or whether this was part of his intimidating-dom thing, she didn't know. Either way he'd gotten her adrenaline flowing.

"No more talking unless I ask you a question or you need to use your safeword. Do you think you can do that?"

"Yes."

"Yes, what?"

"Yes, sir?"

"That's better," he said, stroking her ass. "Alright, let's get started."

She could hear him rubbing his hands together excitedly. Then it occurred to her, maybe he was getting them warmed up for...

Smack!

Ouch, yes, he'd been warming them up to spank her bottom.

His palm struck her posterior again, this time bringing more of a sting with it. She wanted to ask why he was punishing her, but after that last reprimand she didn't dare speak.

As if he'd read her mind he said, "I'm spanking you because you, Charmaine, little tiger, have been a very bad girl."

He slapped a hand against her hind end, this time harder. She braced her arms against the chair, steeling herself for the blows.

"This is for setting a fire in your kitchen."

Thwack!

"This is for passing out while your house was on fire and almost killing yourself and a building full of people." He gave her an extra hard smack.

"This is for changing the locks and not giving your manager the key."

Thwack! She had to admit the list was getting long, but unfortunately she knew he was only getting started, so she sank down into the plush back of the chair and gave herself over to the sensations.

"This is for not cooperating with your friendly neighborhood fireman when he tried to remove you safely from the scene."

Swat! With every fiber in her being she wanted to protest that she'd already been spanked for that offense, but she knew better than to argue during a punishment spanking.

"This is for letting a practical stranger tie you up and take you God knows where. What sort of judgment is that?"

Thwack! Hey, that wasn't fair. She let a little whine escape, an expression of protest. Good, he'd better let that slide. He'd totally set her up for that one.

"And this is for losing your purse."

That last swat was the hardest. Her butt cheeks felt as if they were on fire now. She sighed with the satisfaction that only came from being given a spanking you know you deserve. He caressed her bottom, soothing her tender flesh with a light touch. "Poor little bottom, having to take the brunt of your bad behavior," he said, and she couldn't tell whether he was showing kindness or mocking her pain.

Before she could decide, he growled, "Now I'm going to fuck you," and tugged her panties to her knees. "Step out of them." She shifted and wiggled her legs so her underwear would fall to her ankles, then she kicked them off and stood still again. She held her breath in anticipation as she heard him unzip his pants and then felt his erection press against her naked ass.

He leaned back and entered a finger into her wanting slit. She'd always found being treated like a bad little girl a turn on. Now, after being spanked, her pussy was practically dripping wet so his finger slid in easily.

"You're nice and wet. That's a good girl," he said stroking her waist with his other hand.

His praise warmed her insides and she shivered with pleasure at his words.

"And do you know what good girls get?"

She hesitated. Was she supposed to answer? He'd told her to keep quiet.

He must have sensed her confusion because he said, "It's okay. If I ask you a direct question I expect you to answer."

"No, I don't know what they get."

"A good fucking." He draped his body over hers so that every part of him touched a part of her. His cock poked hard against her backside and she couldn't help but think it would feel better inside her. He cupped her face with his hand from behind and stroked her cheek. Eagerly, she captured his thumb between her lips and sucked on it.

"You're a greedy girl, Charmaine. Do you want a good fucking?"

She hated to release his finger, but she needed to answer him so she did. "Yes, please, Daddy," she moaned. "I need a good fucking."

"That's what I thought," he crooned into her ear then stood up. She heard the rustling of a foil wrapper then felt her pussy lips being spread wide.

"Such a pretty pussy," he said then pressed the head of his cock into her opening.

Being spread apart and inspected like that filled her with a mixture of embarrassment and forbidden pleasure. Mr. Fire Fighter was rather bold. Perhaps she'd read him wrong when she'd thought he might be too "goody-goody" to be any fun. He made *her* blush, and that wasn't easy to do. As his cock slid inside her a gush of relief shot through her whole body. Finally, she'd gotten her wish.

In seconds he'd sheathed himself completely inside her wet, throbbing channel. Her muscles gripped him tightly and he began to move in and out at a steady pace, the friction between their bodies almost too delicious to bear.

He fisted her mane and pulled her head back as his hips ground against her ass. His balls slammed against her clit, but it wasn't enough, she craved more, more pressure, a firmer touch. She didn't dare reach down and touch herself there, though she knew just what she needed. If she did, he would probably yell at her, maybe spank her and her ass was already too sore for that. If she didn't come, maybe she could go to the bathroom afterward and finish herself off.

She had to hold on to the chair because he fucked her so hard she had to work to hold her own. The force he used aroused her even more, and just when she thought she would be able to climax, he pushed inside her one last time with a shiver, then stopped. They both stood silent, panting, until his penis slid out of her and he pulled up his pants and walked into the kitchen area.

He picked up a kitchen towel and wiped the sweat off his forehead then turned to look at her. She'd collapsed into the offending chair, forgetting for a moment how distasteful it was. She felt tingly all over and kinda dizzy, like when you just get off the tilt-a-whirl at the fair. You've just had the thrill of your life, but you're slightly unsteady. Her clit still hummed, not having experienced the relief she'd craved, but she felt happily used and abused nonetheless.

Hunter opened the refrigerator and pulled out a beer. He took two long sips and she scowled at him. "Aren't you going to offer me one?"

"You don't need one. Would you like some water?"

She rolled her eyes. "Sure." His reprimands were a bit tedious. Lucky for him she was attracted to him with that hard body of his plus the hero thing was cute.

He set the beer on the kitchen counter. "So did you come?"

Her eyes widened. "I enjoyed myself," she said perhaps too defensively.

He shook his head lazily. "It's okay. Lots of women don't come from intercourse alone."

"I beg your pardon." She did not need a patronizing lecture about women's sexuality from him. She'd been with plenty of guys. Most of them didn't care one wit if she came or not. What was with this guy? Did he plan to save the world one female orgasm at a time? His arrogance annoyed her.

He walked toward the chair until his hulking frame towered above her so she was forced to look up at him. She couldn't help but admire his handsome physique with a dusting of curly chest hair, and an impossibly flat stomach. Then he sank to his knees so that his eyes were level with hers.

He held her gaze. "I want to make you come." He spoke with an intensity that stirred something deep inside her.

Before she could respond, he buried his face between her legs and began kissing her inner thigh. Her instinct was to grab his hair, to bury her fingers in his luxurious hair and pull him to her, but he grabbed her by both wrists and stopped her.

"No hands, let me know if I need to restrain you," he said.

"That won't be necessary," she breathed, settling her hands on the armrests of the chair. His tongue snaked up one thigh then down the next. Charmaine didn't usually feel vulnerable when a man's face was in her crotch. Normally it made her feel powerful, but in this situation she was struck by how much control he'd taken over her body, and a part of her wanted to protest. Just as she was about to, she felt a wet, velvety touch between her most delicate folds. He flattened his tongue and lapped up her sex like a big, thirsty bear eager for a drink. He licked her slowly and purposefully, and every centimeter of sensitive skin he touched exploded like a barrage of fireworks.

Her muscles loosened and her body surrendered to him. Fine, he could do with her whatever he wanted, this insufferably gorgeous, holier-than-thou God of Fire. But just when she decided to give in—he stopped. Silent curses ripped through her head. Not again!

Sitting back on his heels he said, "I have an idea."

Dazed and drunk with lust she asked, "What?"

He winked at her. "You'll like it, but you have to trust me. It's gonna seem a little tricky at first." Taking her by the hand he pulled her out of the chair and he sat down in it.

"Hey!" she crossed her arms over her chest. No one usurped Charmaine Bainbridge, no matter how sexy he was.

"Relax." With that he reached down and pulled a lever on the side of the chair extending a footrest under his legs. He looked exceedingly comfortable all laid back in his chair, just like grandpa watching a football game.

"Make yourself at home," she said sarcastically.

"Don't mind if I do," he said closing his hand around her wrist and pulling her toward him. "Now, I'm going to set you on top of me."

She frowned skeptically.

"Trust me." He was repeating himself, but she shrugged. What the hell, she was curious as to what sort of kinky thing he had in mind now.

"Here. Put your head in my lap."

She gave him a look. His cock was starting to come to life again.

"Come here." He lifted her onto his lap with her head near his crotch and her feet hanging over the top of the chair. He'd positioned her so their mouths aligned with each other's genitals. He opened her legs so her pussy hovered right over his waiting mouth. His warm breath blew against her swollen sex and she shivered with anticipation.

"May I suck your cock?" she asked. She'd been wanting to taste him ever since he wouldn't allow her to in the car. Forbidden fruit always tasted best.

"Yes. It will be a blessing to quiet that mouth of yours," he said, though this time he sounded like he was teasing. Wanting to impress him, she pushed his pants out of the way and took him into her mouth. First she licked all around the head then swirled her tongue around the shaft. His cock hardened again in her mouth, occasionally twitching with his desire. Once her saliva had moistened him completely she took him all the way to the back of her throat, taking care not to scrape him too hard with her teeth.

Cupping her knees with his hands, he spread her legs apart and lowered her wet pussy down over his face. She groaned, her cry reverberating around his thick shaft. Splayed wide above him, she flinched at first when his tongue invaded her opening. But the more he licked and tongue-fucked her, the more everything else melted away, the only thing remaining in her consciousness was his mouth and her needy pussy. It made it difficult for her to focus on sucking his cock.

He ran his tongue up and down the length of her sex, nipping at her folds before sucking her plumped clit into his mouth. What he did to it then she wasn't even certain. All she knew was that it made her writhe atop him in ecstasy. He conquered her with his mouth, and she would do anything, anything if he would just keep doing it. Unable to stand it anymore she let his cock fall from her mouth, the words "Please, Daddy!" erupting from her lips. "Please don't stop!"

His fingers dug into her ass cheeks and his tongue and lips worked her little nub over and over, tracing the most delicious little circles imaginable. Each stroke filled her with bliss, and she squeezed her eyes shut. In a rush of sensation, her climax overtook her and her body was racked with waves of pleasure. The ecstasy went on and on, spreading all the way to her fingertips and toes until finally her clit became so sensitive that she tried to wriggle away, tried to stop him. He resisted and continued licking her until she squealed, "Please, Daddy! Please stop!"

With a chuckle he released her. Her heart continued to race, and she collapsed in an awkward position on top of him in the chair with her head in his lap. He must have sensed her discomfort because he helped her get right side up, curled her into his lap and held her, with one arm under her knees and one arm curled around her back. She was so spent that she allowed herself a rare moment of vulnerability and snuggled against his chest.

"Did you like that?" he asked.

She nodded, not trusting herself to speak.

"Good," he said stroking her hair.

They sat together quietly, and he began rocking the chair. It was pleasant sitting there with him like that, peaceful. She and Hunter had bantered back and forth ever since they'd met, but this was different. She enjoyed the rare moment of intimacy and didn't want to do anything to break the spell. Not having to be "on," to be able to relax and just "be"—she liked it.

After about ten minutes the chair stopped rocking, and Hunter began to snore. Charmaine puzzled over what to do. Usually in a situation like this she would call Rollins and have him take her home, but these days she didn't really have a home. Her mother's place felt foreign and lonely.

She watched Hunter while he slept. He was gorgeous, and he had just made her come like she hadn't come in years. Maybe she should stick around for more of that. It wasn't like he'd asked her to leave… While his lap *was* cozy, she knew she'd sleep better in a bed. The memory of Lawrence kicking her out fresh in her mind, she decided it might be better not to wake Hunter. Careful not to wake him, she gingerly climbed out of the chair, and tiptoed into the adjoining bedroom.

As she lay down on his bed, she felt a bit like Goldilocks inviting herself into a stranger's home. Hunter hadn't invited her to stay, but oddly, she felt more at home here than she did at her mother's place. Before she fell asleep she thought about how intoxicating his lovemaking had been, even in that bizarre position in that god-awful chair. She'd never had sex in an easy chair before, but she'd never been given oral sex with such glorious results before either. They clearly had a lot of the same kinks, and something about Hunter's raw masculinity made her set aside her snobbishness in deference of her animal attraction to him. And she fell asleep listening to the sounds of his grizzly bear snores coming from the next room.

CHAPTER SIX

The next morning Hunter woke up in his chair. It wasn't the first time he'd fallen asleep in his chair, but his pants weren't usually unfastened when he did it. Then the memories from the night before came flooding back to him. *Charmaine.*

He scanned the room, but didn't see her. Typical party girl, must have called her driver after he'd fallen asleep, had him take her home. He sighed. Charmaine was a handful, and now she showed herself to be that elusive sort of female, the kind whose motto was to love 'em and leave 'em *before they could leave you.* He recognized that hardness in her, the way she cloaked herself in Kevlar, thinking it would protect her against the world. Unfortunately, there were things in life you couldn't be protected against. Heartache being one of them.

Standing up, he stretched and went to the refrigerator. He opened the door, hoping to find orange juice, but only discovered half a carton of milk and a few beers. Taking out the milk he opened an overhead cabinet. Maybe some cereal. Nope, just a few packages of saltines and an almost empty box of Oreos. Time to go to the store. He downed the rest of the milk, and tossed the empty container in the trash.

He was heading to the bathroom when he glimpsed Charmaine lying in his bed asleep, tucked into the fetal position. Her presence caused him to stop short. *She'd stayed.* Had he misjudged her? He thought she was long gone and figured he'd never see her again.

Trying not to wake her, he opened the closet door, found some clothes and got dressed. Where were her clothes? She had the covers pulled up so high he couldn't tell if she was still naked. His cock stirred at the thought of her beautiful body, and put his hand on his crotch, unable to help himself.

Dominating her the night before had been supremely satisfying. It was unusual for him to let loose with a girl and do what he wanted. He'd never showed a girl his kinky side so early in the game. Most girls weren't up for the rough way he played. They would have seen him as abusive, and in his line of work he had to be careful no one leveled accusations like that against him. But each time he'd raised the stakes last night with Charmaine, she had surprised him by matching his intensity. Before he knew it he was doing whatever it took to control her, and with her big personality, he'd had to release his dominant side on her. She was such a little brat, he couldn't help but want to tame her.

His cock throbbed in his hand. The way she sassed him with that mouth of hers made him want to shove his dick between those succulent red lips. He closed his eyes, thinking about the hard fucking he'd given her. She'd taken everything he'd given her, including her punishment. He could still just see her adorable ass all splotchy and red from his handprints.

When he opened his eyes she was awake and staring at him. "What are you doing?" she asked, eyes glued to his hand closed around his erection.

"Nothing," he said, refusing to be embarrassed about having his hand on his cock. "About to get some breakfast. I don't have anything here. Wanna come?"

She looked from his eyes to his crotch then back up at him, a grin spreading across her face. "Sure. That's kinda creepy, you know?"

He shrugged. *Fuck that little princess. This is my place, and I can stroke myself if I want.*

"Could you be a hero and grab me my clothes? I think they're on the floor in the other room." She pointed to his living room.

"No problem," he said tensing at the word hero. Damn, she knew how to push his buttons. Feeling like the hired help, he picked up her clothes and brought them to her.

Taking the chivalrous route he took his toothbrush into the kitchen to give her some privacy and the bathroom to get dressed. "I'll be in here when you're ready."

"Thanks," she said.

After he brushed his teeth in the kitchen sink he sat down on the couch and scrolled through the messages on his phone. He would have loved to have watched her dress, to have taken her again, but something held him back. A nagging feeling in his gut told him he'd read her wrong. He doubted she'd morph into the clingy type, but he wasn't sure what to make of the fact that she hadn't yet disappeared. Charmaine Bainbridge was nothing if not mercurial, and he feared she was playing him, he just wasn't sure how.

"Ready," Charmaine said as she entered the room looking like a sunny day after the rain. No trace of the hangover she was bound to have showed on her face, and it was difficult to detect any hints of the walk of shame her previous night's clothes might give away. Rather, she looked like the picture of health and good behavior.

"Wow, you look great," he heard himself say.

"Gee, thanks," she said wryly, as if he shouldn't sound so surprised.

They took the rickety elevator down to the bottom level, where she asked, "So where are you taking me for breakfast?"

"There's a little diner around the corner called Doc's. Sound okay?"

She nodded. "Perfect. It will be my treat."

"Oh no. I invited you, I'll pay."

"But…" she started to protest but he cut her off.

"I asked you, so I'm paying. End of discussion."

"So it's like a date?" she touched his arm flirtatiously.

"Exactly, plus you don't have your purse. Remember?" He touched a finger to his head.

"Oh yeah. I forgot."

He laughed at her ridiculous flippancy. The rich really were different. He wouldn't have been able to think of anything else if he'd lost his wallet.

It was a short walk, so he offered her a hand and they strolled over to the diner, enjoying the marginally cooler morning air with the knowledge that in an hour or less a thick, heavy blanket of heat and humidity would return to reclaim its chokehold over the city.

When they arrived at Doc's, he opened the door for Charmaine and they stepped inside. The cool air of their air conditioning whipped across their skin and made Charmaine's nipples harden, but he pretended not to notice. His favorite waitress waved to him and pointed to a table where they could sit. He led Charmaine to it and they slid into the overstuffed plastic booth.

Charmaine retrieved one of the cheery yellow, laminated menus and studied it intently. "What are you getting?" she asked, noticing he didn't need a menu.

"Egg white omelet, bacon, and orange juice," he said. She nodded and went back to perusing the menu.

The waitress brought them coffee, and she winked at Hunter when Charmaine ordered a Dutch baby cinnamon apple pancake and hash browns, but he didn't think anything of it until she brought their food. He stared at her plate piled high with a dome of delicious-smelling pancake with a sweet filling. The whole thing was swimming in syrup and covered in powdered sugar. Then there was the big pile of hash browns.

"What?" she snapped, calling him on his dropped jaw.

He wasn't sure how to respond. He didn't meet a lot of women who ate like ten year-old girls. "Nothing, it's just you don't look like someone who would eat that."

She doused the pancake with even more syrup. "Yeah, my personal trainer would kill me for it, but right now I don't really give a crap," she said rubbing her temples.

Aha, so she was human. He knew she'd have a hangover today. "You have a personal trainer?"

She nodded and shoved a bite of her pancake into her mouth.

"That you listen to?"

A smirk began at the corner of her mouth as she chewed then she took a sip of coffee. "I didn't say *that*, but I do pay him to whip my ass."

He almost choked on his orange juice as he visualized a personal trainer wielding a whip, landing a blow on that delicious rear end of hers. A pang of jealousy stabbed at him. "How's that working for you?"

She shrugged then pointed at her body with a flair. "What do *you* think?"

"I think you're hot. And I think you know it."

"Well, duh," she said spearing another sugary bite. "Want some?"

"No. Thank you."

"Let me guess. You're very particular about what you eat," she said as she popped the bite into her mouth and closed her eyes to savor it.

"I try to eat clean," he said more defensively than he intended. "Being in good shape is essential to my job."

She waved her fork in the air. "Yeah, yeah. Mr. Buzzkill, party of one."

"What is your problem? Just because some of us eat like grown-ups that's no reason for you to act like a child."

Shooting daggers at him with her big blue eyes, she stuck her nose in the air and resumed eating her pancakes.

"Hey, what was that last night when you called me Daddy?" Even as he asked, something in his stomach clenched, and he felt the familiar twitch of his cock.

She froze, then after a minute said, "I don't know what you mean."

He could practically see the walls rising around her heart, protecting her. Maybe she didn't remember—it was possible with all the alcohol and in the heat of passion— but he wasn't letting her off the hook that easily. Leaning across the table he said in a low voice, "When you were begging me—you said, 'Please, Daddy'."

Two pink spots emerged on her cheeks, but still she didn't say anything.

"I'm not making fun of you. I'm asking, Charmaine." He leaned back and casually tossed his balled up paper napkin on the table. Raising a brow, he said, "To be honest, I thought it was kinda hot."

"You did?" She looked him in the eye now, and he saw something akin to hope there.

"Yeah," he said shrugging his shoulders.

"It's just that I used to have a relationship like that… a long time ago."

"What kind of relationship?" He gathered she wasn't talking about her relationship with her biological father.

"With an older guy. He was a dom. Do you know what I mean?"

He nodded, knowing deep down that if it wasn't for his career choice he'd probably be a dominant in the BDSM scene. Instead he tried to keep those tendencies in check and sublimate his urges in other ways. Sometimes, like last night, he did worse at that than others.

"Well, it was that sort of relationship. He was my daddy dom, and I was his little girl."

"How old were you?" he asked making sure they were on the same page and not talking about some pedophile.

"Eighteen. It's been several years."

"How old are you now?"

"Twenty-four. You?"

"Twenty-nine. But you liked it?"

"Yes, I have several friends who are into that sort of thing. I just haven't been into it lately."

"I could see how you would do well to have the guidance of a daddy." He stirred his coffee and took a sip.

"What does that mean?" she snapped.

He laid a hand firmly over the top of hers. "Exactly what you think it means."

He could almost see the smoke coming out of her ears, but he stubbornly pressed on.

"For example, you should probably lay off the drinking."

Her eyes widened and she pushed her plate forward. "We are done here," she said with the conviction of a mob boss and scooted out of the booth. Before he could stop her she smiled at the waitress and borrowed the woman's cell phone. Damn that charming little vixen! He grabbed the check lying on the table and hurried to the front to pay. Before he finished cashing out, Charmaine had flown out the front door.

Outside, he found her pacing up and down the sidewalk on the corner. She looked as mad as a bull the toreadors had already stabbed, but had yet to finish off. Injured was when they were the most dangerous. He approached her anyway.

She glared at him. "You don't know me. You think just because you fucked me you can make judgments about my life, tell me what to do. Well, you are sorely mistaken Mr. I-Think-It's-My-Job-To-Save-The-World!"

"That's not what I was doing..."

"Oh yeah? From where I was sitting that's *exactly* what you were doing!"

"Charmaine, I just wanted to help."

"I don't need your help, and I don't want it," she seethed.

He was about to try again when a tricked-out black Lincoln Navigator rolled to a stop in front of them, and a guy wearing a tie got out, walked around and held the door open for Charmaine.

"Rollins! Am I glad to see you!" Charmaine enthused, giving Hunter a dirty look over her shoulder. She climbed into the car and slammed the door. Rollins returned to the driver's side, and moments later the Navigator pulled out into traffic, leaving Hunter standing alone on the corner wishing he'd kept his big mouth shut.

CHAPTER SEVEN

The car only moved about half a block before Charmaine felt a jolt then was flung against the partition between the back and front seats. Something crashed into them. Charmaine lifted her head and realized she was wedged between her seat and the one in front of her. As she started to extract herself, the pain in her head made her realize she must have banged it pretty hard. Putting her hand to her forehead she could feel a nasty bump starting to form at her hairline. Looking around to get her bearings, she noticed that the majority of the driver's side of the backseat was smashed, accordion-style, to within inches of her face. How did that happen? Objects seemed to sway in front of her, and everything seemed as surreal as melting timepieces in a Dali painting.

Suddenly, her door burst open. It was Hunter, and through a dull haze she wondered what he was doing here.

Then his arms were around her, cradling her like a sleepy child, and he lifted her from the car and set her gingerly on the sidewalk nearby.

"Are you okay?" he asked, radiating concern.

"I think so," she rubbed the swelling knot on her head.

"Okay. Stay here," Hunter ordered.

She started to nod, but that caused fresh pounding in her head, so she stopped. Before she could say anything else, Hunter ran toward her car, which now looked more like a dented sardine except it was the side and not the top that appeared rolled up.

Rollins. Oh no, she'd been too out of it, too concerned about herself to see if Rollins was okay. Clearly another car had hit them and, as she took in the situation, it looked like a parcel truck had barreled into them at the intersection just yards from where Rollins has picked her up.

What was it they said—the vast majority of car accidents occur within a few miles of home? Hunter's home maybe. Hell, she didn't even have a home anymore. She craned her neck to see what happened to Rollins, but she couldn't see. Hunter had gone around to the other side of the car. She stood up and headed toward the car. Her gait was wobbly but she didn't feel faint, rather adrenaline coursed through her veins and buoyed her. She walked behind the back of the car, and saw Hunter trying to pry the door away from where Rollins sat.

"Is he okay?" she yelled.

"Go sit back down like I said," Hunter fussed through clenched teeth, exerting all his energy trying to unwedge the door, which now resembled a stomped aluminum can.

"Just tell me, is he okay?" she pleaded. Rollins was like a family member to her. There was no one she counted on more. He couldn't be dead… she needed him too badly. Please, dear God, let him be alright.

"He's unconscious." Hunter grimaced as he tried the backseat door. "Find someone with a phone and make sure they call 911."

"Okay," Charmaine said looking around. There were several people who had gotten out of their cars to help, and it looked like a few people had come out of the surrounding businesses. She noted signs for a pawn shop, a fortune teller, not the best part of town to get into an accident.

A crowd had gathered across the street, and it looked like the driver of the truck was over there. He looked fine but shaken up. The front was smashed in, but clearly her Navigator had taken the brunt of the impact.

With so many people around she was sure someone had called 911. Help would be on its way. Hunter had said Rollins was unconscious, but he wasn't dead. She exhaled. It was going to be okay. Somehow.

Then she noticed the trickle of liquid pooling underneath her car. It started to create a new path toward the gutter on the side of the street.

"Hunter!" she cried, panic rising in her voice.

"Yeah?" he was inside the car now. He'd gone around to where he'd gotten her out and climbed in, apparently still working to help Rollins.

"Is that what I think it is?" she asked, but then the smell hit her nose and as dread coursed through her she knew the answer to her own question.

"What? Charmaine, I can't see very well from in here," he shouted from inside the vehicle.

"Gas! Hunter, the gas tank is leaking all over the place."

He tapped on the glass from the inside. She gave him her full attention.

"Run that way!" he pointed away from the accident scene. "Run! At least a block and stay there until I come get you. Do you hear me?"

Dumbly she nodded and started to run. Then it occurred to her—if Rollins and Hunter were in that car if it exploded…

She kept going in the direction he told her, but her feet felt like they were in quicksand and she stopped running. How could she leave them there? But what choice did she have, what could *she* do?

Do what Hunter asked, a voice inside her said, and she kept walking.

The whir of sirens cut through the hot, steamy air. She'd never been so happy to hear sirens than at this moment. When she was about half a block away, she leaned against a wall and turned back to face the accident scene. More people were milling around now, seemingly unaware of the danger.

Then she saw Hunter emerge from the crowd with a lifeless Rollins. His left side was covered in blood, and he hung limp in Hunter's muscular arms. Hunter called for people to get back, and they listened to him.

From two different directions, a fire engine and a police car pulled up to the scene. Blue, red, and white lights flashed and sirens blared. What looked like dozens of firefighters jumped from the rig.

Hunter laid Rollins on the pavement several hundred yards from the scene and went back to confer with the other firemen. About that time an ambulance arrived, and a pair of EMT's placed Rollins on a stretcher and started to load him into the ambulance.

Not without me. She came back to scene and yelled to the EMTs "Wait!"

They looked up and she caught up with them. "Wait, he's my driver. Where are you taking him?" She looked down at Rollins' unconscious body, and her fears were renewed. He sure didn't look like he was going to be alright.

"Ma'am were you in this accident as well?" the female EMT asked.

Ma'am, really? She wasn't old enough to be a ma'am, Charmaine wanted to scream, but instead she said, "Yes."

"Did you suffer any injuries?"

"I bumped my head, but it was nothing."

"You need to come with us, get checked out at the hospital."

"That's sweet, but not necessary. I'm fine." Charmaine said in sweet-as-sugar debutante voice. Then it occurred to her she had no ride to get to the hospital, and she was desperately worried about Rollins. Changing her mind, she said, "Oh, all right. If you insist."

"We do," the male EMT said then asked her to climb onto a gurney.

"Is this really necessary?" Charmaine asked, feeling ridiculously like an invalid strapped to a stretcher over a minor head bump. This was the second time in a month she experienced such treatment over something minute.

"Yes, ma'am."

Enough with the ma'am's. Charmaine started to roll her eyes, but even that hurt, and then she climbed on the gurney. Okay, maybe a trip to the hospital wouldn't be a bad idea. They had good pain drugs there.

The EMT's lifted her into the ambulance and shut the doors. The female EMT rode in the back with them.

As the woman moved closer to the front to sit down, Charmaine whispered, "It's going to be alright, Rollins. Everything's going to be fine," she said to him. Then she thought of Hunter. She wished she'd told him where she was going, but she wondered if he'd care.

He'd done his best to save Rollins, but he was a fire fighter, never truly off duty. She remembered how diligently he'd worked to pull Rollins from the wrecked vehicle. Clearly he'd been stuck and even when pooling gas put his life in danger, Hunter had fought to save a complete stranger.

What was that? Stupidity?

Her heat skipped a beat as the truth resonated in her heart. No, that was selflessness. A concept so foreign to her that she had to roll the idea around in her brain like a lump of clay to try to make sense of it.

A person so focused on doing the right thing, the heroic thing, that he sacrifices his own safety for the good of others. And this was something Hunter chose to do on a daily basis. Her heart fluttered in her chest, and she licked her lips wishing she could kiss him, thank him.

When the ambulance got to the hospital the intake nurse parked her behind a curtain in the emergency room where she waited for almost an hour. The doctor who finally examined her had a full head of curly hair and sparkling green eyes behind his glasses, not to mention an adorable dimple in one cheek. Uncharacteristically, Charmaine barely noticed. Her thoughts were on someone else entirely.

CHAPTER EIGHT

Hunter paced the floor of the hospital's waiting room. Because he wasn't family he wasn't allowed to see Charmaine yet, but he had been informed that Rollins was going to make it. The driver's spleen had been crushed in the accident and his left leg had been broken in multiple places. He was in surgery to repair them, but after a lengthy recovery the doctor believed he'd be fine.

He took a sip of the weak coffee they served in the cafeteria and glanced up at the television. A program on weather chasers played on the overhead television. Normally he would have found it interesting, but right now it was just noise and pictures. Charmaine commanded all his thoughts. He wished they'd let him go back to see her. Even though he knew she would be okay, he wanted to be certain, and he wanted her to know that he cared about her well-being.

At the scene he'd called in a favor from the boys at Fifty-One, the unit who had responded to the scene, and they found out which hospital she'd been transported to. They appreciated his help on the scene and were happy to do him a favor. He'd been through training with one of their lieutenants and his friend gave him the scoop.

So he waited. Family. The idea made him chuckle to himself. Though he'd only known Charmaine for a short time, it was impossible for him to imagine himself a part of the elite Bainbridge family. In fact, the last time he dared date a woman above his station, her family had tried to pay him off to leave their daughter alone. He'd been pissed, of course, but ultimately he'd rejected the cash and wasn't surprised when, soon after, Laura had left for a nine-month European vacation.

He'd known Laura wasn't the one for him, but it infuriated him the way her parents had treated him. There had been few women since, and now he could kick himself for indulging his interest in a girl who was not only wealthy, but famous as well. He must have a self-destructive streak, he thought kicking at a crease in the linoleum floor.

Finally, a nurse appeared from behind the restricted doors. "Mr. Baldwin."

He hurried to her. "Yes?"

"You can see Miss Bainbridge now. I'll take you to her."

She led him through those sacrosanct doors, then helped him navigate through a maze of patients in various stages of illness. He looked around and saw an old man hollering something about suing a fast food restaurant. After that, Hunter kept his eyes on the nurse in front of him. His skin started to itch. Hospitals made him nervous. They rounded a corner and there she was, reclining in the bed rocking a blue hospital-issued gown. Even with a big goose-egg on her noggin she was striking.

"Hey," she greeted him. "I didn't expect you to come to the hospital. You didn't have to."

He stuffed his hands in his pockets. "I know." Maybe he shouldn't have come.

She shrugged. "But it's nice that you did."

He nodded. Even with her big hair and personality she looked small in the hospital bed, almost fragile. Human life *was* fragile, he faced reminders of it almost every day, but it was new to see Charmaine in that light. She seemed the type who would be just ornery enough to cheat death, live to be one hundred.

"Sit down." She indicated a chair next to the bed. "I'm just flipping the channels. They have a DVD player but it doesn't work."

"How do you feel?" he asked.

"Pretty good, except my head hurts like a motherfucker, especially when I move. If I'm still it's better."

"Going home today?"

"Yes, but first, I have to find somebody to take me. They won't let me leave without someone agreeing to monitor me for the next twenty-four hours. I'm thinking about calling Kimberly or Sloane, but I don't have my phone."

"Oh, wait. Yes, you do. I went and picked up your purse on the way here. It's in the car. Not sure why I left it there. Guess I got distracted."

"You have my purse?" Her eyes brightened. "They gave it to you?"

"Yep."

"But what if you had been someone wanting to steal my things? I mean you're a guy. They know it's not your bag."

He grinned. "They know me. One of the benefits of being a firefighter. People trust me."

"Oh," she let that sink in.

"You know you don't have to call your friends. I don't have a shift today or tomorrow. I could monitor you…" The minute the words left his mouth he wanted to bite them back. What the hell was he thinking? He wasn't her boyfriend. He may have crossed the line offering to do that.

To his surprise, she beamed up at him. "That would be lovely."

A nurse flipped back the curtain. "I'm working on your discharge papers." She turned to Hunter. "Are you the one who's going to take her home?"

"Yes," he nodded, still trying to process his offer and her acceptance.

"Good. She needs to be monitored for the next twenty-four hours. Be sure she's lucid, not vomiting, the headache doesn't get worse. Here is the list of symptoms you want to assess." The nurse handed Hunter several pieces of paper stapled together. "If she shows any of these you need to bring her back. Most likely that won't happen, but when a person is concussed we take every precaution we can."

"Got it." He took the papers from the nurse. "Don't worry. I'll take good care of her."

"I'm sure you will," the nurse said and left in a flurry.

"They seem busy," he commented.

"Mmm," Charmaine responded. She was now glued to the television. He turned to see it was a fashion show about the latest in women's shoes.

What had he gotten himself into?

● ● ● ● ● ● ● ● ● ● ● ● ● ● ●

Charmaine woke up, and it took a minute for her to remember she was at Hunter's place. The throbbing in her head had diminished, but the pain was still there, dull and nagging. By the long shadows cast across the bed she could tell is was near dark. The ordeal of the accident had taken more of a toll on her than she expected. Between that and the hangover she'd been nursing, she slept almost the whole day.

What had Hunter been doing all day? She heard the television playing softly in the next room. She got out of bed slowly, still wearing the same clothes she'd had on for two days now. She needed someone to bring her some things, but Rollins, her go-to source for such things was in the hospital and wouldn't be at her disposal again for weeks, probably months. She groaned.

Hunter must have heard because he called to her from the next room, "Hey."

She padded into the living room barefooted. "Hey," she answered, rubbing her eyes. "How long have I been asleep?" she asked, plopping down on the sofa next to him.

"Since noon." He reached over and touched her leg, and she felt his concern in that one simple movement.

"I'm starved. What's for dinner?"

He chuckled. "I don't know, princess. I didn't want to leave you so I didn't go out for provisions. We could always order pizza."

"Chinese. Do you have any good Chinese food around here?"

"Chinese it is. There's a great place a few blocks from here, and you're in luck. They deliver."

"Oh thank God! I feel like I could eat a wildebeest."

"You really are a tiger, aren't you?" He tugged at a strand of her hair and she smiled. "That, I'd love to see, by the way."

"What?"

"You eating a wildebeest. I think I have a menu around here somewhere." He got up and rifled through a drawer in the kitchen. "Aha!" He produced the menu and handed it to her. She told him what she wanted and he called in the order. They watched television in a comfortable silence while they waited for their food to be delivered.

He was watching a war movie, Black Hawk Down, and didn't offer to change the channel for her. Though she'd seen the movie before and didn't care to see it again, she didn't say anything. It was awfully sweet of him to take care of her, and she didn't want to appear ungrateful. Plus, she had better manners than that.

The food arrived and they ate on the couch with their feet on the coffee table. Charmaine chowed down on her shrimp fried rice. Hunter dug into his garlic beef and finished it in record time. His manners were atrocious, inhaling his food like that, but since it was consistent with the caveman-who-drags-you-back-to-his-lair quality that made him so appealing, she didn't say anything. Plus, nothing was worse manners than pointing out someone's bad manners.

Hunter was different from any other man she'd ever met. He was raw and tough and heroic, and made no apologies for who he was. He made her stomach flutter, and it had nothing to do with her dinner.

She stared at his full lips and wanted to reach over and kiss him, nibble and nip at that sexy mouth of his. But her head still throbbed, and she didn't want to appear too eager.

"How's your head?"

"Still hurts," she said with a wince.

"Okay. Let's get you some ice."

"Sure, thanks."

"What's your address?" he asked.

"Ugh! I don't have one, remember? My apartment burned down."

"Fine, but do you know the address?" When he pointed at her head she got it and recited her address obediently.

"I'm supposed to ask. You should probably go lie down again after you finish eating."

She let a sly smile creep across her face. "Will you join me?"

"No funny business, Charmaine. You're here to get better, so I can make sure you don't stroke out or whatever."

Sticking out her bottom lip, she said, "Yes, sir." Then she thought she saw him shift in his seat uncomfortably. Was he getting a boner? When he got up and went into the kitchen she could see she'd been correct. Yep, when she'd pouted and called him sir, he'd gotten aroused.

Putting on her most innocent face, she opened her eyes wide and batted her eyelashes at him. "You know, you really are being a very good daddy. Taking such good care of me…" She twirled a lock of her hair flirtatiously.

"Yeah?" He removed an ice tray from the freezer. "Well, it's too bad you couldn't be a good girl for me earlier today."

His words hit her like a slap. "What do you mean?" Her spine straightened.

"At the scene of the accident. First, I told you to stay seated on the sidewalk, and you didn't. Then I told you to walk a couple of blocks away and you didn't."

She huffed. "But if I had stayed sitting down on the sidewalk you wouldn't have known about the gasoline!"

He shrugged. "Regardless."

"But, but…" she sputtered, unable to think of what else to say. She *had* completely disregarded his instructions.

"You can't have it both ways, Charmaine. If you want me to be a daddy to you, you have to follow my rules. That's how it goes. Or else, you have to take your punishment."

She grimaced and touched her hand to her forehead in case he'd forgotten about her head injury. "But, you can't punish me with my head like this. I'm hurt. I have been in a car accident, Hunter." Her words came out measured for effect.

"I know. That's why I offered to care for you, and that's why I'm going to give you a punishment holiday and postpone your punishment until you feel better."

"You are?"

"Yes, now let's get you back in bed." He shuffled her back into the bedroom, carrying an icepack.

Once they were in the bedroom, she stood by the side of the bed. "I'm sick of wearing this dress," she said, and pulled it over her head. *Let's see if he can resist this body.*

"Here, I'll get you a T-shirt." Hunter ducked into his closet then came back with a grey T-shirt with Dallas FIRE emblazoned across the front as well as a pair of cotton broadcloth boxer shorts that looked like they would swallow her.

"Thanks," she said and took off her underwear and bra. Standing there, naked, she'd hoped to get a reaction out of him, but he just handed her the clothes as if she were his sister. Fine, if he insisted on ignoring the sparks between them, so would she. She pulled the boxers up and slipped the shirt over her head. The boxers were too big, but the T-shirt was super comfortable and smelled like him—woodsy, like the outdoors.

He pulled the covers back for her, and she burrowed under them. She was already tired again. He placed the bag of ice on her forehead. The rush of extreme cold caused her to catch her breath, but as she adjusted to it, she felt better. It didn't take away the pain completely, but it did ease it. "Thanks," she said through closed eyes.

"You're welcome. Let me know if you need anything else." Then she felt his lips on hers. It was a sweet kiss, almost chaste, as he enveloped her in his care.

"Goodnight, Charmaine," he said at the doorway then flipped off the light.

"Goodnight, Hunter."

She snuggled down farther into the covers, and relaxed. So he'd punish her when she got better, big deal. For now, she reveled in the fact that today, someone cared for her. For the first time in a long time she felt secure as she drifted off to sleep.

CHAPTER NINE

"What's wrong?" Kimberly asked, concern filling her big brown eyes. "Are you still suffering from that concussion?" It had been three days since she left Hunter's and her head felt fine now. Kimberly had urged Charmaine to meet her for lunch, using the familiar "wedding plans" ruse, but Charmaine had feared Kimberly intended to give her the third degree instead.

"Not really," Charmaine sighed. "It's that freaking firefighter, Hunter Baldwin." She said his name in a sing-songy voice.

"What about him? I thought things between you two were progressing." Kimberly leaned forward in her chair.

"They are, I guess. I'm attracted to him." She sighed, glancing over at the fresh pastries in the nearby counter. Kimberly had chosen a bakery that also boasted a lunch café for their meal today. Usually the site of the delectable baked goods would put a smile on Charmaine's face, but not today. She didn't have much of an appetite.

"So what's the problem? Seriously Charmaine, he sounds hot." Kimberly asked, fanning herself with the paper menu. They'd chosen to sit outside to get a table quicker, and the August heat was inescapable.

Blowing her bangs out of her face Charmaine said, "Well, when we started talking about the daddy thing, he told me I should stop drinking." She made a "can you believe him" face, and was surprised when Kimberly lowered her eyes to the ground.

"*What?* You don't think he was *right*, do you?" Charmaine sat with her mouth open and waited for Kimberly to respond.

Tentatively, Kimberly began, "Well Charmaine, it wouldn't be a bad idea for you to cut back, maybe just a little."

Charmaine sat up straighter in her chair. "Unbelievable! You're on his side," she accused Kimberly with a healthy dose of righteous indignation.

"Look at it from his perspective. He probably blames your drinking for you setting that fire in your apartment. He *is* a firefighter so it's his job to prevent that sort of thing, and the other night… how much did you drink? Did you do anything stupid?"

Charmaine pouted. "I don't know. I didn't have that much. I remember everything." She bit her lip sheepishly. "Oh yeah, but then I left my purse at the bar."

"You see? He's just trying to look out for you." She laid a hand on Charmaine's arm and said gently. "Honey, it wouldn't be a bad thing for you to stop drinking, or at least try some moderation. Moderation can be a good thing."

"But moderation is boring!" Charmaine stomped a foot and it was Kimberly's turn to sigh.

"Maybe, but it wouldn't hurt you to grow up a bit, love."

Charmaine glared at her. "Et tu Brutus? Great. Now I've got a pretend mom and a pretend dad. Yippee." Sarcasm dripped from her words.

"I'm only saying that you seem stuck lately in some self-destructive patterns, and if this guy could help you change that and do better for yourself, I don't see the harm. He sounds like a good influence, to tell you the truth."

"I don't need a good influence," Charmaine railed.

"Okay," Kimberly said putting her hands in her lap. Changing the subject slightly she asked, "Why don't you and Hunter come out to dinner with me and Charles? Charles is dying to meet the fireman who rescued our fair Charmaine—not once, but twice now!"

"He didn't exactly rescue me after the accident. I could have gotten out of the car myself." Charmaine crossed her arms over her chest.

"Well, he rescued Rollins. From what you said his life may have been in real danger."

"Even though I'm grateful for what he did for Rollins, I'm not sure if I'm even going to see Hunter again," Charmaine said with a huff. She was resentful of all the attention everyone gave Hunter for being the big hero. Sharing the spotlight wasn't her thing.

"Why not?" Kimberly clucked at her disapprovingly.

"For one thing, he thinks he owes me a punishment, so I'm not looking forward to *that*."

"Why a punishment?"

Charmaine rolled her eyes. "For not following his orders at the scene of the accident. He wanted me out of the way, and well, I didn't do precisely what he said."

"He just wanted to keep you safe," Kimberly said.

"I know, but I was worried about Rollins. I had to see what was happening," Charmaine protested. "You'd do the same if it were Charles in the car."

Kimberly lifted a shoulder, acknowledging Charmaine might be right.

"How is Rollins by the way?" She looked around. "Wait, did you drive here?"

"Oh, God yes. In a rental. It's the worst. And Rollins has a broken leg and some internal injuries. I went to see him at the hospital and it was too depressing. He probably won't be back until after Christmas!" Her face fell just thinking about it. She felt like she'd lost her best friend and her parents all in one person, and the fact that she depended so much on an employee characterized her life as one, sad and two, lonely, and three, pitiful. The third one might have been redundant of the first, but she thought it bore repeating.

"Christmas? That's four months away."

"I know. And it could be even longer," Charmaine wailed.

"Wow. I didn't even know you could drive." Kimberly looked at Charmaine like she was a bug underneath a microscope—parts of Charmaine's life remained a unique mystery to her friends. They'd never known anyone else who didn't drive. In Dallas you had to drive to get anywhere.

"I barely can."

"That's scary," Kimberly said and Charmaine nodded. She could tell Kimberly was wondering who in the hell would let her behind the wheel. Charmaine wondered the same thing. She hit a parked car the first time she took her driver's test, and it had been five years before she tried again. Her father had bribed her to do it with a brand new Mercedes S-class, and she'd taken the bait. Though why he cared whether she drove or not, she'd never know.

"So when are you supposed to get this punishment?" Kimberly asked.

"Friday, but I may just blow it off," Charmaine said.

"Charmaine Bainbridge, you cannot blow off this guy. No matter what you say, he has saved your life twice, and then he took care of you when you had a head injury. No guy does that!" Then as an afterthought she asked, "You didn't have sex with him then, did you?"

Charmaine shook her head tentatively. No, they hadn't had sex when she'd been at his apartment after the accident, no matter how hard she'd tried to tempt him.

"So he's not in this for sex Charmaine, which means he really likes you."

Charmaine was quiet. She hadn't thought of it that way, she'd merely felt rejected when he hadn't slept with her. Just one more thing Mr. Perfect wanted to deny her.

"I haven't met him yet, but he seems like a good man, and when's the last time you had a *good man*?" Kimberly gave Charmaine's hand a squeeze.

Charmaine didn't answer. Tears burned at the back of her eyes. She knew the answer to that, but her lips wouldn't form the word. *Never.*

Her father wasn't a good man, and neither were the scores of men she dated. Oh, some of them were nice enough and there'd been some harmless fellows mixed in there with the bad boys. She'd thought Preston was good, but looking back she saw more and more chinks in his armor.

If Hunter was such a good man, why did she want to fight him with everything she had? She looked up and realized Kimberly was still talking.

"...can't use the man. After all he's done the least you can do is meet with him. Use your safeword if you have to. You owe him that much, Char."

With a sigh she acquiesced. "Fine."

"Would it help to see him with me and Charles? Make the date more casual, less intense?"

"Yes."

"Friday night then?"

"Friday night."

"It's a date."

When they got up to leave Kimberly wrapped her arms around Charmaine. "Char, darling, I've known you a long time. It has been a long time since you've let anyone in. I don't know if you're still nursing a broken heart because of Preston or if it's something else, but I love you and I want you to be happy. Don't just slam the door on this guy because he wants to help you be your best self, okay?"

There they are again—those blasted tears. Charmaine fought to hold them back. Leave it to Kimberly to get her feelings all worked up. Normally, she succeeded in ignoring them, crushing their very existence. Yet Kimberly had known her a long time and loved her despite her flaws. She swiped at her eyes, sniffed, and managed to say, "Thanks" before giving Kimberly a kiss on the cheek and skulking to her rental car.

• • • • • • • • • • • • • • • •

That same afternoon Hunter and Mitch were lifting weights over at the gym in the firehouse. Mitch stood behind Hunter spotting him as he lifted two twenty-five in a military press. With a grunt Hunter hoisted the barbell over his head.

"So how did things go the other night with Charmaine?" Mitch asked.

Hunter shrugged.

"C'mon, man. She seems like a hellcat, that one."

Hunter shook his head, "Yeah, a real handful. How about you and her friend?"

"Sloane? She's cute, but I got a real friend vibe from her. She's fun to talk to, though." They moved to another station, picked up a pair of seventy-five pound dumb bells and started doing bicep curls.

"But you and Charmaine—I could sense real chemistry there." Mitch grinned.

"You just won't quit, will you?"

"Why should I?"

"Because I'm not sure it's going to work."

"Why?"

"She's a rich girl. I've been down that road before."

"You're not comparing her to Laura, are you?"

"So what if I am?"

"No comparison. The two are completely different. Laura was uptight, from an uptight family. Charmaine is a wild child." Mitch pointed a finger at Hunter. "She would be good for you, and who cares how much money she has? To me, that would be a bonus. A pro, not a con."

"Maybe." Hunter paused. "Rich people are different. She's spoiled beyond belief, and I don't think she has any purpose. She's flighty, ya know?"

"But she's gorgeous. Do you know how many guys would give everything they had to tap that?"

"Yeah, well I may have mentioned she needed to stop drinking," Hunter said with a grimace.

"Really?" Mitch tossed his weights on the floor, and they bounced lightly.

Hunter wiped the sweat from his neck with a towel. "Yeah, stupid—I know."

"Man, I don't care if she's a raging alcoholic that is not cool to do the first time you hook up with a girl." Mitch shook his head disapprovingly. "When it comes to women you can't be so controlling. Or so stupid."

"I know." Hunter wondered if his need to dominate would scare Charmaine away. He was too controlling and he knew it, and Charmaine Bainbridge had no intention of being controlled by anyone. It didn't seem like they were all that compatible.

But when he'd taken care of her after the accident, things had been great. He'd known she was going to be a spoiled, pain-in-the-ass patient, but she surprised him by being relatively well-behaved. She had tried to seduce him, and that was cute. But even though his cock was game, he controlled his impulses and ignored her advances. No matter how much he wanted to fuck her into the next week, her health took priority. Her brain didn't need the jostling around he would have given her, so he slept on the couch.

Ever since then he couldn't keep his mind off her. He kept picturing that sassy face she made—with her full, ripe, red lips, and wild multi-colored hair. And that ass. Dammit, he couldn't stop thinking about that juicy round ass.

"Hunter!" Mitch brought him out of his thoughts.

"Yeah? Sorry, I'm distracted," Hunter said.

"I can tell. Maybe it's for the best," Mitch said taking a sip of water.

Hunter drank from his water bottle too. "What do you mean?"

"Dating a woman who has more money than you'll ever make, that's got to be hard."

Mitch was right. He'd already seen glimpses of that when Charmaine had argued with him about who would pay for dinner. At the same time, it didn't bother him that she had gobs of money. "You're right. It would never work."

"It's too bad. She's smokin' hot." Mitch said.

Hunter nodded. "Yeah. She and I are supposed to get together this Friday."

Mitch squinted and gave him a wicked grin. "I'm not countin' you out yet, buddy. I think you've got it bad for this girl."

"Shut up." Hunter tossed his sweaty towel at his friend.

"Man, you gotta up your game if you want this one," Mitch teased.

"I don't see you sewin' up all the ladies," Hunter retorted.

"Oh, okay. How 'bout a little one-on-one?" Hunter nodded and they headed toward the indoor basketball court.

CHAPTER TEN

Friday night rolled around and Hunter had picked Charmaine up at her mother's place. They drove to an Italian restaurant and were now seated across from Kimberly and Charles. Going on a real double date like this made it feel like they were a couple, and though he had doubts about Charmaine, Hunter liked the dynamic.

Kimberly was attractive, with dark eyes and long brown hair. She radiated a sort of kindness, and Hunter found himself thinking she'd make a good mother someday. Charles had a muscular physique, which told Hunter they'd have a penchant for fitness in common. Apparently he was some big deal ex-military guy who now ran his own construction company, and Kimberly was a writer.

They began with drinks, and Hunter tried not to say anything to Charmaine, but he silently started counting her drinks when the first round of margaritas arrived. After some small talk and a plate of quesadillas for an appetizer, the girls got up from the table. Charles and Hunter watched them go. As they turned a corner Hunter turned to Charles. "So I think Charmaine hopes you can give me some pointers about this whole 'daddy' thing."

Charles grimaced and shook his head. "I know. It's not like I'm some guru or anything. Some doms mentor other doms, but that's just not my style. That said, ask me anything you want, and I'll try to answer your questions."

"Got it. I don't think I'd be down with that mentoring thing either." Hunter took a sip of his drink.

Charles shrugged. "What is it you want to know?"

Hunter shook his head. "I'm getting the whole dominance thing. It's the daddy part I haven't done before. What's different there?"

"I think it's more about caretaking and less about dominance for the sake of dominance. Kimberly and I fell into it naturally. I'm not sure how exactly, but Kimberly started finding things on the internet—blogs, pictures—of people who favored the Daddy/little girl dynamic, and it resonated with both of us. She'd send me pictures when I was in Iraq. So for us, it was a way to stay connected while I was away, and to share our fantasies."

Hunter considered this. "That sounds like a good idea."

"For me, being a daddy dom is about caring for your little girl, being proud of her, supporting her, and pleasing her. Kimberly is the center of my world, and I'd do anything to protect her. If there's any way I can guide her or help her out, I will. In return she is submissive to me in the bedroom. Outside of it? Sometimes the dynamic continues, but I have a son who's around a lot, so more often that side of our relationship takes place at the end of the day when he's asleep. Her submission is her gift to me."

"It sounds great, but I can't see Charmaine being submissive outside of the bedroom *ever*." Hunter laughed at the thought.

"You're probably right, but you might be surprised. The girls have a group of friends who either have a daddy dom or who want to have a partnership like that. I've been around these girls long enough to know—sometimes it's the ones who want to be in charge outside the bedroom who make the best subs. For them it's hard to find a man strong enough for them to feel comfortable surrendering control. She has to really trust you for it to work."

"That makes sense. Any advice on earning her trust?"

"Pay attention to her cues when you play with her. She'll let you know what works with her body language. If you're attuned to her she will bond with you more quickly, and don't do any of those stupid mind-fuck things some doms talk about on the internet. That's a recipe for mistrust unless your sub already knows and trusts you."

All this was valuable information, and Hunter tried to process it and think of what other questions he had.

Charles continued, "As you're getting to know her likes and dislikes, you might ask about her fantasies, have her send you some pictures of what she likes. That worked well for us."

Good idea. Fantasies were easier to share if you didn't have to say them or describe them. Sharing an image of someone else doing something was safer than asking for something kinky face to face. "Before they come back, what's the best piece of advice you've got?" Hunter tapped the side of his glass.

"Taking care of her is the most important part. Since she's giving up control to you, offering you her submission, you must honor that and treat her with the utmost respect. She's placed her trust in you, and you need to cherish that."

"I know."

"Watch her body during a scene, pay attention to her signals and learn what she responds to. A lot of it is about being in tune with her as an individual. The rest of it is about being nurturing, protective…" he gestured to Hunter. "I figure you've pretty much got that protective thing going on already."

Hunter smiled wryly. He did, didn't he? The more he learned about being a daddy the more he realized how suited he was for it. "What about punishments, corrections?"

"That's up to you. Some people are more into it than others. Considering your sub, you may need to be strict with her."

"I don't know how well you know Charmaine, but she could sure use a spanking or two," Hunter said.

Charles laughed. "Oh I've known her a long time. If ever a girl needed taking in hand—*it's her.*"

Hunter grinned. He was starting to like Charles. "Correcting her is a full-time job."

"No doubt. Kimberly is as much as I can handle. I can't imagine Charmaine." Charles looked off into the distance as if trying to visualize dominating Charmaine. He shook his head. "Nope. Better you than me. It's gonna take a special guy…" He lifted his glass to Hunter and they banged cups and drank.

Hunter swallowed. "Thanks. I think."

"Oh, I meant it as a compliment. You're going to have to be strong for her. As tough as she is, as glamorous as she wants people to think her life is, Charmaine's had it pretty bad. Other than the money, life has dealt her a difficult hand."

Before Charles could say more, the girls returned from the ladies' room.

"You're not talking about us, are you?" Charmaine teased.

"Of course we are. Same as you were talking about us," Hunter retorted.

Kimberly winked at him, which told him he'd been right. A moment later a raucous sizzling heralded the arrival of their waitress with two big iron skillets teaming with fajitas. Hunter's mouth watered, and he ate more than his fair share of the delicious beef. The girls had chicken, but they stuffed themselves just as much.

"I couldn't eat another bite," Charmaine groaned.

"Me neither," Kimberly said. "Hey, did I tell you about Lucinda?"

"What about her?" Charmaine asked, taking a sip of her second margarita which was almost empty.

"She's going to be here in Dallas, performing a week before the wedding."

"She'd better be comping us tickets." Charmaine narrowed her eyes.

"Of course she is," Kimberly responded.

Charmaine turned to Hunter. "Our friend, Lucinda Lake, is a famous pianist. She performs all over the world, so she's always traveling. It's hard for her to find the time for us with that big career of hers." She shot a look at Kimberly. "I know you were worried she wouldn't be able to make it to your wedding." Then she looked back at Hunter. "Kimberly and Charles are getting married in Acapulco in a few weeks."

"We'd love for you to come," Kimberly drawled.

Was it his imagination or did Charmaine kick her friend under the table as she said through gritted teeth, "Yeah, that would be fun!"

"Mexico?" Hunter repeated.

"Yep, it's taken us three years to get married. We finally decided to just go the destination wedding route. The hotel provides a wedding planner who will handle the details, and for us it will be like a vacation. At least that's what they tell me. I'm just going to show up in a monkey suit wherever they tell me." Charles laughed.

"That's the way to go." Hunter clinked glasses with him across the table.

"Men," Kimberly teased. "They don't understand everything that goes into planning a wedding."

"Let's keep it that way," Hunter said with a wink.

"It's much easier on the bride if the groom stays out of the way and lets her plan it." Charmaine widened her eyes. "I don't know how Kim just turned over the reins to Kanye like that. I would never have done that. I'm way too controlling."

"I know, right?!" Kimberly touched Charmaine's arm in agreement.

"Seriously Hunter, Charmaine's bringing her plane down. You should come!" Kimberly enthused.

"I'll see what I can do about work," Hunter hedged. Charmaine hadn't seemed excited about the prospect of him accompanying her. He'd have to feel her out later.

When the waitress asked if they'd like another drink, Hunter noticed Charmaine shake her head "no" as she smiled at the waitress. She had an easy grace to her that came from having a privileged upbringing. The girl was a lady through and through, no matter how wild her behavior was at times. At her core she was a princess. But did he want her to be *his* princess? Did she even want that?

As they left the restaurant, they walked out with Kimberly and Charles before going their separate ways. Charmaine invited the other couple to join them for drinks at another spot, but Charles said, "I've got an early day tomorrow. No way I can keep up with you tonight and make it."

"Please." Charmaine begged like a purebred puppy.

"No, I've got to get up early tomorrow too." Kimberly gave Charmaine a big hug.

"It was nice to meet you both," Hunter said sincerely.

"You too," they said in unison, then away they went, arm in arm.

Hunter reached out and took Charmaine's hand which seemed to surprise her, but she clasped her hand around his. He led them through the parking lot to his car. "They're a nice couple."

"They are. The best. I'm so glad they're finally getting married. So many things have stood in their way, most of all his ex-wife. It will be so good for them to finally get hitched. It will be good for Charles's son too."

"How old is his kid?"

"Benji is nine. He's with Charles's ex."

Hunter furrowed his brow. "Wow, an ex-wife. That's got to complicate things, sharing custody and all that. I've got some buddies at the firehouse that have to deal with that. It's okay for some of them, but for others—man there are some mean-ass bitches out there."

"Tell me about it. Charles's ex is one of those. She's a piece of work."

"When I get married, I want it to be forever. I'm not doin' that twice."

Charmaine stopped walking, took her hand back and stood with her hands on her hips. "Don't you think everybody feels that way when they get married?"

He shrugged. "I guess so."

She screwed up her mouth. "Well, if everybody thinks that—why do you think you're going to be so different? Fifty percent of all marriages end in divorce. Those aren't great odds."

Placing his hands on her cheeks he bent his head so that their lips were almost touching. Controlling her face, he spoke with an intensity he hadn't felt since he'd been at the fire academy. "Because when I want something I go for it. I make it happen, and failure is not an option."

Then he kissed her. Combining her breath with his, he slid his tongue between her half-parted lips, and then he moved one hand behind her waist and he pulled her head to him with the other. Kissing her plump, juicy lips was the most sensual experience he could remember. They had just the right amount of firmness that they felt like heaven when his lips touched hers.

He felt her relax in his arms and as he held her, he knew he had to make her his. But would she agree?

CHAPTER ELEVEN

Charmaine robotically fastened her seat belt, dazed from the passionate kiss Hunter had just planted on her. Whew, her legs had gone all Jell-O on her, and she'd been afraid she might slide to the ground. A side effect from her concussion last weekend or pure lust? Difficult to determine.

"Where will you take me next?" Usually she would have told him where she wanted to go, but for some reason, tonight it pleased her to let Hunter take charge of their evening.

"I thought we could go back to my place. You still haven't received that punishment I owe you." He raised his eyebrows suggestively.

Her heart sunk. A punishment? That didn't sound like a fun time at all. She was no pain slut, and she had a feeling he would inflict some pain if given the opportunity. Using her safe word was always an option. Nah, she couldn't have him thinking he was too much for her.

"Fine," she said, trying to keep her voice as neutral as possible.

When they got to his place they took the rattle-y old elevator to his apartment. Once inside, Charmaine felt the buzz of happiness. His place was growing on her.

"Why don't you go into the bedroom and take off your clothes," Hunter said as casually as if he asked her to hand him a paper towel.

"Just like that?" she asked in a voice that dripped sarcasm.

"Just like that."

Her heart rate sped up. How arrogant could he be, just assuming she was going to get naked for him? Who did he think he was? Clearly he didn't know she had considered standing him up tonight.

"You should at least offer me a drink," she snipped.

"I'm sorry. Where are my manners? Would you like some water, Charmaine?"

"Water?" She crossed her arms over her chest. "I was thinking beer or some wine…"

"I'm sure you were but you've had enough to drink tonight, tiger."

"You're an ass, you know that?" she asked, pressing her lips together in anger.

"So I've been told. Do you want some water or not?"

"Ugh. Fine, I'll take some, but I'm not getting undressed!" She huffed loudly and went to sit in the ugly recliner, trying to shut out the pictures in her head of the way he'd pleasured her there. She wanted to stay mad at him.

He brought her a glass of water with two ice cubes in it. She took a sip then set the glass down on the coffee table. Hunter tilted her chin up toward him. "Hey," he said.

She gave him a pronounced pout. "What?"

"Don't be like that," he chided her.

"Like what?" she said, sticking her lower lip out as far as it could go.

"All pouty and bratty, like a naughty little girl."

"Why? What will you do?" she said, her interest growing.

"I might have to spank you with my belt."

"With your belt?" Her blue eyes grew huge.

He nodded. "Now, please go into the bedroom and take off your clothes. If you don't want to take off your top you may leave on your blouse, but off with your skirt and no panties."

The way he'd taken control of the situation, firmly yet gently, captivated her. "Well, since you asked nicely…" she said and went into the bedroom where she took off all of her clothes. Unsure what to do next, she lay down on her tummy on the bed.

She heard him come into the room, then heard the "ziiiiiiip" as he yanked his belt out of his belt loops. No one had ever hit her with a belt before, and she wasn't sure she could take it. *Remember you have a safe word*—Kimberly's advice rang in her ears, and she took a deep breath. Breathing always helped her get through a spanking.

"Charmaine, what are you being punished for?"

She wanted to roll her eyes and offer a smartass retort, but she squashed her obnoxious side and answered dutifully, "For not following your instructions after the car wreck."

"That is correct. Anything else?"

"Being bratty?"

"Exactly."

She lay there, quietly on the bed for several minutes trying not to tense up her muscles, a challenge since any second she anticipated a leather strap would wallop her butt.

Then it came. The impact of the belt cracking against her buttocks. Ouch! It hurt, but not as badly as she'd expected. She exhaled and reminded herself not to hold her breath.

Another swat came down, this time she could actually feel the supple texture of the leather against her backside. It made an impression that was both pleasurable and painful at the same time. She writhed on the bed, eager to experience more.

"See? It's not so bad is it?"

"No, sir."

Thwap! The slapping sound resonated throughout the room.

Thwap! The lashes were beginning to sting. She imagined her bottom must be turning pink by this point, and she was getting wetter as her arousal built.

Thwack! That one hit lower on her ass and she prayed he wouldn't go onto her thighs. Thigh spankings could be killers.

Fortunately, Hunter was no sadist, and he kept his swats to her rear end.

His smacks were starting to burn, and now she made a small cry with each one.

He must have realized she was getting close to her limit because with one final whack he asked, "What have you learned from this?"

"To listen to what you say, do what you ask, and not be bratty."

He sat down heavy on the bed next to her. "That about sums it up." He curled his body next to her and rubbed his palm over her reddened flesh which now felt like it was on fire. His caresses served as a salve, mitigating the pain, and she moved to press her naked body against his clothed one.

"Thank you, Daddy," she said playfully.

"You're welcome, Kitten."

She stroked his cheek with her hand. "Kitten?"

"Yeah. You're a tiger most of the time, but when I tame you, you turn into the most adorable little kitten." Her heart fluttered in her chest, and her pussy throbbed with need. At that moment there was nothing in the entire world she wanted more than to be his kitten.

She wrapped her arms and a leg around him and kissed him deeply. His light stubble tickled her cheek, and their mouths melded together joining them, making her want to be one with him completely. "Daddy, please," she whispered in his ear as she clung to him.

"Please what?" he asked mischievously.

"Please take me. Fuck me, Daddy." Her loins were on fire and she had no pride left, no inhibitions left to stop her from asking what she wanted.

"I like it when you ask for what you want. That's a good girl," he said as he pulled away and stood by the bed.

Once he moved away the cool air from the room hit her where his warm body had been and she whimpered. But when she saw that he was merely undressing she breathed more easily. He unbuttoned his shirt slowly and deliberately, every inch of skin he unveiled accentuated by the ripple of his muscles underneath.

How committed he must be to working out, for his body looked like he could be on the cover of a fitness magazine. No beer belly for her daddy. She smiled to herself. This was the first time she'd thought of him as her daddy or her anything for that matter, but at that moment she wanted them to belong to each other.

"Give me your hands," he ordered.

Automatically, she sat up and gave him her wrists.

He picked his belt up off the floor and wrapped it around her wrists, attaching them to one another. The leather felt so strong, so cool against her skin she almost purred out loud. When he was finished he buckled it, restraining her hands.

Stepping just out of reach he unfastened his jeans and let them drop. Kicking his pants to the side, his cock poked out hard against the cotton fabric of his underwear. Charmaine licked her lips wanting to touch him, to taste him.

"Lie back and put your arms above your head," he said in a throaty tone.

She stretched her arms over her head, luxuriating in the cool feel of the sheets against her tender posterior.

"Spread your legs for me."

His words sent a thrill dancing through her. With her arms overhead, legs splayed wide, she would be exceedingly vulnerable. He'd be able to do anything he wanted to her. She loved it.

She opened to him, and he touched her with his fingers, first tracing the delicate folds of her sex, then entering her with one finger, then two. His movements were slow, teasing, and once his fingers were inside her, she started to lift her hips urging him to fuck her with them. As good as he felt inside her, she needed the friction against her quaking walls and wanted him to do more than just fill her.

"Be still," he corrected her, but then rewarded her gyrations by pushing his fingers in and out of her slit.

She closed her eyes and lost herself in the pleasure. He flicked his thumb across her clit, which sent a jolt of ecstasy surging through her. Oh God, he was good—fucking her with two, possibly three fingers, while he rubbed the outside of her cunt with his thumb.

"I love how wet you are." He growled.

"Mmm," was the only response she could manage. Her nipples hardened and she wished he had three hands so he could touch them too.

He shifted positions and held her leg with one hand and continued finger-fucking her with the other. Then she felt a new sensation at the top of her front vaginal wall. It felt as though he were tickling her inside with each thrust. A delightful, sexy, delicious form of tickling, like having her clit massaged, but different.

Soon Hunter started moving his hand in and out at such a rapid pace that it felt like a machine was fucking her. Oddly, it didn't hurt. Rather, it felt like she was floating in heaven. "Oh, Daddy please don't stop!" she cried thrashing her head from side to side.

He chuckled. "Not a chance."

Her pelvis bucked involuntarily, and he laid his other hand on her hip to keep her still. Adding a flick to her clit, his ministrations continued until her body began quaking. Her entire body seemed to contract and convulse around his hand, even parts she'd never felt before. A warm gush of fluid seeped from her as she came, gasping for air. Her bound hands reached for him. She wanted to draw him to her, hold him against her to help her ride out this exquisite wave of pleasure.

His hand remained inside her until all her tremors subsided, then he withdrew and lay down beside her, his erection poking against her side. She could see the wonder in his eyes at the intense delight he'd brought her. He held her close, and she managed to get her bound wrists around his neck. They kissed, less searching, more connected this time. She hoped he could feel the gratitude in her kiss.

When her breathing returned to normal, he bent his head to kiss her breast. Taking her nipple into his mouth he licked the tip with his tongue then circled it as he suckled her, and ended with a sharp bite that made her cry out. The combination of pleasure and pain was back and her pussy began to cream for him yet again.

He inserted a finger inside her again. "Still wet for Daddy. Time to take my pleasure now." He grabbed a condom from his jeans pocket and rolled it on. Lifting her legs, he hooked each over his shoulder and entered her with one long stroke. The intrusion made her jump, but then she settled back to enjoy the ride.

His cock moved in and out of her, his pace leisurely drawing out the pleasure that resulted from each thrust. Underneath him she lay there reveling in her submissiveness. He'd given her an orgasm, a huge one, and now it was his turn. She was happy for him to use her for his pleasure however he saw fit.

Leaning forward, he shifted his position so that he supported himself with his forearms, freeing up his hands. He reached across her chest and took her nipples between his fingers. Pumping himself hard into her, he pinched her nipples until she cried out. A rush of divine sensations soared through her body, and she felt as if she were flying.

When he twisted her nipples, she shrieked and squirmed under him so hard she would have come up off the mattress if his weight had not held her down. With each stroke, each twist, she came closer and closer to another release until finally her defenses broke down and her climax shattered her into a million dandelion particles wisping in the breeze. She held on by a thread and rode every ripple of ecstasy until she was utterly spent.

A few moments later she heard a catch in his breath, then he pushed into her one last time before he stilled. He stayed inside her a few moments and she thought she might die of happiness. Then he pulled out, removed the condom and tossed it in a nearby trash can. When he lay back down he clutched her to him, making a spoon with his body against hers and whispered, "That was your reward for taking your punishment so well. Did you like it?"

She tucked his hand between her breasts and sighed. "I loved it."

CHAPTER TWELVE

Charmaine was lazing by the pool at her mom's condo when her phone beeped. She considered not answering it because it was her generic ring, but at the last second she picked it up. "Hello?"

"Hey Charmaine?" a familiar masculine voice inquired. It had been several days since she and Hunter had dinner with Kimberly and Charles then finished the evening with her punishment and mind-blowing sex. She'd been hoping he'd call, more than she liked to admit.

"Yes," she examined her pedicure, pointing a toe femininely as she admired her new coral nail polish.

"It's Hunter."

Her heart began to beat faster and she swung her legs over the side of the chaise. He had her attention now. Trying to maintain her composure, she said in a mildly flirtatious tone, "What can I do for you?"

"I wondered if you might come down to the station this afternoon. There's something I'd like to discuss with you."

"That's really short notice," she said, and as soon as the words left her mouth she wanted them back. It was a bad habit of hers to be contrary.

"Well, anytime then. You name it," he said agreeably.

"Oh, I *guess* this afternoon will work," she said. "Text me the address." She almost asked him if it was casual dress but thought better of making a snarky comment. He agreed and as soon as they hung up she gathered her things and went inside to shower and change.

After she cleaned up, Charmaine looked through the closet in the guest room where she'd parked most of the clothes she'd brought to her mother's place. Usually she dressed in eye-catching fashions with vibrant prints and loud colors, but today she felt the need to tone it down a little. She chose a pale blue, linen, tank dress and matching Jimmy Choos with a five inch heel.

Thirty minutes later her substitute driver, Clyde, aka not-Rollins, pulled the loaner limo into the driveway of the address he'd given her. The nondescript building was constructed of cream and tan bricks with two large bay doors which housed two red fire engines.

Being this close to the fire trucks with all their lights, gear, and gadgets made her feel like a schoolgirl on a field trip. Several men busied themselves around the truck. One looked to be polishing something, while another appeared to be fixing something.

Everybody she saw looked busy, but she intercepted a handsome man in a "Property of Dallas FIRE" T-shirt exactly like the one she'd swiped from Hunter. The man looked like he was in a hurry. "Excuse me," she said.

"Yes?" He looked very serious, and she could already tell from the atmosphere this was not a frivolous place.

"I'm here to see Hunter Baldwin. Do you know where he is?"

"Lieutenant Baldwin? I'll see if I can find him for you. In the meantime why don't you come with me?" It was more a directive than a question, and she did her best to follow him, though his stride was much faster than what she could manage in her high heels.

Just as they were about to enter the building, Hunter opened the door and came outside.

"Hunter!" she said with a big smile. "There you are."

He smiled back and the other man, happy to see that she'd found who she was looking for, turned to her and said, "Have a pleasant day, ma'am." before getting back to whatever he'd been doing.

Hunter took her by the elbow and moved her to where they weren't blocking the door. His touch electrified her skin, and she tried not to frown when he took his hand back and placed it in his pocket.

"What did you want to see me about?" she asked.

"I've been thinking about this daddy/little girl thing, and I think I'm down for it."

"You are?" She'd discerned they were heading in that direction, but it was good to know that he felt that way too, that he was interested in that sort of relationship.

"Yes, but for it to work we have to establish some ground rules, some parameters."

"Alright." There were always rules in these sorts of relationships, all relationships really, she just hoped she could abide by the ones Hunter imposed.

He knitted his brows together and looked at her as if he wasn't sure he'd heard her correctly. "What did you say?" he asked, apparently surprised that she would agree so readily.

She weaved an arm through his and gazed up at him flirtatiously. "Well, maybe I'm okay with that, maybe not. Let's hear what they are."

He smiled down at her, then leaned in, his lips coming closer and closer to hers. She closed her eyes certain he was going to kiss her, but instead he stood up again and said, "Hey, Mitch." to a guy passing by without a shirt on.

Charmaine recognized him as Hunter's friend from the bar where she'd left her purse. She looked Mitch over with his glass-cut six-pack abs and bulging pectoral muscles. "Hey, what's the deal with your friend?"

Hunter eyed her suspiciously.

She chewed on a fingertip as she took the firefighter's full inventory. "He's hot. Do you think he might be up for a threesome?"

Hunter glared at her. "Are you serious?"

"Why not?" Charmaine looked at him innocently.

Hunter grabbed her by the wrist and dragged her through the door into the firehouse. When he found an empty room, he slammed the door behind them. "What is with you, Charmaine?"

She traced the hair on his forearm ignoring his burst of temper. "What? I don't know what you're talking about." She blinked. "I thought guys dreamed of threesomes."

"Really? You want to fuck my friend? Everything is just a game to you. Fuck this guy, then that one. Why not add Hunter's friend to the mix?" He shook his head and yanked his arm away from her.

"I like to have a good time. What's wrong with that, Daddy?" There was a challenge in the way she said the word "daddy."

"What's wrong is that you don't take anything seriously. I can't count on you to behave for five minutes. I ask you about taking our relationship to another level and you respond by wanting a threesome? Woman, you are unbelievable."

"Maybe you need to punish me," she said, her voice trembling. Perhaps she'd become addicted to his spankings. Was she behaving badly just to get his attention? She didn't know what had gotten into her leering at Mitch like that. She didn't really want him. Hunter was the only man she wanted, but her impulsiveness came out and screwed things up.

"Maybe I do," he said, pushing up his shirtsleeves. He strode over to the door and their eyes locked in a battle of wills as he pressed the button to lock it. "Pull up your dress and lean over that table."

Her eyes didn't leave his as she slowly inched her dress up over her hips. It would wrinkle, but she couldn't care less. She heard a catch in his throat as he noticed she wore only a G-string. From behind he must have quite a view.

He stood behind her, and smacked her rear end with the palm of his hand.

She yelped, and he growled. "Not a word. Not a sound out of your mouth. Do you hear me?"

"Yes, Daddy," she purred.

As he continued to swat her, her pussy grew wetter and wetter with each strike. She could feel the blood rushing to her nether regions, her lips and clit swelling with desire with each smack he delivered to her posterior. She wanted to cry out, but she didn't dare, so she bit her hand instead.

First he struck one side then the other. Then he swatted her sit spot, and she wanted to howl, but somehow she muffled herself—for him. She didn't want him to get into any trouble, and she assumed his boss wouldn't approve of him making her scream locked in a room at the fire house. Toward the end, she wiggled her legs farther apart, straining, wanting him to touch her sex, to stroke her.

"Such a greedy little cunt," he snarled, and her body shivered at his dirty talk. Then she heard the rip of a condom wrapper and felt the mushroom head of his cock against her opening. She arched her back, urging him to take her. The spanking had been enough foreplay, she wanted him to take her *now*.

He pulled her G-string to the side and pushed inside her. She gulped as he stretched and filled her, then she grabbed the sides of the desk and held on. He took hold of her hips and began thrusting deep and fast into her pussy. Her walls clenched around him, and she was grateful the desk stabilized her body; without it she wouldn't have been able to push back. His hips bucked relentlessly, and she couldn't remember ever being fucked so hard by anyone, and that was saying something considering her list was pretty damn long. He reached around and rolled her clit between his fingers. Back and forth, side to side, pulling it, pinching it. Her body tremored with pleasure, and she thought she might lose her mind completely. Then the world exploded into a climax that shook her to her core. She spasmed, her body no longer under her own control, but under his.

Her orgasm had been almost violent, but it had clearly been nothing compared to his. With a huge final thrust he came. He was silent for several minutes, and she relished still feeling him inside her. But soon his breathing returned to normal, and he withdrew.

Stepping back, he tossed the condom in the wastebasket and pulled up his pants. She gingerly stood up and pulled down her dress. Turning to face him, she wrapped her arms around his neck and kissed him hard on the mouth. He returned her kiss hungrily, invading her lips with a passion that made her dizzy.

Moments later he pulled away and took her hands in his.

"Thank you, Daddy."

The corner of his mouth crept up. "For what?" The sex appeared to have abated his anger, at least for now.

"I needed that."

"The fucking?" he raised a brow.

"All of it," she said. "So what were those rules you wanted to talk with me about?"

His eyes darted to a clock on the wall. "I don't know if we have time now… I've got to get back to work. Tell you what, I have two days off starting on Saturday. How about you come over to my place Friday afternoon, spend the weekend with me, and we can discuss it further?"

"That sounds perfect," she said and headed for the door, his hand in hers. He opened the door for her and she left, and she wasn't thinking about how awful the loaner car was or how much she missed Rollins. Nope, her mind was on Hunter. She even considered giving herself permission to hope that maybe, just maybe, things could work out between them. *If* his rules weren't too steep...

As she walked away, she made sure to add just enough wiggle to her walk to give him something to think about for the next two days.

CHAPTER THIRTEEN

To prepare for their weekend date, Hunter sent Charmaine an email. He liked Charles's idea of emailing about sexual ideas and fantasies, and he'd spent a lot of time on the internet lately learning about doms and daddy doms. Hell, he could get sucked in and spend hours on Tumblr. He even skipped a workout the other day he was so entranced.

The one thing that had eluded him was all the stuff about using toys. He'd never used anything other than ropes and handcuffs in his sex play, and he wondered if Charmaine expected him to bring out vibrators, floggers, whips, etc. So, in an attempt to be direct, he sent her the following email:

Hey Kitten,
When you come over this weekend, bring your favorite toy you'd like me to use on you, okay?
Hunter

Attaching a picture of a daddy humming his little girl's clit with a bulbous vibrator, he debated where or not to sign it "Daddy," but decided against it. Things were going fairly well between them, but he wanted to be certain she could agree to his rules before he took on that role officially. If there was one thing he learned from the internet it was that people were serious about their BDSM. Hunter had always done things his own way, so he wouldn't tolerate anyone putting restrictions on him, telling him how he had to do things, but he understood about safety. Hell, he was a fireman for God's sake—safety was of the utmost importance to him. He'd never put Charmaine in harm's way.

An hour later Charmaine sent him the following reply:

Okay, Daddy. Whatever you say.

xo,
Kitten

Whatever you say. He snickered at that. If only Charmaine were that obedient. She was a complicated woman, and he was growing more and more attracted to her complex personality all the time. He loved making her submit to him. Sexually, she was a dream partner for him, and he got hard just thinking about her. She was gorgeous, responsive, enthusiastic, and her rockin' body didn't hurt.

It was Charmaine outside the bedroom he struggled with. At first, he'd thought her alarmingly shallow, but he now recognized that there was more to Charmaine than he'd originally believed. Much of her callous bravado was part of a calculated act she put on to cover her real insecurities.

Something told him deep down Charmaine needed someone. She clearly needed guidance, and from what he'd seen, she didn't have anyone in her life to provide it or to hold her accountable for her behavior. Was her self-destructive behavior a cry for help or was she just looking for attention? He'd developed compassion for the pretty little rich girl, and he'd nominated himself as "Daddy," but he wasn't sure how well she would accept his supervision.

Charmaine certainly didn't have a submissive nature in everyday life, so he knew it would be a challenge for her to give up control. Perhaps bringing her own toy to a scene would give her an element of control and make her more comfortable.

Late Friday afternoon she arrived at his place with her new driver in tow. The guy carried three large Louis Vuitton bags in various shapes. Hunter refrained from shaking his head, but he planned to have her naked most of the weekend so he had no idea why she needed all that stuff.

Taking in the array of luggage, he took a deep breath. He needed to pick his battles with her, and the amount of luggage she brought wasn't one of them. In fact, loathe as he was to admit it, her princess-like behavior was one of the things that endeared her to him so much.

"You can set those over there." Hunter pointed to a corner of the room, and the driver deposited Charmaine's luggage on the floor where Hunter indicated.

"I don't get a drawer?" Charmaine teased, batting her long eyelashes at Hunter.

"Don't push it," he responded, smiling at her bravado.

Charmaine thanked the new driver for his assistance then told him he was free for the weekend.

"Thank you, ma'am. If there's nothing else…"

"No, I think we've got it, haven't we Hunter?" She threaded an arm through his. "This weekend I have this big, strong firefighter here to take care of me."

"Enjoy your weekend off. I'll see to whatever she needs, and I'll return her by Monday morning."

"Very good, sir. If you say so," the driver said, then took his leave.

After he was out of earshot Hunter asked, "How is the new guy working out?"

Charmaine untangled herself from Hunter and plopped down on the couch. "I don't know. He's fine I guess."

"What's his name anyway?"

"I don't know." She frowned and hugged a pillow to her.

"Seriously?"

"I don't want to have to get to know someone new. I want Rollins back!" She sounded like a five-year-old.

"Charmaine, you really don't know his name? He's been driving for you for a week and you don't know his name?" Was she that self-involved?

She cut her eyes then answered. "Fine, I think his name is Bill Richards." Then she added snottily, "But I'm not positive."

"You have to stop calling him 'the not-Rollins' and start calling him Bill."

When she turned to face him her eyes flashed. "I don't want to get used to someone else! I want Rollins back." Her reaction to Rollins' departure from her life was more intense than he'd expected.

"He'll be back, Kitten. But in the meantime you have to deal with the man who took his place, even if it's only temporary."

"He's not even that good of a driver," she sniffed.

"Where did he come from?"

"A temp agency."

"Yeah, they may not get a lot of requests for drivers."

"What if he doesn't come back?" The look on her face was that of a basset hound with her big, sad eyes, and he thought he saw a hint of tears forming.

"Why? Has Rollins told you he might not come back?"

"No, he says he's coming back. It's just that…"

"Just that what?"

"Just that sometimes people don't do what they say they're going to do."

He thought about that. "Yeah, but I have a feeling you can count on Rollins." The guy struck him as every inch the loyal servant.

"I hope so," she said, but she still seemed troubled.

He wanted to take her mind off her worries. "Can I get you something to drink?" he asked wandering into the kitchen.

She flashed him a naughty grin. "A margarita?"

"How about some water? You wanted to play, and you know it's not the best idea to mix alcohol with the kind of things I have in store for you," he said, filling up two glasses of water from the tap.

She frowned. "Fine, but you should really get some tea or lemonade.

Something more exciting if you're having company."

"I'll take that under advisement, Miss Bossy Pants." He winked at her. "That reminds me—we might as well get this out of the way."

"What?"

"One of the rules I have if you want me to be your daddy dom is that you will have a maximum of two alcoholic drinks in one sitting."

"You're kidding," she said giving him the best example of bitchy resting face he had seen yet.

"No, I'm not. I was actually going to say no drinking, but I thought that might be too much of a change."

Her eyes widened, and she looked at him like he'd lost his mind. "Uh, yeah."

"So what do you say? Think you can handle that?"

"I don't know. Can I think about it?"

"Sure." He'd expected more push-back from her on the drinking issue. Maybe she wanted help reining in her behavior.

"What else?" she asked, joining him in the kitchen.

"I'd like you to agree not to see other guys."

"Will you stop seeing other girls?"

"I will. I think for us to see how this will work it would be best not to be distracted by other people."

She nodded. "I agree. What else?"

"I'd like you to refrain from using drugs, unless prescribed by a doctor."

She frowned, but didn't disagree. "What else?"

"I want you to be productive. What time do you wake up each morning?"

"Really? Why does that matter?"

"Because I believe people should have a purpose and that doesn't mean sleeping the day away."

"I get up before noon."

"And if you are not drinking more than two drinks at night, not doing drugs, and coming home at a decent hour, then you should have no problem getting up by eight."

"Eight? Eight o'clock in the morning?"

"Yes."

"Okay, that's not happening. How about ten?"

"I'll meet you in the middle—nine." He folded his arms over his chest. "That's my best and final offer."

"Best and final, huh? Alright, fine. I'll wake up at nine, but you're not very fun, you know," she pouted, sipping her glass of water then setting it down on the counter.

"Really, I'm not very fun?" He drew her to him, placing an arm around her waist. Crushing his mouth against hers, he kissed her hard, his pelvis pressed against her, and his cock immediately hardened. His tongue dove into her mouth, claiming her, swirling ardently against hers. He felt her give in and her body sank into him.

He stepped back, breaking the embrace. "I'll show you fun."

They were both breathing hard, and he sensed that through their kiss, she had undergone a transformation. Gone was the impish brat, and in her place stood a grown woman who desired him, wanted him to dominate her. He could see it in her deep blue eyes, on her now-passive face. He retrieved her water glass and handed it to her. "Here, drink more. You'll need to hydrate."

Obediently she gulped it down, and he took a sip of his. "Now what toy did you bring me?" She sashayed over to her bags, and rummaged through the smaller one before bringing him a small leather sleeve.

He unsnapped the closure and pulled out a silver implement with a wheel of sharp tines on one end. Unable to keep from grinning he nodded his approval. "A Wartenberg wheel. Nice."

"Have you used one before?" she asked.

"No, but it looks interesting." He was going to enjoy torturing the most sensitive parts of her body with it. Then he pointed toward the bedroom. "I want you to strip naked, go in there, and lie down on the bed." She headed for the bedroom, but he called to her, "Oh, and Charmaine—I want you to crawl."

"Yes, sir."

Without hesitation she began unbuttoning her blouse, her eyes glued to his. She let her shirt fall to the floor and revealed her magnificent breasts concealed by a pink lacy bra. When she lowered her jeans he could see she wore matching panties that highlighted her magnificent hourglass figure. She bit her lip nervously as she unhooked her bra and let it fall to the floor then tugged her panties down so they fell at her ankles. "How's that, Daddy?"

His chest tightened, and his heart skipped a beat at her words. The title was growing on him, and he never would have predicted how much he liked it.

"Can I call you that?" she asked. There was something so poignant about her when she was so vulnerable. She went from entitled princess to lonely waif in seconds. Her desire, her need for him to be her daddy struck a chord with him. He wanted to protect her, care for her, but her neediness made him angry. Not at her, but at all the people who had eschewed this beautiful, vibrant woman and made her feel unworthy of love.

He reached out and touched her cheek. "Yes, you may call me that." The intensity of her gaze unnerved him. Did he have what it took to be her daddy? He would give it his best shot, but in the back of his mind he worried he would let her down.

Needing to lighten the mood, he smacked her on the bottom and said, "Get going."

Obediently, she dropped to all fours. With a slightly exaggerated shake to her hips Charmaine crawled into the next room, giving him a glorious view as she went.

CHAPTER FOURTEEN

The whirring of Hunter's window air conditioning unit filled Charmaine's ears, and her senses seemed more alive than usual. As she lay naked on his bed, the masculine, woodsy smell of him wafting under her nostrils from his sheets, everything seemed more in focus. Perhaps the difference was that she was stone cold sober, but she had a feeling it had more to do with the handsome lieutenant in the next room.

Hunter's presence made her heart race, and butterflies flutter in her stomach. It had been a long time since a man had affected her so strongly. Her pattern was to toy with men, dangling herself in front of them like catnip before a feline, but usually, once she got what she wanted from the interaction, she retreated.

Oh she engaged with them, flirted, had sex, but often she kept hidden her darker desires, her need to be dominated by a special daddy. Yeah, she didn't normally reveal that. She didn't usually trust guys not to go running to the press with her kinks. So what was it about Hunter that made her let him in, expose her true self?

She'd been asking herself that ever since the night she'd gone home from the bar with him. Why did she slip and call him Daddy? She hadn't played that game since Preston, and that had been years. Yes, she craved it sometimes, but she'd learned to squash those cravings, sublimate those urges and find other outlets for that side of her. Living vicariously through her friends in the Daddy's Girl Club was one of those outlets.

After that first night with Hunter, her need for self-preservation kicked in, and she'd lashed out at him when he'd delivered his opinion about her drinking. Deep down she'd known he was right, but she wasn't ready to trust him. But Kimberly showed her Hunter might be a good addition to her life.

She wasn't ready to let him control her life, but she decided that she could trust him for some daddy dom/little girl play. He seemed like an honorable guy, the type of guy who, because of his profession, had a lot to lose as well if their kinkiness became public knowledge. Because a part of her liked him tending to her, sexually and otherwise, she wanted to give him a chance. It was nice feeling like someone was concerned about what choices she made. In her experience, most people only cared what she could do for them, not what they could do for her.

Hunter walked into the bedroom with only the silver wheel in his hand. It looked to tiny in his huge hand. He'd taken off his shirt and wore only a pair of navy athletic shorts. They were baggy and didn't allow her the full view she would've liked, but she refrained from complaining.

"I'd like to tie you up before using this on you. Would that be alright?"

Her mouth began to water, and she answered, "Yes, sir." Please, yes. She loved to be tied up, and if he used rope all the better. She loved the white silky rope one could purchase at the hardware store.

He opened the drawer of his bureau and pulled out a couple of coils of light brown rope. He passed it over her wrists one at a time, and she recognized the smell of hemp. That made more sense, somehow she could only picture him using utilitarian rope like that.

He bound her wrists to the corners of the bed on either side of the headboard. "Try that," he said.

"This one's too tight," she indicated her left wrist which was being squeezed too tightly for proper circulation.

"Thanks for telling me," he said as he untied that one and retied it a bit looser. That he took great care to get her bindings exactly right was not lost on her. She enjoyed watching the serious expression on his face as he worked, and felt fortunate he spent his time doing something for her. Not only was the man handsome, but he was also someone who had chosen to help others for his profession. He was a good man, and she hadn't had the chance to be around a lot of men like that during her life. She was more acquainted with men who measured their value through their bank accounts rather than their character, so Hunter had given her a fresh perspective on a man's worth.

She relished his movements as he tied her ankles, one by one to the end of the bed. He'd stretched her, spread eagle, to all four corners of the bed. A chill of trepidation ran up her back, she didn't usually let men tie her up. It could be dangerous, and while her love life was on the wild side, her safety wasn't something she took lightly.

He stood at the end of the bed admiring his handiwork. "Would you like me to blindfold you or can I trust you to close your eyes when I say?"

"You don't have to blindfold me, but it will make things darker if you don't want me to see."

He laughed softly. "See? I knew you'd have an opinion." He withdrew a black scarf from inside the same drawer where he'd found the rope.

"You're so prepared. Were you a boy scout?"

He raised a finger to his lips indicating she should be quiet. "I took a special shopping trip for this weekend."

She perked up, feeling a child-like delight that he'd gone to extra trouble preparing for their weekend. "Really?"

"Yes, now hush." He motioned for her to lean her head forward. She complied and he tied the black scarf around her eyes then adjusted it. "Nod your head if that's good."

Unable to see anything even with her eyes open, she nodded her head.

"Now lie back and be a good girl for Daddy."

His words shot pleasure through her veins. There was a primal place inside her that cried out "Yes! I can be a good girl for Daddy!" but she remembered his request for her to be silent so she merely nodded again.

"Now, once I start, you may speak. I want to hear your responses to what I'm doing. But keep it confined to us, to what we're doing here in this room. No snappy dialogue, okay?"

Hmph! He meant her sarcasm. Fine, she'd behave. "Yes, sir."

"Okay."

She expected him to start with the Wartenberg wheel, so she was surprised to feel the soft touch of a feather on her arm. Mmm. It felt luxurious gliding up and down her arm then sliding over her torso and traveling across her other arm. A deep sigh escaped her lips, and her muscles relaxed as she sank down into the mattress.

The feather tickled across her chest and belly before brushing over her legs and tickling the bottom of her feet. Each time it passed over her pussy she was curious if he would show it special attention, but he didn't. He gave her breasts and her cunt the same treatment as the rest of her body.

What he did to her felt as good as any spa treatment she'd had, yet better, since he was the one giving it. She luxuriated in playing the role of captive, and the anticipation as to what he would do next intoxicated her. Perhaps she didn't need alcohol after all… at least not when she was with him.

The palm of his hand slapped against her inner thigh. *Slap! Slap!* More slaps landed on her leg, stinging her tender flesh. She strained her pelvis toward him eager for him to swat her mound, but he didn't. He was driving her insane with lust—she wanted him to touch her so badly.

The bed shifted as he crouched over her, his knees planted on the mattress. The smacks of his hand trailed up her body and when he slapped at her breasts she reveled in the sensation, arching her back hoping he would recognize her desire for more.

Swat! One hand smacked the left breast, then the right. Then he cupped one in each hand and flicked his thumb across her hard, tight buds. She yearned for more, and as if reading her mind he pinched each nipple, twisted slightly, and pulled. Her erogenous zones squealed in her brain, the exquisite result of pleasure and pain, and she began to pant. Wriggling underneath him she panted, "You can slap my face."

This must have taken him off guard, for her request was met with silence. She had shocked him, gone too far in voicing her desire to be used, humiliated. She felt her cheeks warm with shame. What woman asked to be slapped in the face?

Then his hand made contact with her face. It wasn't hard, and it didn't exactly hurt. It was more stunning and forbidden. Men weren't supposed to hit women in the face, and women weren't supposed to like it. As his other hand landed on her other cheek he snarled, "You know, you are a very bad girl."

"I know, Daddy. Please punish me." Being able to be the bad girl she'd always known she was freed her. Every nerve ending she had was on fire, and she wanted him to spank her, mark her, humiliate her any way he saw fit. That was the only thing that could fulfill her now.

She felt the weight of him to the left of her head. "Give me that mouth. Open it," he growled, taking her face under her chin and turning it toward him.

His erect cock slammed against the side of her cheek and she eagerly adjusted her position so she could take it in her mouth. Her tongue busily licked at the head, wetting him before he enthusiastically thrust himself between her lips then pushed farther and farther down her throat.

She wanted to impress him, show him how proficient she was at sucking cock, but he distracted her by pinching her nipples between his fingers. She let out a groan.

"That's a good girl, you're doing fine," he said continuing to torture her nipples.

Just when she thought the muscles on the sides of her cheeks would give out he withdrew and she could feel him get off the bed.

Soon he came back and she felt the cold, metal of the wheel upon her flesh. *Finally.* He began with her arm, rolled it up her forearm, across her shoulder, and it fluttered over her neck, the tickle of that delicate skin sending a chill through her body. She arched her back, aching for more.

"Mmm," he said, giving voice to her thoughts.

He dragged the tiny wheel between her breasts down over her belly. He drew row upon row sideways across her stomach as if he were a farmer preparing a field for planting. "*Oh God, how I want his seed,*" she thought, amused at how quickly her brain linked everything with sex.

Her breathing grew deeper and her heart raced as she wondered what he was going to do next. He rolled the wheel up and down one leg, then the other. Her pussy creamed and she whimpered with desperation. He had to touch her there or she might die.

Then her prayers were answered. The metal wheel rolled up her leg and over her mound. He dragged it up and down her outer pussy lips. It produced a sensation that made her want to "oooh" with pleasure and "ouch" with pain at the same time.

When he got to her clit, first he rolled the wheel bumpily over the swollen bud. It felt good but she wanted more and lifted her hips in a silent request. After a few passes of that she felt him spread her lips apart with his fingers, and then he went to work. He pressed down harder with the wheel as he rolled it across her clit. The pressure made it almost hurt, her little button was so sensitive. She didn't dare complain because it felt too good, and she didn't want him to stop. He made tiny "x's" on her most delicate little button, and before long she screamed out, tugged at her bindings, and shook as an intense orgasm overtook her.

He rolled the tool over her pussy until her orgasm subsided and she was too sensitive to take any more. Then she tried to close her legs and she yelled, "Stop! Stop!"

Though it wasn't precisely a safeword, he respected her wishes and took the tool back to her breasts. She shuddered as she realized he wasn't finished with her yet. That climax had wrecked her. She was sweating and spent, but as he tormented her nipples with that blasted toy she felt herself becoming aroused again.

The tines of the wheel poked at her nipples. He pressed hard enough that the tips of her breasts were getting sore. The more he worked them the more sensitive they became and the more pleasurable the experience. As she lay there, bound and blindfolded, he practically put her into a trance as he toyed with her. She was aroused, but not feverishly so.

"I'm going to fuck you, and I'm going to come all over you. I want to see your body dripping with my cum."

She wriggled underneath him. Oh god, she wanted that, wanted him to claim her with his seed. "Yes, Daddy. Do it, please," she begged.

He loosened the bindings on her ankles, then she could hear the ripping of a condom wrapper.

"I'll take it off before I come," he said.

When he entered her, she moaned with the satisfaction of being filled with him. He hooked her legs around his waist and fucked her with deep, hard strokes. Unable to touch him, she relaxed and allowed the blissful sensations to envelope her. He fucked her deep and hard, alternating from quick strokes to long, almost painfully slow strokes intended to draw out her pleasure and tease her mercilessly, making sure she always wanted more.

He pinched her sore nipple, which sent an electric current straight to her pussy, and she clenched and convulsed her muscles around his cock. He pinched her other nipple and she cried out as she climaxed again. Behind the blindfold she watched brilliant-colored crystals shatter into a million iridescent shards of light, and rapturous tremors shook her entire body. When she stilled, he withdrew and she knew he would come soon.

"I want to see. I want to watch you come, Daddy."

He removed her blindfold and she squinted up at him, trying to adjust her eyes to the low light. Hunter straddled her just above her breasts.

He wrapped his fingers around his cock and stroked himself, his eyes staring intently into hers. She wanted to look away, to watch his cock explode, but she couldn't drag her eyes away from his. His expression never changed, even as something wet hit her skin.

She trained her eye on his cock. The white, silky fluid spurted from the tip, and he directed it onto her breasts. Her heart filled, for she loved him marking her with his viscous offering, claiming her as his own. Oddly, it made her feel almost loved.

When he was finished, Hunter untied her, and kissed each wrist as he handed them back to her. She shook them and rubbed her wrists as her circulation resumed its normal patterns. Hunter collapsed on the bed next to her, and within minutes he was asleep.

Lying there, in his bed decorated by his seed, Charmaine couldn't remember feeling so content. She'd finally found someone she knew she could love, who might be able to love her back. Now, if she could just keep from destroying it.

CHAPTER FIFTEEN

"As much as I like to see you naked all the time, I don't want you to be cold. You can wear my bathrobe if you want. It's hanging on a hook in the bathroom."

She giggled. "It *is* kinda chilly in here," she said running into the other room. It was Sunday afternoon and spending the weekend with Charmaine had been intoxicating.

She came back wearing his bathrobe. The arms were too long and the whole thing swallowed her, giving her a "Dopey" appearance. Whatever makeup she'd had on had worn off during their escapades, but she looked more beautiful than ever. He'd never had a submissive before, and he found the experience quite intoxicating.

He sat down in his recliner and patted his lap for her to come sit down. She tiptoed across the room and settled herself in his lap. Hugging her to him he asked, "What was that you were doing walking on your tiptoes? You remind me of a ballerina." he teased.

She laughed. "No, I've always done that, walked on my toes, ever since I could walk."

"No kidding?"

"Yeah. I think it helps me be able to wear really high heels, because I'm used to putting all my weight on the balls of my feet. Someone once told me it's some sort of brain damage, but I don't know. Maybe *that's* what's wrong with me." She smiled.

He laughed. "There's nothing wrong with you."

She pulled back. "Tell that to my parents."

"What's the deal with your parents? I don't know much about your dad except that he's super rich and has been married lots of times. And I don't know anything about your mom except that you're staying at her place. Where is she?"

"Some hokey retreat out west. Her latest thing is 'spirituality' and she's all into the healing clay or something. I think she's in Taos or somewhere near there. A few years ago she connected with her past lives in California. She's a flake."

"Spirituality doesn't sound like a bad thing."

"The way my mother does it—it is. Everything she touches turns to crap. She's a selfish, manipulative woman who's been jealous of me since the day I was born. She regrets having me, she said that to my face when I was ten. Something like that, you don't forget."

"I'm sorry." He stroked her hair. "What about your dad, is he any better?"

"That's a good question. Kinda like asking which is worse—the Wicked Witch of the West or Darth Vader."

"That bad, huh?"

"Yeah. He's here in Dallas, which might be worse because he's always trying to inflict his other families on me."

"You mean his other kids?"

"Oh yeah all seven of them and his ex-wives. Most of them hang around. They don't leave like my mom, and they all act like one big, happy family. It's scary, kinda like a cult."

"Wow. So your dad has eight kids?"

"Yeah, my life is fucked up. How about yours?"

"Maybe not quite so fucked up, but everybody has family crap, Kitten. My dad's dead. He was a firefighter too, died when I was nine. I don't remember him all that well, except when I was little, he used to slap my momma around and I used to wish I was old enough to protect her."

Her face wrinkled in sympathy. "That sucks. I'm sorry. How did he die?"

"A fire. Burned over ninety percent of his body in a warehouse fire. The doctors said it was a blessing he didn't survive."

"And you still became a fireman?"

"Yep."

"Wow, that's intense."

"Yeah, I guess it runs in my blood."

"But not abusing women…"

He grinned, "Hey, I like to slap you around a little. I just don't want to hurt you. Maybe my dad was a dom and didn't know it. Didn't know how to channel his impulses. I don't know, but I've wondered about that."

"How about your mom, is she alive?"

"Yeah, she lives here in Dallas. I go see her a couple of times a month. She cooks a nice meal for me. She works for a nice family in Highland Park, has been with them for years."

"Wait, what does she do?"

"She's a maid."

He watched as something dark crossed Charmaine's face.

"A maid, really?"

"Yeah, it's good, honest work and no one knows more about how rich people need help than you do." He poked at her ribs playfully.

She smiled a decidedly fake smile and nodded. "Yeah. I do. Excuse me, I have to go to the bathroom," she said popping off his lap and scurrying into the other room.

Well that was weird. Was she that much of a snob that the fact that his mother was a maid bothered her? His pulse quickened. His mother was a good woman, one of the best, and he wouldn't stand for anyone dissing her.

He gripped the arms of the chair and reminded himself that all Charmaine had done was go to the restroom. Her negative reaction had been subtle, but he thought he knew how to read her by now. Reading your sub was one of the biggest rules of being a dom.

When she returned she sat on the couch next to him rather than in his lap.

"Hey, was that weird that I just told you my mom is a maid?" He asked trying to clarify, give her the benefit of the doubt.

She shook her head and made a face. "No, of course not. Why would you think that? I'm not a total snob."

He studied her body language. Nothing there to indicate that she was lying. He chewed the side of his lip for a minute then said, "Okay. I just thought you seemed kinda weird about it."

She shook her head. "No, in fact, I'd like to meet her sometime."

"Sure." He tried to picture his mother meeting Charmaine but he couldn't even envision them in the same room. They came from such different worlds.

"Hey, did you really want to go to Kimberly and Charles's wedding the other night or were you just being polite?" she asked.

Grateful she changed the subject, he responded, "I didn't get the feeling you wanted me to go."

Her jaw dropped. "You've got to stop imagining these things! Of course I want you to go."

"When is it? I don't know if I'll be able to get time off work, but I can ask, and see if somebody can swap shifts with me."

"It's in two weeks."

"That's coming up soon. I don't know if I can get an airline ticket, and this close they ought to be astronomical." He scratched his chin.

"Oh, that's okay. We'll take my plane."

"That's right, I forgot." He'd known she was rich, but it never occurred to him how rich. He was starting to think her net worth might be difficult to fathom.

"Yeah. That is one of the rare good things about my father. His company has several private jets that I can use whenever I want." She shrugged. "Bonus!"

He stammered, "Th-th-that's great. I'll bet it makes life easier when you have your own plane."

She bobbed her head. "I guess technically it's not mine, but yes—it does if you want to go anywhere."

He stared at her like she was from another planet. "I guess I don't ever go anywhere." All he did was work and workout.

"Maybe you need to get out more." She giggled. "Do you have a passport?"

"Yeah."

"Good, it will be fun. You liked Charles, right?" Hunter nodded. "Then you'll probably like James who is Marley's boyfriend, Mason who Nellie belongs to, Lucinda's daddy Colin—well they're all daddies the ones I'm telling you about. Sloane will invite Rocco and he will dis her and won't come. She is totally in love with him, and he's not into her. Then there's Natron. You know Natron Dakers from the Vipers?"

"Sure." Only someone without eyes wouldn't know Natron Dakers, especially living in Dallas where the star wide receiver lit up the field every week at Vipers' Stadium. Plus, his smiling face shined down on Hunter from billboards as he drove to work and every time he turned on the TV. The guy hawked everything from toothpaste to underwear to sandwiches.

"Well, he'll be there with his little girl Carmen. She's an artist, a really good one, and the Vipers have a bye week so he's going to be able to come."

"Cool." Something about when she mentioned Natron struck a nerve with him and he couldn't put his finger on it. What was it about Natron and his girlfriend—Carmen. He wasn't sure but he knew it would come to him.

• • • • • • • • • • • • • • •

Later that night, after he'd dropped Charmaine off at her mother's condo, Hunter took a load of laundry to the Laundromat down the street from his apartment. He brought a couple of Sports Illustrated magazines with him to read while he waited for his clothes.

The Laundromat was almost empty, a middle-aged lady sat with her nose buried in a girly-looking book, and Hunter set his stuff on the other side of the room. Some cheesy elevator music played in the background. He could have done without that, but the place was convenient and he could always bring earbuds if it really bothered him.

He threw everything into one big washer, added some detergent, inserted his coins and sat down in one of the plastic chairs and started reading. He skipped through the golf stuff. He was more of a basketball fan, but he liked football too.

In the middle of the magazine was an article about Natron Dakers. Since he and Charmaine had just been talking about the superstar he perused the article, which chronicled Natron's comeback from an injury the previous year. They described how he got back into playing shape after being sidelined. A workout nut himself, he was interested in the exercises Natron had done in the pool. He'd like to incorporate some more swimming into his own fitness routine.

The washer pinged, and he transferred the wet mass of clothes into the nearest dryer. He sat down across from it and was mesmerized for a moment by the multi-colored clothes tumbling around in an imperfect circle. He was thinking that it reminded him of a kaleidoscope when it hit him. And suddenly, he remembered it like it was yesterday, remembered it as clear as day. He knew why Charmaine's mention of Natron stirred something inside him.

About eight or nine months ago, he'd been at work and his unit responded to a call that turned out to be what he termed a nuisance call. They drove up to a duplex-type house in a neighborhood to find two tipsy girls standing over a poor excuse for a fire in the front yard. Apparently, in a squabble with one of their boyfriends, they decided to burn the poor guy's stuff, and the boyfriend had just arrived on the scene.

These sorts of situations were often volatile, and he'd been the one nominated to have a discussion with the participants. He went over to talk to the ladies and gentleman in question while another firefighter put out the fire with a fire extinguisher.

When he asked them how the fire had started the pretty girl with the wild hair had admitted she started it. The girl he now knew was *Charmaine*. She'd drunkenly called him "occifer" and said she'd done it because her friend's boyfriend cheated on her friend. Later the other firemen recognized the boyfriend as Natron Dakers. Putting together the pieces of the puzzle, the girlfriend must have been Carmen. He wondered how Natron managed to patch things up with Carmen. Those two girls had been majorly pissed at him. Setting his things on fire was an immature thing to do, and Hunter had told them as much, but people did what they were going to do.

He'd given Charmaine a warning, but she clearly hadn't followed it because he'd had to rescue her from another fire when she'd accidentally lit up her apartment. A nagging feeling tugged at his gut. He'd dedicated his life to fighting fires. How was it possible that he was falling in love with a woman who was so often recklessly and irresponsibly starting them?

He tried to tell himself that people make mistakes, but in the back of his mind he kept coming back to the truth. You don't change people. They are who they are. And Charmaine Bainbridge was trouble of the worst kind.

CHAPTER SIXTEEN

The driver opened the door, and Charmaine stepped out of the limousine. Everyone of importance in Dallas society would be present for the Lucinda Lake concert tonight. As she stepped onto the red carpet, Charmaine knew she looked stunning in a dazzling floral Elie Saab couture gown. Hunter followed behind, and as they approached the concert hall flashbulbs burst and various photographers called her name. "Charmaine!"

Hunter offered her his arm. She took it and plastered on the "public" face she'd learned to wear as a child and turned on the charm. The media presence at the event was on the sparse side, so she and Hunter were able to run the gauntlet in a matter of minutes.

When they got inside away from all the cameras she turned to Hunter. "You okay?"

"Yeah," he said, straightening his tie. "I've never been on a red carpet before." No one would be able to tell that by looking at him. He might not exactly be comfortable in his tuxedo, but he wore it well. She'd already caught several ladies eyeing him appreciatively, and she didn't blame them. He could give any movie star a run for his money.

Squeezing his hand, she said, "You're being a good sport."

"Gotta do what I can for my girl," he said, and her heart leapt. She loved when he called her "his girl." It was at once endearing and old-fashioned, with an undertone of possessiveness that made her hot.

Charmaine greeted various acquaintances and friends and introduced them to Hunter. "I'll let you know if it's someone whose name you should try to remember," she whispered before an older couple came by to chat.

Several people who did not usually make a point to speak to Charmaine came up and introduced themselves to Hunter. Gossips. They didn't recognize the man with her so they said hello to try to get the story on her date. Ugh, she hated the fakery of high society, but that was the way it worked.

She hoped to run into some of the other girls before the show, but so far she hadn't seen them. Hunter checked his watch and urged her to go inside the theater and find their seats. Charmaine had seen to it they got some of the best seats—the box closest to the left side of the stage. They were elevated slightly, and the view was extraordinary. An usher showed them to their seats.

Marley and James were already there, seated next to their empty ones. Charmaine introduced the couple to Hunter, and they sat down.

"Nice seats," Hunter said.

"They are. This is where I sit during opera season."

"You go to the opera? Really?" He appeared shocked.

She gave him a playful bop on the arm. "Darling, I'm a socialite. Of course I go to the opera." Then she added, "And the symphony," for good measure.

"Wow. I didn't know who went to things like that, I guess now I do." He sighed uncomfortably. An awkward silence fell between them, and he studied his program intently.

"The reason it's best to sit on this side of the theater is that from this side you're able to watch the pianist's hands when you are at a concert like this one. The people sitting in the front box on the other side won't be able to see them, and with a pianist, that's half the show."

He feigned fascination. "I did not know that."

"That's okay. Most people don't." She smoothed her dress then made small talk with Marley who was seated on her other side.

A few minutes later Hunter pointed to a name on the program and asked her, "How the hell do you say that?" He chuckled as if the name was funny.

"Let me see." She looked down and said simply, "Rachmaninoff."

"Rock what?"

"Rachmaninoff. Why? Do you not know who that is?" She began to laugh, but caught herself.

He stiffened. "How would I know who that was?"

"He was a composer who created some of the most difficult music to play *ever*. Only the most gifted and accomplished pianists can play his music."

"Again, how would I know that?"

Talking loudly, over her and Marley, he said, "Hey James, do you know who the heck Rachmaninoff is?"

Hunter butchered the name pretty good, but James must have heard him because he responded, "Yes, he's a composer."

With a grunt Hunter stood up and stormed out of the box.

James looked confused. "What did I say?"

Charmaine shook her head. "He didn't know who he was. I'm not sure what's wrong. Sorry y'all." Hunter had embarrassed her by walking out on her like an angry child.

Marley put a hand on Charmaine's knee. "Don't worry about us. We don't care."

"Somebody should tell him my mom's a piano teacher," James said in solidarity.

Charmaine said she would, but when the lights went down Hunter's chair was still empty.

● ● ● ● ● ● ● ● ● ● ● ● ● ● ●

He came back about fifteen minutes after the beginning of Lucinda's performance, whispering, "Sorry," as he slid into his seat.

He'd missed the arrival of Nellie and Mason, and Sloane who had come in late, which normally would have given Charmaine a tremendous amount of pleasure. She couldn't remember a time when the girls had all gotten together that Sloane hadn't chastised *her* for being late. But tonight she'd been too concerned with Hunter's whereabouts to truly enjoy Sloane's social faux pas.

Charmaine took Hunter's hand and whispered, "Are you mad at me?"

He shook his head and focused on the performance.

"That's Lucinda," she said, stating the obvious. He'd missed the introduction where the president of the Van Cliburn international piano competition, based in neighboring Fort Worth gave a long list of Lucinda's accomplishments, including winning the Van Cliburn several years ago at the tender age of eighteen. Winning that prestigious competition launched her career and the Van Cliburn people were always quick to claim her as "their" star, the one they created.

Lucinda had come onstage wearing a white column of silk that contrasted beautifully against her dark hair, and the audience welcomed the international superstar with fervent applause. No one knew how to bring their own back to the fold better than Texans.

Then Lucinda sat down at the Shigeru Kawai, the grand piano she required wherever she played. The moment her fingers touched the keys the audience was transported to another dimension. Lucinda had become quite the diva, but as the notes floated through the air, Charmaine remembered why Lucinda was the first pianist in the world to become a household name. Her music made the audience feel the piece and left all who heard her changed in some way.

"She's really good," Hunter whispered, and Charmaine nodded and nuzzled closer to him. During the rest of the show Charmaine tried to forget about Hunter's blow up earlier and enjoy the music. When the concert was over they took her car to The Capital Grill for a special late dinner with the star and her daddy, Colin.

They started with drinks because they knew Lucinda and Colin would be coming later after they finished up at the theater. From across the table James said to Hunter, "Hey, that Rachmaninoff thing, the only reason I know that is because my mom is a piano teacher."

"Rock who?" Marley asked.

"See?" James said and everyone laughed, including Hunter.

"Just a composer," Charmaine said.

"Oh, I don't know much about that sort of thing, but I did love hearing Lucinda play. She's incredible!" Marley said.

Everyone echoed her sentiments, and Charmaine thought Hunter looked more comfortable once he realized that Marley didn't know any more about composers than he did.

Mason, who was a financial advisor, sat on Hunter's right and Charmaine worried they wouldn't find much to talk about, but before she knew it they were engaged in an animated conversation about basketball. A few minutes later, Hunter excused himself from the table. Mason started talking about some financial stuff with James and Charmaine decided it might be a good time to use the restroom.

She got up from the table and went to the ladies room. After she finished her business she washed her hands and started to powder her nose when the door swung open and socialite Millie Golden traipsed in. Millie was one of her mother's contemporaries and a terrible gossip. Charmaine had always disliked her.

"Well if it isn't Charmaine Bainbridge as I live and breathe!" Millie exclaimed, encroaching upon Charmaine's personal space to air kiss her cheek.

Charmaine didn't bother to air kiss back. "Hi Millie," she said in a lackluster voice.

"Who was that handsome man I saw you with earlier at the Lucinda Lake performance?"

"Just a friend," Charmaine said, hoping that would be enough information, but knowing better.

"Oh, come now. You know I'll find out, so you might as well tell me. Who is he?" Millie prodded as she looked in the mirror and applied a coat of garish red lipstick.

Charmaine released an exasperated sigh. "Fine, if you must know—his name is Hunter Baldwin. He's a fireman, a lieutenant actually."

"Mmhmm, going for that prime beefcake. I bet he'd look good on a calendar, wouldn't he? But what would your father say about you slumming like that?" Millie hit Charmaine's arm as if to say "you naughty thing."

"My father doesn't comment on my personal life," Charmaine said coldly.

"Oh come on. We both know that's not true," Millie said.

"Have a nice evening, Millie." Charmaine ended the conversation and strode back to the table where she took her seat. *The nerve of some people.*

Hunter came back to the table just in time for Lucinda and Colin's arrival. Lucinda had changed out of her white gown and now she looked the picture of chic in a navy tailored pantsuit. Her daddy, Colin, was dapper as always in a smart Hugo Boss suit. He was at least two decades older than Lucinda and had a full head of hair that was the envy of every man above forty. And if it was touched with grey, that only made him appear more distinguished.

Charmaine still thought of him as Maestro Colin Bond, for as a child her grandmother had taken her to watch him conduct the orchestra. She couldn't remember which orchestra, but she recalled how vivacious he was onstage. The man had presence that easily commanded a room, even if that room was Carnegie Hall. It still amazed her that he'd left his wildly successful career to manage Lucinda's. The man was still in his prime, and Charmaine secretly wondered if he missed being in the spotlight himself.

"Lucinda, you were absolutely fabulous tonight!" Nellie gushed. "Wasn't she Mason?"

"Phenomenal!" Mason enthused. Everyone else added their praises for her impressive performance.

"Thank you," Lucinda said with a smile and sat down. "It's always a successful performance when I don't make any mistakes."

"My dear, don't be so modest, your friends already know you don't make mistakes," Colin teased.

The group laughed, and Charmaine decided that Hunter was integrating with her friends without much trouble. Their dinner was delicious and the rest of the meal passed without incident. Afterward, in the car on the way to his place, Charmaine took a moment to patch things up with Hunter.

"Hey, I'm sorry about that thing with the composer," she said, taking his hand.

"Yeah."

"It's not still bothering you is it? You saw that Marley didn't know who he was either. No one cares."

He faced her, his eyes troubled. "I care."

"But why?" she asked, baffled. She hoped they could put this behind them.

"Because we come from two different worlds, you and me."

Charmaine shrugged, shaking her head. "So?"

"So—it matters, Charmaine. You come from this world with private planes, drivers, culture. I'm from the hood."

"I'm not sure you're really from 'the hood,' but I don't see what difference it makes, Hunter."

He took his hand back. "Charmaine, my mother is a maid. You employ maids. I grew up on a street with drug dealers, a lot of the people I went to high school with are in prison. We're from two different sides of the tracks."

"I don't care!" Charmaine said, her heart felt like it would beat right out of her chest. *No, no, no. He can't be breaking up with me.*

"I don't know if I can live in your world, Charmaine."

"You don't have to! We don't have to go to concerts or whatever. We can do whatever you want," she pleaded, hating how desperate she sounded.

"It's not just that. It's everything."

"What else?"

"I remembered something, and it's been eating away at me."

"What?" She held her breath.

"Do you remember when you and Carmen burned Natron's things outside her place?"

"Yeah," she said, wondering how he knew about that. She didn't remember telling him. "Wait, was that…"

"Yes, I responded to that call. I was the firefighter who gave you the warning."

Her eyes widened. *Oh crap.* Her stomach sank as if someone had just thrown a brick in it. No, this couldn't be happening. Now he thought she was some kind of fire bug, or worse—an arsonist.

"Not even a year later, Charmaine, and you were setting fire to your own apartment!"

"But, that's not fair. That was an accident!" The tears stung her eyes, but she refused to let them fall, swiping at them.

"It doesn't matter. The point is—you're reckless. And irresponsible. And that's never going to change." His face took on a sadness that stabbed her in the heart. He *was* breaking up with her.

"Yes, I have changed! Did you notice that I only had two drinks tonight? Two drinks like you said! We were at that restaurant for like three hours! I could have had five drinks if I'd wanted or six, not to mention before the concert. C'mon, Hunter you have to give me some credit. I'm trying!"

"Well, that's true. I did notice, and I'm proud of you." He smiled and touched her cheek lightly.

The car pulled up to Hunter's apartment building. "I think I need to be alone tonight," he said.

"Hunter, no! Let me come in," she pleaded.

He held out a hand. "No. I have a lot to sort through."

It felt like a sinkhole had opened up beneath her and she was being sucked down into hell. "Okay. Are you still coming to Mexico next week?"

"I don't know. I need to think about it. I'll let you know."

"Um, okay." She sat back against the seat, shocked at what he was saying. She'd gone to the concert tonight with him thinking everything was okay, but now she realized he'd been upset with her from the beginning.

He leaned over, kissed her on the cheek, and said, "Goodbye, Charmaine." When he closed the door she knew he was gone from her life forever.

CHAPTER SEVENTEEN

Hunter's gut twisted into knots as he took the elevator up to his apartment. He couldn't stop replaying the evening in his mind...

They'd been sitting in the dining room where he and Mason were talking basketball.

"LeBron's a beast," Mason said.

"I know. Can you imagine if he played another sport like Jordan played baseball? He would be the sickest wide receiver! He'd make Megatron look bad," Hunter said.

"Oh man, that would be insane," Mason agreed.

The waitress brought a plate of appetizers and Hunter excused himself to go to the restroom. After he'd already exited the private room, he walked into the main dining room of The Capital Grille and realized he had no idea where the bathroom was located.

He stopped to ask a passing waitress. She pointed. "Down the hall and to the left." Followed her instructions and he came to a door that looked like a restroom. He opened the door, saw they didn't have any urinals and proceeded to one of the stalls. After completing his business, the door to the bathroom opened and he heard a sigh. Strangely, it sounded like a woman. He zipped up his pants and peeped through the crack in the door.

Crap! He was in the ladies room. He must not have been paying attention. The door opened again, and through the crack in the door, he saw Charmaine come in the door. Double crap!

He lowered the seat quietly and sat down on the toilet. His best chance was to leave once Charmaine went into a stall. Sure, she'd think it was funny he went into the wrong bathroom, but he'd rather she not know. He already felt like a fish out of water, and he didn't want it getting any worse.

The door of the stall next to him opened with a squeak then he heard the sound of the lock turning. Whew! He was just about to leave when another lady walked in. Dammit.

He sat back down, determined to wait until Charmaine left. Then he'd walk out regardless who was in there. It had been an honest mistake. Soon Charmaine exited her stall and he could vaguely see her washing her hands and checking her makeup. Then another woman entered the bathroom. Lord, this place was like Happy Hour on a Friday night.

Then the woman started asking about him. Charmaine hedged, but the woman pressed on. "Mmhmm, going for that prime beefcake. I bet he'd look good on a calendar, wouldn't he? But what would your father say about you slumming like that?"

"My father doesn't comment on my personal life," Charmaine stated flatly.

"Oh come on. We both know that's not true," the woman said.

"Have a nice evening, Millie," Charmaine said sharply and stalked out of the restroom.

The woman sniffed, as if she didn't appreciate Charmaine's hasty exit and disappeared into one of the stalls.

His face burned as he opened the door of his stall and marched over to the washbasin to wash his hands. He didn't care who saw him in here. He tugged at his collar, trying to loosen the tie that threatened to choke him.

What was Charmaine's problem? She should have defended him more. Slumming, my ass. He made a good, honest living and he had nothing to be ashamed of. He hadn't expected Charmaine to be ashamed of him either, but now he wasn't so sure.

He ran his hands under the cool water then dried them with a towel before storming out of the bathroom. His blood pumped fiercely through his veins, and something tore at his gut.

It didn't matter what that woman thought. It was what Charmaine thought that mattered to him, and she hadn't disagreed with the woman. He'd embarrassed her at the concert with his lack of knowledge about classical music and symphonies. She'd tried to play it off like it didn't matter, but it did. He felt out of place in her world. Holed up together in his apartment, things had been fine between them. No, better than fine. He'd been falling in love with her.

But now that he'd had a taste of her world he realized it would never work out between them.

• • • • • • • • • • • • • • •

A few days after breaking up with Charmaine, Hunter's chief called him into his office at the station.

"Sit down, Baldwin," the chief said brusquely.

Hunter tentatively dropped into a chair across from him, not liking his boss's tone. "Have I done something wrong, sir?"

"Not wrong. Just possibly inappropriate."

Hunter eyed him suspiciously, wracking his brain for any possible infractions he could have performed. Other than spanking Charmaine while he was on the job he couldn't think of anything. And even if she was mad at him for breaking up with her, she wouldn't be mad enough to report him for that. Charmaine hated authority. It wouldn't be her style to rat him out by going to the brass.

The chief pulled out a newspaper and showed him a picture of him and Charmaine from the night of the Lucinda Lake concert. All he noticed was how great Charmaine looked. His chest tightened.

"You see this?"

Hunter nodded.

Chief pulled on his reading glasses and read, 'Fire Lieutenant Hunter Baldwin escorts socialite Charmaine Bainbridge to the Lucinda Lake concert two months after he saved her from a fire in her penthouse apartment."

Hunter shrugged. "Yeah, so?"

The chief sat back in his chair and removed his glasses. "Hunter, this could easily be construed by the public as you taking advantage of the situation. I've received a few calls, and this is a concern."

"Really? Who has been calling you?"

The man shifted in his chair. "Thornton Bainbridge for one."

Hunter rolled his eyes. "C'mon Chief. Charmaine doesn't get along with her dad, so he's going to stick his nose in and control who she goes out with behind the scenes? Because his own daughter doesn't want anything to do with him. Don't you see, chief, this is a ploy to control her life. Don't get sucked into that nonsense."

"Hunter, he's not the only one. I'm asking you to lay low if you're going to see this girl. I'm not going to forbid you from it, but I am asking you not to be so damned public about it."

"Not a problem, sir. I broke up with her anyway," Hunter said, hanging his head.

"Then why didn't you say something?" he blustered. "Keep me from yakking on and on about it. Probably for the best, son, but I'm sorry." He glanced at their picture as he tossed the newspaper into the wastebasket. "That's some kind of woman."

Hunter stood up, and the chief motioned he was free to go. "Don't I know it," he muttered on his way out the door.

Outside in the common room, Mitch was shooting pool at the billiard table that had recently been anonymously donated to the fire department. Hunter joined him and Mitch racked up the balls for a new game. "What did chief want?"

Hunter ran a hand over his hair. Under his breath he said, "He told me not to see Charmaine anymore, or to be more private about it. What the fuck is that? Last I checked they can't tell us how to run our personal lives."

"But I thought you broke up with her." Mitch indicated the triangle of multi-colored balls on the table. "You break."

Hunter picked up a pool cue. "I did, but they can't tell me how to live my life. That just pisses me off." With that, he hit the balls too hard with the stick, the red one bounced on the ground. "My bad," he said, picking it up and placing it in center of the table.

"So he told you to break up with her?" Mitch asked and leaned down to take a shot.

"Not exactly. He told me to keep it on the down low."

"So what's got you so upset?"

"Her dad called and was raising hell. That guy's a real asshole. I mean she told me he was, but I guess I didn't get the picture."

"But if it's over I don't see why any of this matters," Mitch said hitting the three-ball into a corner pocket.

Hunter fumed. He hadn't been able to stop thinking about Charmaine. She haunted his dreams, and everywhere he went he thought he saw her. *Wanted to see her.* He took a shot and completely missed the ball he was aiming for.

Mitch laughed. "Thing is bro, I don't think you two are done, not by a longshot."

Ignoring him, Hunter asked, "Did you know that she was the one who set a fire nine months ago that we were called out for?"

"What?" Mitch's mouth dropped open.

"Yeah. She set Natron Dakers' crap on fire!"

"Man, you're fucking with me."

"No I'm not. Her friend Carmen is Natron's girlfriend. They thought he cheated so Charmaine came up with the bright idea to set it on fire in the yard. Can you believe that?"

"Yeah. You know what they say about a woman scorned. Guess I was off that day, cuz I don't remember that one."

Hunter slammed his fist on the pool table capturing the attention of the other guys on the other side of the room. "Sorry," he apologized and took a deep breath.

"Dude, you are not over her." Mitch shook his head. "Don't blame you, really. That's the kind of woman gets under your skin and there's nothing you can do about it." Mitch banked another ball into the side pocket. "It's like poison ivy, ain't it? You can't stop itchin', can you?"

"I can't be with a woman like that. She's careless, irresponsible, and she's from a different world than I am. It will never work…"

"But if you're in love with her, none of that matters. Dude, that's what people who are in love do to each other—they drive each other crazy."

Hunter lined up his next shot. "Like you know all about love. Who are you, our resident Dr. Phil?"

Mitch shook his head. "Nah, I've just known you for the past six years is all. Go ahead and keep fighting it, but I know a man in love when I see one and you've got it bad."

• • • • • • • • • • • • • • •

The day before he planned to go with Charmaine to Kimberly and Charles's wedding, he received a text from Charmaine.

Any chance you're still coming to Mexico with me tomorrow? Planes all gassed up and ready to go. Keeping a seat warm for you…

He responded:

No, thanks. Maybe I'll see you when you get back.

Her response:

That's what I was afraid of. (Sad face)

Just seeing her sad face emoji on his phone wrenched at his heart. But this was better, he told himself. If things weren't going to work, it was better to break it off now, before their attachment to each other grew stronger.

CHAPTER EIGHTEEN

Asking for that third glass of champagne felt liberating—a big "fuck you" to Mr. Don't-Drink-More-Than-Two, who turned down flat her offer of a free trip to Mexico via private jet with a girl who, by the way, is a knockout.

Bringing the crystal flute to her lips, Charmaine smiled wryly, the bubbles tickling her throat as they went down. She thought of all the people who said she should stop drinking and wanted to take a selfie with her champagne flute, reveling in her rebelliousness, but she wasn't up for it. She was going to be crappy company for Kimberly and Charles's wedding.

Kicking off her shoes, she dragged her perfectly manicured toes across the luxurious carpet of the Bainbridge Enterprises jet. She had foolishly arranged for the plane to take her and Hunter to Mexico a few days early, planning the trip while her friends had to work so they would be alone. She scrunched up her face, recalling her plans to initiate Hunter into the Mile High Club.

Well, she'd fucked *that* up. Fucking things up was what she was best at.

This was why she only slept with "unsuitable" men, why she stayed out all night, why she tried to lose herself in the alcohol, the drugs. It helped numb the pain.

The pain that had begun with her father leaving her and her mother. Her mother drilled it into Charmaine's head that her father abandoned her, and he had, emotionally. The fact that he was the source of the golden checkbook—that made their relationship more complicated. Her father used his money to control her, to buy her love, to tell her how to live. It was the one way he stayed in her life, and the one reason she didn't shut him out entirely.

She was no fool. She liked the money, loved the lifestyle she lived. Hell, it was the least the bastard owed her. He'd never given her what she really needed, what she truly craved.

When she was seven, after wetting her pants at school for the third time, her mother had taken her to a psychotherapist who specialized in children from "broken" families. Dr. Gardner was an upbeat blonde with a bob haircut who wore huge pearls around her neck. She'd told Charmaine that in most families the mommy and daddy birds flew away every day and brought home worms to the nest to feed their baby birds. But, according to Dr. Gardner, her family consisted of three people, a mother, a father, and a child, who all needed worms. Her family consisted of baby birds eagerly thrusting their sharp beaks up, mouths open squawking, pleading for worms, but there was no one to bring them worms. In her family, the mommy and daddy bird had no worms to give. In fact, they too, needed worms. And there were never enough worms. The baby birds were never being satisfied. They couldn't share the worms because there wasn't enough to go around.

Even at age seven she'd gotten it. Her parents were selfish, and they weren't going to change. Charmaine quickly realized she would have to get attention elsewhere. Occasionally, she would latch onto a kind teacher, but for the most part she took advantage of her position. She was pretty and rich, always wore the nicest clothes, had the newest toys, and most kids wanted a piece of that. Girls wanted to be her friend and as she got older boys wanted her too, but in a different way. She learned to use them the way they used her, all the while guarding her heart. She manipulated the boys who followed her around, and made them do her bidding. But all that changed when she'd met her first daddy.

Preston had been old enough to be her father, and in fact he was the father of one of her classmates. Scandalous of course, but causing trouble was Charmaine's strong suit. She'd been a senior in high school and had just turned eighteen when they met.

She had been attending a ball honoring one of the season's debutantes, Claire Copeland, who was also a friend of Charmaine's. After the girl's presentation, Charmaine weaved through the crowd near the bar hoping to snag a drink. She was under-aged so it was a thrill to score a glass of white wine from a waitress's tray as she walked by. Bored, she retired to a corner watching dozens of admirers flocking around Claire.

That would be her in a few years. The thought did little to buoy her spirits. After all, what was the point of making your debut anyway? A voice whispered in her ear, "You're much prettier."

She turned, a smile already plastered on her face. Compliments were a drug to her. She knew it was a weakness to be so pliable to flattery, but vanity was her Achilles heel. "Why thank you." She held out a hand to the silver-haired gentleman who had spoken. He looked familiar, but she couldn't place him.

"Preston Harris," he said enveloping her hand in his. Warmth radiated from him and a tingle danced up her arm.

"Charmaine Bainbridge," she said.

His eyes twinkled. "Oh, I know who you are."

She brightened. "Are you a friend of my father's?"

"We're acquainted, but I believe you know my daughter, Eve. I believe you are in the same class."

"Ah, yes. That's where I recognize you from the Ashcroft School." Despite the fact that he must be twenty years her senior, she couldn't help but notice how handsome he was. Seeing an opportunity, she gave him an invitation. "I'm desperate for a smoke. Would you like to join me?" She waved toward the bay picture window to their right, beyond it was the Country Club's pristinely manicured golf course. It was pitch black outside, and her stomach tightened at the prospect of getting into mischief on one of the greens. She could already imagine the grass stains they could make on her yellow silk gown.

"You're as much trouble as they say," he noted, a hint too serious for her. Had she misjudged? She thought there had been flirtation in his voice.

"I'm sure I don't know what you mean. I simply want a cigarette," she said coldly and turned to go, but he stopped her with a hand on her arm. She looked down at his hand, intending to tell him to let her go, but something stopped her. Her eyes met his, and she paused, anticipating his next move.

"Come with me," he said.

She wondered if he might do something untoward. She hadn't particularly appreciated the way he'd manhandled her, and she looked around to see if any of the other guests had noticed it. The people around them appeared immersed in conversation, and the tinkle of laughter and clinking glasses floated in the air as if nothing happened.

Preston marched out of the room. She supposed he expected her to follow him, and for some reason she did. It felt as if an invisible force were drawing her to him. He opened the door for her and led her outside. "Do you have a cigarette?" he asked.

She nodded, rummaging in her Judith Leiber clutch. She brought out a smooshed pack of Marlboro Lights. He pulled a package of matches from his pocket and with a flick of the wrist he lit one holding it out for her.

Placing the cigarette between her lips, she leaned forward and sucked the flame through the thin column, then blew smoke into the air above her. "Thank you. Would you like one?"

He slid his hands into his pockets and eyed her thoughtfully. "I don't smoke."

"But you had matches," she frowned.

"I like to be prepared," was all he said.

She took a deep drag from the cigarette, the rush of nicotine felt incredible as it hit her bloodstream, and she relaxed her shoulders as she exhaled.

"You know smoking is bad for you."

She shrugged. "Who cares?" If anything, the dangers of smoking made the practice *more* attractive to her.

"You strike me as the sort of girl who lacks discipline." He stroked his chin. "Does that sound like a fair assessment?"

She shrugged again. The man was becoming tedious. She'd thought he'd be interested in ravishing her in a dark corner on the grounds, but instead he wanted to lecture her. No thanks. "What business is it of yours?" she asked haughtily, and stubbed out her cigarette with the heel of her shoe.

He took her by the arm and pulled her close to him. "A girl like you could benefit enormously from a touch of discipline." His velvet words magically soothed her irritation.

She stood still. "What do you mean?"

"For example, you know smoking is bad for you, yet you do it anyway. You even flaunt your misbehavior."

"So?" Her breathing grew shallow. Where was he going with this? Her heart pounded in her chest.

"I'd like to take you over my knee and spank you for that," he growled into her ear.

A dim signal in her brain told her this man was crazy, that she needed to run, get away from him now, but instead she breathed, "Do it."

He pulled her to a nearby retaining wall, sat down and uttered, "Lift up your skirt," through gritted teeth.

She felt her eyes widen, but she hoisted her dress up to her waist.

He reached for her and tossed her over his knee. She wore a thong so she knew she was giving him a show, her entire ass out for him to see. Plus they were only a few feet from the door they'd exited. What if someone walked out that door? They'd be met with a view of her spectacular ass bent over Preston Harris's lap. The idea brought a flash of heat to her groin, and she wriggled in his lap.

Holding her with one arm, he swatted her ass with the other hand. The first slap didn't hurt too badly, and she realized this was the first time she'd ever been spanked in her life. Her own father had shown little interest in disciplining her, neither had her mother. They generally handed her off to nannies who didn't dare harm her in any way.

Preston's hand felt like a large paddle and by the fourth or fifth blow her bottom cheeks were beginning to ache. "Ouch!" she yipped, struggling slightly. He held her tighter and continued punishing her bottom.

Thwack! His smacks stung her behind and her cheeks warmed, telling her they were probably red by now. "How much more?" she whined.

After the next swat he stopped and rubbed the skin of her sore cheeks. His palm caressed the whole of her bottom inch by inch, and the sensation was nothing short of divine. She sighed and wriggled happily in his lap. Clutching his leg, she hugged him to her.

When he righted her, she threw her arms around him and kissed him hungrily. With an arm around her waist, he kissed her back then pulled away. "Give me those cigarettes."

"Later," she said kissing his neck.

With both hands he took her by the shoulders and pushed her away. He stood and adjusted his suit. "Now," he said in an I-mean-business tone.

"Okay, okay," she grumbled then she opened her bag and handed them to him.

He pocketed them and held out his hand. "Time to return to the party."

"But…" she protested.

"Enough." He pointed in the direction he wanted her to go.

She pouted. What was this all about? Why had he taken her out here, pulled up her dress and spanked her bottom if he intended to send her away? With a huff she got up and stormed past him. She opened the door for herself hoping it would slam in his face behind her.

She didn't see him again for the rest of the party, and for the next week each time the phone rang she hoped it would be him. But he never called, and she gave up hoping. The father of a schoolmate was hardly an appropriate romantic partner, but she noticed more each day that the boys at school seemed unbearably immature compared to Preston Harris. There was something about the way he took her in hand and spanked her bottom that intoxicated her. Was she some sort of weirdo?

Then one day she received an email from Preston asking her to meet him after school. He picked her up two blocks from school. She remembered him resting a hand on her knee, but other than that he behaved appropriately. He took her to a hotel and, without preamble, asked her to disrobe.

Whenever she remembered it, her heart beat rapidly and she could almost feel her adrenaline flowing as freely as it had that day.

"Charmaine, I like to discipline women. Normally I wouldn't dally with someone so young, my daughter's age. I recognize it is unseemly."

"Age doesn't matter," she'd insisted. How foolish she'd been.

He'd shaken his head as if he didn't want to argue over the matter and brushed her hair away from her face. "But there is something about you, Charmaine my pet… It feels as though we're kindred spirits, as though you will benefit from this as much as I will."

The attention from this older man made her feel important. Eager to please him, she agreed with everything he said. He explained the concept of a safe word, and asked her about feelings on a variety of sexual matters. Then he'd tied her to the bed, flogged her, and had his way with her. Charmaine hadn't known such pleasure existed.

He'd taught her to submit to him, and in return he mastered her body, introducing her to a delicious new addiction—the combination of pleasure and pain. She became his little girl, and he became her daddy. For the first time in her young life she felt cherished, and she allowed someone to steal her heart.

She shuddered at remembering those feelings, but her heart ached now for Hunter the way it always had when she thought of Preston, when she remembered what it felt like before she'd given up on happiness.

Preston told her he planned to leave his wife the next summer and they would be together. He'd wanted to continue the charade of his own family life until his daughter, Eve and Charmaine graduated. He spoke of taking her to Paris, saying he wanted to propose to her at the Eiffel Tower, and spoil her rotten.

And while she'd known it was wrong to cavort with a married man, she convinced herself Preston's marriage was already over. The feeling she experienced when she was with him was too intoxicating to consider walking away. She couldn't help it that they met when he was already married. Charmaine convinced herself that was just an unfortunate detail in the grand scheme of their happy ending. Preston made her feel loved, protected. Finally someone looked out for her, someone cared and wanted to protect her. Someone who was there for her.

Until he was cruelly and unexpectedly taken from her.

And now things had fallen apart with Hunter. She'd gone and fucked things up with him. It was true that trouble seemed to follow her around, but deep down she knew she invited most of it. It was her fault she lost Preston, and it was her fault Hunter had rejected her. Sometimes she wondered if she was addicted to the drama that seemed to unfold in her wake. She loved the rush of doing something naughty, something forbidden. The only downside was when it was followed by remorse. Oh how she hated that sick feeling in her gut that resulted from shame over her own behavior.

Did addicts feel this way? Sure, booze and pills were part of her problem, but it was really the drama, the attention, and the chaos that was her addiction. A therapist had once called it self-sabotage, but she didn't know any other way to live.

To punish herself, she conjured up the image in her mind of Hunter's face the first time he called her "Kitten." She hugged herself tightly. How she loved when he called her that. It made her want to curl up at his feet and purr. Yes, he had been harsh in his judgment of her, but he'd also been tender. With him she'd felt secure, loved, protected—even more than she'd felt with Preston.

Might as well put him out of your mind, she thought, helping herself to another glass. *Time to find some hot cabana boys to take your mind off your troubles.* With a solid effort, she steeled herself against the wave of tears that threatened to fall, and chugged the champagne.

She opened her compact and reapplied her lipstick. It was time to move on with her life, and she needed to look good doing it. Dabbing at her eyes with a tissue, she realized that might be the only thing of value she ever learned from her mother.

CHAPTER NINETEEN

Hunter had the next day off. In fact, he had the whole week off because he'd asked for the time so he could go to Mexico. Now he was looking at a week of nothing to do but think about Charmaine in Mexico without him. He planned to do a lot of working out to occupy himself and keep his mind right. He'd become so infatuated with her that he had to keep reminding himself what a bad idea it was for them to be together.

But images of Charmaine in a string bikini kept popping into his mind. Pictures of her laying on the beach, legs spread slightly, the water swooshing up on her wetting her nipples causing them to harden. He could just hear the lilt of her laugh as the waves sluiced onto the sand and swirled gently between her legs.

The ringing of his phone startled him out of his daydream, and he picked it up. "Mom."

"Are you in Mexico yet? I was hoping to catch you before you left," she asked anxiously.

He made a face. "Don't worry about that. I'm not going."

"What? Why aren't you going?" she asked.

"Charmaine and I broke up," he said.

"Why? I thought you really liked her." Disapproval crept into her voice.

"I do, but it would never work, Mom. She's too rich, too careless. We come from different worlds, we're too different."

"What difference does that make?" she asked.

Her question surprised him. He expected she would understand better than anyone. She'd lived with the same family working for them for fifteen years. She knew what life was like on both sides, and how different it was.

"I don't fit in. I'm not comfortable in her world and she's not comfortable in mine," he said definitively.

"Then you make your own world together!"

"What?" Her reaction surprised him.

"You're not letting that bad experience you had with Laura a while back sway you, are you? Because those people were horrible. Not everyone with money is like that, son."

"Alright, but why are you so worried about this?"

"Because I want grandchildren one day, Hunter, and I want you to be happy. You've been happier these past few months than I've seen you in years. It's because of Charmaine, isn't it?"

"I don't know," he said, not wanting to admit what they both knew was true.

"Can you still go to Mexico?" she asked.

"I don't know, Mom. Listen, Charmaine is a mess. She drinks too much, she's spoiled as hell, she's reckless, childish…" He went on recounting the ways Charmaine was an unsuitable partner, and all the reasons they couldn't be together.

His mother listened patiently and when he was finished she said, "That's fine, son, and in case you've forgotten, you have faults too. The only question I have is this—do you love her?"

Hunter was winding down after his speech, and he took a deep breath before he answered, "With all my heart."

His mother said, "Then get your butt on the next plane to Mexico and tell her. Son, relationships take work. They aren't easy, do you remember living with your father? Whew! He was something else. But when you find somebody who makes you happy you've got to hang onto them, you know?"

"Yeah, Mom. I do." He'd been afraid to fight for Charmaine, afraid the world would laugh at him, but now he realized that was all in his head. Sure, not everyone would understand their relationship, but as long as he and Charmaine did, that's all that mattered. He needed to fight for his girl—for them.

"Hunter?"

"Yeah, mom?"

"You don't think she's an alcoholic do you?" She sounded worried.

He laughed. "No, Ma. I think she's just a party-girl who gets out of control sometimes."

"Well, you like to control everything around you, so you two sound perfect for each other."

They talked for a few more minutes. She asked him to run by and change out the batteries in her smoke detector before he left, and he agreed. Just before they hung up she said, "Hunter, baby—you were ready to let go of a woman you love just because of social standing and what people think? Like you're not good enough because I'm a maid, and we're not the Rockefellers?"

"I don't know, Ma. There's more to it than that…" he hedged. "She's a real handful."

"Well, I know I didn't raise you to think that way. You are a noble and honorable man, Hunter. Better than your father ever thought of being, and you need to hold your head high and fight for yourself and fight for her if you love her. Of course she has flaws, but everyone does, including you."

He chuckled. "I'm sure I do."

"Yeah, but you balance each other out, you help each other. That's what partners do."

"Okay, Mom." He hung up the phone and started packing.

• • • • • • • • • • • • • • •

The flight to Mexico was uneventful. Once the plane landed, Hunter grabbed his carry-on and headed for the car rental counter. Minutes later, armed with a bottle of water and a map, he found his way to number forty-eight, which was a white Ford Focus. He got in and punched the address Charmaine's travel agent had been kind enough to share with him into the GPS system adhered to the dashboard. The woman's phone number had been conveniently located at the bottom of an email she'd sent both him and Charmaine. Apparently no one had informed her that he'd cancelled his trip, which worked out in his favor. He hoped to surprise Charmaine, and he couldn't wait to see the look on her face when he walked through the door.

Part of him knew he should have called her to tell her he was coming, but if she didn't want him here, let her tell him to his face. That would give him the chance to argue with her, to convince her how much they needed each other.

It took him about thirty minutes to reach the beaches. He would have appreciated the view of the water crashing against the shore if he hadn't been so focused on Charmaine and what he wanted to say. He loved her. It was both as simple and as complicated as that.

As he got closer he consulted the map. He'd changed the settings on his phone to international and the GPS should direct him there, but he knew it was never a good idea to put all his faith in technology.

"Destination on right," sang the voice of a Mexican woman in stilted English. "You have arrived at your destination."

Looking up at the mansion, he shook his head. The rich really were different. Leave it to Charmaine to rent what must be a fifteen thousand square foot house for herself for less than a week. The building rose at least three stories high and resembled a palace with a barrel-tiled roof, surrounded by fuchsia bougainvillea. He parked the rental car on the side of the driveway, strode up the walk, and rang the bell.

A short Mexican woman wearing a maid's uniform opened the door. "Hola!"

"Hola," he replied. "I'm here to see Charmaine Bainbridge."

"Si, Senorita Bainbridge this way." The woman stepped back and opened the door for him. Hunter stepped past her and into a cavernous entrance hall.

The woman led him through a luxurious outdoor living space, a mild sea breeze brushed across his face. He could see the infinity pool and the ocean beyond it. The view was spectacular. The location of this place alone must have set her back what would have amounted to half a year of his salary.

They came to a table already set with copious amounts of fruits and a spread of appetizers, including nachos, one of his favorites. The woman motioned to the food and said something in rapid-fire Spanish. Though he didn't understand a word she said, he realized she was offering him something to eat. Absentmindedly he shook his head no, "Gracias."

Laughter rose from the pool area and he recognized Charmaine's voice.

The maid indicated a pitcher of what looked to be margaritas and an icy tub of Corona *cervesas*, complete with limes inserted in their long necks. Another laugh came up from the swimming pool, a deeper sound, that belonging to a man.

His gut clenched with the greasy sense of jealousy. "No, thank you," he said pushing past the maid. When he reached the edge of the pool he saw her. Charmaine was doing a frog-like stroke underwater while two young men looked on. One wore a cap that said "YOLO" and the other had a hipster-like beard. They were sun-burned and each held a Corona as they hung onto the side of the pool.

"Hey bro," the guy in the cap said lifting his beer to Hunter in a salute.

"Whasup?" the one with the beard asked, though it was more a greeting than a question.

"Not much," Hunter said through gritted teeth. Studying them he determined they were barely twenty, if that old.

Charmaine's head bobbed above the surface of the water, and she drew in a long breath.

"You've got company," hat-guy said with a smirk and jerked his head in Hunter's direction.

She turned toward him and her eyes grew wide and she gulped. "Hunter."

"Hello, Charmaine," he said, trying to maintain an even tone.

She smiled nervously. "I thought you weren't coming."

"I can see that." He flexed his chest muscles and gave each of the boys a pointed look that was meant to intimidate. He could tell it worked as they scrambled out of the pool.

"Hey, we're going back to the beach," bearded guy said after climbing out of the pool. He grabbed a beer from the tub. "One for the road."

"Sure," Charmaine said to them. "You don't have to go…"

"That's okay," hat-guy said. "We'll see you later," he said, stuffing a nacho in his mouth. He snagged a Corona on his way out too. "You kids have fun."

Hunter rolled his eyes, and his fingers curled into fists. *Keep your cool, keep your cool.*

An uneasy silence hung in the air between him and Charmaine. Her eyes darted anxiously from one side of the pool to the other. He followed her gaze wondering what she was looking for, but saw nothing.

"What? Have you got more guys stashed around here?" he sneered.

She rolled her eyes. "No," she said lifting her chin defiantly. "Though I don't know why you'd care. What are you doing here anyway?"

He took a deep breath and released it. "I came to apologize for ending things so abruptly. Why don't you get out of the water, and come up here so we can talk?" He gestured toward a comfortable-looking loveseat in the shade.

"Can you get some towels from Lupe please? I think she forgot to bring them."

He looked around, but didn't see any towels. "Where is she?" he asked.

"I don't know, but if you go inside and yell for her you'll find her."

Unaccustomed to giving servants orders he whispered to Charmaine, "Her name is Lupe?"

She nodded.

He walked back toward the house taking in the lush garden, which comprised the large outdoor space. The smell of tropical blossoms lingered in the air, and for a moment he had the feeling he was on vacation.

He slid open a door and called, "Lupe!"

Lupe rounded the corner with an armful of plush beige towels.

"Ah, just what we were looking for." Hunter indicated the towels and offered to take them from her. At first she shook her head, she would do it, but Hunter insisted and they both knew she was no match for him. Finally, she let him take them and she uttered several more things in Spanish which Hunter didn't understand so he nodded, smiled, and said, "Gracias!" and took the towels back to the pool.

To his surprise, Charmaine was still in the pool when he returned. The temperature outside was hot, but she might be afraid of catching a chill as she got out anyway. Fine, he'd be chivalrous and bring her a towel. She treaded water near a ladder and as he grew closer he noticed the cause of her anxieties. She wore only a bikini bottom, her magnificent breasts bobbed freely in the water as she positioned herself to get out of the water.

Rage rose from his stomach and spread through his core until he exploded. "Really, Charmaine? Really?" he asked, anger bubbling in his voice. His hand shook as he held out a towel for her.

"What?" she snapped, avoiding his glare and turning her nose up as she used the ladder to ascend from the water. Holding her shoulders back proudly, she displayed her naked breasts in all their glory. Her nipples hardened as the breezy air hit them and water droplets fell from her wet skin onto the stone surface surrounding the pool.

His cock twitched despite himself while he balled his fists involuntarily. He could feel his temperature rise. "You're entertaining those guys half-naked? Do you even know them?"

Charmaine wrapped the towel around her chest and moved past him breezily. "It's South America. Nobody wears tops around here."

Mexico wasn't in South America, but Hunter was more concerned with Charmaine's new male friends than he was her faulty geography. "Who are they?" he fumed.

She sauntered over to the pitcher and poured herself a margarita. "I don't know. Just some guys we met on the beach. They're staying close by." She waved a hand, simultaneously dismissing his concerns and indicating a house down the street.

"So you've just met these guys, these *strangers* and you're already undressed with *two* guys? And we've been apart, what—less than a week?"

She sighed. "God, you are no fun." Placing a hand on her hip she asked in a bored tone, "So is that why you're here? To play the role of resident buzzkill?"

"Charmaine, if you want a relationship, you're going to have to be more serious about things. Clearly, I can't trust you."

"Trust me to do what? You and I are not together. We're not exclusive. In fact, you broke up with me. Anyway, I told you! I was just tanning, having a little fun. Maybe you should get back to that apology," she sneered.

Maybe we should be exclusive, he thought but didn't say it out loud. He ignored her jibe and stared at her drink. "How many drinks have you had?"

"Aww. Daddy's going to count my drinks now," she mocked.

He closed the distance between them and gripped her hand that held the drink. "Oh, you bet I am."

For an instant he saw a mixture of fear and excitement in her eyes, but it was quickly replaced by defiance. She jerked her hand away spilling the drink all over the ground. "Now look what you made me do," she fussed.

Just then a new set of voices warbled up from the beach. Hunter let go of her hand and glanced up to see the trio of Sloane, Carmen, and Natron trudging back from the beach. Charmaine's house was a regular party house. Why was he not surprised?

"Hey, if it's not our friendly neighborhood fireman." Natron flashed his million-dollar grin at Hunter, while Carmen and Sloan waved in greeting.

"Hey, man. Good to see ya." Hunter shook hands with Natron. Carmen and Sloane gave him welcome hugs, which was more than he'd gotten from Charmaine.

"How was your flight?" Sloane asked looking at Hunter, then at Charmaine.

The tension in the air was thick, and everyone except Natron fidgeted uncomfortably.

"Fine," Hunter answered, and offered no additional conversation. He'd come here to make things right with Charmaine, not charm her friends.

"What are y'all up to?" Charmaine asked her girlfriends, lifting her brow in a "save-me" sort of way. Hunter was beginning to regret coming to Mexico.

"I think we're going out to dinner," Sloane said. "I'm going over to the hotel with Carmen and Natron. Y'all want to come?"

Charmaine began to answer but Hunter spoke over her. "I need to have some time with Charmaine to sort things out. I'm going to have to claim her for dinner this evening."

Her three friends' eyes widened in unison. "Okay," Sloane said in a way that indicated she thought Charmaine was a lucky girl to have a man "claim" her.

"Maybe later though. I'll call you," Charmaine said, shooting Hunter a dirty look.

Natron nodded. "Yeah. You two work it out, and if you have time come see us at The Princess. They've got some good food over there." He picked up something from the outdoor buffet and took a bite. "Mmm. Not that Miss Lupe's not a good cook, too. Mmm. I'm going to have to run six miles tomorrow." He shook his head and popped a tortilla chip in his mouth. "But damn, it's worth it."

Carmen nudged him playfully on the arm. "You *are* on vacation."

He laughed. "Vacation on a bye week. Woman, I've got to stay in playing shape." He looked longingly at the buffet. "And that is not easy."

The conversation stalled out and Sloane said, "Well, let's go then."

Natron looked down at his wrist, pretending he wore a watch, "Yep, look at the time. I'd better get these women out of here so y'all can have your little pow wow." Carmen linked an arm in his and he lifted the other elbow for Sloane who slid an arm through his and they took off through the house, giggles trailing behind them.

"I just thought of something I need to tell Sloane," Charmaine said and hurried after her friends. "Be right back," she called over her shoulder to Hunter.

Hunter watched her go, feeling like a complete fool. He picked up a beer and sank down into a comfortable chaise-lounge. Taking a big sip, he peered out at the ocean realizing he should have never come.

CHAPTER TWENTY

"Sloane! Carmen!" Charmaine called. They'd gone into one of the six bedrooms to change into clothes to wear back to the hotel. She knocked on the door, but didn't wait for them to answer before barging in. Both girls were in the middle of taking off their suits. Charmaine found them in the bathroom, looking in the mirror and comparing tan lines.

"Oh my God, y'all. Hunter just showed up. What am I going to do?" she whined.

"That sounds like a *good* thing, so why are you freaking out?" Sloane asked, rubbing lotion on her pink shoulders.

"First of all, he saw me with those two guys..."

"Which I knew was a bad idea," Sloane said to Carmen as if Charmaine was not in the room. "What were you planning to do with them? Two total strangers, Charmaine... they could have drugged you, raped you, murdered you, videotaped themselves doing any or all of the above. Where is your judgment, girl?"

Carmen made a face, but nodded in agreement.

"Okay, fine so that wasn't the smartest move. But I didn't know Hunter was going to show up here! He told me he wasn't, and he basically broke up with me. What was I supposed to do?"

"Maybe not find another guy right away," Carmen said sympathetically.

"Or two," Sloane snarked.

"But he broke up with me! He doesn't get a say," Charmaine insisted.

"Have this argument with him then." Sloane was already tired of the drama.

"Well, I think he's mad about more than just that," Charmaine chewed on an impeccably polished nail.

Sloane gave her a what-now look in the mirror.

"I kinda didn't have my top on," Charmaine grimaced.

"Oh no!" Carmen said.

"You ignorant slut. What were you thinking?" Sloane asked.

"I was just having fun," Charmaine whined. "There was no touching. It was innocent."

"Yeah, only because he interrupted you three," Sloane said.

Charmaine's face fell. "But what do I do now?"

Carmen took Charmaine's hands in hers. "You have to apologize, honey. You've hurt his feelings, embarrassed him, and he doesn't trust you."

"I've really fucked things up, haven't I?" Charmaine said.

"Um, yeah," Sloane agreed as she applied a coat of mascara.

"Maybe I should just send him home…"

"No, don't do that!" Carmen exclaimed. "Honey, Hunter Baldwin is the best thing that's ever happened to you. Don't give up now."

"She's right," Sloane said.

"But I'm just going to fuck it up again, I always do. Maybe I should just end it now and save both of us the trouble," Charmaine said, picking up a T-shirt off the bed and pulling it over her head.

Sloane whirled on Charmaine. "God, you are such a fucking princess! How dare you just throw away a man like that?" Her face a mere inches from Charmaine, she spat, "Do you know what I would give for a man like that to care enough about me to fly down to Mexico to set things right with me? And you just take it for granted. He fights for you, even when you're down there half-naked with two other guys! Most men would have left already, but you just don't get it. You make me sick!" With that Sloane snatched a sweater off the bed and stormed out of the room. "C'mon Carmen. Let's go!"

Sloane slammed the door behind her, and Carmen touched Charmaine on the shoulder. "It will be okay."

"So, I've been kinda stupid, huh?" Charmaine looked to Carmen.

Carmen shrugged her shoulders but nodded. "Pretty much." Charmaine knew Carmen didn't want to hurt her feelings. She was sensitive and kind that way, but Sloane's outburst had made her realize how selfish she was. She hadn't been thinking about how fortunate she was, and she could see how it would be difficult for Sloane to empathize with her.

To the outside world it looked like Charmaine had it all, while Sloane had had to work for everything she had in life. As much as she hated to admit it, Sloane was right. She should be more grateful that Hunter had come into her life. Even though she was afraid—afraid of him leaving her, afraid of becoming too attached, afraid of getting hurt—she owed it to them both to give him a chance and hear what he had to say.

"Thanks," Charmaine gave Carmen a hug, and they walked down the stairs together.

They parted ways at the bottom of the staircase. Carmen winked at her and whispered, "Good luck."

With a knot in her stomach, Charmaine took a deep breath and walked back out to the pool.

• • • • • • • • • • • • • • •

When Hunter looked up at her, his eyes flashed. "I see you've decided to get dressed," he said nastily.

Charmaine ignored the snide remark. "Would you like to walk on the beach and talk?"

"Fine," he said, the anger still registered in his voice, but it was somewhat tempered. Good, she needed to distract him. He followed her out onto the sand. They had already walked a few paces together when she held out a hand for him to hold. He gritted his teeth and refused to take it. Crap! He planned to make her pay for this one.

"I'm sorry. That was stupid of me, I admit, but I didn't know you were going to be here," Charmaine said, trying an apology.

"Sorry you did it or sorry you got caught?" He took a swig of the beer he carried.

"Got caught? This is my rental house. It is a free country, well I think it is… Anyway, you broke up with me. Technically, I can do anything I want." She had been calm, ready to make nice, but now she felt defensive again.

"So this is how you respond? You go fuck a bunch of strangers the minute you're free? That just shows how little I meant to you, Charmaine. How little you think of me, and of yourself." The disdain in his eyes cut her to her core. It didn't sound like *he* thought much of her.

"I didn't fuck anybody," she said miserably.

"You and I both know that was just a matter of time." His face filled with disgust. "A matter of time," he repeated.

She huffed and turned on her heel to go back to the house, insulted, but also humiliated because he was right.

Hunter grabbed her arm and whirled her around to face him. "Dammit, Charmaine! Don't you walk away from me." He held her by the forearms, too strong for her to get away. She wanted him to stop saying these things to her. If what he said was the truth then she didn't want to hear it.

"There is more to life than pleasure," he hissed.

She tilted her chin defiantly. "Oh yeah. What's that?"

He pulled her to him and kissed her temple. "Love, Charmaine. Love."

Her bottom lip quivered. "I'm not sure I know what that is."

Giving her a squeeze he whispered, "I know. We'll have to work on that."

Unable to meet his eye, she stared out into the ocean, watching the waves crash over the top of each other several yards from shore. Tears welled up in her eyes. Angry at herself for showing emotion, she brushed them away.

He cupped her chin and forced her to face him. She waited for the lecture, but instead his lips crashed against hers, his tongue hungrily seeking her own. Her resistance lasted a mere second before she opened her mouth to him, kissing him back with a fervor she'd held back in the past. She had missed him so much. When she thought she'd lost him forever, she'd minimized her feelings for him, tried to convince herself the loss was less than it was. But she'd lied to herself, and now she drank him in, realizing how thirsty she had been for him.

She wound her arms around his neck and he drew her hips into his so they were almost dancing together in the sand. "I'm sorry," she whispered, this time meaning it with her entire soul.

"No, I'm sorry. I shouldn't have shut you out like that. I've been doing a lot of thinking, and I need you, Charmaine." he responded hoarsely. He sank to his knees and pulled her down with him. "Dammit, I love you."

"You *love* me?" she gazed at him incredulously.

"Yes, God help me, but I do." He smiled at her and she planted a massive kiss on him and pulled him to her. Passion coursed through her, and she tore her lips away to scan the beach to see if they were alone. She didn't see anyone else on the beach.

Hunter lay on his back with her straddling him. He reached up and took one of her nipples into his mouth, biting it gently through her T-shirt.

"Hunter!" she scolded. "What if someone sees us?"

"What a time to get all prim and proper," he said gruffly. Then he rolled them over in the sand, pinning her beneath him, his legs between hers.

"Let me up," she fussed. Someone could come along at any minute.

He kissed her again, igniting a fire inside her that melted her resolve. Why was she even fighting him? She might have done this very thing with one of those boys from this afternoon if she'd had more to drink, if they had hit it off. Why was she being such a prude with Hunter? Frustrated with herself, she pushed all thought from her mind and allowed herself to feel.

Her nipples hardened and her pussy throbbed, wanting desperately to be touched, filled, fucked. She opened her mouth wider and slid her tongue alongside his, showing him she would be his willing accomplice.

When he came up for air, he asked, "Do you really want me to stop?"

Breathing heavily, she shook her head. Eschewing his usual foreplay, he shifted the crotch of her bathing suit aside, pulled his shorts down, and entered her with his cock. It had been so long, and he'd made her wet with his kisses and his hard, sexy body pressed against hers. She was so ready for him that when he pushed inside her, he sheathed himself to the hilt with his second stroke.

She arched her back and hugged his torso tightly with her legs, wanting her skin touching his in every way possible. He fucked her hard and fast. The act was not about giving her pleasure, rather it was about claiming her as his. His frenetic pace was so dominant that it spurred her lust further. No, he hadn't played with her clit or spent extra time preparing her, but right now that turned her on even more. "Fuck me, Daddy," she cried out.

His hips plowed into her time after time, and soon she felt her muscles clenching around his cock and sending shockwaves of satisfaction down her legs, leaving her with a warm glow that permeated her body. She lolled her head to the side, lapping up the ecstasy with each of his thrusts. A few moments later, he let loose a groan as he found his release. He kissed her again then withdrew and sat on the sand next to her.

With a flip of his wrist he pulled his trunks back up, and she pulled down her T-shirt. She repositioned herself so she could lay with her head in his lap. He stroked her hair, and they both gazed out at the ocean silently listening to the sounds of the surf lapping at the shore.

A few minutes later an older couple strolled by, walking hand in hand. After they had passed by and were out of earshot, Charmaine sat up and looked at Hunter. "What if they had come by a few minutes earlier and seen us?" She let her jaw drop, horrified at the prospect.

Hunter shrugged. "We'd have given them a thrill?"

Charmaine shook her head. "Why does it feel like you and I switched places?"

He laughed and put his arm around her, hugging her to him.

She smiled, but something nagged at her. Quietly she asked him, "Hunter, what is it you want from me?"

He stared out at the ocean. The sun started to go down, setting the sky ablaze with slashes of red and orange. It took him so long to respond that she was about to repeat the question when he said, "I want you to let me in."

Her heart skipped a beat. She expected him to say that he wanted her to love him or to let him love her, or even to change who she was. Those requests would have been easier. Instead, he was asking her to open up to him, to trust him with her true self.

She squinted in the glare of the falling sun. "I'm not sure I know how to do that."

He reached out and took her hand in his. "I will help you."

"Okay," she said doubtfully. "But first, you need to learn how to relax and remove that stick from your ass."

He gave her a harsh look, but then said playfully, "I'm not sure I know how to do that."

They both laughed and she squeezed his hand, and they watched the sun until it dipped below the horizon.

CHAPTER TWENTY-ONE

The smell of skirt steak greeted them as they walked back to the villa. The delicious aroma wafted onto the back porch. "That smells amazing, I'm hungry. How about you?" Hunter asked.

"Sure. I guess we worked up an appetite," Charmaine giggled.

He winked at her. "Great. I need to have a word with Lupe, and I'll be right back."

"Okay. I'll go wash up," she said and disappeared up the stairs.

Hunter meandered his way through the big house, following the smell until he found the kitchen where Lupe was busy cleaning up.

"Lupe, it smells divine!"

"Gracias, Senor." She took the compliment in stride, but he could see it pleased her by the way her eyes twinkled.

"When you finish cleaning up in here, you may go."

"Go? Missy needs me here until eight," Lupe said.

"It's okay. Missy and I need some privacy this evening." He palmed her a handful of pesos. "You will probably get the afternoon off tomorrow too." He grinned.

Her eyebrows arched inquisitively. "If it's alright with missy."

"It is. I have a surprised for her," He gave Lupe a conspiratorial look. "I don't want her to know."

"Ahh." Lupe's eyes widened. "I won't tell. Missy can call me if she needs me. I live close by."

"Thank you, Lupe."

A few minutes later a lovely, freshly showered Charmaine ambled into the dining room wearing a colorful caftan that reminded him of a long, flowing tie-dyed T-shirt. "That was fast," he said.

"I had to get that sand off me. It was up my crack," she laughed.

"Good, I'm glad you're more comfortable."

She pulled a chair out from the table and was about to sit down when he stopped her. "Ah, ah, ah."

"What's wrong?"

"If we're going to get this relationship back on track little girl, you need to remember your place."

The skin at the corner of her eyes wrinkled. "And what's that?"

"You are the little girl and I am the daddy. Your behavior in my absence has been unacceptable, and you know it."

"And?" she asked, folding her arms over her chest.

"And if you would like this to continue I will have your full compliance for the next two days. You will be my slave and you will do whatever I ask of you."

She furrowed her brows.

"But first you deserve a spanking."

"Really, Daddy? Before dinner? I'm starved."

"Before dinner. Now go lean over the table."

Sulkily, she obeyed.

"Flip up your robe."

With a sigh she lifted the voluminous skirt of her caftan until it was almost over her head. He stood behind her marveling at her freshly sunned bottom. She wasn't wearing underwear, and he appreciated the easy access.

He glided a hand over the luscious globes and thought he felt her press her ass into his hand. As much trouble as Charmaine caused, he believed that deep down she craved discipline. She might not be aware of it, but he was certain of it.

"How many swats do you think you've earned?"

"Probably twenty," she grumbled.

"That sounds about right," he said and landed the first one on her rear end. Her muscles tensed under his hand. "Relax, Kitten. You know it will go easier if you do."

She exhaled a long breath and he smacked her again. This time she uttered a barely audible squeak. He smiled to himself. She was so cute when she tried to hold in her cries.

His palm hit her buttocks again with a thwack. Her ass pinkened and started to glow. If she had a sunburn this spanking would have been torture, but her skin had browned in the sun, turning a gorgeous bronze color that suited her perfectly.

When his hand connected with her skin it brought blood to the surface and released her adrenaline, endorphins—it made for an intoxicating cocktail in the blood, and she would need it for what he had in store for her.

He smacked her bottom until he reached twenty swats then smoothed her warm, glowing cheeks with his fingers, stroking them, kneading them until she practically purred.

"Oh, Daddy, that feels so good."

He leaned over and kissed the small of her back. "Good. Now go get Daddy some dinner." He gave her ass a final whack and settled himself into the chair at the head of that table.

Charmaine righted herself, her billowy robe ruffling around her, covering her body like a shroud. "What about Lupe?"

"I gave her the night off. I'd like you to serve me," he said, realizing she'd probably never served another person a meal in her entire life. It would benefit her to try new things.

She pursed her lips quizzically then muttered, "Okay" with reluctant compliance.

She sauntered into the kitchen with the gait of a lady of leisure rather than that of a waitress. She returned a few minutes later with the plates Lupe had presumably left out, barely aware of their presence, and they looked like they might spill at any moment. He held his breath as the plates wobbled in her hands and reminded himself he wasn't trying to make a waitress out of her, only to remind her who was the dominant in this relationship.

The plates clattered as she set them down on the table, placing one in front of him and the other at the place next to it. Both had already been set by Lupe with a cloth napkin and tasteful flatware. As she attempted to sit down for the second time Hunter stopped her again.

"What is it now?" she whined.

"I would prefer that you kneel by my side."

"You're kidding me, right?" Her face contorted with snark.

"No, I wish I had a collar and a leash, but since I don't, you can just behave like the free little kitten that you are."

She stared at him like he had lost his mind. "Do you want me to eat out of a bowl on the floor too?"

He smiled indulgently, "That won't be necessary. I'll cut up your food and feed it to you—after I've finished my meal."

Her eyes bulged.

"Go ahead and kneel," he directed her. "Oh, and off with that robe thing."

She threw the big garment over her head and lay it on the wood floor then proceeded to kneel on it.

He enjoyed watching her struggle with her natural personality tendencies and her desire to be submissive, to please him. It was like watching personal growth before his eyes. Plus, she looked ravishing with her light bikini tan lines, and though he wouldn't admit it to her the beauty of her bare breasts had been enhanced by her reckless tanning excursion. His mouth watered and it wasn't from the beef on the plate in front of him.

The steak was as tasty as it smelled, and he quickly plowed through his vegetables, rice, and meat. "Darling, would you please go get us some water for our meal?"

"Sure," she grumbled, eyeing his plate with envy.

"What was that?" he prodded.

"Yes, sir," she said with a false brightness.

"Thanks," he said and started cutting up her meat.

She returned, bringing two glasses of water with her. She set them both on the table. "Will there be anything else?" Good, she's getting with the role, sounding like a real server.

"No, but thank you. You may resume your position."

She knelt beside him. "May I rest my head on your leg, Daddy?" she asked sweetly.

This made him suspicious. Her head so close to his crotch... Who knew what his manipulative little wench had in mind. "After I feed you. Now, place your hands behind your back and open wide."

She smirked. "I like when you ask me to do that, Daddy."

He laughed, speared a bite of her food and placed it between her eager lips. She chewed hungrily and when she finished that bite she said, "Thank you, Daddy. That was yummy," and opened her mouth wide again.

He fed her another bite and watched her close her eyes and savor the flavor of her food. His cock stirred in his swim trunks. Damn, she was such a sensual girl. He thought of how her eyes fluttered when she climaxed. He readjusted his pants to accommodate his growing erection and filled the fork with more food.

"I love when you feed me, Daddy," she cooed.

His throat went dry. "You do?"

"Yes. Daddy knows what to put in my mouth."

He shook his head. "You're being a bad girl, you know that?"

"I thought I was being good." She pretended to pout.

"You're both good and bad at the same time. That's why I love you so much."

She wrinkled her nose with pleasure and opened her mouth for another bite.

He fed her over half of what was on the plate before she told him she was full. They both drank their glasses of water, and Hunter tossed his napkin on the table. "When you were in the kitchen, did you see if there was any dessert?"

Shaking her head she answered, "I'm all the dessert you need."

He loved her playful, seductive ways. "Fine, you can put your head on Daddy's lap now."

Her face lit up and she snuggled close to him resting her cheek on his leg.

"You *have* been a very good girl during dinner, Kitten."

"Thank you, Daddy. I did try." She gazed up at him with big puppy-dog eyes that reflected her desire to please him.

His heart lurched. It went against her nature to submit, but somehow she craved it all the same, and he felt eternally lucky to be here with his beautiful princess in paradise. He stroked her hair, holding her head close to him.

Slowly, she ran a hand over his leg, his muscles contracting beneath her touch. Then she began planting soft, feathery kisses on his skin. Her touch electrified his senses as he allowed her to explore his lap.

Her fingers travelled across his legs, dipped under them, and came to rest on the bulge resting between his legs. She traced the outline of his erection, and when it tented his pants at her eye level, she giggled.

"You make me so fucking hard," he groaned, feeling his cock might explode before he even got to fuck her.

"I like that." Her smile stretched from ear to ear. Gazing up at him through heavy lids, she asked, "May I please suck your cock, Daddy? Please?"

"Hell, yes you can." He pushed his trunks down and his erection bounced toward her with newfound freedom. "And you asked so nicely," he praised her. She nodded and took the head of his cock between her plump lips.

She slid her tongue around the head, lapped up a drop of pre-cum and slowly took him deeper and deeper into her mouth. He leaned back in his chair to enjoy her attentions. Earlier he'd been concerned with putting her in her place, and she'd done a good job obeying his instructions. Now he wanted to revel in that stunning and talented mouth of hers.

He allowed her to use her hands, so she cupped his balls in one hand and jerked him with the other while her magical mouth licked and sucked him until he came close to shooting his load. Then he took back control. Straightening in his chair he fisted her hair and guided her head back and forth over his cock.

"Clasp your hands behind your back," he ordered her, and she complied. Her eyes met his and he saw pure passion there, pure joy in being a vessel for his pleasure. He pulled back her head and held it just in front of him as he jerked his cock to completion, spewing strings of semen on her pretty face. He expected her to make a face, but she tilted her chin proudly and caught his semen on her cheeks as if it were a normal part of any facial she might receive at one of the five-star spas she visited. How he loved this lusty side of her.

He scraped the white fluid from her cheek with his finger and held it before her mouth. With a seductive wink she enveloped his finger with her mouth and sucked his cum into her mouth and swallowed it.

"Good girl," he said and handed her a napkin and she wiped away the rest.

"Did I please you, Daddy?" she asked.

He patted his lap. "Come sit." She climbed up off the floor and into his lap where he held her and kissed her cock-battered lips. "Yes, you made Daddy very happy, but that's just the beginning."

"I really wish I knew what you had planned," she said, wrinkling her brow. He winked at her. "I'll bet you do."

Hunter asked Charmaine to take their plates to the kitchen while he made a call to Natron at the hotel. When he was finished, he took the still-naked Charmaine by the hand and led her upstairs. When they got to the master bedroom he instructed her. "Put on a bikini and use the restroom. I have to go round up a few items, but soon you will be indisposed for a while."

Her eyes widened but she said, "Yes, sir." She was so obedient that she must still be feeling recalcitrant from being caught half-naked with those two boys earlier. He took his suitcase into another bedroom and opened it to find the rope he'd brought with him. He'd hoped for an opportunity to use it on her, but this afternoon he realized he needed to *make* the opportunity. It was time for Charmaine to see who was in charge in their relationship. He needed for her to see how much he cared about her, and in her case, tough love was necessary.

Grabbing a white bandana from his bag, he took that and the rope into the master bedroom. Charmaine stood in the middle of the floor wearing a white triangle top bikini with a tiny bottom that barely covered her ass cheeks. Her hair was wild as usual, the blonde streaks more pronounced after a few days in the sun. The white of her suit contrasted beautifully against her tanned skin and she looked devastatingly gorgeous, like a Greek goddess making a rare earthly appearance.

"Lie down on the floor," he said, keeping his voice hard and firm.

She looked down and made a face. "It's a tile floor. That looks really uncomfortable. Can't I lie down on the bed?"

"Floor," he insisted.

With a big, dramatic sigh she lay down on the cool, tile floor. He knelt at her feet and rolled her onto her stomach and tied her wrists behind her back. He enjoyed rope work, with its methodical, repetitive movements and especially the results—a beautiful, helpless female completely under his control.

His experience dominating women in the past had been limited, and it didn't compare with this. The games he'd played with women had been all about meeting his needs—the need to dominate and the need for sexual satisfaction. But with Charmaine, his focus was more on her needs. He wanted to teach her discipline, and most importantly he wanted to please her.

Moving to her feet, he began tying her ankles. Usually he bound her with her legs apart, and he guessed she was confused at this point, wondering why he was tying her legs together.

"Daddy, why…"

He cut her off. "Quiet. You don't get to ask questions now. In fact," he pulled the bandana out of his pocket, turned her over and propped her up to a seated position. "I'm not interested in hearing you right now. Open your mouth."

She opened it wide, beginning to protest, but any sounds she made were muffled by the cloth he installed across her mouth, and then tied behind her head. He stood up and stood back to survey his work. Charmaine sat with her hands bound behind her, this made her breasts jut out proudly in front of her, her feet were stretched out in front of her reminding him of the Playboy looking silhouette that adorned the tire flaps of countless eighteen wheelers worldwide. The gag in her mouth was the finishing touch. It went perfectly with the flicker of anger in her eyes.

A doorbell chimed, and Hunter winked at her and held up a finger indicating "just a minute." Not waiting for her to respond, he left the room and went downstairs and opened the front door to find the smiling face of Natron Dakers. The two exchanged handshakes, and Natron breezed past him into the villa carrying an athletic bag over his shoulder and a long skinny pole in his other hand.

"Were you able to find everything?" Hunter asked.

"Man, I hooked you *up!*" Natron set the bag on the ground and gave Hunter a high five.

"Really? I wasn't sure you'd be able to find everything. I mean, these aren't things you find at the local tourist shops."

"Naw, man. It's cool. The concierge at the hotel pulled it all together for me." He shrugged. "For a big enough tip, those guys can find just about anything."

Hunter pulled out his wallet. "Thanks, man. What do I owe you?"

Natron brushed it off. "Nothing, man. You gonna use this stuff on Charmaine?" He laughed. "It is my gift to you." He shook his head. "If ever there was a girl who needed a whoopin', it was her."

Hunter nodded in agreement. "Amen to that."

"Hey, can I see her?" Natron asked with a mischievous grin.

"She's kinda tied up." Hunter hesitated, then he and Natron laughed at his unintentional pun.

Natron slapped his leg, still laughing. "All the better."

Hmm. Maybe having Natron see Charmaine all tied up would be somewhat humiliating for her, but it wouldn't be nearly as bad with her bathing suit on as it would be if she was naked. It wouldn't hurt Miss High and Mighty to be knocked down a rung. "Sure. C'mon."

Hunter picked up the athletic bag and headed for the master bedroom, Natron in tow, still carrying the long thin stick. When they entered the room and Natron saw Charmaine sitting on the floor tied and gagged, he busted up laughing. He pointed at her, and her eyes blazed. She started squawking something, but they couldn't understand it because of the gag.

Having some sympathy for her plight Hunter approached her, loosened her gag, and let it fall down her neck in front of her.

"What the hell is he doing here?" she spat at Hunter.

Hunter tried to bite back his smile. "Natron owed me a favor, and I called it in. That's all. He just wanted to say hi."

Natron was still laughing.

"What is that in your hand?" Charmaine snapped at Natron.

"Hey, don't shoot the messenger, okay? I'm just the courier here," Natron said.

Her head swung to face Hunter.

Calmly, Hunter said, "I believe it's a cane."

Charmaine's eyes widened with fear. "A cane?" She looked back at Natron like she wanted to kill him.

"Alright, I'm gonna go now. Uh, Charmaine, good to see you again."

Charmaine sniffed, turned her head and tilted her nose up in the air.

Natron gave her a sarcastic bow, and he left the room. Hunter followed and walked him to the door. "She doesn't like you very much, does she?"

"Aw no, but me and Charmaine—we're good. She's just used to being the star, ya know? Her ego doesn't like it when ole Natron comes into the picture, but deep down we're friends. I just like to fuck with her is all. It's fun yanking her pigtails, ya know?"

Hunter nodded. "I do."

"But, for real. Carmen and I care about that girl, what happens to her."

"I only want the best for her, Natron. I do."

"Alright. Just don't go messing her up so bad she can't be in the wedding. Ew! Kimberly would kill me dead if you go fucking her up where she can't be a bridesmaid."

"No marks, I promise."

"K, just have her at the wedding. Kimberly says the rehearsal dinner is no big thing, just have her there by Saturday morning, okay?"

"You got it, and thanks again."

Natron pulled Hunter in for a hug. "Man, you're like steel. You ever play football?"

"O-line in high school. Left tackle."

Natron nodded a new respect in his eyes, and handed Hunter the cane. "Yeah, I can see that. Well, alright. See ya later, man."

"Later." Hunter closed the door.

Inside, Hunter took a moment to get his mind right. He tapped the cane lightly against his wrist. Before he used it on Charmaine he wanted to be centered, not angry. He took several deep breaths then climbed the stairs. When he got back to the bedroom, Charmaine still wore a scowl on her face.

"That attitude will do you no favors, Kitten."

"Speaking of favors, why does Natron owe you a favor?"

"How quickly you forget. Don't you remember? My team put out the fire when you and his girlfriend decided to torch his things?"

This jolted her. "Oh yeah," she said, her voice uncertain. Had she already forgotten? He shook his head. She was impossible.

"Don't you worry about Natron. He was just helping me. You have no reason to be angry with him."

She scoffed. "Except that he laughed at me."

"And do you know why he laughing at you?"

She screwed up her lips. "Why?"

"Because you're usually so high and mighty, so it's funny to see you helpless, unable to fend for yourself."

"That's funny?"

"Yeah, to someone you give a hard time to, yes."

"Hmph!"

"You might want to cut him some slack. He said some nice things about you."

"He did?"

"Yeah. What have you got against Natron anyway?"

"I don't know." She rolled her eyes. "He's so showboat-y."

All of a sudden it became clear to Hunter. Charmaine wasn't used to sharing the spotlight. She was a local celebrity, and an only child. Natron Dakers was one of the biggest celebrities on the planet, and he upstaged her. His girl was jealous, not that she'd ever admit it. He decided to change the subject. "Enough about Natron. Time to get back to your punishment." He lifted her up to a standing position. "Walk over toward the bed."

"With my ankles tied together?"

He couldn't wait to use the cane on her and to get that gag back in her mouth. He walked up behind her and growled in her ear. "Now!"

With a squeak she hobbled over to the bed with short little strides that reminded him of a Geisha girl in a tight kimono, her hips wiggling with every bit of progress she made. When she reached the bed he barked, "Now bend over."

"Wait!" she shrieked. "What about my safe word?"

"What about it?"

"It's red. If I say 'red' you have to stop." He could hear the panic in her voice. The cane really scared her.

"Yeah, but you're going to be gagged so I won't hear it. Maybe stamp your left foot three times if you need me to stop."

"Daddy, canes are supposed to be awful! I can't believe you got a cane!"

"I can't believe just days after we broke up you're cavorting half-naked with strangers. But I won't miss it if you stomp your feet."

He walked over and stood behind her, close, with his body touching hers. Then he leaned over and repositioned the gag in her mouth. She started to mutter something into it, but he slapped her on her bottom and she quieted down with a whimper.

POOR LITTLE DADDY'S GIRL

Stepping back, he peeled back the bottom of her bathing suit and let it drop to the floor. To tease her, he slowly ran a hand over her firm, toned cheeks. Damn, how he loved her curves. Part of him wanted to take her, forget about the punishment, but the rational part of his brain wouldn't allow it. Charmaine needed discipline, and there was no way she was going to receive any if he didn't administer it.

Taking the cane in his hand he tapped it lightly against her rear. He watched her exhale. Poor thing had no idea what she was in for.

Since her hands were tied just above her bottom, he repositioned them higher, making her bend at the elbows a bit more. With her arms completely out of the way, he brought the cane back then smacked her rear end with it.

Her sharp squeal was muffled by the gag, but he couldn't miss the tone. Everyone said the cane hurt badly, and clearly they were right. He struck her again slightly above where he had initially made contact. A thin pink line was already forming on that spot. In an effort not to hit the same place twice, he hit lower, on her sit spot and her whole body jerked.

"I am punishing for behaving like a common street whore."

Another swack. He peeked around at her face and saw there were tears forming in her eyes. "Charmaine, you are an incredible woman. You don't have to trivialize sex and spread your legs for every guy that passes by."

She mumbled something that sounded like, "I didn't."

He gave her another flick of the cane. "Maybe not, but that's the message you're sending running around without your top on. That's dangerous if that's not your intention. If that's not what you're selling, you're giving off the wrong impression and you're going to get yourself raped. There are a whole lot of guys out there who are not nice guys, Kitten."

The whole time. He watched her left foot like a hawk. Not once did she pick it up to stomp it so he gave her another swat. The sound the instrument made was so minor compared to the swollen pink welts it left, it showed to be quite a powerful tool for getting one's point across.

"You need to be smarter than that. And you must respect yourself more than that. What if they'd taken your picture and sold it to the newspapers?"

At this, she turned and looked at him, shocked. To his surprise, he could tell she hadn't thought about this before, and she broke out in fresh sobs.

He gripped the cane harder. How could she be so out of it that she hadn't thought that through? He was torn between wanting to punish her further and comforting her. Seeing her so bereft tugged at his heart strings, but he stayed true to his course and gave her a final swat to the lower thigh.

Then he set the cane down and found a bottle of aloe after sun lotion in the adjoining bathroom. He rubbed the cool, creamy substance between his palms and applied it to her bum. The instant the lotion touched her skin she relaxed and melted into the bed.

Once she appeared to have calmed down, he rummaged in his bag for something. Finding the toy with the flared end and some lube he stood with his pelvis against her ass. Rubbing her juicy flesh had given him a hard on, and he wanted her to feel it.

He pressed his erection against her cleft and was pleased when she pushed back, bringing her own need into the equation. With his hands he opened her cheeks wide and entered her anus with a well-lubed finger.

She groaned in protest, but he paid her little mind. After a moment or two the tight muscular ring eased and he fucked her ass with his finger. She writhed with pleasure underneath him, and soon he removed his finger, lubed up the toy and inserted it ever so slowly.

Her whimpers turned to moans as he worked it in. Once the toy was deep inside her ass, he gave her sore rump a slap and growled devilishly in her ear, "Who's got a stick up their ass now?"

CHAPTER TWENTY-TWO

Holy crap that cane hurt like a motherfucker! Charmaine groaned into the soggy bandana stuffed in her mouth. Each strike stung like a million freaking bees all attacking her ass at once. Her butt had to be bleeding by now.

Should she use her safeword? Or her safe stomp, as it were. She might have to, because she wasn't sure how much more she could take. Then, finally, he stopped. Hopefully that was an end to the lectures, too. Hunter meant well, but if he expected her to be perfect, she knew she would disappoint him. He began to rub a silky cream on her aching bottom and she melted into the down comforter that topped the bed. The contrast of his tender caresses with the evil bite of the cane was startling. Oh how she needed this—a man who could handle her, then love her to pieces. Since she'd lost Preston, she hadn't found a man who was strong enough to take her in hand, especially one she admired.

She could manipulate most men into doing whatever she wanted. But Hunter was different. She respected him too much to try to manipulate him, at least not very often.

Suddenly, she felt her bottom cheeks being spread wide. How humiliating! She squeaked into her gag, conveying her displeasure. Then he entered her asshole with his finger and fucked her little hole. This took her from uncomfortable to incredibly turned on all in a matter of minutes.

While his intrusion was unwelcome, he knew what he was doing because the sensation started to feel incredible. Soon she felt his hips, and his erection pressed against her bottom. Eager for him to fuck her she backed her rear end up so that their bodies touched in several key areas.

To her disappointment, he lubed up her ass and inserted a toy in her anus. She would have preferred his cock inside her pussy, but Hunter was calling the shots tonight. Wanting to be a good submissive, she ignored his snide remark about her now having a stick up her ass.

She felt his hands at her ankles. As he unwrapped the ropes, she realized he was freeing her feet. Good. She felt like a nitwit walking with those teensy steps she'd had to take earlier.

"I'm going to lift you onto the bed," he said before hoisting her onto the bed on her stomach, her hands still tied behind her back, the toy still inside her.

At first this felt fine because the bed was so comfortable. After the sun and the alcohol she'd had earlier in the day, her body soaked up the coolness of the fabric against her skin. But just as she got comfortable he lifted one of her legs and tied it again.

He bent it behind her and secured it there. She realized the bottom of her bathing suit, which had been around her ankles was gone, leaving her pussy and ass exposed. Both ankles were now connected to her wrists, which stretched her body in a way that wasn't exactly comfortable. When she pictured what the bondage must look like her heart skipped a beat.

Hell, he'd hogtied her! Wasn't that what serial killers all did to their victims? This was more hardcore than what he usually did to her, and a chill ran up her spine. She wanted to ask him what he was going to do to her, but with the gag in her mouth she couldn't, and her anxiety level rose.

She heard him rummaging around, but even when she craned her neck she couldn't see what he was doing so she closed her eyes and waited.

She didn't have to wait long before she felt the whip of something against her right leg. Experience told her it was a flogger of some kind and she looked over her shoulder to see her assumption was correct.

"Grunt twice if you want me to stop." Hunter stood next to the bed wielding a leather flogger. He looked amazing, his muscles bulged as did his crotch. She tried licking her lips, but she'd forgotten the wad of fabric in her mouth. His physique was superb, with its well-defined ripples and hard, cut planes. She wanted to touch, lick, and explore every ridge and every valley of his muscular frame. The outline of his cock pulsed and she felt a wanton thrill course through her body and settle between her legs. She knew she was probably dripping onto the comforter by now, but she didn't care. In fact, that would make her daddy happy.

The flogger came down again, and she lay her head back on the bed, intent on enjoying his ministrations. He whipped both legs and then her arms, making a circle around the parts of her that were available to him. The tails slapped against her flesh with a clicky thud, but their bite was not as bad as it sounded. They might turn her skin pink, but there was no danger of them breaking the skin. But she loved how they made her nerve endings come alive. In her estimation, a proper flogging was better than the best massage.

She felt him set the flogger on the bed next to her, then he rocked her onto her side, untied her bikini top and tossed it on the floor. Now she lay sideways with her limbs tied behind her, but her breasts and belly were facing the end of the bed, giving him access to them.

Before he picked the flogger back up, he ran his hands over her breasts, kneading them under his palms. Being tied up and helpless always aroused her, so her nipples hardened the moment he touched them, but to her frustration he ignored the tight little buds and started flogging her stomach and chest. Her moans came out as whiny little cries, and he smiled with satisfaction at the mixture of frustration and lust he inspired in her.

When he had marked her thoroughly with his whip, he flipped her back onto her stomach and pulled her head toward the edge of the bed. He had never worked her over this well before, and she was beginning to feel the floaty edges of that other dimension he sometimes took her to. She wondered what he planned to do next, but her anxiety had dissipated into a hazy sort of trust.

His hands fiddled with something behind her head, and suddenly her mouth was freed from the hateful gag. Finally!

"May I please have some water, Daddy?" she asked, trying to wet her mouth with her tongue.

"Certainly." He left then came back with a bottle of water. "Open your mouth."

She complied, and he poured a small amount of water into her mouth. She almost choked on it, but did better with the next two sips he gave her.

"Good job. You have to stay hydrated, Kitten," he said, caressing her cheek. God, she loved the feel of his hand on her face, loved when he took her face in his hands and kissed her... She closed her eyes to fully appreciate his touch.

"Now we're going to put that little mouth of yours to work," he said, and she could hear the lust in his voice. Before she could open her eyes, she felt his rock hard cock smack up against her cheek. She moved her mouth to capture it between her lips. She wanted him, any part of him inside her somehow. It didn't matter how or where.

He chided her cheek with his hand. "Ah, ah, ah. No. Be still and I will feed it to you, you greedy girl."

With a whimper of frustration, she held her head upright and opened her mouth obediently, waiting for the gift of his cock. He presented her with only the tip and she closed her lips around it, suckling his mushroom head, lavishing the tender underside with attention from her tongue before running it up and dipping into the slit of his cum hole. When she heard a deep groan erupt from the back of his throat, a sweet satisfaction overcame her.

His cock pushed deeper inside her mouth and she continued to lick and stroke him with her tongue. He pulled back then pressed inside again, fucking her mouth, and she imagined he was fucking her pussy. Her cunt throbbed with pleasure as he moved in and out of her lips, pushing farther and farther back until the end of his rod hit the back of her throat. She knew he loved the feel of that, and she focused on opening her throat wide and breathing when he slid back out.

He fucked her for a few minutes, and when he pulled out she gasped loudly for air. "Good girl. I don't want to choke my kitten. Well, not too much." He laughed and she smiled wanly, the muscles in her mouth aching, needing a break.

She dropped her head to the comforter and felt his weight behind her on the bed. With trepidation she remembered the butt plug that was currently inserted in her. "What are you going to do to me, Daddy?" she asked with trepidation.

"Nothing I haven't done to you before." This eased her nerves slightly.

She felt him settle behind her, and he drew her hips back closer to him. Her pussy pulsed with the need for him to fill her and as she felt the head of his cock enter her, she quaked with need. He drove into her so slowly that she trembled with anticipation, wanting him all the way inside her.

She knew better, but unable to control herself, she cried, "Deeper, Daddy, deeper!"

Instead of going deeper he pulled back a tad and smacked her sore bottom.

"Oow!"

"Don't tell Daddy what to do, Kitten. We've already established that you do not know what's best for you, haven't we?"

"Yes, Daddy. I'm sorry," she whined.

"Trust Daddy."

"Okay."

Then he plunged back into her, all the way inside, and her pussy clamped down on him.

"You keep that plug in your ass, Princess."

"Yes, sir," she answered weakly. Unsure she was in control of any of her bodily functions anymore, she attempted to squeeze the plug.

"You want to be a little whore?" He grabbed a hank of her hair and pulled her head back as he impaled her on his cock. "Then you be Daddy's little whore. No one else's," he growled.

He rode her hard and fast. Each thrust sent her to another dimension, and she started to drift away, embarking on a lust-induced trip with chemicals firing in her brain that trumped any drug she'd ever tried. He rocked her body with a climax that lifted her to new heights of pleasure before dropping her back to earth, wrung out and spent.

Hunter continued to pump into her hard and fast. He held her hips and rammed his cock inside her like a man possessed. She lay there and endured his onslaught in the hazy aftermath of her own climax, but unexpectedly her body grew aroused again. As if without her consent she felt herself travelling up the mountain again, coming closer and closer to a another release with each frenetic thrust of his cock, until finally, with a moan and a shiver, she flew over the other side of the cliff. Every muscle she had contracted, her arms and legs jerked, and she almost wept from the intensity of her orgasm.

"Take it," he panted, and with one final stab he stilled inside her, his hands holding tight to her legs. He breathed heavy as he withdrew, tossed aside his condom, and began slowly unfurling the ropes that bound her. He gently returned her arms to her, resting each by her side, then he released her ankles and allowed her to stretch her legs out. She was about to roll over onto her back when he stopped her. "Wait," he said and slowly pulled the toy from her rear end. The sensation was both pleasurable and slightly painful as the bulbous head evacuated the tight exit. She made a small guttural sound and he got up from the bed and went into the bathroom to wash off the toy.

She flipped onto her back and stretched her arms over her head as far as she could. Then she did the same with her feet, and crawled under the covers, feeling both used and fulfilled, a glorious combination. When Hunter came back, she was almost asleep. He climbed into the bed behind her and curved his body against hers, making them fit together like two pieces of a jigsaw puzzle.

He kissed the top of her head and stroked her hair. "I should have never let you go, and I'll never do it again," he whispered in her ear. "You're Daddy's girl, Kitten. Never forget that."

CHAPTER TWENTY-THREE

The next morning Hunter brought Charmaine a delicious breakfast tray with Lupe's specialty tomatoes and spicy cheese omelets, homemade tortillas, and orange juice.

"How sweet of you to bring this to me." She yawned. "Are you going to join me?"

He winked at her. "I like having a chance to spoil my girl. And you were such a good sport last night, I wanted to be sure you got the sleep you needed. I ate earlier."

He left Charmaine to her breakfast and went back to the kitchen to tell Lupe she could have the afternoon off. He was checking his email on the back patio when Charmaine appeared in a striking yellow bikini. "Join me for a swim?" she asked.

"Only a light one. You'll need your strength for what I have planned for you today."

Her eyes widened. "So should we stay at the house and swim in the pool?"

"That would be a good idea."

She sauntered outside, assuming he would follow, which he did, admiring her delectable ass in her thong. Later, he would show her what he thought of her taking the lead. Today was the day he would truly master his bratty little girl. He'd woken her up with the cane the night before, but he'd been careful not to leave any lasting marks.

The water in the pool sparkled in the sun, bright triangles of light hit him in the eyes and he pulled on his sunglasses.

Charmaine dipped her toe in the pool. "You know, Daddy—I swim in the pool at home all the time. I had my heart set on a swim in the ocean. Would that be okay if I make it a very short one?" she asked batting a fringe of lashes at him.

He sighed. "You know you're adorable, don't you?" She captivated him with her zest for life, the way she embraced new experiences, going a hundred miles per hour as if it had never occurred to her there were other speeds.

She tilted her head demurely, with modesty that was clearly false. "I've been told a time or two."

"Very well." He held up a finger. "You promised short."

She nodded and held a hand out for him, and he enclosed her tiny paw in his enormous one. "I love it here," he said as they made their way toward the sea, the brisk ocean breeze whipping across their bodies.

"Me too," she beamed. "We should come back again."

He squeezed her hand and they ran into the surf together, the roar of the waves echoing in the ears. She pointed to a school of porpoises jumping out of the water. "Look!" There were three of them and it looked as if they were doing tricks. They watched them for a while then swam parallel to the shore for a bit. After a gentle reminder, Charmaine obediently swam back to shore and they trudged through the sand back to the house.

Now the fun could really begin.

• • • • • • • • • • • • • • •

Hunter's hand hovered in the air, about to strike the match. Charmaine had played with fire a time too many, and the time had come to teach her a lesson about respecting nature's most magnificent, yet dangerous force.

Naked, bound and gagged, her eyes glistened in fear as she waited for what he would do next. She had no reason to fear him, not really. No one knew the power of the flame as well as a firefighter.

He struck the match against the flint and was rewarded with an orange-yellow glow and the smell of sulfur tickling his nose. Holding it between two fingers he reached for a candle from the bag Natron had brought him. His eyes fixed on the lit match as he said, "You've shown repeatedly that you like to play with fire." He extinguished the flame by blowing on it. "Today, I'm going to teach you something about fire." Charmaine's face had lost all of its habitual nonchalance, which brought him immense pleasure. He'd gotten her attention.

Fire was not something to be played with. It was not a toy, but a power he'd seen destroy countless lives not to mention damaging billions of dollars' worth of property. Today he would provide her with the most valuable lesson he could teach anyone—respect for fire. Charmaine would learn what it was like to be on the receiving end of the flame rather than the one igniting it.

Where to start? He'd tied her to the bed spread eagled and her pussy shone with damp arousal and her breasts strained against the rope bra that held them. He removed a large white dildo from the bag, applied some lube, and inserted it between the lips of her juicy opening. She moaned over the gag, and he inserted it slowly so that he could acknowledge her reaction to every inch as he plundered her sex.

"Now let's find something for the back door," he said knowing that would get a rise out of her. This time he turned back to the bag, ignoring the big bright eyes he knew flashed at him from behind impossibly long lashes.

He brought out a gold toned butt plug that flared out into a red gem at the end. After adding some lube to it, he started to push it gently into the anus of his captive.

She whined, and he shushed her and began stroking her clit with his fingers. She fidgeted until he found the right tempo and motion—tiny circles got a better reaction than straight strokes or pressure and wiggles. His attentions loosened her up and she rolled her eyes back in pleasure when he pushed the plug past the tricky ring of muscles. Her eyes flew open and he smiled benevolently at her as he seated the rest of it in her ass.

"Keep that in there." He wagged a finger at her. "No pushing it out."

She fumed, but he distracted her as he bent down and kissed her neck then breast, her nipple beading to a hard point begging for attention. He suckled her for a moment and slipped the dildo in and out of her pussy, making her hips jerk with desire.

He fucked her a few more times then left the dildo buried in her delightful cunt. His cock pulsed as he took her in, with all her holes filled. If only he had three cocks he'd fill her like that every day—ass, pussy, and mouth.

With a flourish, he lit one of the candles.

She started to moan with dread.

"Kitten, do you need to use your safeword?" He asked, half-serious, half-mocking.

With a nasty glare she shook her head "no."

"Then behave yourself. I haven't even done anything yet." Though he avoided her gaze, he could still feel the daggers she shot him.

The first droplet of wax fell on her stomach, and she flinched. He moved the candle in a circle, dribbling tiny drops of liquid fire across her belly. She moaned again and wriggled against her bonds.

"You can't get away," he said, proud of the professional job he'd done with the ropes. With practice, he'd come a long way since he and Charmaine had first gotten together. He dripped a path to her chest and was pleased to see her breasts rise, eager for the scorching liquid to land upon them. Turning the candle he placed a few drops on the skin next to her areola, and watched in fascination as both the wax and her nipple hardened simultaneously. His mouth grew dry with lust, and he righted the candle and took a sip of water.

Back to work, he dribbled wax across both breasts, relishing her squirms and squeaks. Her muffled utterances were increasing in volume, squeals of excitement mixed with pain. Each time he asked if she wanted him to stop she shook her head "no."

He worked her whole body with the wax—her feet and the inside of her arms proved the most sensitive until he came to her pelvis. When a drop landed just above her mons she shrieked through the gag, and her eyes danced with pain. He moved lower and when a droplet hit the hood of her clit she groaned with pleasure. A deeper sound, more satisfied than the others she had made, and he prided himself on reading the signals she gave him.

With such favorable results he dripped more wax on her outer pussy folds and watched her grow wilder and wilder the closer he came to her center. She threw her head from side to side in ecstasy and lifted her hips as best she could so her skin could touch the melted wax. Her muscles quivered around the dildo buried inside her and she began to push it out.

His cock throbbed in his pants. When he could contain his lust no longer, he yanked his pants down and stroked himself with his free hand. Charmaine seemed to have floated off into another world so he removed the dildo and gave her a final dribble to her pussy entrance then blew out the candle and set everything aside.

He climbed onto the bed between her legs, bent over her, and ignoring the wax that covered her body, kissed her neck. Her eyes were closed, and she moaned, acknowledging his presence. He unfastened her gag and asked, "Do you see, now, how fierce fire can be?"

Eyes still closed she nodded. "Yes, Daddy. You're smart."

This made him laugh. After what he'd just done to her, "smart" wouldn't be the first thing that came to his mind. "Thanks, Kitten. Now I'm going to fuck that greedy little pussy of yours."

She giggled and nodded in agreement. Then it occurred to him why she seemed to be in la-la land. He'd sent her off to sub-space, same as he'd done the night before with the cane and the flogging.

This made him stiffen even more, and he grabbed her hips and entered her slick, welcoming cunt. He'd grown to love fucking her while she was tied up, loved how helpless it made her. In real life Charmaine was larger than life, but when he had her pinned down and she let him fuck her any way he saw fit, he knew he could tame his fiery lioness.

Gurgles of pleasure escaped her throat, and her pussy clamped down on him as she sped toward an orgasm. He took one of her breasts in his mouth as he began to nibble on her, her body trembled with fulfillment. The only part of her body she could move, her head, thrashed wildly on the bed and she cried, "Daddy!"

He continued to pump her full of him. "I love you," he said.

"Love you too," she said. His body froze. She'd never said that before. Was she drunk with the chemicals of sex and pain or did she sincerely return his love?

Slowly, he resumed fucking her, told himself it didn't matter. He gave her cheek a soft slap. "Charmaine," he said trying to get her to open her eyes.

It took several minutes for her to respond, but when she did she seemed faraway. He thrust into her with less enthusiasm now, and later, when he came quietly inside her, he wondered if she would remember what she'd said.

CHAPTER TWENTY-FOUR

Charmaine must have fallen asleep because when she opened her eyes Hunter was staring at her. He had an arm draped across her and he was wide awake. Huh. Usually it was the man who fell asleep after sex, but then it had been she who had endured all that hot wax and a staunch fucking.

Exploring her torso she found she still bore the wax drippings.

"Lupe is going to hate me. That stuff is a bitch to clean up." Hunter ruffled his hair.

"She is," she giggled.

He raised a shoulder—what-are-ya-gonna-do?

"So, it's the rehearsal dinner tonight. Since I'm in the wedding party I'm supposed to be there."

"Oh no, you're mine tonight."

She frowned.

"I got the okay from Kimberly. They don't mind."

"But…" Kimberly might have said it was okay, but Charmaine knew it wasn't. "Are you sure?" You only got married once—or at least that was what people hoped on their wedding day, wasn't it? This was a big deal. Surely Hunter could teach her a lesson some other time. Couldn't he? Crap. She hated having to choose between him and her friends.

"I'm sure. Besides, I have something planned. Get dressed and we'll go soon."

With a slight huff, she gave in. He helped her remove the wax, sweeping most of it into a wastebasket then they scrubbed the rest off in the shower.

"What should I wear?" she asked noticing that he'd donned khaki pants and a sport shirt.

"Not beachwear. Something you'd wear to dinner."

She put on a peach-colored maxi dress that looked great against her tan and some rhinestone sandals. Adding a pair of large turquoise chandelier earrings, she met him by the front door.

"Hubba, hubba," he said, reminding her of middle school. Even the dorky things he did endeared him to her.

He took her in his arms and kissed her sweetly. "Thank you for trusting Daddy to take care of you today, and for staying with me tonight. I know how important your friends are to you."

The corners of her lips curved upward in spite of herself. "You're welcome, Daddy."

They took his car, and she didn't mention that her rented car was more luxurious than his. It didn't matter. All that mattered was that he was here with her. Just yesterday morning, feeling rejected, she was determined to get Hunter off her mind. Today, they were together and he was paying her all sorts of attention—the kind of attention she needed.

And even though she didn't want to miss the rehearsal dinner, she liked how he was taking charge of the situation. He must have something special planned.

They left the villa by mid-afternoon, and after they'd been driving for about half an hour she piped up. "How do you know where you're going?"

"I don't, other than the GPS."

As if on cue, the computer-toned female voice from the GPS sounded, "In half a mile turn right."

They both laughed. "You guys are so lucky someone invented that. Now you don't have to ask directions. A machine just calls them out to you," Charmaine said playfully.

"Isn't that the truth?" he concurred.

They followed the robotic woman's directions until they arrived at a sign for a seaside café. Hunter helped her out of the car then led her hand-in-hand up several outdoor staircases. As they rounded a bend Charmaine gasped.

The ocean stretched before them, but they were about halfway up a cliff. Two bodies falling out of the sky in front of her was what made her catch her breath. She looked down in time to see the splash as their bodies hit the water.

"Cliff divers! How did you know I wanted to see the cliff divers?" She punched him in the arm and liked that he looked pleased with himself.

"I read your tweets."

"You do?"

"Sometimes."

She gave him her prettiest smile and they found a table at the outdoor café. "That's awfully sweet, Daddy. Please may I have a cocktail, Daddy? I really want one of those beachy type drinks with the umbrella in it."

He screwed up his mouth pensively before acquiescing. "Just one." He held up a warning finger.

When the waiter came by he ordered them two rum runners, and they watched the local divers catapult their bodies two by two off the top of the cliff and plummet over one hundred feet into the swirling sea below. The entry point was so far down they couldn't even hear the splash of the water when they hit. The blue-green water of the ocean was incredibly gorgeous and she couldn't think of a lovelier place to spend an afternoon.

"I have no idea how they do that. I'm terrified of diving, even off the low dive at the Country Club pool." She shivered.

"I think it looks fun." Hunter gave the waiter a tip and took a sip of his frothy drink.

She grimaced. "I think you've lost your mind." But secretly she was proud to be with such a brave man. She shouldn't be surprised by his reaction. After all, the man did run into burning buildings for a living.

"There's something I want to tell you about, Charmaine. An incident from my past that I probably shouldn't have let come between us, but I'm afraid I did."

She set down her drink. Hunter hadn't talked much about his past. She chalked it up to what a private person he was, but now that he wanted to reveal something to her, she gave him her undivided attention.

"A few years ago, I had a girlfriend named Laura. We weren't that serious, but we'd been together for about a year when her parents tried to pay me to stop seeing her."

Charmaine felt herself grimace. What kind of people would do that? With a sigh, she realized she was all too familiar with exactly the sort of people who did that—controlling, ridiculous people who thought they could rule the world because they had money. "What did you do?"

"I turned it down, of course, but soon after that, she went on an extended European vacation and I never saw her again."

"So they paid her off with the vacation?"

He nodded.

"Were you heartbroken?"

"Not really. That just made it clear we weren't right for each other, but it soured me on wealthy people. I think I was letting my prejudice against rich people color my judgment when it came to you."

That made sense. Rich people could be even bigger assholes than people without such extensive resources. She tucked a hand in between his. "Thanks for telling me that. And by the way, I don't think you have anything to worry about with my family."

"Oh yeah, why is that?"

"No one in my family cares enough about me to bother to pay someone off." She bit back a bitter laugh.

Hunter squeezed her hand and leaned over to kiss her. He made her feel so safe and loved that she hated to even think of her family while she was with him.

She was glad when he changed the subject by pointing out one of the cliff divers' daring tricks. For the rest of the afternoon, they laughed and talked and watched the divers until the shadows grew long, settling heavy on the ground around them. When the diving performances started occurring less and less frequently, Hunter pulled his chair back. "Ready?"

"Sure," she said. "Where to next?"

"I need to feed you, but later I have a surprise."

She gulped. She would do almost anything with him—the hot wax had proven that. It had been painful, yes, but something she could handle. In fact, she'd enjoyed it. The whole experience had been surprisingly erotic, and if he'd wanted her to be more serious about fire—*fine*. He'd made his point. She'd stop playing with matches like a naughty girl, but she might like him to try the wax on her again one day…

As they arrived at the car, a band of dirty children ran up to them begging for money. Some of them were barefoot and their clothes were ragged. Charmaine opened her purse and gave them each a handful of pesos. They favored her with wide gap-toothed smiles ran down the road, whooping at their good fortune.

"I'm surprised you did that," Hunter said, getting back into the car. "I wouldn't think you'd encourage ruffian behavior."

One corner of her mouth turned up. "Normally I wouldn't."

"But…?"

"Being here with you, I feel happy." She reached up and touched his earlobe between her fingers. "I can't be this happy and not share it. We are so fortunate, and I have so much… how can I not share that with people who have so little?"

"I'm proud of you, Kitten." He leaned over and kissed her.

"Thanks, Daddy."

They got in the car and he drove them to their next destination. When they pulled into the driveway of a grand resort she realized she'd been daydreaming most of the ride. The rum had glazed her senses slightly and she'd sank back into the heady, steamy memories of earlier—the heights to which Hunter had aroused her and the intensity of the pleasure he'd brought her.

Before she knew it a valet opened the door for her. Hunter gave over his keys, and they disembarked. He offered her his arm in typical escort fashion and she tucked her hand in the crook of his elbow.

"Do you know where we're going?" she asked.

He squeezed her arm gently. "Of course. When are you going learn to trust Daddy, Kitten? Let me be in charge, or I'll have to gag that pretty little mouth of yours in public."

She giggled. "You wouldn't!"

He gave her a devilish grin. "Oh, but I would."

They walked through the lobby, and he did seem to know where he was going. First, they passed through the indoors, then they followed an outdoor walkway amidst some of the most beautiful gardens she had ever seen. The sunlight was fading but she could still appreciate the fragrant blooms in their many vibrant colors.

Turning a corner, they came upon an outdoor dining area that looked like a restaurant. "Oooh! Is this where we're going to eat?" She clapped her hands.

Before he could answer she heard several people call out her name. She looked around suspiciously. Surely the damned paparazzi hadn't staked out their restaurant. She was well-known in Dallas, but she wasn't a big enough celebrity for anyone in Mexico to care about her.

Just then Nellie and Marley appeared, grabbed her by the arm and dragged her into the restaurant. "You've got to sit with us," Marley said with a sorrowful look thrown over her shoulder to Hunter.

"Yes, we'll fill you in on everything you missed at the rehearsal," Nellie said. Kimberly's wedding had to be the biggest thing she'd been involved with since her last pageant.

"Oh, okay. I'll be right there, girls. Hang on just a minute." Reluctantly the two girls backed away, then started giggling again on the way to their table.

Charmaine planted her feet wide and placed her hands on her hips. "What is going on?" She drew out each word, a pretend reprimand on her face.

He winked at her. "Go sit with your friends. I'm sitting next to Mason. It will be fun."

"Did you have this planned all along?"

He nodded.

"So why did you make me think that we weren't coming?"

"I want you to trust me, Charmaine. Trust that I know what my baby girl needs. I wouldn't have let you miss this, Kitten. I know how much your friends mean to you."

"Thank you, Daddy." She kissed him dutifully on the cheek, and he escorted her into the rehearsal dinner.

That evening as he watched Charmaine with her friends, he was overcome with how much love he had for her. For years he hadn't had a personal life, but Charmaine had opened up a new world for him. She reminded him how to have fun. Now he had a girl he adored, a girl he could protect, someone who needed him. And he wanted to make her his. But first he had to convince her she was worth it.

CHAPTER TWENTY-FIVE

The wedding went off without a hitch. Kimberly and Charles took their vows beachside amongst a small group of friends and family. Charles's mini-me son Benji, was the most adorable best man Charmaine had ever seen in his boy-sized tux. Charles himself was handsome as ever, his blond, surfer-style good looks fit perfectly against an ocean backdrop.

Kimberly, a vision in her ivory shantung Vera Wang gown with the fitted sweetheart bodice and mermaid skirt, carried a bouquet of lavender orchids. Charmaine got stuck wearing lavender, not her favorite color, but she had to admit the bridesmaids' dresses were lovely and they complemented the bride beautifully with their Easter egg palette of pastels.

The seafood dinner afterward had been scrumptious, and the band had kicked off Kimberly and Charles's first dance to "L-O-V-E" by Nat King Cole. Charmaine was seated next to Hunter on one side, and Carmen on the other.

"My money's on Natron and Carmen," Sloane said from across the table. They were discussing which couple among their friends would be the first to have kids.

"Yeah, we'll start our own little basketball team, won't we baby girl?" Natron leaned over and kissed Carmen's cheek.

Carmen laughed. "Not until after we get married. Maybe Kimberly will want to give Benji a little brother or sister to play with before he gets much older. Or Nellie. I can see it being Nellie and Mason."

Nellie's eyes almost popped out of her head. "Me? Why the hell would I have a baby? I have too many things to do, plus I couldn't ruin this figure!" The beauty queen smoothed a hand across her impossibly slim waist, and Charmaine chuckled. Nellie's vanity knew no bounds, and rumor had it she had shoved Lucinda out of the way to catch Kimberly's bouquet a few moments earlier.

"It's okay, baby. We don't have to have kids any time soon," Mason soothed Nellie.

"I should hope not," Nellie huffed.

At the next table, Lucinda and Colin were clearly having a disagreement. What started with raised voices had developed into a silent stand-off between them, and even though Charmaine wondered what they were fighting about, she decided to steer clear of those icy waters.

"May I steal you away?" Hunter whispered into Charmaine's ear.

She gave him a small nod, pushed her chair back, and excused herself from the table. Hunter led her to the corner of the tent where they watched Kimberly and Charles on the dance floor. Wrapped in each other's arms they appeared madly in love. She wondered if her parents had ever been that happy. Perhaps at the beginning, but something had gone terribly wrong. Something had gone wrong in all six of her father's marriages, so it had to be him. Something was wrong with him that made him incapable of happiness. Was she the same way?

She watched Kimberly's arm placed comfortably on Charles shoulder as he held her close, his hand resting on the small of her back. They had been through so much in their time together—his injury in Iraq, custody fights over his son, wedding delays. But their difficulties had only made them stronger. People like Kimberly deserved to be happy, not people like her.

"What are you thinking about?" Hunter asked turning her face toward him.

To her humiliation tears glimmered in her eyes. She tried to smile them away. "They sure look happy."

His brow wrinkled with concern. "They do, but what is bothering you?"

"Nothing," she sniffed.

"Really? That's how you're going to answer Daddy?" He shook his head.

"Okay, sorry. Bad habit. I just wonder if I will ever have what they have." She inclined her head toward the newlyweds.

He took her in his arms. "Stop that, Kitten. You'll have it, and you'll have it with me."

"But what if I'm like my father? What if I'm incapable of love?"

"You stop that right now or I'll throw you over my shoulder and haul you out of here like I did the first day I met you."

"I'm serious," she pouted.

"So am I. You are nothing like your father. Underneath all your bravado, my dear, you have a heart of gold."

"Don't tell anyone," she snarked.

"Your secret is safe with me," he winked.

"But my father has been married six times," she started up again.

Before she could say anything else, Hunter's muscular arms took hold of her and he upended her. Suddenly the world was upside down, and she watched his black dress shoes below marching off with her. "Wait!" she screeched.

He smacked her bottom with his palm. Fortunately for her, the crinoline petticoats underneath her dress protected her, and it didn't really hurt. As they passed out of the ballroom she saw Carmen giggling at them and Natron giving Hunter a thumbs down sign, though it was probably a thumbs up—to her everything was upside down.

Hunter stopped in the hallway and she heard him press the bell for the elevator.

"You can set me down now."

He ignored her.

They got into the elevator and she sighed.

"I told you not to keep going," he said calmly.

It was her turn not to say anything. Stubbornly, she decided to remain silent until he set her down.

He strode down the hall on the eighteenth floor, unfazed by her extra weight. He wasn't breathing harder or showing any signs of fatigue. She was relieved when he pulled a key out of his pocket and she heard the door click open.

Inside the door he set her gently onto her feet, turned her body and unzipped her dress. The strapless color concoction fell to the floor. She stepped out of it, while he stepped around it. "Take off the rest," he said in a hoarse voice.

A ripple of pleasure ran through her veins. That he wanted her so much, that she affected him like that—it made her want, with every fiber in her being, to please him. She unhooked her bra and slid down her panties.

He pointed at the bed. "Lie down."

She kept her eyes trained to his as she sat down on the bed, scooted back then reclined onto her back.

The he spoke. "I know you're trying to push me away. You don't know how to let someone love you. You've never had that, but I'm going to prove to you that you're worthy of being loved. I'm going to love you every day for the rest of my life. Now spread those legs, Kitten," he said and she could hear the lust in his voice.

She opened her thighs and he came to rest between them. He petted her cheek and bent his head to taste her sex. His tongue lolled around, exploring her folds, teasing her until she felt an urgency like none other. She hugged her to him and whispered, "I love you, Daddy."

Sucking her throbbing bud between his lips, he rolled it around in his mouth, pulling, licking, daring her to come. He entered her with one finger, attacking her pussy with his mouth and his hand, grinding his scratchy face against her delicate skin. It didn't take long before she erupted in a cascade of bliss. Holding his head tightly in her hands, she rode out the spasms of ecstasy, falling, falling into that peaceful space where she was loved.

CHAPTER TWENTY-SIX

Charmaine glanced down at her phone and heaved a loud sigh, but the receptionist's attention remained glued to her computer. She sighed again, but still received no reaction from the ageless blonde with the razor sharp pixie cut and the blood-red lips who sat at the sleek desk at the mouth of Thornton Bainbridge's office.

It was typical of her father to make her wait. He used every opportunity at his disposal to remind her how powerful he was and how indebted she was to him for everything she had. She'd long since learned to sing for her supper and fawn over the great man when it suited her, but also she knew how to push his buttons when it behooved her. She cleared her throat loudly. "How long does he expect me to wait? He asked me to come here, the least he could do is see me," she grumbled.

The latest gatekeeper threw Charmaine a patronizing smile that was reminiscent of the Grinch who stole Christmas. "I'm sure he won't be long."

Charmaine huffed and went back to playing the candy game on her phone. A couple of weeks after she'd come home for Kimberly's wedding, her father had summoned her to his office. She hoped his accountant hadn't tattled on her again. True, she had been putting off working on the information the guy had asked for, but when it came down to it—go to Mexico or pull together a bunch of tax documents—who wouldn't opt for exotic travel?

Listening to another one of her father's lectures was not high on her list. He really needed to learn the art of the email rant. Then she could just delete it. She giggled to herself picturing herself deleting her father's emails one after the other. Sadly, she didn't think she'd ever gotten an email from him. She had, however, received several from his various minions.

Just as she uncrossed her legs and realized her left foot was asleep, her father burst through the double doors of his office. "Charmaine!"

His exuberance startled the receptionist who jumped in her chair. Thornton didn't appear to notice as he strode toward his eldest daughter, arms outstretched as though he intended to give her a bear hug.

Charmaine stood, her left foot tingling angrily. "Dad."

He hugged her and she managed to give him a half-hearted pat on the back. The hug was as impersonal as it was odd. She'd never known her father to be a hugger. When they drew apart he ushered her into his office, and her left foot started to awaken, and her left side was besieged by pins and needles which made her limp, gritting her teeth in agony.

Her father frowned at her like she was Quasimodo as she dragged her stinging foot behind her, but he didn't say anything. Typical. Ignore anything that makes you uncomfortable. Charmaine sank into the chair across from his desk, and then blanched at the hardness of its seat cushion. She fell for it every time. The chair looked super comfortable, but once you sat down it felt like you were sitting in an unforgiving wooden church pew. Just another of Thornton's psychological warfare tactics utilized on those visiting his office.

Thornton perched on the side of his desk so he towered over her. More psychological warfare—*I'm so much higher up that you.*

"If this is about the tax stuff, I'm sorry. Kimberly got married in Mexico, and I put it off..."

He raised his eyebrows, and she realized that not only were her taxes *not* what he called her in to discuss, but she had just given him ammunition for yet another lecture. *Great.*

"I see."

"That wasn't what you called me in to discuss, was it?"

"No, though I am disappointed to find out you haven't done what I asked." His lips stretched into a thin line.

"I'm sorry. I'll get it done this week." She squirmed in the uncomfortable chair.

He nodded curtly, got up and settled into the huge leather chair behind his desk. "So he didn't tell you?"

"Who tell me what?"

"That fireman of yours."

The beat of her heart picked up its pace. "I have no idea what you're talking about."

He rested his elbows on the desk and steepled his fingers. "He came to see me the other day."

"What?" Her stomach lurched and she clutched the arms of her chair.

"Yes. He came to tell me to stay out of your relationship, to stop interfering."

"He did?" Hunter hadn't mentioned anything about that to her, and she wondered why not.

"Perhaps he thought it was better to keep the conversation man to man." She shrugged. "What did you say?"

Rubbing his chin, he said, "At first I was angry with him for telling me what to do, but now that I've had the chance to consider it further, I must say I respect the man for having the balls to march in here and give me a piece of his mind."

"You do?" The only men she knew her father respected were fellow captains of industry, and he didn't *like* most of them. He had a snobbish disdain for anyone he didn't believe was living up to their potential, a factor he seemed to feel only he was capable of judging.

"Yes, I do. You like this man?"

Dumbstruck, she merely nodded.

"Alright fine, I won't interfere." He picked up his phone dismissively.

"That's it?"

"Unless you have something else. Your stepmother will be expecting you at the family Halloween party."

"Which one?" she muttered under her breath, though she knew that his fourth wife, Isabelle, the mother of two of her younger sisters and a younger brother, hosted a Halloween party each year and invited all of Bainbridge's children.

He ignored her, and as she grabbed her bag and prepared to go, something occurred to her. "Hey, what exactly did Hunter say when he was here? What made him think you were interfering?"

Her father sighed and spoke to her as if she were a child who didn't understand the world. "A photo of you two was in the paper recently, and I feared he might be taking advantage of you."

"Taking advantage of me? How would he know you thought that?"

"I called his chief."

"You did what?" Ire bubbled just under the surface of her skin.

"Charmaine, you know how much you're worth, how much I'm worth. It is my job to look out for our best interests."

She glared at him across the desk. "You are unbelievable, and you never change."

"You may not want to hear it, but someone needs to look out for you."

"Well, from now on it will be Hunter. Consider yourself relieved of duty," she snapped as she stood and headed for the door.

"Fine," he said with a dismissive wave of the hand, and he went back to his phone.

She slammed the door of his office with all the force she could muster.

POOR LITTLE DADDY'S GIRL

• • • • • • • • • • • • • •

When she got home, Hunter was at her apartment waiting for her. The repair work had been completed while she'd been in Mexico, and she moved back in to the high rise last week. The whole time she'd been at her mother's place, she hadn't received a phone call, a text, nothing from her mom asking how she was. Charmaine assumed her father would have told her about the fire, but maybe not.

"What's the matter, Kitten?" Hunter asked wrapping her up in his arms.

"Nothing," she replied shaking off the baggage of parental failings.

"I'm not sure if I buy that, but I have a surprise for you." He opened the refrigerator and pulled out a moderately priced bottle of champagne.

She eyed him suspiciously. "You bought that for me?" Hunter didn't exactly have champagne taste. He was more of a barley and hops kind of guy, and he didn't exactly approve of her drinking.

"For us. Where are your glasses?"

"Over here." She opened an overhead cabinet in the kitchen.

With his long arms he retrieved a pair of Baccarat flutes and placed them on the counter.

"Are we celebrating something?"

"Yes." He winked at her and popped the cork then poured some of the frothy liquid into the glasses. "I just got the word that Rollins will be back at work near the end of next month."

"For real?" Joy and gratitude flooded her. "How did you know?"

"He called. I have a feeling Rollins is going to report to me from now on."

"That's weird," she said, a bit jealous.

"I'm just teasing. He probably left you a message. I guess he just wanted me to know. He credits me with saving his life, though I think that's quite an exaggeration."

"Awww. So you're his hero. That's sweet." As excited as she would be to have Rollins back, she couldn't stop thinking about her conversation with her father earlier, and she blurted out, "I went to see my Dad today."

"How's he?" Hunter asked innocently.

"Fine. He told me you came to see him." She crossed her arms over her chest.

"Oh, he did?" he asked, and handed her a glass of bubbly.

"He did. I think he was impressed you stood up to him. Not a lot of people do that."

"I'm always going to stand up for myself, and you too. I've been through the whole controlling family with money thing before, and I'm not going to let anyone mess with us, Kitten."

"I love that. No one has ever stood up to him for me before, not even my mother." She beamed and held her glass to her lips. She loved how the bubbles tickled her throat as they went down. "I love you, but I wish you would have told me."

"I love you, too, and you're right. I would have, but I think I needed time to cool down. Your dad is a real ball buster."

"Don't I know it!" Impulsively, she said, "Hey, new topic. I was thinking, maybe you should move in with me." Then, nervous what he might say, she set down her glass, hooked her arms around his neck and kissed him hard on the mouth. He cupped her ass and lifted her up onto the counter. She wrapped her legs around him, pulling him close and when she ground her hips against his abdomen, she heard his breath catch in his throat.

He leaned back, a wicked grin on his face. "I can't exist in this girly, frou frou place." He started unbuttoning his pants.

Her heart soared because he hadn't said no exactly. Taking his cue, she lifted her blouse up over her head and tossed it on the counter. Pouting prettily she said, "I love your place, *but…* your little kitten has *needs*."

This made him chuckle. "You have needs, huh? Well, right now you need to stop talking and let me fuck you senseless." He touched a warning finger to her lips and she widened her eyes to show she was complicit with his plan.

They hurriedly dispensed with the rest of their clothes and he picked her up and tossed her on the new sofa. "Need to christen this anyway," he teased.

She nodded, wide eyed, showing great restraint by not saying anything—just like Daddy asked.

Usually, he tied her up to fuck her, so it was a treat to be able to run her hands over his body. Her skin became electric when it touched his, and she caressed the hard, sinewy muscles of his neck and back. As he entered her she grabbed his biceps and held him tightly as he rocked in and out of her. Having been separated for several days, her climax overtook her quickly and she rode the waves of pleasure, whipping her head from side to side.

"I want you so bad, Charmaine. I want you always," he whispered and gave one final thrust as he came.

Afterward, Charmaine pulled out a faux fur blanket and cuddled up next to him on the couch. Twirling her fingers in his chest hair, she summoned her courage. "Maybe we could get a place together."

"Together? That sounds good. But what names would we put on the deed?" He hugged her to him.

"I don't know," she said continuing to play with his chest hair absent-mindedly.

"We'd need the same name, don't you think?"

When she looked up at him, a wide grin spread across his face. Her heart thumped so loudly she knew he'd hear it. "You mean…?"

"I mean, would you ever consider leaving the Bainbridge name behind, and maybe becoming, I don't know, a Baldwin instead?"

She punched at his arm, but he caught her fist before it had the chance to land. "You're teasing me." She pouted, her heart beating like a cornered rabbit. This was too important for him to tease her about.

He shook his head. "Nope."

"Me? Become Charmaine Baldwin? Marry you?"

"Yep."

"I haven't even met your mom," she said. The comment seemed off topic, but she was searching for holes in what he was saying. He couldn't be serious about marrying her. Did he have any idea what that would entail? The lawyers, the prenups, the media?

He shrugged. "That's okay. My mom was the one who convinced me to come to Mexico to patch things up with you."

"She did?"

"Yes, silly girl. So what do you say?"

"I would say yes, but, Daddy, I am such a fuck-up. Why would you want to marry someone who's as big a mess as me? Plus I'm so high maintenance."

He sighed, exasperated. "Don't you think I know that? You need me to keep you in line." He raised a brow and swatted her derriere. "Smack that cute little ass of yours when it needs it."

She chewed on her lower lip. "You might have to do that every day, but what about what you need? Surely it can't be all the headaches that I give you."

He pulled her close, enveloping her in his big, strong embrace. "You want to know what I need? I need you! I don't care if you are a pain in the ass. I consider it a challenge. You are mine and I want to make it official."

He got up from the couch and pulled on his pants then he went and got a box off the counter that she hadn't noticed earlier.

When he knelt down in front of her, her heart caught in her throat.

"I knew better than to pick out a ring for you. We can do that later. But in the meantime, I got this for you," he said, handing her the box. It was thin, but wide, and she opened it to find a simple blue collar with a small silver bell on it.

He winked. "I thought it was perfect for my little kitten."

Her eyes lit up and she squealed with delight. "It's so cute! Please put it on me, Daddy."

He fastened it behind her neck. "The bell doesn't really make noise. I thought that might drive you crazy."

She giggled in agreement, and her hand rose to her throat touching her new collar. "I love it, Daddy. It's perfect."

"I'm glad you like it." His mouth found hers, and she melted into his arms. The amount of love he had to give was boundless. Somehow she'd found a man with an endless supply of worms, among other things. She kissed him with every fiber of her being and vowed to do her best to be a good girl for him from now on.

THE END

Stormy Night Publications would like to thank you for your interest in our books.

If you liked this book (or even if you didn't), we would really appreciate you leaving a review on the site where you purchased it. Reviews provide useful feedback for us and for our authors, and this feedback (both positive comments and constructive criticism) allows us to work even harder to make sure we provide the content our customers want to read.

If you would like to check out more books from Stormy Night Publications, if you want to learn more about our company, or if you would like to join our mailing list, please visit our website at:

www.stormynightpublications.com

Made in the USA
Middletown, DE
24 November 2015